To Ian

SARAH MACPHERSON

THE UNBELIEVABLE MYSTERY OF
The Black Prince's Ruby

With All best Wishes
(via Bunny e Pat)

Sarah Macpherson

A Catalogue record for this book is available from the British Library.

First edition

ISBN: 978-1-3999-6072-4

This book was professionally typeset on Reedsy.
Find out more at reedsy.com

To Ian, much missed.
And to my wonderful family:
John, Caroline, Katherine, Lara, Markus,
Alec, Molly, Honor, Daisy, Archie, Ivo, Harry and Jed

Contents

Acknowledgement

I have had immense help and encouragement through many years of research, mainly by our erstwhile French neighbour, the late William (Bill) Norris, ITV reporter and author of nine books on real-life unsolved mysteries ('A Talent to Deceive' and 'The Mystery of the Lindberg Baby'), who translated ancient Spanish documents for this book, while I unravelled the French Pyrenees equivalent. Without his encouragement this book would not exist.

I must thank my talented crown painter and support: Colin and Liz Legge. My editors: Egie and Deirdre Skipwith, Julian and Penny Morgan. My wonderful code breakers: Caroline Gray, Teresa Hester, Nicolette Lyne and Lynn du Pré. My main supporters: Jonathan and Debs Loader, Hilary Finzi.
And lastly my cover design artist and adviser Katherine Bolder.

*** DISCLAIMER ***

Having started life as a treatise of English History of the late Middle Ages, I found I could not prove the spoken word (a common problem with History), despite new research into French and Spanish documents. So I had to consider making this a Historical Novel.
All my characters are real (except my narrator, the Hermit), their dates, ambitions, loves, battles and treacheries are already part of our rich History. I have long studied King Edward III and his two remarkable sons, the Black Prince and John de Plantagenet. However 'The Black Prince's Ruby' proves the Middle Ages belief in Holy Relics, Superstition and the true existence of Templar Treasure.

I

Part One

CAST OF CHARACTERS

King Edward III of England was 54 years old at the time of our story and had reigned for 39 years, since usurping his father, Edward II. He was arthritic, irascible and looked older than his years. He was forever stroking his long grey beard, reaching to his breastbone, as he groomed it into a point. His moustache was thick. He wore his hair down to his shoulders.

Wisely and almost uniquely, Edward kept his sons well occupied in helping him run the country, for he had no intention of being usurped himself.

Among the crowned heads of Europe, Edward expected to be treated as the most senior monarch. He had instilled a sense of family destiny and unswerving loyalty, which was to be most displayed in his fourth son, John of Gaunt.

Edward's daughter Joan, his daughter-in-law Blanche, married to John of Gaunt and her father The Duke of Lancaster, all died of the Plague.

***

Edward, The Black Prince, was Edward III's son and heir, holding the titles of Earl of Chester, Duke of Cornwall and Prince of Wales. He was 36, with a head of fair curly hair, he was to become a hero of folklore. His military genius was such that (frequently winning battles against overwhelming odds) ultimately the French refused to fight him. His strength on the battlefield was one of the many reasons for the suspension of the Hundred Years War.

As a boy, he had once dreamed of becoming a Templar Knight, but that ambition was thwarted when his French great-grandfather, King Philip the Fair, ordered the destruction of the Templars.

Edward felt indestructible, until a strange weakness in his limbs caused them to swell, until he could no longer fit into his distinctive black armour, bearing an English lion upon the helmet. He was married to Joan, the Princess of Wales, called the Fair Maid of Kent, who bore him two sons. The first, Edward, died after falling and hitting his head on his fifth birthday, though the official reason given, was the Plague. The second son, Richard, would later become Richard II.

The Black Prince and his wife held a brilliant Court at Poitiers, in the principality of Aquitaine, in South-West France. This former province of the Roman Empire, a medieval duchy, became an English possession when Eleanor of Aquitaine divorced the French King Louis VI and married Henry II of England, taking her lands with her. It remained in and out of English hands for 300 years, until the end of the Hundred Years War in 1453.

Templar connection: His grandmother, a Princess of Castile, told stories of seeing Templar Treasure in the two crypts below the bones of St James the Apostle, in Santiago de Compostela.

***

John of Gaunt, Prince John of England, Earl of Richmond, Earl of Derby, Earl of Lincoln, Earl of Leicester, High Sheriff of England, later to become the Duke of Lancaster, was aged 26. He was born the fourth son of King Edward III and was now the third surviving son, after his brother William had died young.

He was a fair-haired serious young man, with a wise head on his shoulders. Under his father's tutelage he had become an able administrator and diplomat. As the years passed, his father relied on him more and more to run the country. He also served under his brother, as a military commander. Later, when the Black Prince fell ill, he led the army, but without the success of his brother.

He was first married at 19 to Blanche of Lancaster, the Duke of Lancaster's

4

daughter and heir, receiving four of his titles and considerable lands from the union.

At this point the couple had 2 girls, Philippa and Elizabeth, of whom the former was to have the greatest influence on the European bloodline. Another baby was due in two months. It would be a boy, who would later become Henry IV.

When Blanche died, John of Gaunt married twice more and by doing so, founded a dynasty that produced many European Kings, as well as monarchs of England. His son John de Beaufort would become the second ancestor of generations of English Kings and Queens. Family loyalty above personal gain, was John of Gaunt's banner and creed.

He was a patron of Geoffrey Chaucer, later paying for the author's house and his family's upkeep, while Chaucer filled almost every hour of the day writing.

His memory lives on, as John of Gaunt's badges, a portcullis, was depicted on the back of a 1p coin. It is also the symbol of the House of Commons.

His sister Joan, his wife Blanche and his father-in-law Lancaster, all died of the Plague.

***

King Pedro (The Cruel) of Castile, aged 32, second cousin to King Edward III, was quick tempered, violent and ruthless, with a reputation for mindless cruelty. With a large triangular face and a long straight nose, he was not a handsome man. Within the family he was good company, but was known to be tetchy with any ordinary mortals who dared to cross him. Undoubtedly, he helped his country's merchants and traders to prosper, using many of the ideas he had learnt from England. It was his lack of tolerance with his nobles that made him many implacable enemies, who he would lure to meetings to murder them.

At the age of 14, he was chosen to marry King Edward's daughter Joan, but she died of the Plague en route to Spain. Thereafter he had children by a succession of different women. His wife, Blanche of Bourbon, was imprisoned after only a single day of marriage, without even having the dubious pleasure of being bedded by Pedro. Later he carried his three daughters by Maria de Padilla (whom he swore he had married secretly) everywhere with him, in case they were murdered. He was left with no heir. When his bastard half-brother, Henry of Trastamara, was chosen by rebellious nobles to fight for the throne, Pedro did not even remain on the battlefield to lead his troops. As was his habit, he left his soldiers to fight on their own. For many years, he carried on a constant series of totally inconclusive wars against his chief 'bête noir', King Peter II of Aragon. Pedro was depicted as 'King of Jews' by his half-brother, due to the prevalence in his country of Jews and Moors, as traders and merchants, confidants and Tax Collectors.

Like his father and most of the other Kings in Spain, France and Portugal, he spent his life plotting to seize the Templar Treasure that had been permanently hidden by the Holy Order Knights, upon the Pope's instructions.

His father, King Alfonso XI, persuaded the Pope to install his own bastard son, Don Fernando, aged 10, as Grand Master of the Order of Santiago, but the boy was true to his vows, and refused to give up secrets of the Treasure.

Shortly after he had inherited the crown, Pedro murdered his half-brother, the Grand Master Don Fernando, as well as his father's mistress, who was Don Fernando's mother. He then installed the brother of his own mistress, de Padilla, as the new Grand Master, causing a split in the Holy Order.

His father Alfonso XI of Castile died of the Plague.

Connection with Templar Treasure: King Pedro's grandfather and the Princes' great uncle were brothers. They had both been taken as children to see the Templar Treasure, in the crypts underneath the bones of St James the Apostle, in Santiago de Compostela.

***

King Peter IV of Aragon, Count of Barcelona, King of Valencia, Duke of Athens and Neopatras, King of Majorca. He was called 'Peter the Ceremonious' and known for a jewelled dagger, always visible at his considerable waist. Aged 47, he was of medium height and square build, with an unusually large head. His father, Alfonso IV of Aragon, had divided his vast kingdom between his two sons.

Married four times, he had five daughters and two sons, by the Princesses of Navarre, Portugal and Sicily. He became used to constant political intrigues throughout his life.

He gained much land by overthrowing or allying with his neighbours. He regained Roussillon and by deceiving his brother-in-law, added Majorca to his possessions. He was never a man of his word.

Having a murderous enmity for King Pedro of Castile, he joined Pedro's half-brother Trastamara against him, with the promise of one sixth of Castile as his reward.

He wrote a 'Chronicle of Peter IV' and was probably the best read of all the European Kings of his era. As an Astrologer and Alchemist, he was at the cutting-edge sciences of the age. Earlier, he had attempted to appoint his own man as the Grand Master of one of the Knights' Orders, but was unsuccessful. His later years were spent ensuring that he kept neutral in any fighting that involved England.

His second wife, Leonor of Portugal, died of the Plague.

Templar connection: His great-uncle had been a Templar Knight.

***

Geoffrey Chaucer, at the age of 24, Chaucer had already served at Court in a number of official positions. A gifted linguist, he became invaluable to the King. Short and of slight stature, with long dark hair, tied back and intense brown eyes, he was trusted and able to carry out foreign negotiations, especially with France, Italy, Flanders and Spain. After release from his imprisonment in Spain, while carrying Calveley's orders, King Edward raised him to become Squire of the Bedchamber, in those times a personal post. He carried the King's communications to foreign leaders, under royal protection.

He was the perfect choice for King Edward, who had set himself the hugely difficult task of standardising the multitude of different English dialects. Chaucer had to come-up with written English, capable of being used for official documents from then on. He went on to invent a narrative style which was new to English Literature. At this time he was writing his early works: 'Book of the Duchess' and 'Roman de la Rose', mostly translations. His own writings were encouraged and sponsored by John of Gaunt.

Many years later, he accompanied the royal family on a pilgrimage to Santiago de Compostela, which stimulated his most famous work, 'The Canterbury Tales'.

Geoffrey Chaucer and John of Gaunt became brothers-in-law towards the end of their lives, when Prince John married his 3rd wife, Katherine Swynford, who was the sister of Chaucer's wife Philippa.

Philippa Chaucer died of the Plague in Spain.

***

Sir Hugh Calveley, aged 51, proudly called himself the 'Giant of Banbury', where he was born and is buried. A famous medieval figure, reputed to have been seven feet six inches tall, with projecting cheekbones, red hair, and long teeth. He ate continuously and drank to an extent that would paralyse most mere mortals. As a younger man he travelled far and wide to jousting tournaments, where his speed belied his size. At 26 he was knighted, after army duty in Brittany. He decided the inactivity of peacetime was unbearable. He gradually attracted a body of skilled would-be warriors around him, all seeking a cause. Some were the disaffected sons of Squires, many were grandsons of Knights Templars and a few were intended for holy orders. They became his family and found a mercenary life adventurous and rewarding. They were, or became, outstanding horsemen and fearsome fighters. Calveley taught them defensive riding skills that would have graced a circus ring. He called his cavalry the 'Free Company', some also called them 'The White Company'. They were free to fight for anyone who would pay them, whether their cause was popular with the English authorities or not.

When Calveley was 34, King Edward took the decision to use the mercenary and his Free Company to his own ends. He preferred them to fight on his side in future. To do this he had to pardon Calveley of 'all felonies, trespasses and outlawries, committed before 1353' and granted Letters of Protection prior to service for the King. He sent him on secret foreign missions to ambush and harry his enemies. Sometimes he paid them himself or lent them to his allies to fight alongside their own troops.

Calveley became a personal and trusted friend of the King and received many royal favours in times of peace. He served in varied administrative roles: Seneschal of Calais, Captain of Brest, Governor of the Channel Islands and even for a short time, Admiral of the English Fleet. He and his Company campaigned in Gascony, France, Flanders and Spain.

He was a kind, chivalrous man, honoured among men and possessing great strength. He became a friend with a monarch as easily as with a common soldier, for this they all loved him. King Peter of Aragon approved of his marriage to his eldest daughter Constanza and appointed him the Count of Carrion, giving him all the lands in that district. The marriage was evidently not a success, because she later married King Frederick of Sicily. Perhaps being a better prize for King Peter.

Calveley remained a mercenary. For an enemy, it was often easier to pay-off the Free Company, than to defeat them. He and his men always had their price. But the King of England always had the first call on their loyalties.

Templar connection: He and his men heard many stories of Templar and Cathar Treasure, wherever he travelled in France and Spain. He was the grandson of a Crusader.

***

King Abu Said, ex-King of Granada, in the south of Spain, was in his 40's and travelled with his son **Hassim,** who was his weapons expert.

They were *Muslim Moors*, whose ancestors had invaded Europe from North Africa and Arabia, five hundred years before. The Moors brought their learning, universities, architecture and culture with them. They were tolerant of all other religions, including Christianity. They improved agriculture as well as commerce. Over the decades the Christians, including the Templars, had gradually started to drive them out of the rest of Europe, retreating to their strongholds in Spain. The biggest rupture came when many Spanish Moors rallied to the cause of Saladin, the Christians' enemy, during the re-taking of Jerusalem. The Templars and other warrior Knights vowed to drive them from Spanish soil. By 1367, the Moors had fought and lost most towns and cities in the northern areas of Spain.

The Moors began quarrelling amongst themselves and several of their provincial Kings tried to usurp each other.

Having driven out the Muslims, the Holy Knights were often given any of the vacated lands. They were held responsible for re-populating them with Christians, which made them both popular and very rich. Merchants would pay high prices to take over such prime sites.

The balance of wealth and power in Spain began to tilt away from the noble families, with their feudal system. Instead of favouring the merchant classes, as had happened in England, the riches of the country were now in the hands of the Holy See.

When tales of vast Templar Treasure began to leak out, several Christian Kings of Spain plotted to infiltrate the Orders and gain access to their undoubted wealth. As a Holy Knight must be celibate (except for the Order of Santiago) the Kings found themselves unable to appoint their legitimate sons, should they be needed to continue a royal bloodline. It became the fashion to attempt to install a very young illegitimate son as Grand Master, a ruse to get to the money. These Grand Master appointments had to be voted on by fellow Holy Knights and ratified by the Pope. Kings needed to be held in good odour with the Pope and extremely cunning to ensure such success.

Abu Said overthrew his brother-in-law, the rightful King of Granada, for ordering the execution of his sister. Abu Said only ruled Granada for two years, before the crown was re-gained by the rightful King and he was banished. He tried once more, just escaping with his life and with a price on his head, dead or alive.

Abu Said became paranoid about his own safety, frequently choosing to travel in disguise. He became a facilitator for King Pedro of Castile, the only Christian monarch who kept company with the Arab Moors, as well as his friends the Jews. He undertook all Pedro's unpopular business, tax collecting and bullying the population for more money. His son became especially useful to the King of Castile, because of his military skills. Hassim kept the secrets of refined gunpowder, both in his head and on his person.

Both men were very dark skinned. Abu Said was of medium height, with sharp narrow eyes. Hassim was thin, angular and tall, with large brown eyes that seemed forever watchful. Until now, Arabs had not allowed the mysteries of the alchemy involved in making gunpowder to ever fall into enemy hands. They had first used it against the Crusaders, driving them out of Jerusalem. Now, whichever western power could attain the refining recipe, would be able to spend the time and resources inventing powerful weapons to use it. They could become invincible. The raw material, saltpetre, was a natural rock deposit, found only in parts of Spain and in hot eastern countries. For years, King Pedro of Castile had honoured a trade agreement with his cousin Edward of England to export a small amount of natural saltpetre to England, for experimental purposes.

Now, since the Arab ex-King of Granada and the Christian ex-King Pedro of Castile had no money, no armies and no facilities to develop this *magic powder*, they reasoned that the King of England would pay handsomely for the formula. Surely they would concede to their condition, to re-install them both on their separate thrones.

***

Juan de Padilla - Grand Master of the Holy Order of Santiago was aged 36. He was brother to Maria de Padilla, whom King Pedro said he had married. Pedro certainly accepted her three daughters as his heirs. They always travelled with him, for there was a constant threat of assassination, especially from King Peter IV of Aragon.

In 1357, in one of his first acts as King, Pedro executed his father's mistress. He then he murdered her son, his half-brother, who was the proper Grand Master of Santiago. Pedro's father had managed to put this bastard son, Don Fernando, in place aged 10, having had the required special dispensation from the Pope. The boy grew up loyal to the Order and would not reveal the secrets of their Treasury. King Pedro had no hope of persuading the Pope to accept his candidate, de Padilla. So he announced the appointment himself, which was illegal. This caused a split in the Order. Twenty knights backed the King and de Padilla and the rest voted another Grand Master from amongst themselves. The Pope accepted the second leader. The problem for the Holy Knights, was that one of their vows was 'to protect the person of the King'.

De Padilla was 29 when he became the Grand Master, but he did not have access to their headquarters in Ucles, in the province of Cuenca. However, the safety of the two to three thousand pilgrims a day to and from Santiago de Compostela came under his daily administration.

Over the years, he managed to finance King Pedro's troops from the donations of money and jewellery pouring into Compostela. These were kept in a series of locked wooden boxes in a strong room. But he never got entry into the secret treasury, where Christianity's biggest secrets from Jerusalem were hidden. This was a vast crypt-like cave underneath the Holy Relics of St James the Apostle. The key was held by the other Grand Master. However, de Padilla did discover an interesting parchment in the library, placed there by the Knights Templar. It was headed, 'Inventory of Shipment from Jerusalem'.

The Templars had placed the treasure in the crypt on the premise that their secrets would never be revealed, by order of the Pope. It was the most protected Holy Site in Christendom.

The items in the Inventory were blasphemous, heretical, astonishing and were never allowed to see the light of day. That would have been any Christian's view, but would that have been a Muslim's view?

Muslims believed in God and the Old Testament, but not in the reincarnation of Christ.

There was one Muslim who would sacrifice anything to handle the most heretical Christian relic. It would win him great favour among his fellow Muslims. It would prove once and for all that Christians were wrong about Christ rising from the dead. It would win him back his crown. Abu Said

12

played a devious game. But then, so did King Pedro. De Padilla, the Joint Grand Master of Santiago was a pawn in every man's game, including that of King Edward, when he saw a copy of the Inventory.

<u>Templar connection</u>: When the Spanish Knights Templars were disbanded, a group of twenty-three Templars joined the Order of Santiago instead, including de Padilla's grandfather.

***

Edward of Alpath, Archer of Arden. Royal Envoy to Prince John of Gaunt, the uncle of King Richard II of England. Sent to Santiago de Compostela to find an old soldier/spy.

***

Elderly Hermit/Spy, driven out of his wits by years of abuse by the suspicious monks. He is our Narrator. Was he a spy?
Could he remember the Templar Treasure?

PROLOGUE

The Year 1385.

He is a wreck of a man, an old hermit, crouching down in his hovel beside the Pilgrim Path to the Spanish Monastery of Santiago de Compostela.

The Camino.

He furiously bats away an imaginary intruder with his elbows, swaying this way and that. He believes he is shouting out his defiance, his abuse. In fact, his vocal cords hardly work:

'No! No! DON'T you lay ONE finger on me!'

He weaves violently on his haunches, until he finally falls over in a tangled heap, caught up in the torn gown he wears.

Slowly, his bedraggled old hairy face emerges from the dirt of the floor, snarling at his attackers:

'You son of Hades! I've TOLD you! I don't WANT to remember! '

Again, he flinches away and in a flash he covers his face with a bony arm. A true soldier's instinct to danger.

It takes time, but he manages to calm himself a little, mumbling from inside the bag of rags he calls clothes:

'Can't you hear me? YOU!'

Getting no reply, he re-arranges himself, sits up and physically digs in his mind for his dignity. He thrusts out his bush of straggly white hair that flows from his face towards his shoulders:

'I'm an old man. Leave me ALONE! Don't you understand?'

The old hermit must have imagined a satisfactory reply, because he hangs on to what remains of his cloak and agrees to settle back down on his haunches in his favourite position.

He begins, at last, to attempt to puzzle his head for his memories:

'If I have to.

Who am I? You ask...

Maybe, just maybe, I was THE BLACK PRINCE once'

He turns his head away and mumbles to himself, *'So why am I forsaken now? Here? Am I quite MAD?*

By the Stynx river of Hades, surely I don't have to fill my head full of gore and bloody armour again.'

At last, he turns back to face his imaginary adversary. Determined to fire some of his own questions. But his voice and even his whisper desert him, so the rest of his tirade comes out only in his head:

'If I am a Prince, just what are these rags I wear. An ancient cowl? God's clothes?

Maybe I'm a Monk and not a Prince at all?

In this devilish place, surely not!

My life is HERE now, inside these four derelict walls with endless Pilgrim feet passing by and never noticing me?

My world has come down to the cracks in the parched earth beneath my feet, my pitted toes, no shoes, no hope.'

Suddenly, he does manage a hoarse whisper:

'WAIT!' He's remembered.

Very slowly, he drags back the folds of his old worn cloak and reveals the one special secret he carries next to his heart, hidden from all the world.

A cat, with one furry paw trustingly laid in his own hairy leathery hand. Both paw and hand are a burnt-brown colour, they oddly blend together as if they belong to the same animal.

She never moved when he fell.

'Now you know, she calms me. She has brought me some peace. At last, I know it exists.'

Suddenly he looks up sharply, really fiercely. One shaky finger pointing to the outside, towards a random clutch of other dishevelled huts alongside the Pilgrim Path, the homes of other beggars:

'Don't you DARE tell my Secret to those other hermits here.

They'd EAT a cat! I'll tell you, they'd eat anything!'

He protects his furry companion once more, a little roughly, kneading her brown fur with his clawed fingers, until she mews a tiny protest.

She shows her small face and he places his gnarled old hand over her eyes, slipping it down the side of her throat. His bony fingers curl upwards to feel tenderly along the length of her whiskers. Friends again.

All of a sudden he hears unmistakable noises from the outside and his mind veers back to attack:

'I don't like what's going on out THERE!'

As he talks, a cloud of dust rises from the path below, as a score of armed soldiers pass by carrying an emissary flag. He sees it. That is the Royal Banner of England galloping by! He is sure of it. The escort ride urgently to reach the Monastery before nightfall.

The dust sweeps its way into his hovel and entirely engulfs him. Like many times before, he splutters and mutters his own personal curse on the Santiago Monastery walls that tower over the hot dry countryside.

INTRODUCTION

Spring, in the year of our Lord 1385. The snows are melting in the Pyrenees and across the narrow, dangerous passes that lead from France to the sunny uplands of North-Western Spain. A thin stream of humanity threads its way towards a holy goal. These are pilgrims. Once, they took a different route and trod eastwards to the city of Jerusalem, seeking the memories of Christ himself. But the defeat of the Crusaders in 1187 and the banishment of Christians from the Holy Land had changed all that. Now their devotions had to be directed to a mere Saint, but certainly no ordinary soul.

St James was one of the first Apostles, the closest to Jesus and brother of John the Evangelist, who was credited with bringing Christianity to Spain. Working miracles and healing the sick, he became the first Apostle to be martyred in Jerusalem, in AD 44. Now his bones lay in the Cathedral of Santiago de Compostela, venerated and adored by the thousands who tramped along the Pilgrim Way.

From Germany, Holland, Italy, and France they came, some walking over two thousand miles. Even from England, though that country had in recent years established its own pilgrimage to the shrine of the murdered St Thomas a'Becket, immortalized in Chaucer's *Canterbury Tales*. And like the pilgrims of that saga, these were a solemn band.

Though tired and footsore, they found the energy to frolic. Their needs were catered for by willing servants and prostitutes at the inns and at the Abbeys and Hospitals placed along the way. This was no casual affair. From the building of bridges to the provision of armed protection from brigands, the annual pilgrimage to Santiago had become a well organised event. The church may have frowned on its more licentious aspects, but it turned a blind eye in deference to the greater cause of devotion and sacrifice, as long as Confession was said at the next church.

However, for some along the way (and there were many), neither the purpose of the pilgrimage nor its diversions meant a jot. These were no holy men. They were wretched outcasts from society, wayside hermits who lived in tiny flat-stone shelters they built for themselves, patiently waiting for the alms that might give them one more day of miserable life, although most would have welcomed death.

All but invisible to the passing pilgrims, the hermits sat cross-legged beside the path in silent supplication. Their beards white and wild, their skin tanned to leather and their body hair grown to resemble the fur of wild beasts. They never begged openly, never pleaded for help. They just squatted patiently behind their empty bowls, oblivious to the world around them. Every now and then a kindly pilgrim would step from the path to drop an unacknowledged offering in the bowl.

Religion meant nothing to these old men. Their apparent pose of prayer and contemplation concealed a mere vacuum of thought. They existed. That was all. Very few bothered to consider what had brought them to this pass, the world of normal lives, of work, of families, had long since faded from their memories. One thing they feared and one thing only: they dreaded the prospect of being buried alive.

It was no idle fear. Each evening, all along the pilgrim routes, bands of young monks set out from local monasteries equipped with handcarts, spades and little wooden crosses. Their mission was to gather up any travellers too old or sick to reach sanctuary by sunset. But they also provided a mobile burial service for any pilgrims who had died on the road that day. The dead were buried by the side of the path in a State of Grace, for, by decree of the Church, all their sins were forgiven if they died on a pilgrimage. The young monks would look for their details gathered from the pouches around their necks and mark their graves with wooden crosses.

It was entirely different for the hermits. The young monks only had to check they were still alive. Given their condition and a lack of medical knowledge among the postulants, it was sometimes difficult to tell…not for them the funeral blessing and the planting of a wooden cross. Instead, the hermits would be thrown into the nearest wood to be devoured by wild animals, or else pushed beneath a layer of mud in one of the many marshy areas nearby. Some woke-up while being eaten, or choking to death in the slime. Rule 1: *Don't go to sleep in the evenings*. Such was the life and death of the average hermit, along the pilgrim trail.

But what happened to our cat-hermit?

Yes, he *had* been the Black Prince, for a while.

II

Part Two

Chapter 1 - Santiago de Compostela

The Monastery of Santiago de Compostela was built in 1103 for the monks who served the great Romanesque Cathedral. It completed the West and North sides of a square, with the existing cloisters to the East. The statues of the Pratarias completed the southern façade with the South door. The square was further extended on the North side, to a busy working garden with a pleasant apple orchard.

The Great West gate of the Monastery was the gateway to the outside world.

In this year of 1385, the nightly spectacle in the Monastery courtyard is not to be missed. But it is a cause of grave embarrassment to the Abbott. Especially when it happens to be witnessed by any important visitor.

Look! Can you believe that jumble of legs? Bare legs on display in front of the Great West gate. Boisterous and scandalous. What's even worse, these puny limbs belong to young monks of the Holy Order of Santiago de Compostela.

They are busy slipping and sliding in the dirt. Thanking their lucky stars the elderly Abbott turns a blind eye. He has absolutely no option. There is no other way of opening the gate.

The army of excited young postulant monks fling themselves against the Great West gate, pushing, attempting to persuade the groaning rumbling hinges to move just a little. Naturally, they are excited at the prospect of being free of the grey walls of the Monastery, even just for a while. They slip, fall and try again. With their habits carefully tied up high between their legs, the trick is not to get their cowls too dirty.

What a question! How old is the mighty wooden gate? Nobody knows. It is all of thirty feet high, in two halves, each side twelve feet wide and held together with the weight of a hundred domed metal studs. Each stud nearly the size of a man's head.

It's a constant wonder the hinges put-up with the abuse they endure at Eventide, everyday. Certainly they seem to howl and groan in ever louder protest. Gradually they wind themselves open just enough to let the scampering crowd of running legs through. The novices were free for an hour. They seemed to spare no care for the state of their small handcarts. Ancient rough waggons they pull behind them. For the wooden wheels wildly hurtle and bounce along the dry stony ground.

They're on their usual mercy mission, day-in and day-out, to save the latest crop of Pilgrims along their road.

This unseemly exodus is permitted each evening by the elderly Abbott, who is possibly very wise. He currently has a surfeit of teenage novices studying in his monastery. Besides, the Monastery cannot afford a new West gate.

In fact, both the injured and the dead pilgrims are quite safe in the quality of the treatment they receive. The injured are loaded very carefully onto the carts and brought back to the monastery. The youngsters are quite capable of digging a grave beside the Pilgrim Route while saying the correct words for a burial for those more unfortunate who had died on the path to St James.

But the treatment of the old wayside hermits, in their individual hovels, is regarded more as a *sport,* than a duty. Incorrect confirmation that a hermit is actually dead, was responsible for more than one either being buried alive, or thrown to the wolves before his time.

Our cat-hermit, in his hovel near the far end, they leave well alone. He usually looks alive enough. But like the rest of them, he is left with a constant terror of what they might do to him.

It takes an hour or so before the dusty handcarts return to the monestry, with their load of pilgrims. Creating eddies of swirling dirt around them as they go. Every evening the carts and the wide flagstones in the courtyard of the Monastery have to be scrubbed down with beer, to keep them clean.

The Abbott is a tiny fellow and fastidious to the extreme. Like many men with small feet, he has a prominence about his stomach. His own importance is of no matter to you or I, but let us say, his dignity weighs heavily upon himself. His chief feature is a noticeably large conk of a nose, donated to him by his mother, which he twitches in his Holy Quest to keep everything spic and span. The daily cleaning of every cranny in his Monastery is a legendary chore in Santiago de Compostela. Even the studs on the doors have to be immaculately polished.

The splendid upper chambers, used for entertaining distinguished visitors are also regarded by the Abbott with a fierce fussy pride. Every day, whether there are visitors or not, the walls are brushed tenderly with bunches of feathers, for they are entirely covered in tapestries. These are already more than a century old, depicting monastery life in Santiago and were the Chief Monk's pride and joy.

But on this particular late spring day, the monastery at Santiago de Compostela has an unusual visitor, a Royal Envoy carrying secret papers. He is an Emissary from Prince John the Protector of England, Uncle to young King Richard II.

It was the Emissaries armed escort who covered our hermit in a cloud of dust, as they galloped to reach the Monastery before sunset, three nights before.

The Englishman is certainly tall and strong-boned. He bears the callused face-scars of a warrior upon his right cheek (the mark of an Archer) and a distinctive double cleft in the bulb of his chin, like two deep craters in his flesh. So deep they look like injuries too.

He towers over his host, who rubs the crick in his neck while he has to appear to listen to this foreigner's request. In truth, the Abbott finds himself distracted by the arresting impression of this Englishman's strange-coloured eyes. At first glance he could be taken to be blind. They are a shade of opaque sea-blue and look so other-worldly, that people must stare and wonder what colours he sees. Surely, if the centre of your eye is so very Aqua, would that not make the green of a tree appear mid-blue? Was the sky not green? Or perhaps a light yellow?

Edward of Alpath is in his late thirties, born near the Forest of Arden in Warwickshire. He was one of the Archers of Arden, an area containing several villages, which the inhabitants referred to as the 'Centre of England'.

They grew them tall in Arden and fed them well. The local population was granted the freedom of the royal hunting in the Forest of Arden. This was a unique privilege in these Middle Ages, when royal deer and wild boar were guarded with jealously.

Prince John of Gaunt, the Duke of Lancaster, had nurtured these young men. Allowing them to catch and kill his best red meat from the forest. It was an experiment to see if he could *grow* his own regiment of archers, his own bodyguards and his aides. He needed big-boned, tall, strong individuals who were practised in using the Longbow.

There must have been something special about the soil. The yew-wood around the Ardens was pliable and springy, without being too soft and yielding. It was more awkward to cut, but an ideal combination to construct the most lethal long-distance weapon of the time, the Longbow.

You could always tell an Archer. His overdeveloped shoulders came from pulling the Longbow and his right-hand cheek was callused from the firing position. For he was taught to touch the gut to his lips to get the perfect line of fire. With every firing, the nails on his right-hand fingers would scrape across his cheek.

Back in England, there had been difficult times for Prince John of Gaunt. He was uncle to the rebellious teenage King, Richard II and official Regent, for his nephew was not yet of age. But, he was being challenged and undermined by the King's wild friends at Court. Encouraging Richard II to criticize his uncle's foreign policies.

At last, the pressure of the unsuccessful Hundred Years War against France, came to a stalemate. A pause caused by bouts of insanity afflicting the new French king, Charles VI. With much rejoicing, the army was brought home and stability finally returned, with the marriage of the young King Richard to Ann of Bohemia, the French king's daughter. Prince John, Ruler/Protector of England, became more popular again.

At last, in 1385, Prince John of Gaunt felt the time had come to pursue his own personal claim to the throne, as the King of Spain, based on his 2nd marriage to the rightful Queen. She was the daughter and heir of the late King Pedro of Castile, who had been usurped by his illegitimate half-brother, Henry of Trastamara.

The English army made preparations to sail to mainland Europe once again. But first, the Prince had some unfinished business at Santiago de Compostela. He sent his most trusted Emissary to investigate the problem. This was a treacherous, secret business. So secret, it required a plan to hoodwink the Monks of Santiago.

Edward of Alpath confers for hours with the the monks and pours over monastery documents for several days, with no success.

His urgent quest, is to look for traces of a certain old soldier, last seen at Santiago de Compostela in the year 1366, 19 years ago. But he is not about to reveal that to the Abbott.

On the fifth day of the Royal Envoy's visit, one fine Spring evening, the young postulate monks set about their tasks, with their usual will and wanton bare legs. Making the Great West gate groan ever louder. They have special orders this time.

They deal with all the infirm pilgrims first. Eventually checking the hermits. Three of them approach the tiny shack at the far end, the furthest one along their stretch of road. They tow their battered handcart behind them, with tools rattling on its flat-back.

The old cat-hermit, deliberately prises his aged hooded eyes as open as he can, to prove he's still alive. He is not going to be taken, not yet.

But, they catch him by surprise. Two of them bend down level with his ears and blow into them, one on each side.

He jumps and growls a base animal warning at the intrusion. What mischief is this?

Instead of laughing and leaving him alone, as they had done in the past, the young devils grab him underneath his arms and legs. They lift him like a bag of bones and swing him up, onto the cart.

Shocked and panic-stricken, he calls out in a high quivering tone that's too weak to hear. It comes out as a desperate whisper:

'I'm not dead! I tell you, I'M NOT DEAD!'

He kicks and he lashes out, but his efforts, like his limbs, are too feeble. He begins to pour with sweat and gives a *'meow'* in distress.

'It's alright, old timer. We know you are alive.' They laugh at his confusion. *'It's OK, we've been told to bring all of you beggars into the monastery. Mother Mary old man, you smell! Maybe you'll get a wash!'*

This he could not tolerate.

'I'm not going into that monastery!' He manages a rasping croak that is totally ignored. *'Put me down at once!'* There's something else he wishes to say, but his voice is weak from lack of use. He has not spoken for ten years. It's useless to protest, there is nothing he can do.

As they turn the cart around and pull away from his shack, picking up speed, the old man is facing backwards. He sees the small brown head of his cat emerge from the depths of his tiny hovel. It wonders where he's going, blinking in the rays of the evening sun. The old hermit raises a shaking spidery hand into the air in protest and opens his lips to cry out, but nothing comes.

'Brown Fur!' he is saying, *'Brown Fur!'* He mouths another *'meow'* at her, as the distance between them grows. He closes his eyes again. Perhaps it's a bad dream. He disappears back into his thoughts.

When had she first arrived? How long had it been? He shook his old head. He didn't know anything anymore, except maybe that she had chosen him.

One early evening, she had walked tall with her tail brushing right past him and selected his hovel for her litter. There was not enough room for eight of them in there, he kept meaning to tell her, what with him, her and six kittens. Naturally he ended up pressed against the wall.

Nobody else knew she was there, for she went out hunting at night. She was a good mother, bringing in rabbits, voles and all manner of birds. When her babies had gone into the great world outside for themselves, she still brought in harvest mice and small snakes, placing them at his feet. It seemed as if she was now taking on the responsibility of feeding him, her big baby. Either she thought his digestive system could take only a little red meat or

28

perhaps, as there was only one of him, she would only need to provide one portion. Either way, he was only used to bread, some biscuits and a few cooked vegetables. The usual pilgrim offering. All she occasionally did, was to dab her tongue across the top of his biscuits. She did enjoy being invited to inspect his food.

He remembered how he had wanted to smile at her. Gradually he had achieved it, but the skin on the side of his face had cracked into deep lines, open and sore. He had not smiled for years.

At night he would lie alone for hours at the back of his tiny dwelling. Suddenly she would wake him by climbing over or through all angles of his elbows, hands, hips and fingers, to nestle down inside his arms. On a cold night he did not know which of them was keeping the other warm. By caring for him, she sparked his dormant brain cells. He thought the world of her. The world slowly came back to him just by thinking of her. Flashes of battles, wars, limbs and bloody mayhem sprang at him among a muddling clamour in his head. They distressed him. He was too used to nothingness. Amnesia had its own blessed peace. He did not want to accept chaos. At times he thought his brain was out of control. Was he mad, after all?

He had felt the warm body of another living being in his arms at night and her brown fur calmed him. For her sake, he struggled not to flinch and cry out in his sleep. For he was afraid she would move. His head was full of fearsome flashing colours and noise. Time and time again he tried to calm himself. Gradually he had developed the idea of forcing his bad thoughts to one side and out of the way entirely. Like a page already read, *accepting* and moving on. He wanted to concentrate on another scene, a far quieter scene. He wanted to forget the smell of blood.

For the sake of his sanity he dug for good memories. He must have had good times. He tried and tried, until he finally saw a twittering of bobbing blue tits, dancing around the grass for a speck of water from the rain outside his shelter. He smiled at their antics and pastoral pictures of his childhood opened behind his eyes and slid fleetingly into his mind.

On the way back with the cart, the young monks had collected two pilgrims for medical attention and nine hermits. Some of the surprised old men still struggling for freedom. All are confused, but manage to endure their journey cross-legged, trying their best to convey a look of puzzled dignity and distrust. However carefully the young monks pull the carts, their passengers are forced to hang on grimly to the sides, as they buck over stones and bump into the holes in the road. Pulling their carts behind them, the postulants bring their precious cargo back to the monastery in good time, before sunset.

The Royal Envoy has been searching the Monastery parchments for days, with no sign of what he sought. And of course, he cannot possibly reveal to the clucking Abbott the secret of what he is *really* looking for.

'*What a wild goose chase!*' he calls out loud in exasperation to the group of monks in the Tapestry Room.

'*I am so sorry, Your Eminence,*' replies Brother Peter approaching. He is a large monk who looks a little like a fat full-stop, '*I assure you, we have made every effort to trace this man you seek. You must tell Prince John that we have tried.*' He catches the taller man's thunderous look and his voice trails off.

'*Yes, yes...*' fusses the Englishman with impatience, '*but you do not understand the urgency here.*' He turns smartly around to face the elderly Abbott head on. '*You signed in sixteen of our army men with dysentery in 1367, but not one of them is signed out! Yet we know only two returned to England.*' He looks hard into the Abbott's eyes, '*I do not believe all the others died.*' He pauses, '*Prince John told me he had given you a good endowment, to look after them. Is that not true?*'

'*Sire, Sire, I assure you, it is recorded!*'

'*Surprise, surprise!*' the Emissary murmurs to himself.

'*Perhaps you will find the one you seek among the beggars.*' Rotund Brother Peter speaks-up once more, tugging uncomfortably at his belt. He shrugs. '*It is the only other possibility!*' He sighs and puffs out his cheeks. There is no pleasing some people. He has done his best. '*He's probably dead long ago, Sire.*'

Whereupon Edward of Alpath lets loose a roar of frustration, '*I can see no excuse for him being a beggar beside the road when Prince John paid you to look after him!'*

With bulging eyes and rattled nerves, the monks are instantly convinced the Envoy is about to attack them. Poor Brother Peter is being yelled at, full force in his fat face, as the Envoy continues:

'And I still cannot understand, why your records are so bad.'

'But Sire, you must understand, we had the Plague here for two years,' the little Abbott hurriedly interposes, now quite worried at the tone. *'Anyway, I gave an order this morning to bring all the hermits that live outside our walls in.*

You can take a look at them for YOURSELF!' His voice trails off, as his attention is taken by an arresting sight. The arrival of a group of Novitiate Monks, carrying nine hermits between them. Each old man sitting perched upon the crossed-arms of two young monks. The novices have to position themselves sideways to get through the doorway.

As the awkward procession enters the chamber, the Abbott instantaneously claps his hand to his prominent nose and mouth, as a waft of hermit-smell assaults his fastidious nose. He is unable to speak, so Brother Peter hurriedly orders the monks to deposit their charges along the walls.

'No! No! Not there!' shrieks the Abbott, all in one breath, without inhaling. He is terrified of soiling his precious tapestries, so the old men are shuffled and pushed towards the centre of the room, even nearer to the Abbott, who's now in some distress. He very much wants to breathe.

Rotund Brother Peter comes to his rescue. He digs deep amongst the voluminous folds of his cowl and tugs out a considerable length of teased, raw sheep's wool. It has been hidden for emergencies and sometimes used to blow his nose. He winds it twice around the Abbotts rather large nose, tying it at the back. However, there is a far bigger problem than the ridiculous appearance of the Abbott, whose head now resembles a sheep's posterior.

It does occur to the Englishman straight away that the hermits all have long matted beards, whiskers all over their faces and they are all dressed in rags. Each one is cross-legged, bare-armed, motionless and looking at the floor. They all look alike. How can he identify one man when they all look old, confused and appear as if each one had come out of the same pod?

31

He finds himself consciously taking only light breaths, for the smell is rancid. I must concentrate, he thinks. He racks his brains for an answer. And then it comes to him, it's obvious!

He snatches off his jerkin, revealing the emblem of the Royal Standard of England upon his chest: the three long black lions, one above another, on a yellow background.

He walks up and down the room, giving them all a good look at his chest. Surely any old English soldier would react to the flag of the Royal Household? But nobody looks up. It's impossible to get their attention. They look completely blank, as if they're in another world. Perhaps they are.

In frustration, he starts once more with the old hermit at the far end. This time he bends down low and with both hands, carefully lifts-up the heavy old head, peering into the long bearded face. He does this to each hermit in turn. When necessary, he gently opens their eyes to see the colour. It's hopeless. They are unrecognisable.

'You've lost him!' he rounds on Brother Peter, with venom in his eyes and pokes him in the stomach.

Highly offended, with tension and tempers boiling over, Brother Peter runs out of the Tapestry Room in the greatest dudgeon, before he breaks his vows of Peace-to-all-Men. He disappeared down the stone circular steps, slipping and sliding at a gallop.

Then it happens and he does not even notice! He is half-way down the stairs, when a small bundle of fur on four legs passes him, going up. The monk is so distracted with forbidden swear-words that he does not see it. If he had stayed longer in the chamber, he would have witnessed the cat clambering into the well of his master's lap, onto the hermit's crossed legs. Brown Fur goes to the hermit at the far end. It is then that the English Envoy realises with a shock, he has found his Man! It's the Cat-Man!

Now he remembers what he had planned to do next, but he dare not expose him. For he knows of him as a Thief and an English Spy. Left behind by the King of England to steal the famous treasures of Santiago de Compostela. Now what is he to do? Somehow he must get the hermit out of there, before they recognise him.

In a moment of inspiration and with a flash of light, he reaches into his tunic and pulls out his dagger. In fright, all the monks cry out and pull back a pace. *'No! No!'* calls out the Abbott from beneath his woolly face. Nobody is going to get knifed in cold blood, under *his* roof! Bravely, he moves between the Englishman and the hermits.

'It's alright, Abbott,' laughs the Emissary, *'I only want to take a bit of hair!'* Saying this, he starts down the length of the room once more, stopping in front of each man in turn. He lifts the first face once again and expertly carves off a section of beard, leaving each hermit with an unsightly inch-wide bare stripe down the middle of his chin. One by one the old men wake-up in a rage. By the time he has shaved a piece off the seventh beard from the right, he has his man! A man with a double-cleft chin, like his own and several old scars on his pathetically thin arms.

'This is my Father!' he exclaims totally unexpectedly.

Good ploy! He doesn't have a father.

But the Envoy's declaration ignites utter confusion and fury between the Abbott and the other monks. At no time were they aware this stranger was in fact only looking for his lost father. Obviously, he is not on any Royal Mission at all! All those hours spent trailing through their monastery documents.

So, this is the Cat-Man!

Portly Brother Peter would have identified the old man instantly, if he had not disappeared in fury. This was the fellow monk, who had tried to rob the Holy Treasures from the Crypt, years ago. He was the only monk who ever had a cat. But the connection is not made.

Meanwhile, the cat is shooed away and the hermit is carefully carried-off for a bath, meowing as he goes.

At last the Englishman has the old man to himself, to attempt to recover his mind and to unlock the secrets of a spy.

The very future of England depends on it.

Chapter 2 - The Madman

I am that Hermit.

And I must be allowed to tell you how I became, Prince Edward of England. How I found the Treasure of the Templars and the magical story of The Black Prince's Ruby. That Holy blood-red Ruby. Forever blessed to bring protection to a wise King.

But I know you will understand, that all I could cling to was that my little Brown Fur had been frightened off, shooed away. Never mind, brave girl, I knew she'd be back!

First of all, let this young man who keeps bullying me, tell you how they worked on my body and my mind. You see, for the sake of England, I needed urgently to recover my memory.

For, to be sure, I was not aware of the methods they used to recover the brain of someone who had suffered unimaginable deprivations over the past 18 years. To be plain, I had become a Lunatic.

I am the Envoy.

My, the old goat is malodorous enough to rot the very clothes he stands in.

Though Prince John himself commanded me to find this Spy, I much doubt he meant me to go looking under this particular putrid bush of iniquity. In these conditions, it is a wondrous thing that his brain still works. Less fortunate for me, he is definitely missing his buttons.

I was never more in need of the team who travelled here with me: a Barber-Surgeon, Prince John's private Apothecary and my own Cook. Confronted with a madman, I must say, they set to with a will, seeming to know exactly where to start. Me, I very much doubt they will have the least success.

My first task is to placate the woolly Abbott. I need his immediate co-operation, although I feel more like tweaking his nose.

You will not believe the yarn I spun him, this old wreck of a man (the tallest tale of all was that he was my father.) He was an old favourite they thought lost in the Black Death, years ago. A passing Pilgrim had sighted him here. What matters is that our puffed-up host believes it, ALL of it.

With my Royal Warrant from Prince John, the Abbott had little choice but to forgive my forceful nature and swallow these gigantic lies. God help me!

He comes up with ideal lodgings for us, because our hermit will not be fit to travel for weeks. Our needs are mainly medicinal and we gratefully accept the Visitor's Lodging House, located on the ground floor, near the kitchens, leading out into the monastery orchard.

This offers us both seclusion and access to their comprehensive planting of herbs in the walled gardens, beside the orchard. He even promises us the King of Spain's bath-tub.

No doubt he is only too pleased to get rid of us, as far-away as possible.

What a splendid affair, the Royal Bathtub! It is not the normal slatted wooden contraption we occasionally idled our time in. It is not even a moveable bath at all, it is a whole room of royal riches. Quite clearly it had previously been reserved for royal backsides and titillations. It turns out to be a breath-taking example of opulence of magnificent proportions. An extravagance of gold and copper glitter.

The entire room is lined with light wood panelling above, with beaten copper, 3 feet high around the lower half and a leaded windows dominating one side. This provides maximum light when accompanied by 8 tall glass candle-protectors, placed around the bath.

The round tub itself is of smooth shiny copper, sunk into a 3 feet high corner unit, surrounded by dazzling sides and a shelf of gold-flakes and a copper mixture. The bath is topped by a heavy wooden lid, that rests against the wall and seals the tub when not in use.

It certainly does not quite outshine our late King Edward III of England, who had both hot and cold taps in his bathtub, at Westminster Palace. But the gold and glitter of this Spanish tub is indeed startling to the eye.

A regime of lotions and potions, massages, soft food and 14 days of bathing is drawn-up by the Apothecary, Barber-Surgeon and Cook, to free-up his body.

My task is to undo the workings of his head! My master, Prince John, did not think to send a brain physician. Nor has our patient any small desire to submit himself to our administrations without a struggle and without great agitation of mind. His strength is feeble, but his *meowing* and his terrified demeanour pluck at our heart strings, as we scramble to manhandle him into the tub. We begin the task with great human pity, for this old soldier has long been deserted in this state by our own country. However this inclination towards Grace and Charity soon swings back and forth between repugnance at the odour and incredulity at the pile of bones we find underneath his rags. I swear, nothing but skin held him together.

Yet he has the strength of the devil to fight us off. We end up having to carry him in a blanket to and from the bathtub. For, to fend off his struggles, we would have broken his bones for sure.

I cannot help remembering the normal rules for anyone intending to take the risk of cleansing themselves in warm water, methinks they hardly apply here: (Not too much sex before bathing and not too little).

The Apothecary picks herbs and flowers fresh from the gardens each day: Comfrey, Lady's Mantle, Marigold, Mint and Yarrow. He uses his infusing pot to enliven the senses and bring out the diverse heady aromas. Then he encourages the concoction to float in the warm bathing water a short minute, before our daily wrestle with the blanket full of bones.

We lower him as gently as possible onto the five large sponges installed inside the tub: the largest one to sit upon and the rest underneath his feet and supporting his back. As you can now imagine, keeping these tethered in place while we lower his pile of bones into the neck-deep water, is yet another abomination of difficulty. It is the cause of many frightful oaths. I do confess to our wickedness on the first day, when we offer the closing of the bathtub lid, if he did not co-operate.

At first, he howls like a wolf from the depths of his tub, until the soft sponges begin to sooth the small hard cracks and fissures of his ravaged skin. For the open sores around the shoulders, where his filthy rags rubbed, the Barber-Surgeon mixes his own lotion of eggs, oil of roses and turpentine. Which sting upon application and cause more misery all round.

After the first week the skin healed and bathing became more comfortable. His body gradually beginning, little by little to fill in the spaces between the bones. His food is simply Leeks and Sops, for his digestion could take no other. With as much boiled-water and ale as he can drink.

Now comes the difficult part. Time for me to try to dig out his Mind, if he has one left. So I start:

'Who are you? Can you remember?' was all I can ask. Untrained in the disturbances of the brain, what else can I do?

'Brown Fur! Brown Fur! Where are you, my Girl? They're touching me! HELP me, my little friend, HELP!' I know I am talking in my head again.

By the third week, he is getting stronger and now eating Pottage and a little Fowl. But there is still no reply and I am fast sinking into a Slew of Despair at the futility of our mission, for our endeavours seem at their most impossible.

Suddenly we find encouragement when he starts to stare at us, making odd noises. They sound like a *Yap* and a low *Grunt*, with the odd string of gibberish, or a very unknown language with clicks and moans. Gradually these turn into loud noises and shouts about nothing.

Are these the workings of his mind starting to switch on at last?

Then the cat comes back.

'Now I have you! What do they want, Girl? I wish they would leave us alone.'

Chapter 3 - Golden Treasure

L ooking back, some many years later, I feel I can at last make sense of my own story. How I rose up to become the Black Prince and then was cast-down to be the lowest, wayside hermit in Christendom.

Here is how this old soldier remembers it:

I began by hating those men in the orchard, especially that young Kingsman. He was bullying me for answers and I resolved to try to keep my peace, if only they would leave me alone. Yet, I somehow felt discomforted by the colour of his eyes. They reminded me of someone.

It took three weeks for them to unbend my legs, massaging them painfully, while the loudness and clamour of my own voice, eventually made me jump. I surprised myself with the noises I was able to make. Did my sounds make any sense?

The man with the strange-looking eyes kept peering in my face and I responded by staring back at him for a reaction to the noises I made. Which words should I use, if I could? The right ones ought to have been be there somewhere. Could I remember any? Frustrated and desperate, I couldn't.

To my surprise, I found myself trying to please that Englishman again and again. It took time, while gradually the Envoy taught me to understand the sounds that came out of his mouth. I copied him and little by little, he began to resurrect my brain and put me back together again. Gradually I realised my mind had stopped fighting him and had started to take things in. Even these poor old bones began to rattle less, for they fed me gruel and chicken broth little and often, very carefully.

When the memories did arrive, they came in a rush of uncontrollable images, tumbling over each other in no discernible order. My limbs twitched, twisted and thrashed out to defend myself against terrible visions and demons. I cried water from my old rheumy eyes, that had long dried up. People came to bathe them.

For a whole day, I remember, I found perfect peace looking upwards, distracted by the beauty of the clouds. Can you believe, I had forgotten there was a sky! Eventually, I came down to earth and located myself in a gently sloping orchard, with apple blossom, crowding the old gnarled trees.

Gradually the pictures in this old head divided themselves into blocks of time and I found out that *Time* quite frequently got it wrong. At first it was not possible to put it in the correct order, but slowly the story of my past life emerged. Later on, the Englishman's demands would begin to make sense.

'Who are you?' the Envoy kept asking, *'Can you remember your name?'*

I shrugged. What did it matter? What I couldn't puzzle out at that point, was why this Englishman was so interested in me and in my life?

Naturally, now that I could start to remember, there was a pressing need to tell my story. It became urgently important to get those violent images out of my poor head, or they would stay to haunt me forever. In the end, the memories seemed just another form of madness.

But still my name was elusive.

Of one thing I was certain. I was NOT this man's father!

'I tell you, I have no son!' were my very first words when I could talk. They were shouted in anger. It was enough of a sadness not to have had a son to teach, a son to impress, not to have any children. A knot grew in my stomach in fury that the Envoy should claim it.

At once the younger man backed-down and held out his hand to calm me, surprised at my shaking anger: *'So, you recall what I said to the Abbott?'* Then he remembered, *'No! No! Of course not!'*

So, eventually I resigned my memory to the inspection. It was obvious, there was some secret in there. What was it? And just why was it that important?

I couldn't make it out. But it wasn't long before it became all too clear. *'So, just what can you remember about the Black Prince and the Templar Treasure?'* he began slowly probing.

I calmed the clamour in my head. Then, quite suddenly, I gasped at the shock of my thoughts. I pointed one finger at my own chest:

'I AM THE BLACK PRINCE!' I revealed incredulously, looking straight into his eyes.

He pursed his lips, nodded a little and then sighing, slowly, shook his head.

I remember all too well what happened next. I physically battered him and attacked again and again. Though in truth there was no strength in me and he just let me.

I fell down upon the grass and wept my frustrations.

There was something wrong here!

Still on the ground, still shaking with the effort, I sighed long and deeply. Puzzled, I knew, I could have sworn I was he…

'The Templar Treasure?' he insisted, hauling me to my feet, not treating me like a Prince of England at all. It seemed I must dig further into the recesses of my mind for even more answers.

'And do you want the BLOOD-STONE?' I suggested tentatively, as that memory came floating by.

'Ah! So you DO have it in there!' He cuffed my head a bit too roughly and laughed in my face.

I didn't like the look in his eye. Trusting my old instincts, warning bells clanged in my head. Was he trying to fool me into revealing my secrets? It flashed into my brain: Now I knew, he must be an enemy agent!

Answering a long-forgotten reaction, in a flash, I leapt at him again, roughly grabbing at the small dagger he carried at his waist. I got lucky and managed to wrap my fingers around the hilt and withdraw it from its scabbard, all in one movement, I pressed it to his throat. I was left shaking with the effort. But I had him! I had never liked him.

A look of surprise fleetingly galloped across his features, as one drop of blood found its way down to his collar.

'Oh! Ho! My friend!' He recovered both his composure and the upper-hand, as he twisted sideways and easily batted me away. He wiped his throat and bent down to retrieve the dagger as I dropped it.

I lost my footing, staggered back onto the grass, rolled into a ball and covered my head with my arms, expecting to be dispatched with his sword at any minute. He shrugged and beckoned me to stand-up. He didn't bend down to help me, so I had to struggle to my feet, the exertion had beaten me into a fit of the shakes.

To my surprise, I didn't get my just punishment. He was clever. He guessed what had made me dangerous.

'You're quite right! You need to see my Authority,' he raised the flat hand of Peace in front of me, as if to keep me away. He reached inside his tunic for a small scroll of parchment, a Royal Warrant, with the King's unmistakeable Seal, for my perusal:

'I, King Richard ll of England commands
my well-beloved Emissary Sir Edward Alpath,
Baron of the Realm, to locate and interrogate
the Trusted Servant of England, Sergeant Petit-Roi.

Signed: Richard R.'

'That's me? Petit-Roi?'
  'So, you're not my Father?'
  'No!'

I tried to control my shakes, as he felt his throat. I don't know what changed his mood, but he leant forward and gravely shook my trembling hand.

'Welcome back Sergeant Petit-Roi. Forgive me and forgive England for leaving you here to your fate, so many years ago.'

I felt an immediate sense of release. I had no need to fight the world any more.

We both sat down heavily onto a bench in that blossom-strewn orchard and I allowed old memories to spill out freely in their own haphazard order.

All I knew was that the Templar Treasure would have to wait, for there was much plotting, intrigue, cruelty and many battles. I had half-a-lifetime of PRETENDING I was the Black Prince to remember first.

'Ah, I remember my two Princes! Prince John and MY Prince, my poor Black Prince. How magnificent they looked riding into battle together, the two brothers side by side. Poitiers, Languedoc.'

I kept wandering-off to the pictures in my mind. A battle here, a beautiful woman there, snow in the Pyrenees. The head of a Saint.

With a groan, he stopped asking me about the Treasure and agreed to let me start at the beginning and tell it in my own fashion. For that was the only way for it all to come back to me.

'I remember the year 1346, when I was a young man,' I said as we settled down for many days of telling:

They were recruiting for the French Wars, village by village they were systematically rounding up every young Englishman in the district, village by village, a cruel method.

I hadn't had the greatest luck, you see. I'd been married for a month to a gentle girl with the softest eyes and a shy manner. I had not had time to break her in before they took me, for the physical side of married life seemed to repel her. She was shocked and weepy whenever I approached her. I remember the frustration all too well. Eventually I managed to bed her, but just the one time. Whenever she saw me after that, she ran to crouch in a corner. What had her family done to her, I asked myself? She went home and her father brought her back with the marks of lashes from his strap. It was hopeless, she still refused to lie with me.

So I walked into the town, even before they came to get me. I must have been the army's most willing recruit. I was still just 19. But in escaping from an unhappy marriage, I had walked straight into the fire. They trained us with whips, for they had only two months to lick us into shape. We practiced against each other with pikes and swords. They whipped us if we gave one inch of ground.

'Look!' I held up my bony right arm in front of the Envoy's face, for him to see the three wide scars running down its length; clearly sword slashes.

'That is the result! Ah yes!' he exclaimed in triumph, 'those scars are written in your army record. That was how I recognised you back there in the Tapestry Room!'

'So it wasn't my double-cleft chin, like yours?' I asked wearily.

'No, that was pure coincidence. You see, I had to make something up. I couldn't risk them recognising you. I believe you're the man they must have kicked-out of their monastery for trying to steal their precious Treasure, years ago!'

I suddenly felt exhausted, and we stopped to answer the lunch-bell. An hour later ,I was refreshed and ready to find whatever my brain could come up with.

I felt along the old sword slashes on my scarred arms and continued:

After being slashed, it was luckily for me I was nearly as strong with my left arm as my right. Five of my fellow recruits were not so adaptable and not so lucky. They were killed, *'accidents in training'* they called it. What punishment we got: They whipped us for mistakes in drill, for an untidy backpack and even for the wrong expression on our faces.

After the two months, in early 1346, we marched four days westwards to the royal port of Southfleet-by-St Clements, where we joined other troops, sailing for Le Treport in the north of France.

Here he interrupted me in a pensive mood which made me stop: 'What about your earlier life? Where were you born? and all that.'

I shrugged. Those memories hadn't come to me yet. I was busy concentrating on my life in the military. I continued:

We arrived in Picardy just in time for the start of a battle beside the village of Crécy-en-Ponthieu. It seemed we were up against a whole army of hardened French troops, spread-out in four battle sections. An overwhelming sight.

We were assigned to the South Section.

At first our Longbowmen found the range of the French heavy cavalry, catching the enemy by surprise. They were lined up a good 300 yards off, too far away for their shorter Crossbows.

Next the Longbows began to target the Axemen before they had a chance to attack on the South side.

'*Charge!*' Despite their immediate losses, they were ordered forward, straight into the killing zone.

I had never seen so many men fighting in such tight order. We were trained never to step back, even one pace. We had no alternatives, our destiny was either to fall and get trampled, or to fight on.

That first time the French blood was up, I remember facing a tall heavyset Frenchman with a body covered in scrolled tattoos, with a dirt-covered beard and a snarling row of iron teeth. I did not have time for my heart to sink. We had to stay strong to keep alive.

I knew he must be one of the Blacksmith's Regiment, with a fearsome reputation. I had to keep my head.

A shaft of sunlight caught the edge of his axe as he swung it in a short arc, aiming at my sword. My reaction was half a second too slow, as I attempted to raise my shield in defence. I dropped to one knee and the wide blade shattered through the top corner of my shield. He wrestled it completely from my grasp and it buried itself, in the shoulder of the English soldier close behind me. As he fell and stumbled back, bellowing on the blood-soaked grass, he created a foot of space for me to collect my wits and to stand-up again.

While my adversary was retrieving his axe, I had the time to snatch-up the dead man's shield. We straightened-up at the same time. I encountered his mad eyes, as he began the arc of another swing of his blooded axe. This time my training took over. I gave my sword a short stab towards his face, as if to strike. He instinctively lowered his arm to defend himself, swaying backwards, in need of balance. In a flash I swung my shield into action, leapt forward and struck him with the sharp end. He lost his balance completely and staggered back against his fellow French fighters.

I had him!

I drew my sword back and drove it towards his tattooed torso, but he managed to defend himself with one arm, which my sword impaled against his stomach. His eyes bulged and the air left his lungs with a groan, as I twisted the blade to remove it.

My blood was up, busy in battle. I took one extra stride, stepped between his sprawled legs, took hold of the hilt of my sword with both hands and stabbed straight downwards, through his heart. A fountain of blood hit me in the eyes. I shook my head urgently to be able to see, while my next opponent came into my vision as he tried to strike at me from the side. Luckily I easily retrieved the sword from my first victim and discovered I had found a certain rhythm of feinting, swaying, stabbing and slashing.

Later I came to understand it as an acknowledged automatic state of a soldier, the *rhythm of war* they called it.

We didn't step back, but neither did we advance as we should. Their overwhelming numbers were beginning to sway us. I could feel the frustration growing around me, as we tried to increase the tempo. It was all very well to be prepared to die for your country, but we dared not lose any more men. There had been stalemate on the battlefield, but gradually I felt the need to take two steps back with my comrades. Oh No!

I tell you, it was our young Commander in the black armour who truly saved us.

'The Black Prince! The Black Prince!' the cheer went up all around us. I remember there was a sudden surge of excitement in the air, as the eldest son of King Edward III of England, wheeled his heavy cavalry around in two sections and swathing their way through the French soldiers from each side. As he encircled them, we found ourselves fighting alongside his snorting, stamping horse. With much practised control of his cavalry, he swung them around with a simple wave of his sword. There was not even a trumpet call to alert the French. It came as a complete surprise to them. And he saved us!

Afterwards, we realised there was no French Cavalry left to retaliate. So our heavy mounted Knights had the initiative on that famous day, at the Battle of Crécy.

Even years afterwards, I have never seen such a capitulation! It was as if a light had gone out, they stopped fighting and violently threw their axes, pikes and swords onto the ground, on-top of their shields, with a great clatter. We couldn't believe they'd given up. Like our south-side of the battlefield, they surrendered!

We left some of our number to march them away, while the rest of us moved to fight on the Eastern Section of the battlefield. Again and again we were re-used, while the valiant Black Prince performed the same pincer movement on the French once more.

We could not believe how many French soldiers we captured that day. They outnumbered us three to one. We were told afterwards that this was the greatest victory for England, that had ever been known.

Later, we marched for nearly two weeks to the English garrison at Bordeaux. Some months later we moved north to our newly-prepared headquarters at Poitiers, where our Black Prince was to set up his Court. We felt we could conquer the world during those long marches.

My life changed as soon as we reached Poitiers. This was to be our permanent base for several years. Many of the soldiers brought their families over. Those without wives were pestered by the camp followers (a gaggle of local French women).

If we went out on exercise for more than a day or two, a whole host of them would follow along behind. They came in carts or on foot, carrying cooking utensils and food, blankets and spare weapons dangling from their waists. Everything seemed to clank as we marched along. We soon got used to their attentions and it put a spring in our step to hear them singing behind us.

We called them the *Women's Regiment*. Like us, the camp followers had their own self-appointed leader: Marie-Elaine. Her very name meant *Strength*, for she was the tallest, the strongest and had the loudest voice of them all. She ruled the female host by divine right, for she had been the Sergeant Major's woman for years. He had lost his life at Crécy, when our cavalry horses had wheeled to the right too sharply in the middle of battle and struck him down. What luck! They said he killed ten of the host before the accident.

Marie-Elaine took a fancy to me, me! I was an ordinary soldier. Why she chose a man with no rank, I couldn't understand. She fooled me and told everyone it was my eyes! It was years before I came to realise the true reason she selected me. I should have been warned by the name she called me, 'Mon Petit-Roi,' my little King.

I was flattered by her nickname for me. The significance never occurred to me. Indeed, I presumed her association with me would pull her status down. I was only a new-horn private, surely she could no longer lead the Women's Regiment? To the contrary, she pulled me up! I became a sergeant myself, yet I was still new to it all.

She had my all too willing services night and day, until I got weak with it all! Oh! What a contrast to my wife! She changed me. I was no longer the uncertain youth.

I became a rebellious, big-headed, crude, beer-loving, one-of-the-boys and a quick learner in the wonderful arts of rough love.

But the usual rowdy camp-life changed very soon after that first year, when the Black Death struck that region of France, for the garrison and the town suffered appalling losses.

Earlier, quite by chance, I had picked up two lost kittens outside the town. One lived in my kit bag and the other I had given to my woman. I swear and declare now that I believe they had a magic about them. I had heard that said. They protected us both.

We managed to keep clear of that dreaded Plague, when all those around us were dying. I even helped with the burial parties in the lime pits and still I didn't get it.

By the end of 1349, there were only a third of us left in the garrison and even fewer women. Those who wanted to go back to England were given their release the following year, when the *all-clear* was given. I did not leave. I had nothing to go back for.

There was a new king, Jean II of France by the following year and we were told to expect more battles ahead. To be honest with you, anything was better than waiting around for the Black Death to come back.

As time passed, my woman Marie-Elaine complained that she was losing her looks. I didn't see it. She was still big and beautiful to me. I can still see her wavy red hair hanging loose to her waist. The only time she tied it up was when she ran at the head of her Women's Army. Ah, she was strong and powerful and she was still my woman.

I remember a particular song she liked me to sing to her. In those days, I had a good deep voice. I sang the man's version in English:

> 'My love is neither young nor old,
> Still fiery hot, not frozen cold;
> It's fresh and fair as springing briar,
> Blooming the fruit of love's desire.

> Not snowy white not rosy red,
> But truly fair for soldier's bed;
> And such a love was never seen
> On hill or dale or country green.'

Then she would sing the woman's version to me, in French:

> 'Ce que j'aime n'est jeune ni vieille,
> meme chaude comme flamme, ni froide comme glace,
> c'est fraiche et belle comme aglantier de mai,
> envermeillant les fruits du beau desir d'amour.

> Ni blanche comme neige, ni pourpore comme rose,
> mais vraiment beau pour la couche d'une fille;
> et pareil Amour oncques ne se vit
> sur colline ni vallon ni verte prairie.'

Chapter 4 - Doppelganger

A t this stage of the telling of my story in the apple orchard, I could see the English Envoy getting restless and more irritated with me, not for the first time I may add.

He sighed and puffed out his cheeks, 'Forget those bits. For goodness sake let's get to the Treasure!'

'I can't,' I replied, 'I'll remember that part when I get there. I don't know when it comes.'

He gave up. 'Oh Well, it's getting late, let's start again tomorrow.' He got up from the bench and stretched his limbs.

The next morning he put his hand up before I could start again. 'Wait! Can't you even remember your name yet?'

'It's Sergeant Petit-Roi. You told me!'

'No! No! The name you were given in England, the one you were born with!'

That threw me. I had no idea. 'No, I can't recall back that far. All I can see is countryside and birds. Oh, I don't know!'

'Alright, alright, keep going old man.'

One blessing, at least he did not call me Father in private.

'In 1355,' I continued, 'our Black Prince, our Master of Aquitaine, planned to win a larger share of France for England. Why not? He had the best army in the world. We had no doubt we would succeed, as we marched into the southern Languedoc region.

It turned out to be a terrible mistake! You should have seen the countryside, it was too poor to sustain the troops. As we marched, our Women's Army were used to scouring the countryside for food. They were the ones who fed all of us each night. They usually rounded up beasts to roast and wrung the necks of hens and ducks by the hundreds. They raided every home near the road. A marching army had to live-off the land. That is the way it was. But this time, there were very few animals to eat. The effects of the Plague had left its mark everywhere. Inhabitants and working farms were few. Sometimes we ended up with cats and dogs and even rats to eat. I tell you one thing, I kept my cat safely in my kit bag. I hid it well, come to think of it, I was always a cat man!

The further east we marched, the more forest we had to cross. The soil was too dry for crops and the people too poor to feed us. We sacked town after town, with no plunder, no riches to show for it. There was no point in taking prisoners, we hardly had enough food for ourselves. Some villages were already deserted from the Plague and the walls of towns like Toulouse were suffering from ill-repair, easy enough to defeat, but with little plunder. We followed the wide open valley of the river Garonne, to the fortress of Carsac, where we had not even gathered enough supplies for a long siege, so we plundered the new town below the city walls instead. It was hardly worth it.

We followed the old trade-route from there to the nearby Roman city of Narbonne, where we fed ourselves from the wares of the traders en-route, but they tricked us. They must have given us inedible spices, for we fell ill in droves. That proved to be the last straw.

Outside the giant walls of Narbonne, we had to turn for home. Undefeated in battle, but brought low by our stomachs.

As long as I have my mind, I will never forget our march back to Poitiers. The towns we had already sacked could not give us more. It took over a week to struggle back into friendly Aquitaine country, where we could rest. What a disaster! We lost half of our men on that journey back. I will not tell you about the state of the poor women. Only to tell you that those men who could, ended-up carrying them on their backs. Some army!

Eventually, over a month later, we returned northwards, to our garrison at Poitiers.

Well, this catastrophe must have been the opportunity the new King of France was waiting for. Reports reached him of our weakened state and he took his chance early the following year.

Can you imagine? He actually took us by surprise. He gathered his whole army and marched into English territory, to besiege Poitiers.

The simple fact was that our Black Prince had been away in England, overseeing the specialist training of a new regiment of Longbowmen and a different Camp Commander had become complacent. Our spies had let us down. The enemy army was nearly upon us.

It could have been the end for us. Our outriders reported the French force was more than three times larger than ours. We would have to defeat overwhelming odds once again. This time, without prior warning and without our brilliant Commander-in-Chief.

But fate smiled on that beleaguered garrison, for our beloved Black Prince returned from England with his new intake of Longbowmen, just in the nick-of-time. So when he got late news of the French host approaching from the north of Aquitaine, we received urgent orders to prepare the ground two miles outside the town. We dug trenches with spiked posts in the front. We dug-up small trees and replanted them at marked intervals to give our archers the maximum chance of killing the French at a distance. We laid false footings along a main forest path, so they would fall into pits if they tried to ambush us from deep cover. It looked like a solid road. It all worked well. The treacherous boggy ground through the trees claimed hundreds of lives, for the enemy was forced to funnel into a perfect shooting zone.

'LOCK! DRAW! LOOSE!', the 6 foot Longbows fired front-on, every 7 seconds, unleashing a perfect storm of arrows, killing anything that moved between 250-350 yards away.

A second company of Archers took aim at their Cavalry from the side, where their armour was known to be made of thinner plate or chain-mail. On that day of the Battle of Poitiers, just as at Crécy, the Black Prince outwitted them. What a Commander he was! Again we took thousands of prisoners. This time, however, we managed to capture King Jean II of France himself. What a victory! It was even better than Crécy, because now we could ransom the French King and sue for peace.

The whole of England welcomed the peace treaty with our old enemy. But peacetime did not suit us soldiers. A good number of us became bored and drunk.

Marie-Elaine led most of the women into terrible drinking matches. She became foul-mouthed to me and to everyone else. I became resentful. But, you see, I did still love her.

Peacetime made me a hard man. I was always picking a fight. I had often punished junior soldiers, when they stepped out of line. But for a sergeant to be publicly flogged was a very rare occurrence.

Now, as I speak, I thank my God that I was!

It happened like this: I was in the garrison at Poitier on a weekly rota for ceremonial Royal Guard duties. I made certain I was never completely drunk on these days, for we knew we would be dismissed from the army if we disgraced ourselves in front of the Prince's Court, or royal visitors.

You understand, the army was my life and my woman was my anchor, or had been. For a joke, fellow sergeants had mixed the drinks for several of us the night before and it was my misfortune to be unexpectedly changed onto Royal Guard duty the following day. It was for the rare visit to Poitier by Their Majesties the King and Queen. We were honoured.

I managed for about ten minutes to stand to attention, between our master the Black Prince and his brother Prince John of Gaunt. They were welcoming their father and mother, the King and Queen as well as the Grand Prince of Rome, escorting them on to high-chairs, overlooking a formal court presentation of foreign royal Princes.

All I can remember is a boiling rage against the guard standing opposite me, for I had just been told that he was responsible for my terrible plight. Not only was I feeling extremely ill, but I was practically unconscious with intoxication. My head, at that moment, was receiving pictures of dancing devils in a red-hot hell.

The rage I felt kept me standing upright, somehow. It was at that moment that I decided it was time to take action, to stop the main dancing devil tormenting me so.

At once, I dropped my weapon with a clang and all the foreign royalty stood and watched me walk unsteadily over and attack the guard opposite me. He was the devil, I could see it clearly and I nearly killed him with my bare hands. Stumbling to cross the Great Hall to get to him in my rage, I managed to knock-over the Grand Prince of Rome and tripped-up two Boy Pages. One of them howled for days with a broken arm, if I remember rightly.

'Flog him!' ordered the King, as I was dragged away. This would be the end of the army for me. I knew it.

The next day, the scene was set. The flogging post was repainted white, to show every drop of my blood spilt in public. At least they did not invite all the visiting dignitaries to witness my punishment, as I was far too lowly a spectacle. But His Majesty and his two sons insisted on seeing justice done.

I was marched past the painted post to stand in front of the King. Here, I was stripped of my sergeant's uniform and stood bareheaded in my wool undervest. Prince John leant over and said something to his father, who shrugged his shoulders. 'Carry on,' he snapped, still furious at the insult I had brought upon his hospitality to his father and to a foreign Prince and his retinue.

I was turned about and marched to the white post. I had been sentenced to fifty strikes. Enough to break every rib, your backbone and to cripple or to kill a man, when the weapon used was a thick iron chain. So, THIS was how it was all to end for me.

Tradition decreed, that the recipient was inspected after every five strikes. He died before the punishment was complete anyway. A pity to tangle the chain unnecessarily.

I had seen these injuries before. If the Sergeant Major who wielded the weapon stood back from you on your left hand-side, he was aiming for your line of ribs on the right side and vice-versa. If he stood level with you, on either side, he intended to break your spine immediately. Otherwise, it was just a matter of time. Was I relieved that he stood back to my left? No! I wanted it over with. It would be the end of me anyway, dead or alive.

The iron chain crashed into my right-side ribs, back and front it caught me, five times. My breath left me and I tasted the saltiness of my blood, as it gushed through my clenched teeth. I felt it well-up and out of my mouth in a fountain of red sickness.

I was rapidly losing consciousness. After five strokes my head was lifted into the air by my hair, to show the King. My eyes were open and glazing over.

Prince John of Gaunt, his younger son, spoke loudly to his father and pointed in my direction, then at his brother the Black Prince.

'Still alive' cried out the Sergeant Major, letting my head fall again and taking his stance level with me, preparing to attack my spine.

'Wait! WAIT!' I was not aware, but it was the King himself who shouted out the order. 'Let me see this man's head again!' and he signalled to his two sons to join him. They walked slowly forward to my flogging post, talking amongst themselves as they approached me.

I felt my hair being pulled upwards once more. I regained my senses, as if coming back from Hell itself and looked straight into the eyes of my King. We both took a good look.

'Untie him and stand him up.'

Cold water was smashed into my face and my poor back. I was ordered to stand to attention.

I couldn't!

Before the water was introduced, my injuries were perhaps happening to another man, on another planet. But the shock of the drenching brought the pain and the blood to the fore. I clutched my right-side and collapsed to the ground, hardly able to take a breath.

Soldiers pinned my arms down as King Edward and his two sons stood over me.

The Black Prince took-off his feathered hat and held it in his hand, as he contemplated my inert body. The three royals stared at me and talked

54

amongst themselves.

I finally lost what consciousness I had been clinging on to, though I could still hear their words as though from a long way off.

'This is the man I was telling you about two years ago,' said the Sergeant Major when questioned about my identity. 'The men call him Petit-Roi behind his back, because they have seen the similarity.'

'Well, well!' said the King. 'I believe you now. He does indeed bear a remarkable resemblance to my son the Black Prince.' He stroked his white pointed beard slowly, thinking. 'Hair, thick-set build and about the same height, I should think.' He waved his hand at the Sergeant Major. 'Look after him and bring him to us when he is recovered.'

Prince John of Gaunt remarked, 'I've only ever seen this fellow in a helmet and guard's cloak. I wouldn't have known.'

'Quite so. But you have to admit that this has interesting possibilities, don't you think?' replied the King. 'We've been looking for a decoy for some time.' He patted his eldest son on the arm. 'We can play all sorts of tricks with our enemies now!'

The Black Prince was not sure that he was altogether pleased by this turn of events, for he was a proud man and enjoyed showing his bravery in battle. After all, his trademark was to expose himself to the enemy, in order to lure them away from an uneven fight elsewhere.

My recuperation took more than two months.

At first, when I woke up, my Marie-Elaine had to breathe into my mouth, in order for me to breathe out. Breathing-in was too painful until they dosed me back to sleep. I was better unconscious.

The problem came when the physician wanted me to stay awake, at least three times a day for treatment. Marie-Elaine slugged me with her fist and put my lights out again when the doctor had gone. Anything was better than the pain. It was blessed relief to know nothing, feel nothing. Inevitably, my jaw developed an ugly lump where she landed her punches, always on the same spot.

'Years later, I still carry that swelling. Look!' I turned to the English Envoy on the bench beside me and encouraged him to feel my old bearded face, as I presented it in front of him.

He nodded, but wouldn't feel it. He believed my story. 'For goodness sake, keep going!' he handed me a tankard of Bragot (a spiced and honeyed Ale), as he urged me on.

Well, I could stand again after two months. But there would be no more foot-soldiering for me. My lungs had been pierced by the broken ribs. I would never be fit enough to march double-time again.

The King had already returned to England by the time I presented myself to my master, the Black Prince and his brother Prince John.

'I have plans for you, Petit-Roi,' laughed the Black Prince.

I thought, how did he know my woman's name for me? That name was our secret!

He caught my puzzled expression. 'Didn't you know? You look like me!'

I shook my head and then I suddenly realised that THIS must be the reason for Marie-Elaine choosing me all those years ago. So, she had seen it. Of course, that was why she called me her 'little King'.

Over the years I had grown even more like him. I could have passed as the Black Prince's double. And that is what I became.

'You will be one of my personal bodyguards, attached to my royal household. You will be trained to impersonate me,' announced the Prince. He was quite proud of the idea now.

'Sire!' I protested.

'What is it, man? I am sure you'd prefer to be alive?' and he chuckled.

'Sire, it's my lungs. I'll never be fit,' I said.

'Oh well, you had best learn to ride, my friend, for that is how I get about. Also, you will have to learn how to copy me.' He turned aside to the Sergeant Major. 'You must get him fitted-up with black armour like mine and he had better ride the quietest of my black horses.' He had three.

I remember, even that one was a devil.

In private, I was coached daily in speech, manners and even taught to walk like him, with a longer step and with my left foot slightly turned out. In public, I wore my normal uniform and helmet and nobody would have guessed our similarity.

There were usually four of us bodyguards attending the Prince at any one time, so the rest of my story was witnessed by at least one of us. Now I witnessed the intimate nature of just how he lived. All of the guards were intrigued by the unfolding story of cheating and lying that went on between royal cousins.

I suddenly realise, I was ready to tell him what he wanted. At last!

I turned to my Envoy on the bench once more, 'Let me tell you the tale of the Treasure of the Knights Templars and how I came to see it with my very own eyes.'

It took him a second to snap to attention, he did a double-take, not quite believing his ears. This was what he had been waiting for.

Chapter 5 - Prince Edmund

'I remember the day all too well,' continued the old soldier. 'It was the 27th January 1367 and we were in Poitiers. I was on duty the day of the birthday celebrations for the Black Prince's five-year-old son and heir, little Prince Edmund. He was the pride and joy of the whole Court. We had royal grandparents, as well as proud uncles and aunts all sitting on chairs in a circle in the cobbled courtyard. The birthday boy faced his father across the circle. He was eager for the games to start'.

'Jouet, Papa! Jouet!' his small voice pleaded.

The tiny Prince hurled his little compact body full pelt towards the tall figure of his father, his arms held high. He had wriggled free of his mother's grasp and launched himself across the small jousting arena. He was brave, for he could hardly run on the cobbles.

'Jouet!'

He tilted and swayed precariously over the stones. Gasping with '*oohs*' and '*aahs*', the seated audience of fifty royal relatives found themselves leaning this way and that, as if to catch the little blonde boy before he dashed himself upon the cobbles.

The audience was there for joint celebrations, for it was also the fortieth anniversary of the reign of his grandfather.

When the young Prince was born, there had been a week of festivities in the courtyard of the vast royal castle. Forty Knights jousted forty Squires. Many of the would-be Knights won their own spurs during the celebrations. This time the scene was a lot less formal. Miniature jousting was on the cards, along with games aimed at pleasing a very special little boy.

He was nearly there, but the little Prince stumbled as he ran, became uncertain and stopped short, while putting his little hands over his eyes. He did not fall, but a flash of light had startled him. His adored parent had stepped forward to scoop him up, but the sun had created a blinding reflection off his father's shining black armour. He had never seen his Papa dressed-up in his armour before.

He was used to watching men in silver body-armour, swords and visors, but this black sword and bodysuit were different. It usually hung on the wall above the open fire, in the castle's great hall. Feeding his growing imagination, he played fearful games of *Fight the Devil* every time he passed the *evil armour*. Some servants encouraged him. Of course these were his own private games.

He wondered at the Lords and Ladies of his father's Court. It seemed to him they were very brave, for they thought nothing of the armour hanging there, just above their heads as they ate. They never even looked up.

Instinctively he knew they would laugh at his fears, so he told no one. Despite having convinced himself that the shining armour moved. If he looked at them for long enough, the black swords slid along the wall. They shook themselves at him. They were scary monsters.

'C'est moi, mon petit!' said the Black Prince, snatching off the chain mail collar that covered his head and shoulders.

The boy peeped between his fingers and found himself lifted up to shoulder height. It was a striking sight in the glinting sun, they both had the same curly blonde hair.

Suddenly in safe arms, the little boy laughed and kicked the black armour bravely to show he wasn't afraid. The audience laughed and King Edward leant over and whispered to his wife in a worried tone, 'Doesn't he talk in English?' She shrugged. 'I do hope so!' grumbled the King, for it was one of his favourite projects back in England, to change the language of the Court from French to English. Master Chaucer was his Chief Linguist.

He had taught them the correct way to speak it, there being so many regional differences. Nowadays Chaucer was kept busy producing official documents in English, instead of Latin.

59

Around the cobbled Jousting Arena, the audience caught the distant sound of musical notes getting louder. From the area of the drawbridge came the high-pitched tooting of flutes and pastoral pipes. As they got nearer, the dancing rondo they played set everyone a-tapping. A way was made and into the arena came a long line of miniature people and musicians on horseback. In among the musicians were clowns and jugglers who danced and fluted as they tumbled. In slow serious procession amidst the whirling throng, fifty pennants, small triangular flags, were held aloft, adding some dignity to this motley, disorderly parade.

The real stars of the show came in pairs behind all the flags. Dressed as hobby horses, the costumes of the court dwarfs were breathtaking. They each had a platform attached around their waists, protruding from their behinds. Grey chain-mail hung to the ground all the way around the platform, except at the front, where from the dwarf's torso, the head and front legs of the hobby horse swung. On each platform was a saddle, upon which stood a trick dog, swaying and barking, trying to keep its balance. Frequently it would tumble off and immediately jump back on again, to the delight and amusement of the little Prince.

At last, a cartload of sawdust was spread on the cobblestones and the jousts could begin. Each hobby horse faced another on either side of a rope. They galloped awkwardly towards each other, carrying a small wooden sword.

The rules appeared to be a bit muddled. Striking a blow on your opponent seemed legal, as long as you didn't flatten them. That was cheating. For the real object of the tournament, was to hold-on to the occupant on your saddle. Whoever got tipped out first, was the loser. So the galloping was not very vigorous and the fighting was more of a dance, with swords carefully poked.

Eventually a winner was declared and challenged to a Champions Duel with the Black Prince. This was the bit the little boy liked best. He had been practising his kneeling for days.

A tiny black horse was led into the arena. It was little more than two and a half feet high and was covered in black war armour. It was a tiny charger for the little Prince!

His father led the boy towards attendants, waiting in the centre. They dressed him too in miniature black armour, before he knelt in front of his father, as he had practised.

Withdrawing his mighty war-sword from his waist, Edward the Black Prince *knighted* his five-year-old son on the shoulders, presented him with a wooden sword and sent him to do battle on his *charger*, for the honour of the King.

Of course, it was all pretence. The little war-horse was led and its tiny rider was strapped securely into a black basket-saddle. The victorious hobby horse met the King's Champion at the lists. But nobody noticed the state of the ground. Many hobby horses' feet had swept the cobblestones clean of sawdust.

The first pass was uneventful, one little sword was wildly swung, but neither the tiny Prince nor the hobby horse could reach each other. Approaching another pass, the little boy wriggled free of his safety strap. He leaned far over the side with his sword and knocked his opponent to the ground. But in doing so, he fell head-first onto the cobblestones.

The audience leapt to their feet.

Almost immediately, the little Prince got up, laughed and ran towards his father. Then delayed concussion hit him and he crumbled to the ground once more. The Black Prince reached his son, picked-up the limp body and looked skywards. His face was terrible, his mouth wide open:

'NO!' he screamed.

The physician ran from the far-end of the courtyard just as the patient awoke smiling. 'Papa, I won!'

The collective sigh of relief was like a passing wind, as everyone bent to take their seats.

Instinctively, the father knew the boy had died and come back to him. Thank God!

Through years of battle and bloody deeds, the Black Prince had never faltered. But now he started to shake. It was an affliction for life, that would never leave him.

The games were over and the tournament done. The audience dispersed quickly, for the weather was closing in. The great hall was expecting them, for there was a feast ahead to honour King Edward.

The little boy was led away feeling happy, all be a little dizzy. He would never forget his birthday.

But Alas! Alas! There would never be another. The fall caused a blood clot on his brain. Deep into that night, unknown to his unfortunate parents, he lapsed into a coma from which he would never awaken.

Chapter 6 - The Throne of Castile

I t was a common enough occurrence. When the intense light of January gave over to yellow clouds, it brought snow to south-west France. So by the time the fifty royal relatives had sat down at the long T-shaped table, a blinding snow blizzard was raging outside. It clattered the drawbridge, safely drawn-up for that night. The wind dashed past the windows and howled through the openings of the arrow-slits, in the thick castle walls. It guttered the candles until guards were found to keep them alight. It was the worst storm in years.

Safe in their ignorance of the awful truth of the tiny Prince's deep sleep two floors above, beside their great fire, the royal party celebrated.

Suddenly, there came an unmistakable clash of swords and the sound of fighting was heard. The Black Prince leapt to his feet. Was this possible? Were they being invaded in this weather?

I was part of the Prince's personal bodyguard. We instinctively closed in around him at the sound of danger, but he urgently waved us away, towards his father, 'The King, the King,' he cried. 'For God's sake, protect the King!'

An unexpected sight filled the doorway. A clean-shaven, dark-skinned Spanish monk, escorted by royal guards. He was a soldier monk, with a scabbard, disturbing the hem of his habit. The intruder wore a densely-woven dark grey cloak. Snow tumbled from his hem and collected on the flagstones around his chain-mail feet. Below his hood, the cowl extended over his shoulders and down the outside of his habit, nearly as far as the elbow. This provided double protection of his upper-body from the vagaries of the weather.

With a spray of icy water that drenched everyone within twelve feet of him, he flung back the left-hand side of his cloak, revealing a white robe with a brown leather belt and a half-body length shield, carried at elbow height. This was decorated with a red rim and gold-embedded studs. In the centre of the shield was a distinctive red cross, made in the image of a sword, with a typical pilgrim's gold seal.

He advanced purposefully towards the King, strangely offering neither bow nor obedience.

There was something wrong here.

My bodyguard's training warned me. It did not look right.

The hairs on the back of my neck stood proud as I sensed trouble.

Quietly, I stepped sideways into the space between the monk and the King. I knew a soldier monk should kneel to a King.

Watching from the side, the Black Prince wondered at him. There was an arrogance about him. The man never flinched, despite facing an array of Kings and Princes. Taking a parchment from his sleeve, he handed it to the nearest guard. My hand lay instinctively on the handle of my sword, just in case.

He spoke in French, not in Latin as a monk would, nor in Spanish as a lowborn country Spaniard would, but in the court language of Europe.

'Sire, this is from His Majesty of Castile'. The man handed over a rough parchment, 'It is for your eyes only, Sire.'
The Prince handed the note straight to his brother John of Gaunt, seated beside him. 'The King of Spain is outside? On a night like this?' The Knight nodded. 'King Pedro urgently requests shelter, Sire!'

'Good God!' called out Prince John, reading the contents of the letter, 'He's lost his third battle in a row. Most of his men are dead in the Pyrenees!' A large hand thumped the table, as the booming voice of the King spoke, 'He's a fool! Why is he fighting in the winter? Besides he's always running from battles. He'll lose his throne like this.' The Knight nodded to the King.

'He has, Sire!'

The women guests let out a series of moans, which disrupted the King's concentration. He shook his head and gestured his hand to the side. 'This is men's business. Let the Ladies withdraw.' Sneaking either a chicken leg or a pastry pie under their many layers of clothing, for the feast had barely begun, the women left, bobbing curtsies as they passed the King.

'Sire,' broke in the Knight, quietly pleading with the Prince, 'he has his Treasury and his family with him! He has NOWHERE else to go!'

'Even if he has half an army with him, there's no room here,' murmured the Black Prince.

'How many men?' roared the King, unable to hear the conversation properly.

'Only a handful your Majesty.' The reply was louder. 'We are all Knights of the Order of Santiago, sworn to protect our King.'

The soldier-monk side-stepped my attentions, pulling his cloak and cowl off his shoulders to reveal a bright Red Cross on his chest, with the same sword design, as was on his shield.

Across his right shoulder, the heavily embroidered unmistakable insignia of a Holy Grand **Master**. It marked him as the head of the Military Order of St James of the Sword, the most important Spanish Medieval Order of Knighthood. He held a position second only to the Pope, answerable only to the pontiff, subservient to no man. Perfectly entitled to look any King straight in the eye. He was more commonly called the Grand Master of the Holy Order of the Knights of Santiago, who guarded the pilgrim routes to Santiago de Compostela. All the guests stood-up. Most of them had never before seen such a senior warrior of the Holy Orders.

The Black Prince sighed and looked to his father for guidance. The King would have to handle this himself. He signalled his bodyguards to back-off, but you could be sure we would stay in watchful distance.

The elderly King lowered his head very slightly at the visitor, acknowledging a higher order in Christendom. It was not a gesture he was used to. 'Grand Master, you yourself are always welcome in our house,' he paused, '...and as King Pedro is under YOUR protection, we cannot refuse him a roof on this night. What in God's name induced him to expose his family like this?'

'Sire, the weather is terrible and Princess Beatrice is ill on a litter!'

'Good God, that man is inhuman!' exclaimed Edward. 'Very well, let him in!'

They stayed at the table while the Prince ordered more logs for the fire and bear-skins to warm and dry his guests.

'He has his Treasury with him, does he?' asked John of Gaunt sarcastically, 'at least that shows a bit of sense!' He got no reply.

All the remaining guests seated at the table, stared in disbelief as a troop of sodden monks entered the lower entrance half of the hall. Their cloaks and cowls were sagging and voluminous, their faces invisible within the hoods. There were seven of them, dripping their puddles onto the mats like ecclesiastical drowned rats. Another monk was stretched out on a very narrow canvas, with a cloak serving as a makeshift tent. He was carried in by four of the Black Prince's own soldiers holding each corner of the stretcher.

The diners looked puzzled. Where were the King and his family? These monks were not what they expected. The Grand Master of the Knights of Santiago stood aside. Altogether, the other 'monks' dropped their sodden cloaks, revealing four members of the royal family of Castile. Ex-King Pedro, Princess Constance (aged 12) and her younger sister Princess Isabella (aged 11). Princess Beatrice, his eldest child and heir (aged 14), lay on a stretcher, exhausted.

Of the others, two nearly black-skinned men were clearly Moors.[1] Many of the recent campaigns in the Iberian Peninsula had been spent regaining land and towns from them. The Templars had fought them in Jerusalem and again back home in Spain. They were regarded as the Christians' greatest foe. How could they possibly be travelling with the Holy Knights? Surely they were sworn enemies?

King Edward signalled to his guards to close in and surround them. We drew our swords in a flash. Ex-King Pedro (known as Pedro the Cruel) of Castile, seemed delighted at the defensive reaction of his hosts. He roared with a merry belly laugh.

If there had been a battle of the Kings, ex-King Pedro would have won easily, for he was a giant of a man. His long aquiline nose belied his forthright nature and bombastic humour. All he lacked was his share of common sense. Those around the table that night were mostly second cousins. They could not help liking cousin Pedro, though they knew him as a man not to be crossed. He was a rogue with the women. In fact his cousins were intrigued to see which *wife* he had turned-up with.

Pedro had rejected his only legitimate wife, reportedly without even bedding her. It was rumoured that he had married at least two others, while plainly still married to the first. He had three daughters whom he dragged around with him everywhere. Though whose they were, nobody could work out. There was also a rumour of his real wife's imprisonment. Quite frankly, they feared for her safety.

Looking back on it, King Edward of England was heartily glad that his own daughter, Joan Plantagenet, sister of the Black Prince and John of Gaunt, had not been able to marry Pedro when they were younger. Nearly twenty years before, aged just thirteen and fourteen years old, their marriage had been arranged to unite England and Castile. But she, poor girl, had died of the dreaded Plague en route to her wedding.

Pedro had grown up to be a difficult and unpredictable man, but undeniably great company at a feast. His bastard half-brother, Henry of Trastamara had called him King of the Jews for he used them to collect his unpopular taxes. In this battle between the half-brothers, bastard Henry had usurped Pedro's crown, picking it up from the battlefield and having himself enthroned as Henry II of Castile.

Around the table that winter night, ex-King Pedro's military policies were found to be questionable, but it was his habit of not leading from the front that his cousins refused to condone. Every time the going got tough, he left the fight. No wonder he lost battles. 'What on earth,' they would ask later, 'was the crown of Spain doing on the battlefield, if the King had already left?'

'A mistake!' said Pedro, 'at least I didn't lose my head as well.'

Perhaps some of them might have preferred it if he had. But for now, he needed to explain the two Moors in his party of *soaking rats*.

'May I introduce my friend His Majesty King Abu Said of Granada, in the south,' he hesitated, 'ex-King, I should say, like myself. The other gentleman here is his trusted munitions man.' He arched an eyebrow at his English cousins who stood in astonishment, 'they travel under my protection.'

What trick was this? King Pedro had an odd temperament at the best of times and nobody trusted him. What was he up to now? These were the three chief protagonists of the Spanish War: the King of Castile, the Grand Master of the Order of Santiago and their chief enemy, the King of the Moors from Alhambra Palace in the south. Surely they would want nothing better than to destroy each other?

The older Arab, who was dressed in a flowing dark red robe trimmed with braid, tapped his chin, nose and forehead before spreading out his hand. 'Salaam,' he said in salute.

At this word, the second Moor flung aside his own robe, exposing an astonishing array of knives, crossbows and pouches strapped around his body.

King Edward was outraged. 'Guards!' he shouted, pointing at the Moors hiding in the clothes of Christian monks. We drew our swords.

'Explain yourselves!' The King of England's voice was menacingly low. Using his Scabbard, he leaned forward and parted the guards in front of him. He needed to be able to see these infidels.

'Cousin! Cousin! I am sure you would not begrudge my three brave girls a welcoming bed this terrible night?' Pedro may have been a trifle dim, but even he realised the situation was tense. The Queen and two ladies re-entered and shushed the girls out of the hall, helping the eldest Princess out of her litter.

Unconcerned, ex-King Pedro launched into a thunderous tirade of his own. 'I see, my cousin England, you are prepared to condemn me for travelling with such fellows.' Indicating towards the Moors. 'You are a fool until you have heard me out.' There was dead silence. Nobody spoke to the King of England like that. He continued, 'I tell you, at this time, these are my only friends.'

The Black Prince walked around the table. 'Cousin, are you soft with fatigue? There is something very wrong here! It is obvious to us that these infidels are your sworn enemies, even if one of them is an ex-King. The Grand Master of Santiago is of course a different matter. He is your natural ally and protector.'

'Ah, de Padilla!' sighed Pedro, 'He's family as well! Let me introduce you to my brother-in-law.' He saw their faces widen in surprise. 'Yes, yes, he is the Grand Master of the Holy Order of Santiago, only he's not the Pope's man, he's mine!' He paused for effect. 'His Holiness has thought, in his wisdom, not to approve my choice. So now there are two Grand Masters and we have a split in the Order. De Padilla here and thirty others fought for me, their King. The rest sided with my treacherous half-brother Trastamara, the Usurper.' He spread his hands towards his little band of refugees. 'This is all that remains. Trastamara has defeated my army and taken my crown. They harried us and blocked our route over the Pyrenees from behind. They knew I would come to you for help and they are ready to ambush your troops if you come to my aid.' He sat down, dejected for the first time. 'I regret, I do not know how I am to regain my throne.'

His mood changed again suddenly, startling his audience. 'You!' he pointed to King Edward accusingly, 'you have been double-dealing in this matter. To think I believed in your *blood's-thicker-than-water* promises. Did you not promise me that Sir Hugh Calveley and his Free Company of English mercenaries would never be allowed to fight against me? You told me you could control them,' he added bitterly. 'They won the day for that usurper. They lost me my crown!'

King Edward looked aghast. He turned to his chief administrator, his son John of Gaunt, 'What happened to that letter we sent with Master Chaucer three months ago? I expected him back a month since. Has anyone seen him?' There was no reply. 'What's- happened- to- Master- Chaucer?' he asked again, slowly.

John of Gaunt looked puzzled, 'We sent him to hand-over your instructions in person. They were for Calveley's eyes only. Maybe he couldn't get back. The highest passes in the Pyrenees have been closed since November.'

'The King of Castile here got through with his family,' retorted his father.

'What the DEVIL has that mercenary Calveley done now?'

Edward was getting wound up, feeling he was losing face here. 'As soon as we heard his company had been paid to fight for Trastamara, alongside your old enemy the King of Aragon, we sent Chaucer. I remember, I personally arranged a free pass from King Charles of Navarre. We sent him with safe passage to deliver my orders to Calveley, telling him not to join your enemies. I ordered him to withdraw!'

'Well, if I am to believe that' said King Pedro, 'then either your Master Chaucer did not get there, or he joined them himself, or possibly Calveley simply ignored your order'.

'He wouldn't dare!' roared Edward, covering both the last two possibilities.

'Well then, dear cousin of England, I know of something else that Calveley wouldn't dare.'

'What is that? What are you talking about?' replied Edward cautiously.

'He is said to be so friendly with the King of Aragon, Trastamara's ally, that he has married the Princess Dona Constanza, the King of Aragons eldest daughter. That mercenary of yours is so thickly embroiled with the King that he has been given the lands and title of the Count of Carrion! What do you think about THAT, from one of your loyal subjects?'

'Good Lord!' King Edward flopped back in his chair. 'The man has betrayed us. He has denied his own country.'

'And, there is one more thing,' added King Pedro, now in the ascendant. 'Your other friend, King Charles of Navarre has betrayed you also. There are three commanders blocking the high passes of the Pyrenees to prevent you reaching Spain to help my cause. King Peter of Aragons army are there, along with Sir Hugh Calveley and his Free Company, as well as your friend King Charles of Navarre, with his personal guards.' For a full minute nobody spoke. They sank into their chairs and waited for the King's reply.

'This is serious. I need at least a week to find out about Master Chaucer. Let us pray he has not been taken hostage, or worse. King Charles has clearly deceived us,' Edward sighed, and waved towards his bedraggled visitors, 'In the meantime, there is accommodation enough for you all. Even the Moors can stay. But be careful, we will all be watching you.' He must puzzle it out. 'There has to be an explanation from Calveley. He is an honourable Knight. If Master Chaucer is in trouble, that means Calveley and his mercenary troops never received my instructions. The King of Aragon is another matter. I know he is a very old adversary of yours.' He nodded towards his errant cousin. 'Peter of Aragon has always desired your land, hasn't he?'

Pedro of Castile nodded vacantly. He was no longer on the defensive. Before their eyes, he grabbed a flagon of wine and downed it. His knees buckled and he fell into an untidy heap in the space beside his chair, with limbs spread-out at oblique angles. The two Moors bent to pick him up, quite used to his behaviour.

'Leave him where he is,' Edward ordered, rising from his chair. 'I'm past the age of wanting to do that every night, thank God.' Now, feeling his age and leaning on his two sons, King Edward left the hall, leading them into his chamber for private instructions. There was nothing wrong with the workings of his brain. He wasn't a successful King for having a blunt head. 'We have some basic questions that need answering.

Why is the Moorish King here? Is it possible he is planning an ambush on us?

Does he have troops hiding outside? Perhaps at this very moment they are surrounding our fortress. If King Pedro has brought his usual Treasury with him and saved it from his enemies, where is it now? I didn't see a Treasury box. If he wants us to get his crown back for him, he had better have something very precious in that treasury of his! If our soldiers are to be sent from England, this will have to be paid for. If he wants Calveley to change sides, he will need to reward him as well and he will only take gold.'

The King sighed. Dealing with a Mercenary was tricky at the best of times, even if he had been a friend. He looked hard at his sons, busy formulating a plan in his head. It had also just occurred to him that this situation was so serious, he might never see them again.

'At first light, I want you to take King Pedro and a troop each, to the base of the Rencesvalles Pass of the Pyrenees, where the pilgrim routes meet.

The armies must be somewhere nearby. Find Calveley and arrange a Parley. I must speak to him personally. I want him back here. I need an explanation from Aragon and Charles of Navarre as well, but I daresay they will not come. Both of you must lay good plans, for they are waiting to ambush you. They will have many a man at their disposal. It will be your stealth against their brawn. King Pedro must go with you, for he may be useful as bait. But do not let him get killed.'

He stood to face his precious sons, both the finest men in the land, 'Once again the safety of the good soldiers of England is in the undefeated hands of my eldest son and his brother. Go with my blessing, seek out the answers to these questions: What has happened to Chaucer? And why are Calveley and his Free Company fighting for the other side?' He extended his right hand, 'May God travel with you.' The Princes knelt for his blessing.

'Ah!' he added, almost as an afterthought, 'make sure you keep a guard on the ex-King of Castile. He may be a cousin, but I trust him not.'

Ordering their troops to be ready to move out at first light, the two brothers sat for hours, discussing their strategy. Eventually everyone, except King Pedro, managed to find the right beds and surprise their wives that night. They had expected their men to end up draped across the hall table, as usual.

Prince Edward, the Black Prince was woken the next morning by his wife. She had not come to scold him in his dishevelled state from the night before, but with the awful tidings of the passing of their precious son in the night-time.

In shock, he grabbed hold of her for balance as he sat up and instinctively reached for his left elbow to stop the shaking. His arm had been trembling all night.

Chapter 7 - A Question of Loyalty

T his time, the English Emissary brought a plate of fresh warm Cracknels to the camomile seat they occupied in the garden. The aroma and a sense of calm surrounded the questioner and the hermit. The tension between them had dispersed as they both took in the sorrow surrounding the story of the little boy and the dangers ahead of the royal Princes. The Emissary was becoming caught up in Petit-Roi's tale. But still he needed news of the Templar's Treasure.

'Patience, my friend,' said the old hermit. Truth be told, he was enjoying himself. For once in his life he was in command of the situation and he found his rediscovered power of speech intoxicating. 'We'll get there, never fear, but if you want to reach your destination you have first to travel the road and I am your only guide. But by all means, we will take a break before I continue. I can wait.'

Muttering under his breath, the Envoy departed, returning ten minutes later with a pair of chicken legs, one of which he offered to the hermit. For a while they ate in silence, then the hermit wiped his lips as he continued:

'But we did not move the troops out at first light. Instead we buried our precious little Prince on the next noontide. He who would never become our King.

Three days later, the Black Prince and his brother John of Gaunt were southbound on a five-day journey towards Bayonne. Accompanied by his bodyguards and two hundred cavalry, plus a still-exhausted ex-King Pedro of Castile and de Padilla (the Grand Master of the Holy Order of Santiago).

They travelled all the way, ensuring to stay within the boundaries of the

Prince's own Kingdom of Aquitane. These lands had been ceded to the English two hundred years before, in 1152, when Eleanor of Aquitaine married King Henry II of England.

'Their union...' he reminded his listener, who knew this perfectly well, 'had produced King Richard the Lionheart, the Crusader.'

Nearing Bayonne, the Black Prince and half the cavalry wheeled eastwards, to pick-up the smaller track beside the Adour, followed by the Pau River. We crossed into the Bearn district and stopped our last night at Salies-de-Bearn, where the warrior Prince sought the bathhouse spa for his weary bones. I had witnessed, with growing concern, the spread of a strange illness that sapped his strength. What was it? Luckily, he found relief from the salt content of the spa waters.

The next morning, we crowded into the courtyard of the hostelry belonging to the hamlet of Peyrehorade, causing the grey-bearded innkeeper to panic when he heard that the cavalry intended to stay. There were no houses at all in this extended farmstead, only three ancient barns. In the smallest of these, someone had put-up an old table for an altar and dragged in some benches. They had stuck the usual shell motifs to the outside walls, as with all places of worship along the pilgrim route and called it a church.

The innkeeper was used to receiving tired and honest pilgrims each night from the month of April onwards. If they stopped around midday, the travellers knew they would not be able to persuade their limbs to walk further.

If any halted there, it was usually to die, or to urinate. Why, wondered the innkeeper, did the sight of the little cross on the church make everyone veer right to spend their water against the wall? The ground on the east-side of the church was covered in nettles.

He had two teenage girls to protect. Now he had a whole army to contend with. That was going to be a problem. He told his wife to fetch all male relatives from nearby Salies and Orthez. 'Take the pony and keep the girls well out of sight,' he ordered urgently. He expected trouble.

But this site had been specially selected by the Grand Master of Santiago, who knew all these routes from his years spent guiding the pilgrims. It offered views for three miles on each side and could be defended if necessary behind its stone walls. It had a secret underground cave from the church, leading underneath the very nettles the pilgrims watered.

Our troops took over the two large barns and we sent our Lookouts to high ground in the distance. The royal visitors made themselves reasonably comfortable in the innkeeper's own rooms. They had seen worse. Our host slept amongst his barrels of ale to, protect them.

There we sat and waited for news of Prince John of Gaunt. Little did the innkeeper know that this army was nothing compared to the one that was making its way steadily towards them. It did not occur to him that he might soon be in the middle of a battle.

Before their troop had split up, John of Gaunt had noticed his brother riding with his feet out of the stirrups. It was a common sign of tired muscles. What was ailing the Black Prince? Usually he could ride all day and night, changing horses three times. He could even fight a battle at the end of a twenty-four hour ride. Was he unwell? The whole troop must have noticed it. Nobody said a word.

Prince John was a diplomat, trained by his father to handle awkward negotiations. This was meant to be a diplomatic mission, requiring all his powers of persuasion. Was he leading his cavalry straight into a trap? Would the protagonists even listen to him?

The letters he carried from King Edward might never be read, if enemy orders were to butcher them on sight.

Next morning, the other half of the force, led by the Black Prince, turned eastwards towards Peyrehorade.

John of Gaunt, with the rest of the cavalry kept to the road straight ahead for Bayonne and beyond. They skirted the centre because of the mass of great boulders that were strewn around the building site of the enormous new cathedral. This was a joint project between King Edward and the French Bishop of Bayonne. It had remained unfinished for more than eighty years. They were completing the buttresses, joining the middle section between the two front towers and the inner arches. At this time there were nearly a hundred English masons working on the massive walls and vaults.

John of Gaunt ordered a flourish of trumpets. The men saw the royal troop with the English flag and the royal pennant they knew so well. A great shout of 'Prince John!' went up.

They clambered down to wave and cheer their own countrymen in a foreign land.

Soon afterwards the cavalry entered an area full of folklore and foreboding. The Nive Gorge, called the *Evil Passage*. Ancient stories told of the cleft in the rocks being gouged out by the panicky hooves of a horse ridden by Charlemagne's nephew Roland, cut off and pursued by the Basques. Here was the famous Roland's Leap of legend. The little army jingled its way along the narrow cut without much thought or local knowledge of its sinister roots. They neither knew nor cared that the small bridge at the village of Bidarray was called Devil's Bridge. But they did know and did care, that two galloping horsemen were seen crossing it half a mile ahead. No doubt about it, they were enemy Lookouts.

'Shall we follow them, Sire?'

'No, no,' said the Prince, 'let us see what their orders are. We must spread out into three units, with half a mile between each. That way we are less likely to be surprised or surrounded.' But there was no army around the first or second bends, as they exited the gorge. Nor was there an army over the next hill.

Eventually their destination was on display before them. In a hollow between the gentler hills and the gigantic starkness of the Pyrenees, was one of the most important through-towns of medieval Europe. The place where several different pilgrim routes converged on their way through the narrow low pass to Roncevaux and Spain. It was a major resting-place on the road to Santiago de Compostela.

Lying as it does at the foot of the Roncevalles Pass, St-Jean-de-Pied-de-Port had the dense Iraty Forest to the south-east. Here eagles and bears preyed on those who strayed from the protected pilgrim's path. Deep snow

76

lay on the heights, but underfoot, through the town, it was no longer white.

As the English troop approached, they could see how the pilgrim paths converged. Each one picked out by way-markers and church walls decorated with shells. They started to see little wooden crosses beside the road, where travellers had died en-route. On hillocks they saw larger stone mounds and more permanent crosses, marking where pilgrims still paid homage to Charlemagne and his nephew Roland, for they were treading in their very footsteps, even though they had lived over 500 years before.

The legend was kept alive by the song Chanson de Roland, sung by pilgrims and locals to ward off evil spirits along the menacing Basque Mountains. This had undoubtedly recently been the location of the army blocking the pass against ex-King Pedro and any English troops he might have gathered.

Tightening ranks, they raised their trumpets with all their flags of England and of the Royal Household attached. With swords drawn, erect in salute and with trumpets blasting, the one hundred cavalry of King Edward left the river Nive. Galloping up-hill, in impressive formation towards the citadel. Risking themselves to exposure across an open space overlooking the town. They meant the enemy to see them approaching. They were faced with fortified barracks, which looked as though it could be almost impossible to get a foothold on, or to besiege successfully.

Almost at once, the great gates of the citadel, hewn into the rocks, were drawn open, as if by an invisible hand. A matching force of one hundred cavalry galloped out in a motley array of foreign uniforms. They drew-up some hundred yards in front of their visitors and held their lances forward. Thank goodness, there appeared to be no King at their head.

'Is that a salute or a challenge?' the English troop commander asked his leader, who had by now, deliberately placed himself at the head of his little army.

For all to see, Prince John removed his helmet, gave it to his commander and replaced it with a crown. It was his own personal coronet, the battle-crown of a King's son. With an arc of his right arm, he deliberately discarded all his weapons by leaning down and distributing them all around him on the ground with a clatter, except for one 3-inch dagger, which he had concealed

77

about his person. Then, quite alone, he rode up-to and right-through the lances ahead of him. They were forced to move aside as he rode by. Their orders did not include the killing of an unarmed King of England and their foreign leader was not to know that this was not the King. The gate was opened for John of Gaunt and closed directly behind him. So far, his gamble had paid off.

Standing in the courtyard was the largest General seen on any battlefield. Not only was he over seven feet tall, but his girth was twice the size of a normal man. It could only be Sir Hugh Calveley, head of the English Mercenary Army. He greeted the Prince with a chuckle of approval, as he strode forward.

'By God, King Edward has sons!'

'A friendly face?' questioned Prince John to himself, dismounting and suddenly feeling dwarfed. Could he trust him? 'We have brought a force to Parley,' he said.

'I fear they will only talk to the King. That was all they would agree to. I'm sorry.'

'Will they talk to King Pedro instead?'

'No! By God. They never want to talk to that man again! They hate him for deceiving them a thousand times. You should hear the stories. They'd sooner send an assassin to Pedro. No! It's only your good father, King Edward they'll sit down and *Parley* with.'

'So, it's a lot more complicated than King Pedro says?'

'I fear the feeling is murderous here,' replied Calveley gingerly.

'By the way, I'm curious,' said the Prince, 'just what orders did you give your troops, outside these gates?'

'They're not *my* men.' Sir Hugh was amused. His whole body shook slightly, 'I think they were trying to salute you, but you appeared to undress!'

'Ridiculous!' snorted John of Gaunt, then he saw the laughter in Calveley's eyes.

'No, no, my Prince. That I assure you, was the bravest action I have ever seen. Quite worthy of your esteemed father,' he nodded. 'Believe me, they would have fought you if they had not thought you were the King of England himself!'

'Are you saying they will only talk to my father? You know better than anyone, he hasn't ridden a horse for five years. I fear he'd never make this journey.'

They heard approaching footsteps. Calveley hissed in a low voice, 'Beware! You know what these Kings are like, they are not keen on the lower ranks.'

'Meaning me?'

The giant warrior nodded. 'They expected a King!'

'Then, I'll just have to bluff my way out of this one,' John murmured as he turned to give his formal salute to the older of the two Kings, now stood before him. He greeted King Peter IV of Aragon and then King Charles II of Navarre. They were accompanied by two pennant-bearers and an escort of ten, led by a Captain of the Guard.

'I gave orders only to admit the King of England. Who are you?' King Charles was disdainful of a small coronet, when he clearly expected a stately crown. Neither of these men had met his father in recent years, thank goodness, or they would have realised sooner that Edward was too old for all this.

'Prince John Plantagenet, Sires.' He bowed low to two of the several rulers of Spain, who he knew had very little power in themselves. [2]

'Be bold. Stroke their vanity,' John of Gaunt could hear his father's old advice, as he had coached his fourth son to be a diplomat. It had always stood him in good stead.

'Oh! Grand Sires of Spain! The King of England awaits you,' he lied with aplomb and paused a little. 'With all Pomp and Crown attended, he requests his brothers in kingship to Parley in his golden tent.' And where, he wondered, was he going to find one of those?

'King Edward is here?'

'No, sires. He is one day's ride away, awaiting your pleasure.' A fib as large as England.

He deliberately did not tell them the location of the Parley, or that the King would not be the one who had to whip these fellows' mighty egos into shape. John of Gaunt needed to gamble that his esteemed brother, Edward the Black Prince *would* be able to.

'And King Pedro?' the older King Peter asked weightily. 'There's no point in going if King Pedro is not there. We plan to denounce him in front of your father and expect him to carry out his execution.'

'Er... King Pedro is there.' Prince John hesitated, taken by surprise at the demand for King Pedro's execution, but he had told the truth.

'See, he's lying. This is a trap!' Charles of Navarre called out to his Captain of the Guard. 'Tell the troop to prepare for Attack!'

Sensing the danger, John of Gaunt lashed out with his tongue, 'I am but a messenger, Sires. If the King of England gives his word, then...' he started to speak more slowly and deliberately: 'King...Pedro...of...Castile...is... present.' But I hope he won't be, he thought.

'Ah!' Calveley jumped with two mighty feet into the middle of the tension. 'So, when do we go? And how many escorts would your Majesties need?' Calveley bowed extravagantly to them. 'Do you wish to take my Company? May I suggest that their presence will not threaten your negotiations with King Edward.'

'No!' replied the two Kings in unison. They turned to one side, took one step away and started to argue. Apparently they each wanted their own soldiers. Prince John realised they obviously did not trust each other. Did this give him more chance to divide them?

'Take heed,' whispered Calveley behind him, 'they plot Assassination!'

John of Gaunt weighed up the possibilities of getting a message to the Black Prince. Would there be an opportunity? King Pedro had to be gone by the time the two Kings arrived at the meeting place. They clearly planned to kill him. But they could see no way of getting the warning to the former King. Besides, the laws of Parley allowed no messenger to be sent back to the enemy, in case an advantage was taken. The English Prince realised that he and his cavalry troop were virtual hostages. Thank goodness the two Kings had no idea where the rendezvous was. A vague idea dawned on him. His English troop was still outside this fortress. Could he possibly get a message to them?

As if reading his thoughts, but to his horror, the great gates swung open and his cavalry entered the citadel. He cursed under his breath. He remembered his own orders: *if the crossed white flag of Parley was offered to them, they should enter peacefully.* Now he had nobody on the outside of the walls. There would be no chance of sending a secret message to his brother. Every move the English made would be closely watched from now on.

Undoubtedly the two Kings were now plotting to kill King Pedro. It was in the lap of the Gods what they would do when they found that King Edward of England was *not* at the Parley. Already in a murderous mood, they would most probably slaughter every one of them. Would they dare to go as far as killing the Black Prince?

That would be a terrible gamble.

On the other hand, John of Gaunt thought gloomily, if a message could be sent somehow, the scenario was just as bad. Finding no King Pedro to kill, they would seek vengeance when they discovered that King Edward was missing as well, wouldn't they? Everything depended on their view of his brother. He prayed that the Black Prince's far-flung fame as a warrior Knight, would have earned their respect.

The next day, his one hundred strong troop outnumbered two to one by foot soldiers and Calveley's company of cavalry. To Parley you had to have equal forces. With the crossed white flags in front, followed by the banners of two Kings of Spain and one Prince of England, the army of three hundred men of different hues left the stronghold of St-Jean-Pied-de-Port.

John of Gaunt's instinct was to order his men to turn and fight, despite the odds against them. He knew he was putting his brother, the heir to the English throne, into immediate danger if he led this army into his camp at Peyrehorade. There would definitely be a battle fought over King Pedro, if nothing else.

Calveley rode up beside him. It occurred to the Prince that the odds would be evened out if the mercenary company could be relied on. If only he could trust Calveley. Would he change sides again? How could he test him?

'Prince John, I have some information.' The mercenary leader saluted. He was riding a white stallion called Pheidippides, nearly eighteen hands high. A horse he was reputed to have bred himself. Indeed it could not have come from the Arab blood of Spanish horses, as it had enough bone to carry him sixty miles a day in full armour and enough blood to keep up.

Deciding to meet his problem head-on and believing attack was the best approach, Prince John let loose with his tongue, 'You are a traitor, Sir!' He needed the truth, right now.

'Of what do you speak?' growled Sir Hugh.

'I talk of Master Chaucer. He carried orders for you from the King.'

There was silence.

Prince John continued, 'Just where is Master Chaucer?'

The Knight measured his words carefully before he replied, 'I have spies everywhere, Prince John. All I know is that Master Chaucer was seen boarding a ship at Bilbao bound for England, earlier this month. Believe me, Sire, I know nothing of my King's orders. I am an English subject first. His Majesty knows well my commitment to my King and my Country.'

'And to whosoever pays you!' came the tart reply.

'The King, your father, knows where my loyalty lies, Sire.'

'Well, that may have been the case, but he doubts it now! I accuse you of directly disregarding an order NOT to fight against our cousin King Pedro. By installing the Usurper Trastamara, his half-brother, you are responsible for the rightful inheritance of a King being passed to a bastard.'

'Master Chaucer never reached me, Sire. Thus, I received no orders from England. When did he come? What route did he take?'

'He left Poitiers in late September, and he carried diplomatic papers with letters of transit from King Charles here.' The Prince caught a thought.

'At least they didn't kill him, if he was on his way back,' muttered the Knight, as his huge stallion sidestepped a boulder. They were travelling through Roland's Gorge.

'No doubt he dispatched a messenger to the King as soon as he landed in England. It should arrive in Bordeaux very soon. He will vindicate me, my Prince.'

John of Gaunt sighed, 'There's nothing I can do until you are officially cleared of this charge. However, at this moment, I need proof of your loyalty, for there is much trouble ahead.' The Prince spurred his horse to end the conversation, still sick with worry about his predicament. He still couldn't trust the Knight. Unexpectedly however, the white stallion caught up again. Sir Hugh spoke, 'Last night, two of my spies reported the whereabouts of your camp at Peyrehorade. I have told no one, Sire. My Sergeant Major also overheard today's orders. *They are to surround your camp as soon as we arrive.* Sire, I must tell you, he also overheard the plan to have twice as many cavalry soldiers travel in secret, half an hour behind us. They are under orders to stay out of sight, until summoned.'

'What treachery is this from these two Kings?' Prince John was appalled.

'It is not King Peter's doing. I am certain he knows nothing. The cavalry behind are all King Charles' men. He gave secret orders.' It was obvious, Calveley earnestly wanted the Prince to believe and trust him.

'How do you know so much?' John of Gaunt wanted to believe him, and felt bitter that he couldn't.

'You can judge my loyalty, Sire. I deliberately did not tell them of our destination today. If they knew, we would be going via the cross-country route, down the small valleys to our right. This gorge, this route, is the long way around.'

So, the Prince made up his mind. Having little alternative, he decided to take the risk, 'Our only chance is to get a message to the camp. Could you sent someone to arrive before we get there?'

'It might be possible.' Calveley was thinking. 'One of my men could try. The message should be in coded, in case he is caught. If only we could create a diversion for the secret cavalry coming half an hour behind us. What we need is some outside help.'

'I have an idea!' the Prince interrupted, signalling for his portable writing tablet. He turned to the mounted officers behind him, 'Close in around me while I write a note, I don't want anyone to see'.

On the front of his saddle, as he rode, he gave himself two minutes to think and then he wrote on a small scrap of papyrus that he always carried on his person. The Prince then tore the note in half and handed one half up high to the large Mercenary, on his tall horse. 'Your message. The other half is for Bayonne, where there are a hundred English masons building that cathedral,' he partly explained, not daring to say any more in case he was overheard.'

'Interesting!' mused Sir Hugh. 'Let me see what we can come up with.' Then, inexplicably, he added, 'We train our horses well here, you know,' and wheeled away.

Five minutes later, the army had nearly reached the end of the Evil Passage of the Nive Gorge, when a shout went up and one of the cavalry horses went hopping lame.

It carried its off-foreleg, like a three-legged dog. Though a horse could walk on three legs, it would have to be in agony to do so. It usually denoted a broken leg.

Calveley had pulled further back along the line. He was now riding beside King Peter, some way behind the unfortunate incident. He announced loudly, with a show of some annoyance, 'We're not stopping the whole cavalry for one horse.' As he passed the offending creature it was hopping about. 'Destroy it!' he called disdainfully. 'Give the man a cross-bow!'

The whole column rounded the next corner, leaving the horse and rider behind, out of sight. They heard the scream of the poor horse, it was distinctive and blood chilling. The noise bounced off the tight walls of the Gorge, echoing repeatedly.

'It's done!' claimed Calveley a few minutes later, as he rode up beside John of Gaunt, further up the line.

'You killed the horse?'

'It was a trick!' laughed Calveley quietly, 'Oh yes, we've got out of many tight corners with my horses. They act well, don't you think?'

'That was an act?' the Prince asked incredulously. 'What if the man's captured? What if he talks?'

'Oh, he won't talk,' Calvary grinned at the Prince, 'you can absolutely rely on this fellow!' he inclined his head to one side and lifted one eyebrow.

'I don't understand. What are you saying?'

'Like all my messengers, he's speechless. They're dumb! You see, I recruit them deliberately. They can't reveal secrets if they're tortured, now can they?'

Aghast and discomforted at the ways of a Mercenary leader, Gaunt took a minute to gather his thoughts. Now, not feeling quite as confident that he was really the one in charge, the Prince deliberately changed the subject, back to the circus act, 'So, what prank did the horses play this time?'

'Oh no! They aren't pranks. They have saved our lives time after time. You understand I cannot tell you all of them, for some tricks are indeed secret. But all our horses are taught to go lame, merely from a touch on their shoulder. Most of them neigh or scream to order and they all lie down, either to protect us with their bodies or to look dead from a distance.'

The Prince was amazed. 'I've never heard anything like it!'

'That is why people believe it is real.' He smiled. 'By now that horse and rider will be half a mile away, down that small valley we passed. That, by the way, is the shortest route back to your base at Peyrehorade. Now we just have to hope like hell, that the secret cavalry behind us has not spotted him.'

'Good God! When will he get there? If he gets there?'

'Maybe half an hour, or an hour before us.'

'An hour is not enough time! King Pedro needs to be well out of the area by then. For goodness sake, his road to Poitiers is along the same path we must take now. My God! He'll meet us coming the other way!'

Calveley comforted him as best he could. 'The Prince, your brother, will work that out for himself. It is up to him now.'

Suddenly the Prince thumped his mailed fist in anger, on his knee: 'Good God! I've forgotten to tell him the Password!'

'It wouldn't have done any good. He can't talk!'

'I should have put it on the note.'

'And risk that falling into enemy hands? No I don't think so.'

The Prince groaned and they both fell silent.

Despite all the evidence to the contrary, John of Gaunt felt things might now be starting to improve. At least there was a glimmer of hope that they might get out of this catastrophe. But what was the truth of it? It was highly possible he was being drawn further and further into a grand plan, a royal web of deceit. He felt his own life was in the hands of capricious fate. He would much rather be on the field of battle, to live or die by his own skills. He needed to be in control and to make his own luck. In four hours time he would find out for himself.

When the troops reached Bayonne and its Cathedral, the cavalry led them right up, over and around all the building paraphernalia. As they marched past the wooden scaffolding, some was knocked over. It was only by chance that no-one was hurt. From all over the cathedral building-site, masons rushed down to protect their tools and their lead. They muttered obscenities at the soldiers. In the ensuing melee, nobody noticed a feather and a slip of parchment being passed by John of Gaunt to the Head Mason.

The two hundred secret troops, reached the cathedral building-site at Bayonne, half an hour after the main army. With not a little glee, the masons had raked over the hoof marks of the earlier army and directed the following troop through the marshes, north along the coast. Almost entirely the wrong way.

Chapter 8 - A Coded Message

Meanwhile, the Black Prince had picked out twenty reliable Lookouts and posted them on the surrounding hills, some 3 miles away.

The hamlet of Peyrehorade was in the middle of a saucer of land, with scrub, gorse and low clumps of bushes dotting the uplands. It provided perfect cover for both the Lookouts on the slopes and their horses tethered in the bushes. Their task was to give the earliest possible warning of an approaching army, probably expected from the West. But you never knew how devious the enemy was. 'Watch out for Bandits around here,' the Officer in Charge warned his men, 'they prey on Pilgrims along this route. If in doubt, there's a Password. And don't forget, no Password, no Access! A single man could well be an enemy spy!'

So it was not a complete surprise when the lookout spotted Calveley's secret messenger, slipping and sliding in a tumble of stones and dust, as he ascended the steep hill to the South. He was in a dishevelled and filthy state, having hit the ground with a sickening somersault when his horse's heart gave out at the gallop. The man arrived exhausted and on foot. His brave steed lay motionless and already pecked by crows, some 2 miles back. Truly dead this time. It was the result of a relentless flat-out gallop, for much of the 30 miles since leaving Calveley's troop.

He certainly wasn't the ideal Messenger after all, for he had no tongue to make himself understood. He was a mercenary after all, in fact his tongue had been missing since birth. Gasping for breath, he remembered his wits and waved the now filthy scrap of parchment, addressed to His Excellency

Prince Edward the Black Prince, from Prince John of Gaunt.

They snatched the message away from him and scoffed at it. There was no Royal Seal and no Password! The four Lookouts lunged forward to make an arrest, but he fought them viciously despite the state of him. He nearly got the upper-hand.

'Password? Password?' they kept repeating as they subdued him. His silence was driving them mad. Still nothing. 'He's a Bandit!'

To his horror, the Messenger was pushed to the ground, tied with a rope and finally flung across the pommel of a Lookout's saddle. They galloped him all the way down the hill towards Peyrehorade, the Black Prince's hamlet. All the while attempting not to die from lack of breath, as his stomach thumped against the pommel, in front of the rider. Flung to earth, he found himself thrown to the ground in a tiny store-room, under close guard. His piece of parchment was properly unrolled by the Officer in Charge, who ran to get his Commander-in-Chief. He wasn't sure what this was.

At once, the Black Prince thankfully recognised his brother's hand. 'A messenger who refuses to talk! What good is that!' He tore at his fair curls in frustration. 'What in God's name is all this about? I cannot understand a word. It's in some sort of *Code*!'

'You won't be able to get anything out of him, Sire,' said the officer.

'Why the devil not? You haven't killed him, have you?' The Prince looked up sharply, a fury building in his voice.

'No, Sire! It seems the fellow has no tongue. He cannot answer you.'

The Prince was silent a moment, then murmured, 'Hard bastards those mercenaries, they use dumb men for messengers!' So, there were no secrets to be tortured out of him, if he was caught.

'Fetch me the man!' he ordered, 'I cannot unravel this message without him. Get me a large skin of parchment and a quill. Mix me some soot!'

Sitting in the Monastery orchard, in the middle of his life story, the old hermit's voice began to croak mid-sentence. As if he had a crumb irritating his throat, he started a violent fit of coughing. His voice got lower and slower.

'Are you alright there?' asked his companion, gently patting the old bones upon his back. Petit-Roi managed to move his head up and down slowly. 'Are you sure?'

'That will have to do for writing...' the hermit did his best. He tried to continue, but found he was getting flashes of colours before his old eyes and jumbled-up patterns in his brain. He felt troubled and started kicking out in agitation. The English Envoy urgently called for him to stop. His voice had lowered an octave and begun to come out in a completely incomprehensible language. It trailed-off, as he suddenly pitched head-first into the grass and apple blossom at their feet.

It took another week of rest, as the old man slept deeply for days on end. When he revived, they fed him Frumenty Porridge and Bread, for that was soft and nutritious. They treated his sore throat with sips of warm Honey, Lemon and Grated Ginger. Still worried about the state of his cracked skin, rather than waking him up for the bathtub, they gently applied a lotion of infused Poppy Petals as he slept.

The Envoy wondered if he would ever be strong enough to get as far as the Templar Treasure! But as the week passed, the story eventually got going again:

I stood guard behind the Messenger when he was carried in and thrown down in front of the Black Prince, in case he caused any trouble.

'My God, he's trussed up like a parcel. For goodness sake, get a move on and undo this man!' he ordered sharply, 'If I am right, he may save all our lives. I do know we have to hurry.'

It soon became apparent that there would be other communication problems. Apart from not being able to talk, there was a handicap in his understanding of our English language. Even though he was a fellow Englishman, getting the mercenary to understand the London tongue was difficult. He must have come from one of those northern regions, or maybe from the far west of England. The sort of dialect he understood would need an expert like good Master Chaucer to properly interpret.

The urgent questions began, as fast as possible: 'Is a troop coming?'

The man shook his head, puzzled.

'How many men?'

Again he shook his head, knitting his brow.

'Maybe it's too fast for him, Sire' suggested the Camp Commander.

'Is a troop coming?' The Black Prince spoke slowly, making riding motions with his arms.

The messenger nodded, his face lit up. Success!

'How..long..before..it..is..here?'

The man went into sign language and began to flap his arms.

'No! No!' It was exasperating. 'Put...up...one...finger...for...each...hour,' instructed the Prince, wiggling his own digits.

The fellow held up one, waved his hand from side to side and shrugged.

'One hour maybe?'

He nodded.

'My God.' exclaimed the Black Prince. 'We have got to decipher this message and act on it, all within the hour.' He was speaking to the officer, but the messenger was starting to understand him better. The man was shaking his head. Suddenly he banged his right fist into the palm of his other hand with some force, urgency written on his rough craggy face.

'Help us!' interceded the Camp Commander, 'he means NOW!'

Down the left-hand side of the parchment, the Black Prince wrote out the code:

2K+C

1½ f +½ C-t

ByrD

(+2dt.BY?)

ChtkEg

CgpE

XK-P

Jericho

Danjouan

As he worked it out, he started writing the translation, on the opposite side of the page. He began from the bottom up:

'**Danjouan** – That's the origin of our Plantagenet name, *Geoffrey of Anjou*. That has a mixture of our two pet names for each other in childhood. John was JOUAN, and I was DANJOU. This is definitely from my brother. Only he could sign it like that.'

The Prince wrote *Prince John of Gaunt,* on the right-side of the last line. Then he started on the next line up.

'**Jerico** – We are to be surrounded! Like the Bible story. Is that right?'

The mercenary shrugged.

'It must be, it has to be,' mumbled the Black Prince, unsure. Confused also by the next coded line above, he quickly turned his attention to the very top of the page:

'**2K+C**' – He looked for help as the man who could not speak, circled his head with two of his fingers and placed them spread-out on the top. 'A Crown? Two Kings, plus Calveley?' That was right!

'**1½f+½C-t** – This looks impossible! What's this one and a half and another half?'

The Commander was ahead of him. 'Could they be troops. There's twenty in a troop.'

The Prince steadied his thoughts for minute and then turned to his Commander, 'How many would we normally expect here for a Parley?'

'Equal numbers. Exactly two hundred from the other side, Sire.'

'So, one and a half hundred and then half a hundred. Could that be 150 foot soldiers and 50 cavalry? Whose cavalry? Calveley's?' he asked and immediately got a nod. 'Thank goodness for that.'

'**ByrD** – could that be *by road*?'

The messenger shook his head and started making square shapes with his hands.

They all looked at each other in frustration. 'Can I, Sire' the Officer reached over and gave the man the pen. He offered him the reverse side of the parchment to write on.

He was probably illiterate, but he must help them. The messenger drew several squares beside each other and then fewer squares above those. They watched him draw a cross on the highest point.

'A church!' exclaimed Prince John. '**By**, *Bayonne Cathedral*? They're coming on the Bayonne road!'

'**(2dtT.BY?)** – That's more numbers. There can't be any more, surely? Two hundred?' he asked the man.

The messenger shrugged and waved his hand sideways again. 'He's not sure. Surely he must have seen an extra two hundred men?'

'Perhaps they are hidden, or following later?' The man shrugged again.

'**dt** – Could that mean a detour, a longer route? Or does it mean they are detained? No, they wouldn't fight them at Bayonne, would they?'

'Sire, can I suggest we leave that one?' the Officer suggested, 'It looks as though something happens to the extra 200 soldiers at Bayonne.'

'Don't forget the question mark!'

'They must have plotted something. Why did Prince John want us to know about soldiers that would not arrive here?'

'To warn us, of course,' said the Prince making up his mind. He turned towards his Commander. 'Order the immediate manning of all defensive positions and have all arms laid ready. I want every man in full armour. Warn the innkeeper to bolt his doors and hide well away from the inn. They'll probably burn it.'

With the orders discharged, the Black Prince, his trusted camp commander and his personal aide, were back at the parchment.

I tell you, we guarded them well, as they puzzled over its meaning. There were to be no interruptions.

'I believe my brother is warning us of treachery on the part of the two Kings and Calveley'

'But this is Calveley's man. He must be on our side!' the commander objected.

'We'll see! Sir Hugh was a favourite with my father, but he has a lot to explain here. He must know he is in trouble over Master Chaucer's orders.'

'**ChtkEg** – Aha! Look at that! The **Ch** on the fifth line from the bottom. *Chaucer*, tick. So Chaucer is *OK* and *Eg* in *England*. He'll surely get a message to His Majesty as soon as he lands. King Edward has been worried, in case he had sent him to his death. Now hurry, we must complete this last part. What I cannot understand, is why we are in danger here? For goodness sake, it's meant to be a peace Parley!'

'**CapE**' – the Prince read. '*GpE* is what the family calls my father, *Grandpa England.*

'**C?**'

'Try it phonetically, **C** equals *See.*

'They think they are going to see Grandpa England?'

'That's it! We have to pretend he's here.'

'Run, run,' ordered the Prince. 'Tell the innkeeper I have a role for him after all. Bring him to me in the church. Now, let's tackle the last line:

'**XK-P** – *K* was *King* earlier.'

'Without King Peter?'

'King Peter's not with them?'

They had all almost forgotten the little mercenary in their midst. He started to shake his head vigorously and made a cutting motion across his throat.

'King Pedro!' They looked for confirmation from the little man. 'That must be it.' The Black Prince hesitated, continuing cautiously, 'they are coming to kill him, the treacherous swine! It's meant to be a Parley. They call themselves anointed Kings, yet they plan to murder another. They don't deserve their crowns. That's it! You read it out to me. It will give me time to think. Quickly! We need to make a plan.'

The Commander took the parchment and read the right-hand side of each line:

2K+C — — — — — — — — — — — —	2 Kings + Calveley
11/ 2f+1/ 2C-t — — — — — — — — — —	150 foot, 50 Calveley troops
BYrD — — — — — — — — — — — —	Bayonne road
(2dt.BY?) — — — — — — — — — — —	(+200 diverted at Bayonne?)
ChtkEg — — — — — — — — — —	Chaucer OK in England
CgpE — — — — — — — — — — — —	See Grandpa England
XK-P — — — — — — — — — — — —	Kill King Pedro
Jericho — — — — — — — — — — —	We are to be surrounded
Danjouan — — — — — — — — — —	Prince John's signature

'There's the two Kings, with 150 of their foot soldiers, plus 50 mounted troops with Calveley. That is as well as Prince John's 100 men?' he asked the dumb mercenary. The man nodded wearily.

'Thank goodness for that, at least.'

'I wouldn't put it passed them to murder us all and take the English crown for themselves,' said the commander, his voice trembling.

The Black Prince looked thunderous. 'Perhaps they are already allied with France!'

'Anyway, they intend to murder King Pedro. Chaucer is OK and we are to be surrounded,' the commander finished with a flourish.

'They cannot be far away now, Sire. Don't you need to get King Pedro away from here immediately?' asked the aide.

'No!' answered the Prince, 'It's too late for that. He'd be seen from miles away.' He paused and added, 'Get the innkeeper to show you the entrance to the secret cave. He'll have to use the hidden door in the church. Quickly!' He turned to the Commander. 'I want King Pedro left down there with a guard. Four men should be enough. They have my explicit orders to kill him if he looks like siding with the incoming troops, or if he tries any signal.'

'Sire!' protested his commander, 'what's on your mind? You risk all this to put King Pedro back on his throne, yet now you don't trust him?'

The Prince sighed and looked around at all of us. 'It is true. This could well be a pro-French plot to murder us all. Just think a minute. They would kill my father, my brother and i, as well as the cream of our forces. The English would be driven out. What a coup for France!' Then he added quietly, 'They could well be successful.'

There were not many of us in that room, but we at once grasped the full extent of his distrust. The Grand Master of Santiago chose that moment to enter and received an unexpectedly frosty stare from the English. They didn't trust him either. Strange Race, he thought. Executed an about turn and marched right out again.

'Put him in there too!' ordered the Black Prince with a flash of temper. Santiago had chosen this ground. He had led them all straight into a trap. The Prince steadied himself. The lives of his soldiers depended on keeping a clear head and his wits sharp.

'What about Master Chaucer, Sire? Where has he been?' asked the commander.

'Thank you, Captain. Of course Chaucer is the very key I need. Let's get this plan together. He must have been detained, imprisoned under guard, or whatever. Unable to get the King's message to Sir Hugh Calveley. Otherwise our Mercenary leader would not have gone against his orders and fought against King Pedro.'

'So they only released Chaucer well after King Pedro's battle was won, clever!' remarked the Aide.

'Yes, my father guessed it all along. He could not contemplate Chaucer's death. The man who imprisoned him was King Charles of Navarre. *He* is the traitor here. He was the one who gave Chaucer safe-passage documents at my father's request. He has gone back on his word, from one King to another. This is a serious breach of honour by a common knight, let alone by an anointed King.'

The Prince raised his hand for silence while he thought for a moment, his eyes scanning the room. Finally they rested upon me. 'Petit-Roi' he mouthed.

I stepped forward and whispered, 'Shall I go, Sire?'

He nodded slowly, and then turned back to the others. 'I have my plan at last!' he declared in triumph. 'I pray our boldness can save the lives of us all.'

The aide, an older Knight, stepped forward and knelt before his Prince, 'Forgive me, Sire, but your father the King would wish me to advise you to join King Pedro in the secret cave. We must save his son and heir!'

'Thank you, good Knight,' replied his master, touching the man's shoulder. 'I have never turned from a fight in my life. Why, I wouldn't even trust King Pedro at this moment, as you know.' He turned back to the Commander, 'No, we have a bold plan and we must embellish it with a bit of acting, my friends.' He leant forward to draw circles on the parchment.

'Here is what we do...'

Chapter 9 - Rough Justice

Half an hour later the report came of a 300-strong force halted a quarter of an hour away, just over the hilltop, out of sight. The Black Prince received the news with satisfaction. 'That makes sense, thank God! At least we have understood that part of the message. That must be Prince John's men, plus the visiting 200.'

'Do you think they are waiting for their extra 200 hidden cavalry to catch up?' asked the commander. 'There is no other reason for them to stop there. We just have to hope those hidden troops have been successfully diverted. If they arrive we are lost.'

'Have more faith,' said the Prince with confidence. 'We have a good plan. First we must draw these 300 troops into our camp, whether they want to or not, follow me!'

The Black Prince looked splendid and carefree mounted on his black stallion. He was dressed in only half armour. Black chain mail with black upper body armour. He was not wearing his helmet with its distinctive lion on the top. His blonde curly hair made him look younger and more vulnerable. All of which was deliberate.

Only it wasn't him. It was *me*, Petit-roi, his double! Trying to look at ease on his favourite fiery horse.

With trumpets and drums loudly sounding our approach, the Black Prince and my four flag bearers, cantered to a stop in front of King Charles of Navarre and King Peter of Aragon. The Kings thought they had stopped out of sight, but were taken somewhat by surprise. Most of their soldiers were on the ground for a well-earned rest.

With a welcoming flourish from the horns, I began as keenly instructed by my Prince, in my strongest, most authoritarian voice. 'My father King Edward of England welcomes you, noble Princes and Kings of Aragon and Navarre. We are indeed honoured. We know you have come to Parley, but we have a tournament for you first!' I turned my head and shouted loudly towards the resting troops. 'His Majesty bids you come and join him for the festivities and feast that we have prepared for all.'

A great cheer went up from the exhausted soldiers, for they had run many miles. Two of my own flag bearers peeled off and re-positioned themselves, one in front of each King. 'Now you see, my friends, you travel the last part of your long journey under the protection of the personal banner of the House of Plantagenet. By the Grace of God, Kings of England, France and Lords of Ireland.'

I wheeled the horse around and set-off at the trot back towards camp. I was riding with the Prince's own standard carriers either side of me, quickly followed by the two flag bearers, beside each King. Everyone was delighted with their welcome by the supposed Black Prince himself and trotted along to catch up. But it was Sir Hugh Calveley's mounted mercenaries who followed behind. The foot soldiers had not yet picked up their weapons or formed into lines. Meanwhile, half of John of Gaunt's cavalry moved into the space ahead of them, while the other fifty horsemen stayed at the rear.

They had successfully *SPLIT* the opposing forces.

'King Pedro? He IS here, isn't he?' asked Charles of Navarre.

'So sorry,' I said. 'His daughter has taken a turn for the worse. She's very ill, you know.' I had to give them an excuse. We had not had time to prepare my speech. 'If anyone asks you questions, make it up, but for God's sake man, sound convincing!' the Prince had said as I departed.

We entered the compound of the camp. 'Such a pretty girl, too,' I added. Sensing disquiet, the King of Navarre looked behind him and quickly registered the lack of his own soldiers about him. He was a youngish man, with a hard head on his shoulders. But, before he had time to think, the group came to a halt. A royal servant took the reins of his bridle and a wooden block was provided on the ground, for him to dismount. An

Equerry stamped his salute. 'His Majesty awaits your Royal Highness, as well as the King of Aragon and your personal Equerries. Sires, this way please.'

Indeed, standing in the dark doorway of the church, there miraculously was King Edward of England. He had his flowing grey beard and his red mantle, crown and well-known sceptre, topped by a dove. Perhaps his beard was not quite as pointed as usual. He turned into the doorway, within a few moments I completed the party, as the two Equerries with their respective Kings followed *King Edward* into the gloomy light of the small pilgrim church.

Prince John of Gaunt and his entourage marched noisily behind us, bowing low to the *King*, who was now sitting on a raised seat in front of the altar. He stepped sideways and addressed the improvised throne.

'I shall do the honours this time *Your Majesty*.' The church door shut solidly behind him. He bowed low to the guests and addressed the figure on the throne. 'Sire, noble father, may I present His Royal Highness King Peter of Aragon and His Royal Highness King Charles of Navarre.' There was much bowing.

'Our noble guests, Your Majesties.' He bowed low again. 'May I present my brother, Prince Edward, Prince of Aquitane, Earl of Chester and Duke of Cornwall.' The real Black Prince stepped forward from the shadows, reached out and deftly removed the mantle, the crown and the dove sceptre from the supposed King Edward and said quietly, 'Thank you, innkeeper.' The *not-so-pointed beard* rushed back to the apparent safety of his inn.

There was a clash of steel as soldiers closed order all around the visiting Kings, to bar their retreat. Without my helmet and without thinking, I went to my usual place, to stand guard beside my Prince. Everyone gasped, as the likeness between us was undeniable. One visiting Equerry suddenly realised they were in imminent danger and went to draw his sword. But we were prepared and took it from his hand. All four of them were disarmed. Their protests were indignant, but of no use whatsoever. They were prisoners.

John of Gaunt strode up to his brother in the chair. 'We have to act fast! We don't have much time,' he said. The Black Prince nodded. Both the brothers knew that if the extra 200 cavalrymen arrived now, there could be a slaughter.

From the *throne*, he started to speak both very quickly and authoritatively, almost mechanically. 'I convene this as a Court of Law upon English soil in this land of Aquitane, which I am entitled to do in the name of my father King Edward III of England.'

Both Kings found their voices at once, 'We came under the flag of Parley! It is the known and accepted law. You have no right to hold our persons.'

Suddenly King Charles realised his personal jeopardy and yelled out a warning at the top of his voice. 'Treachery! You create WAR here!' It was intended for his men outside to come to his rescue. But no shout could be heard. Calveley's men were on guard outside the doors. They had their orders.

On the other side of the camp, the weary foot soldiers were lying around a bull-roast. They were laughing and enjoying the food and ale on offer. They were looking forward to the tournament and entertainment to come. What they could not see was that most of the English soldiers were inside the two big accommodation barns. They were packing up, getting ready to ride-out as soon as possible. No tournament ground was being taped-off, no jugglers or players were readying themselves.

With a much wiser head upon his shoulders, King Peter of Aragon's tone was not so hysterical. 'Why do you hold us? We have done nothing.'

'That is precisely what we have to decide here.' The Black Prince held up his hand, and started speaking quickly once again. 'I declare that this Court will hear submissions from the prisoners and accusations from the Crown. Fair judgement will be summarily carried out.'

'You have no right to punish a King of another country, you know that!' interrupted Charles of Navarre. His point was swept aside.

'You will accept our decision, for you have no choice. Now, who is going to speak?'

King Charles' Equerry stepped forward. He was always the prudent one. He bowed low. 'Sire, Most High Prince of England, this is a case of…'

His speech was waved away and halted mid-sentence. 'Only Kings are permitted the right of reply. Only then may we get to the truth of the matter.' The menace in the Black Prince's voice was obvious and it jolted Charles of Navarre into verbal defence. He knew now he must talk for his life. 'May I remind you, this quarrel is part of a Spanish war of Succession. It has absolutely nothing to do with England! King Pedro was judged unfit to rule. We have joined forces to enthrone his half-brother, Henry of Trastamara,' he paused. 'do you not agree with that?'

The Black Prince nodded sagely.

'All would be well', continued King Charles, as he warmed to his theme, 'we have come to explain why he has been deposed, for we know he is your Kinsman. We are here in good faith and under *your* flag of truce, in order to negotiate peace between us.' He turned to the older King beside him, 'Is that not our case complete?'

There was a nod of approval, 'It is well made!' replied Peter of Aragon.

The Black Prince leaned over and picked up two parchments from a side stool. He stood up and unfurled the first. He began to read, speaking in the same automatic quick-fire voice. 'You are accused...' He was interrupted by a loud rapping on the church door. The Kings looked at each other in relief. Their secret troops must have arrived.

But they were doomed to disappointment. A rough-looking burly stranger was escorted into the church clasping a battered hat. He was no soldier. He and his big boots were covered in dust. He was brought up the aisle and placed right in front of the Black Prince. Whose man was this? He mumbled something about a horse and kept his head lowered. Nobody could hear what he said.

'Please tell the court who you are,' said the Black Prince, 'and what happened today. I believe the safety of our English homeland depends on your speaking the truth in front of these persons.'

Somewhat overawed, the man started slowly in a broad Devonish accent, 'We be working like on that there church at Bayonne...'

'Yes, yes, the Cathedral, we know. And just who are you?'

'Me, um, the Master Mason, Sire.'

The two Kings looked at each other uneasily. What could this mean?

There was no arguing who he was. There was a year's worth of stone and brick dust all over the man.

'You are in charge of the men working on the Cathedral?'

'The men Sire, well they comes and goes for a few months at a time Sire. I stays like and takes me orders from that Frenchman what designs it.'

The Prince turned his gaze towards the prisoners. 'This man must be difficult for you to understand?' he asked courteously. All four shook their heads miserably. They were starting to understand only too well.

'Pray continue, Master Mason. We want the events of the last two days please.'

'Well, ye know there be a centum of war 'orses with Prince John here. They came by us along the path riding westwards around the bottom of the hill below. While sounding their trumpets like. Grand sight it was!' He waved over to John of Gaunt. 'We recognised you Sire! That be yesterday, Sire.'

'A hundred horses yesterday?'

'Yes, Sire. Then 'twas about noontime today Sire, he came back with some more on 'orses. There was more of 'em on foot as well. A good hundred and fifty fighting men, running besides. Bloomin' pesky devils they were.' He started screwing his already battered hat in his hands in agitation.

'Why, what was the matter?'

'Well, what we nairn't understand Sire, was why Prince John here brought 'em to the top of our hill, all through our building site. They were dislodging stones and one of his men brought a piece of scaffold right down with 'is 'orse. Lucky there wasn't one of my men up there. Right dangerous it was!'

'What happened then?'

'All t' men came down their ladders and started shout'n and carry'n on. Then Prince John came over and he said he wanted our attention. He told us to look out for the enemy, half an hour behind. *Save our homeland from destruction,* he said. He gave us his feathers, LOOK!'

The Master Mason held up a small brooch, with feathers entwined around the letter 'J'. Still attached to the brooch was a short message:

Report the outcome immediately to Peyrehorade.
The safety of the Kingdom is in your hands.
Order from Prince John of England.

'We reckoned he'd knocked the scaffolding down deliberately to tell us about the enemy coming along behind.'

'My brave man, don't tell me you fought them?'

'Oh, we couldn't do that! There was a whole army of war-'orses that came an half hour behind Prince John's lot. Reckon we did better an that!'

'What happened?'

'Directed 'em to Soustons, along the coast road to the north. The wrong way!'

'Why Soustons?'

'It's terrible marshy long that way. They'll not know if Prince John has been there before 'em, ye see. They'll not be able to follow the tracks. Good plan, Eh?'

'Why would you send them the wrong way?'

He straightened up and nodded proudly to his Prince, 'We're every one of us English, Sire, working on that church.'

'Your testament is finished. We thank you Master Mason.'

The Black Prince felt a well-known instinct for action. Time was running out. Maybe these extra cavalrymen had been successfully diverted, or maybe it was only a short time before they were re-routed, back onto the right road. The enemy army could be bearing down on them even now. The situation was both evilly dangerous, while desperately urgent.

He rattled off his Judgement:

'You are found GUILTY of abusing the flag of international parley, plotting to murder King Pedro of Castile, plotting to murder King Edward of England, Prince John of Gaunt and all our noble English Knights upon our own territory of Aquitaine. You are obviously allies of the French. Your argument with King Pedro is one thing, but as far as we are concerned you are Traitors to your old English alliances. 'You will be dealt with at once!'

King Peter reacted first. Knocking the guards around him off their feet, though he was unarmed. Out of pure instinct, I stepped in front of my Prince to protect him, but our guards had managed to seize King Peter again. They had to hold on tight.

'Talk then, damn you!' interrupted John of Gaunt, standing in front of him now. He *had* to get the truth of this. The war with France was presently stalled and inconclusive. If *this* was a French plot, they must know it, in order to get the main body of their army back from England to defend their position.

'We only planned to kill King Pedro,' said King Peter defensively.

'You lie! You would have murdered us all, if an extra two hundred soldiers were ordered to run amuck through this camp.'

'They had orders only to hold you, while we found King Pedro. I can assure you, we Spaniards are no lovers of the French. We never have been.'

'I reserve judgement on that. The next evidence comes from this communication I have here.' The Black Prince held up a folded tube with the English royal wax seal upon it. 'It is a copy of King Edward's orders to Calveley. Bring in Sir Hugh Calveley,' he ordered.

The giant mercenary marched in on his own. His sword had not been removed and he was obviously *not* under arrest. That was the moment when the two Kings realised that Calveley had changed sides. Why else would he not be under guard? He was to be a witness against them! What else could you expect from a mercenary?

'Sir Hugh,' continued the Black Prince, 'I now show you these orders from King Edward. It is an exact copy of the communication carried by my father's diplomatic messenger, Master Chaucer. It should have reached you last November.'

'I received NO orders from King Edward of England,' Calveley said emphatically, dropping onto one knee. But he had a mind to keep his head raised, in case someone took an inclination to remove it from his shoulders. 'He is my Liege-Lord. I myself and my Free Company of men, owe England our first loyalty. By God, we so swear it every night in our prayers and every year we make it our oath, in front of the King's representative. Otherwise he would not give us licence to hire ourselves to foreign countries.'

'That is very easy to say, Sir Hugh. I tell you that the contents of this letter ordered you *not* to fight for the usurper Trastamara, against our kinsman King Pedro of Castile.'

'Then we would have been bound to withdraw.'

'That's not true! He lies!' shouted Charles of Navarre. 'He ignored the order. We paid him well. So it suited him better.' He turned to face Calveley. 'I can prove your complicity Sir Knight! Did you, or did you not, ingratiate yourself so much into the favours of King Peter here, that you married his daughter and accepted a noble Spanish title? Do you not bear the name of the Count of Carrion? Bah!' King Charles turned to face Sir Hugh, 'He is thick with our cause! Deny THAT, mercenary!'

The Black Prince called for silence and held up another tube, with another English Royal seal upon it. 'I would like you to know King Charles, that I also have here in my hand a *signed* deposition. It has just arrived post haste from Master Chaucer himself. It seems he has been most fortunate in finding a private ship sailing into Bordeaux, from Bilbao.'

'That's hardly possible!' burst out King Charles.

'Not possible? Why not?'

There was no reply.

'Let me read his statement:

I Geoffrey Chaucer, Yeoman of the Bedchamber to His Majesty King Edward III of England and France, Lord of Ireland, do swear the following account to be true:

I was given one of His Majesty's sealed royal diplomatic bags with a letter for the eyes of Sir Hugh Calveley only. I was instructed to take the sealed bag to Barcelona, where he lodged with his Free Troop of Cavalry. I was to seek him out privately, for King Edward believed him to be in company with the King of Aragon. His Majesty had arranged a free diplomatic passage signed by King Charles II of Navarre. His Majesty handed it to me himself. I left Poitiers with three horses, baggage and two men.

We travelled via the Roncesvalles Pass, through the Pyrenees and entered the region of Navarre. In early November we had just gone through Pamplona, when we were arrested by the King of Navarre's soldiers, who knew my name. We saw

them throw the unopened diplomatic bag into the ditch along the way. One of
our number took ill and died in prison. My baggage and horses were lost, but he
remaining two of us were unexpectedly released on the 10th of January. It was
not until the 25th that we found a ship sailing from Bilbao. His Majesty received
my report on this incident on the 29th of January.

    Signed: Chaucer.'

'I've had enough of this!' The Black Prince's face was dark. He addressed
King Charles. 'YOU signed Chaucer's free passage through Navarre? And
you had him arrested?'

'Yes,' the King looked resigned, 'It was meant as a joke!'

Now the Prince was furious. He held up the doved sceptre of state and
pronounced:

'We find you *GUILTY* of a personal Act of War against King Edward III
of England by violating a Royal Diplomat, whom you yourself swore to
protect under the International Laws of peace. And,' he turned to the King
of Aragon, 'you have always been an enemy of King Pedro. We pronounce
you *guilty* of Colluding!'

There was an awful silence. 'My sentence upon both counts is death!'

He nodded at the two Sergeants-at-Arms. They backed the two young
Equerries away to make space, unhooked cleavers from their pouches
around their waists. They swung them with a high wide-angled swish
and beheaded both young men. Blood spurted from the stumps of their
necks. Their bodies still stood for a few seconds, while their heads made a
hard landing at the feet of their masters and rocked slowly, side to side, ear
to ear. It happened incredibly fast.

Both Kings paled as they stumbled hurriedly away from the heads. Finally
the bodies keeled over, knocking into two guards, who were promptly sick.

'These men have taken your punishment for treachery to the English
crown. I have to say, you are lucky my father is not sitting here now. For
only He can order the execution of another King. And be assured, that he
would.

Lastly, we have the disputed matter of whether you intended to kill King

Edward himself. I am only prepared to mark that not proven', said the Black Prince, 'if you can explain to me, exactly why King Pedro of Castile deserves this treachery, while under our protection?'

'You mean you don't know what he's done?' asked King Charles incredulously, still shaken at the fate of his Aide.

'Tell us!'

'He committed a Holy Sin! He is guilty of stealing a Holy Christian Relic from Santiago de Compostela and of murdering the Archbishop of Santiago, when he stood in his way.'

'My God!' There was a general intake of breath. That was the holiest site in Christendom since Jerusalem had fallen, over seventy years before. 'Surely he did not steal the bones of St James the Apostle?'

'No! He took the Blood of Christ!'

The whole camp was quickly cleared. We left at the gallop, anxious to get out of there. The English Royal Cavalry certainly did not trust King Charles of Navarre.

The Black Prince and his brother accompanied the King of Aragon, who agreed to be a witness at a trial against King Pedro, for a promise of safe conduct. We all dispersed back home, and King Charles withdrew his men back to Trastamara's lines, to fight another day. We travelled the eastern route, back to Poitiers via Orthez and Roquefort.

John of Gaunt rode up beside his brother. 'There's something I do not understand,' he said. 'How did Chaucer's letter reach us so quickly?'

'It didn't!' replied his brother, 'I made it up.'

'Wasn't that a gamble? How did you think of that?'

'Well, there was a line in your note, what was it? **ChtkEg,** told me he was safe and back in England, so I put two and two together.'

'But **ChtkEg** did not mean that at all,' exclaimed Prince John. 'It meant *IN GOD'S HANDS*. It came after the plan to divert the extra troops at Bayonne. *Chance OK Ega*. The diversion plan would work with God's will.'

The brothers started to laugh.

Chapter 10 - Alchemy

Back in the monastery orchard, walking a while amidst the fruit trees with our hermit, the English Envoy was beginning to feel uncomfortable, twisting his head from side to side and feeling the collar of his cloak.

'I feel sorry for those Equerries,' he said gingerly rubbing his own neck. He had a feeling for the misfortunes of royal servants. 'The poor fellows were only doing their job. They weren't responsible for any of that.'

'There's no justice,' agreed the hermit, 'as you'll find out, if only you let me go on with the story.'

'Oh, very well.' The emissary sounded resigned, this was taking too long. 'Is there much more of it before we get round to the treasure?'

'Quite a bit,' said the hermit complacently. The weather in the orchard started to drizzle lightly, but neither seemed to notice the quiet pattering on the apple blossom at their feet.

Now that the younger man was getting caught up with his story, Petit-Roi felt more comfortable, as if the balance of power had shifted in his direction. In fact, he now held all the cards.

'During our cavalry's five-day return journey to Poitiers, King Pedro was carefully kept separate from his accuser, the King of Aragon. Upon arrival and after a long conversation with his eldest daughter, whose strength appeared to be rapidly draining away, Pedro asked for a witness to strengthen his defence. Realising that his crown rested on the matter, the ex-King of Castile requested the presence of the elderly Bishop of Lucon, from a district of Poitiers, to verify his story.

Two weeks later, they were all assembled. Present at the gathering, about to get seated around the table in the great hall at Poitiers, were four Kings, two Princes, one Holy Knight Grand Master, one Bishop, one Diplomat/Linguist and one weapons expert. The matter for discussion was King Pedro's throne. Did he deserve to regain his rightful inheritance? They were the witnesses.

However, as the most senior Ruler, only King Edward III of England could pass judgement on his cousin, ex-King Pedro of Castile.

King Edward was talking animatedly to King Pedro as they approached the chairs. Suddenly he became red in the face and found his temper. As we watched him, a light from the window caught his eyes, and I declare they were ablaze with fire.

In a second, before anyone had even taken their seats, he roughly pushed his pointed old beard out of his way, leaned over and gave the table such a clattering with both his fists, that the jugs and tankards jumped. Wine streamed onto the well-worn flagstones.

'This meeting is worthless!' he roared, bellowing into Pedro's face. 'My God! You have no money AT ALL! No Treasury. No Money. No War! I told you that!'

The Castilian King sat down calmly. He was used to his cousin's temper, but he'd have to keep his wits about him. The question was: Whose wool was he going to have to pull over whose eyes, in order to get what he wanted from this?

'No, No! You have it wrong! You asked me if I *could* pay. I gave you my word, *yes*, I can!'

'What with? Promises again? Baubles? Cheap stories? I can tell you, we are not fool enough to take your promises here.'

'No,' Pedro remained calm in the face of Edward's tirade, 'by negotiation.'

The King of England was stony-faced. 'We'd better sit down,' he said grimly. 'You can't pay my soldiers with pieces of paper.' He started stroking his grey moustache away from his mouth and ran his fingers down his pointed beard. To those of us who knew him well, it was a sign. At least he was prepared to listen.

King Edward touched Sir Hugh's sleeve next to him. 'Here's Calveley, for instance, he only takes gold. If you want his men to change sides, they only take gold.' He looked at the mercenary, and added with meaning, 'or sometimes gems.'

'Perhaps', intervened King Abu Said, the Moorish Arab who everyone had forgotten about, 'perhaps you believe you could re-capture Jerusalem?'

This remark was so out of context, so bizarre, there was a silence as all ten heads swivelled and attached their gaze on him.

Edward addressed him sternly. 'Sir, you have been brought here by King Pedro. If you have something meaningful to say, we will listen. But, I warn you Abu Said, do not mock this table! We all lost grandfathers or ancestors in the Great Crusades for Jerusalem.' There was a clamour of agreement and I caught a warning signal, to move in closer to the Moors.

Abu Said stood-up and held his right hand high to be heard. 'It will interest you to know, I freely acknowledge your Crusaders were the bravest warriors ever seen,' he said, 'but, they never had a chance against King Saladin. Don't you know why?'

Silence.

'It was because of Saltpetre.'

'Gunpowder!' called out Peter of Aragon. He was a well-known dabbler in the science and dark practises of Alchemy. 'They threw firecrackers to frighten the horses. Clever tactics, but not earth-shattering!'

At that moment the meeting was interrupted by the surprise arrival of Geoffrey Chaucer, King Edward's favourite Man of Letters. His clothes and tied-back hair ingrained with dirt. It was impossible to tell what colour they should have been. He knelt at the feet of his King, who duly tapped his shoulder in an affectionate gesture. He was mightily relieved to see him.

The newly returned diplomat greeted the English Royal Princes personally. To the surprise of the other visitors, dirty or not, they kissed him. He then bowed to the assembled foreign Kings and dignitaries.

'Ah, Chaucer!' beamed Edward. 'Truly, we thought you were dead.'

'Apologies your Majesty. I could not get a message through earlier. I was detained in prison and was lucky to catch a ship sailing for Bordeaux.' Sir

Hugh Calveley expelled an audible sigh of relief. He was vindicated at last.

'We give thanks for your safe delivery,' said Edward. He gestured towards his guests. 'I believe you know everyone, except for our Bishop of Lucon perhaps?'

Indeed, Chaucer had heard of this man. A Templar Scholar indeed, he thought. What was *he* doing there?

'I will have your report later,' nodded the King, adding, 'in the meantime, clean yourself up and re-join us. We are in sore need of your skills to take notes, if you please.'

As they waited for Chaucer to reappear, the Black Prince looked over at King Peter of Aragon and caught his puzzled expression. The Prince shrugged at him. When they restarted, the warrior Prince had some questions of his own. 'King Peter, you're always experimenting with your Alchemy. Do you know how this *Gunpowder* is made?'

'Yes, I know the basic ingredients. But the problem is to judge the exact proportions of each, before it will work properly. The whole thing is guesswork and can be very dangerous.' He held up his right hand to prove the point. There was a gap in the middle of his fingers. 'I blew my middle finger off one day,' he said, not without a degree of pride, 'it is powerful stuff. I nearly lost my whole hand'.

'Is it true the Far Eastern countries have had the recipe for hundreds of years?' asked King Edward.

'I believe so. Gunpowder has been used for centuries by the Chinese in firecrackers, just for celebrations. Then, about a hundred years ago, they discovered it was a very effective method of frightening the cavalry horses in the middle of a battle. The Arabs, who had access to natural saltpetre, began to refine it and added the other ingredients that turned it into Gunpowder. This is what was used in the explosives, employed against the Crusaders. You can be sure they made absolutely certain that the secret recipe did *not* fall into enemy hands.'

'If that is the same saltpetre we import from you each year, Cousin Pedro,' said the Black Prince, 'there is too little of it. Without knowing what to mix it with, it's not a lot of use. It will burn, but it doesn't explode, we've tried!'

'Yes,' Pedro replied. 'We have saltpetre caves all over Spain, it's a naturally-occurring mineral. You don't have it in England. That's where I get a lot of my revenues. Other countries pay me well,' he smiled, 'so I give them a little each, and then they ask for more.' He sat back, satisfied with himself. Then he added, 'There you all are, trying to develop your killing machines, and not understanding the basic problem. You must have the correct formula to turn natural saltpetre, which is potassium nitrate, into Gunpowder.'

Abu Said leant over and took a tightly rolled parchment from the folds of his son Hassim's robe. He placed it on the table. He unrolled it very slowly, and showed them the writing:

Formula for exploding powder:
potassium nitrate .... = 74.6 %
charcoal .... = ??.? %
sulphur .... = ??.? %

Signed: Shams al-Din Muhammad al-Ansari al-Dimashqi
Dated: 1320

'You will note' he said, 'that I have blanked out the EXACT proportions of the ingredients. That is our secret, and that is what we are here to bargain over.'

'Now I understand why our ancestors spoke of fighting against dragons and fire,' said King Edward slowly. 'Now it seems they never understood what the great beasts were'. He accepted the facts now, 'Saladin kept his secret well.'

The Bishop of Lucon attracted attention as he leant forward over the table, and began the painful struggle to his feet, helped by his chaplain. He was pointing at the Moorish King. 'Do I really have to get up every time I want to make myself heard?' he grumbled loudly. But it was Edward who posed the questions he was about to ask. 'King Abu Said, may I ask just why would you want to betray your own religion?' He paused while the old Bishop subsided again with a grunt, and the Edward continued with his questions: 'If your own Spanish people have this terrible secret formula, why are your Muslim Moors now being defeated all the time? And why have you only brought us PART of this famous secret formula? What good is that to us?'

'You'll get the rest later,' the Moor replied dismissively. 'Now we are in Spain, my people don't have the time or resources to develop it further.' He looked over at King Pedro. 'First, I have a demand of my own in exchange'.

Wary now, the Black Prince felt his anger rising, what trick was this? 'Well, we know Cousin Pedro here wants his crown back; so what the devil do you want as well?'

'Exactly the same thing!'

'Your own crown back? As what?'

'As the Muslim King of Granada?' Abu Said nodded slowly.

'How, may I ask?'

'With your soldiers my dear Prince.' He smirked.

King Edward leapt to his feet and took his frustration out on the table once more. He was furious when he could not turn it over. 'That's it! That's enough! If you think any Christian King would send his army to place a Muslim on a throne, you're mad!' He spat on the flagstones in disgust.

'My friend King Pedro did.'

Nobody could believe what they just heard.

'What?'

'I told you, King Pedro's Christians put me back on my own throne!'

Even Edward was nonplussed for a minute.

'My God!' He pointed at King Pedro, 'your grandfather was the same. He spent more time with the Moors than the Christians.' He flung his chair backwards, and strode off. There was a hush in the Great Hall, as servants ran in to right the table. There was some scraping of legs, but nobody talked. Equally, nobody wanted to get up and leave.

They knew very well, that never again would they be able to get such a group of Kings and leaders together to sort this mess of petty wars between neighbours in France and Spain, and England. There were many questions, and undoubtedly many truths yet to be laid bare. The trouble was, these cousins were all gifted liars! It was so seldom you could guarantee you heard the truth about anything.

With a resigned sigh, the Black Prince took charge. He was determined they would each show their hand before they left this table. He wished his father had curbed his temper. 'I propose we continue, and we get down to the business of what King Pedro has to offer.' He addressed the King of Castille personally, 'I must say I have heard some fantastic tales about you. Are you going to tell them? Or shall I get King Peter's side of the story first?'

Before Pedro could reply, Abu Said leapt to his feet and clenched his fist at the Black Prince: 'What about my crown? This must be dealt with first!'

'Forget it! Anyway I cannot raise an army without my father's permission, and the King will never give his consent. So that's the end of it!'

Abu Said prepared to depart. 'There's no point in me staying,' he said. 'I'll take my Gunpowder formula to the French instead.'

It was Calveley who intervened. He put one gigantic hand on the Arab's arm, persuasively instead of forcefully, 'Don't go! I think there may be a way out of this, a compromise!'

Abu Said snapped back his rejection. 'If you're thinking of your mercenaries, there aren't enough of them for me! I need a whole army to dislodge that infernal brother-in-law of mine.'

'No, not that.' Slowly, because he was only just formulating a plan in his own mind, Calveley caught the eye of the Black Prince. He would need his support. 'Are you saying it was King Pedro's army that fought to put you on your throne the first time?'

'That's true.'

'Well' continued Calveley, 'if we do call upon England's full army to get King Pedro back to his rightful throne, then he could raise his own army again, to repeat your victory in Granada, and get your crown returned to you.'

'I suppose that is possible,' shrugged the Moor, and inclined his head, 'but wouldn't that depend on you backing Pedro? And it seems you have refused to do precisely that,' he sighed. 'What we need is money or gold you said.

We have neither.'

John of Gaunt intervened. 'If we would consider backing King Pedro, would you pledge your secret formula to us?'

'If he succeeds in getting his throne back and he pledges his army to me,' there was a pause. He nodded slowly and turned sideways to stare full-face at the giant Mercenary at the table, 'Yes, I might consider it, but ONLY if Calveley's troops were ordered to fight for me as well.'

Instantly the mercenary leader knew that the cause was lost, and so did many of the others. How on earth could he persuade his mercenaries to fight for this man, an Arab Moor? Hadn't they spent the last few years helping the Spaniards to drive these people out. Anyway, they would only fight for Gold.

Wisely, nobody around the table voiced their negative thoughts. It was going to be completely impossible to get their hands on that Gunpowder formula. There wasn't a way.

'So,' said the Black Prince, 'we'll have to see how the rest of the negotiations go. You will stay for the rest of the talks?' He was stalling. He had a plan developing in his head and knew it depended on being able to keep Abu Said at the table. 'Besides, the weather is foul outside, we have a feast tonight, and some grand entertainment for you all,' Abu Said sighed and nodded.

The Master of the Royal Household entered with a hurried step and whispered a message to King Pedro, who jumped to his feet. His heir and eldest daughter Beatrice was very weak, and calling for her father. There was a break while more wine was brought, and the two Princes went out to find their father. It was half an hour before King Edward agreed to return to the table, bringing King Pedro with him, with a sympathetic arm about his shoulders. That was a change! But there was no doubt Pedro's daughter was fading fast.

Edward still needed to judge his Cousin Pedro's case, just as long as England's army was not expected to fight for those Moors, those non-Christians. Besides, he knew very well that the others could take no decision without him. He began, 'Before we get onto Cousin Pedro's story, I would like to ask King Peter to tell us how this saltpetre is ever going to be any use to us? As far as I am concerned, our soldiers have found the stuff downright dangerous without the correct formula.'

'It's lethal!' exclaimed Peter of Aragon, holding up his right hand again. 'Let me explain. As you know, I have some interest in alchemy. I have tried for years to make this saltpetre stable enough to use.'

'You must have a source of your own to do that?'

He nodded, 'I have my own saltpetre caves near Barcelona. The first problem is its weight. It is too heavy and impractical to trundle tons of it around a battlefield.' He saw the blank expressions around the great table.

'I'd better start at the beginning. The word 'saltpetre' means 'salt of rock'. It is found in Spain and Arab countries as natural incrustations in caves: a white salty substance that shines like crystal. Arabs call it 'natrum' and 'barud', meaning fiery. They have used it for six hundred years as fireworks, by mixing it with metal, producing a flash. We call it 'potassium nitrate'.

To use it as an explosive in warfare, it should first be purified and then mixed with other ingredients. But the question is, which other ingredients?'

'Some clever devil told us to mix it with urine,' grumbled the Black Prince.

King Peter chuckled, 'What happened?'

'It killed five of my soldiers.'

'The correct method of purification,' King Peter went on, 'the exact balance of saltpetre and other element. What the other elements are, have been my greatest problem. And I daresay, the alchemists in England are in the same state?'

The Black Prince agreed.

'However, it is easier for me, because I have an endless supply of saltpetre in my caves. You English have no chance, you have to import what little King Pedro will allow you. It is heavy, and totally useless in a battle because, by itself, it burns but does not explode. I am more and more convinced that Gunpowder is the answer. If only we can find the right formula, it will be light enough for each man to carry his own supply. If the mixture is correct, it will not harm the soldiers using it. I believe each soldier will eventually carry their own individual explosive weapon into war one day.'

There was a collective shaking of the heads. That would spell disaster.

Everyone would blow their own men to smithereens.

'What a lot of nonsense this is!' growled King Edward, 'there's nothing like an English longbow. It has a range of 250 yards I tell you!'

'At the moment, yes. The suppleness of your English yew, and the huge strength of your bowmen make your army invincible, I must admit.'

Edward relaxed, quite satisfied.

'But,' continued Peter of Aragon, 'I talk of the Future. This formula, if it is correct, will allow your soldiers to carry powder into war. It will be safe for them to use, and you will be able to kill your enemies twenty at a time. Don't you like that idea?'

King Peter pointed to Abu Said, 'He should know! His ancestors answered the call to defend Jerusalem. His lot were on Saladin's side. They used exploding powder.'

The Moorish King of Granada nodded. 'I know my history. The first instance I know of, was more than 200 years ago. Saltpetre was used to burn down our own city of Old Cairo, rather than surrender it to your besieging Crusaders. It was not used to kill them. It just prevented them from occupying our city. The first rockets with Gunpowder were used against the French army of King Louis IX, during the Seventh Crusade over 100 years ago. We Muslims drove your Crusaders back home in 1291. At the port of Acre, north of Jerusalem, we drove you out of the city and onto your ships. We used arrows carrying Gunpowder devices, trebuchets throwing explosives. Gunpowder ignited underneath the city walls.'

'They thought Hell had arrived, I expect,' mumbled John of Gaunt at the far end of the table.

King Pedro joined in. 'My grandfather spoke of projected fire with thunderous noises when he besieged Niebla for nine and a half months. That was at about the same time as Acre.'

'Gunpowder was used at the Siege of Algeciras, wasn't it?' the Black Prince asked. He turned to the head of the table. 'Don't you remember, father, you told us that the Earl of Derby and Lord Salisbury came back from Algeciras talking about it?'

'Yes, that's when we started to get the saltpetre over to practise on, but we couldn't use it.'

'The very first Artillery Masters for Spain were Moors in Christian service,' remembered King Pedro.

'They changed sides?'

'That is true' said King Peter the alchemist. 'My friend King Charles of Navarre has a Moorish Artillery Master in his service right now.'

'Oh no he doesn't!' responded Abu Said forcefully, 'He's here! He's beside me at your table. Let me introduce you properly, this is Hassim my son.'

'He has been working for Charles of Navarre, a Christian?' asked the Black Prince.

'For the past year.'

'Why? For what reason?'

'Because I needed to know which side was stronger, you or them.'

There was a gasp from King Pedro at the other end. 'He was working for my enemy,' he said in disbelief, shaking his head.

'A slippery man', thought King Edward. He asked, 'Which side are you on now?'

'On the side of whoever will regain me my throne, of course!'

'Tomorrow we will continue talking,' said Edward. 'I've had enough for tonight. It's nearly time we called the ladies to feast and be entertained. We will not take a decision on your throne Abu Said, until we sort out the fate of King Pedro.' He saw the Moor looking doubtful, 'It seems to me these two decisions are tied together.'

Letting the others disperse, Edward signalled his two sons to stay behind. As bodyguards, we stayed with them. Our masters were so used to our presence, we were practically invisible to them.

'We have a viper in our nest' said the King. 'I strongly suspect he is spying on us for his Muslim friends. I simply do not believe his story. I want to know everything he does. Our Lookouts have been watching out for them, but we haven't found any others in the area. But you must tell the Captain of the Guard to extend the patrols. We need to hear from our informers if any Moors enter Aquitaine, anywhere.'

'That's quite a tall order,' exclaimed the Black Prince, comforted that his father was still top of the pile.

'Just see that it's done. Arrange it yourself.'

'Yes, father.' He turned on his heel and marched out.

'This man could be plotting a Muslim uprising,' said Prince John. 'He may be planning to lure our whole army to Spanish shores. Now he will know our numbers, our weapons, and could deliver us straight into the arms of the biggest Moorish-army ever seen.'

'I agree', replied the King, 'I already gave the orders to the Lookouts earlier on. Why on earth do you think I left the table?'

The Black Prince chuckled in reply.

The King turned to us. 'Watch that Arab!' he ordered, 'and his son!'

Chapter 11 - The Mysterious Box

Suspicious and wary of all his guests, King Edward delayed their next meeting for three days, providing adequate time for patrol messengers to report back on the detailed state of his Aquitane borders.

No invading Moors had been discovered, but Edward had earned the right to be called one of the most astute Kings who had ever sat on the throne of England. He realised that the enemy could have already infiltrated the region days before and were lying low. His gut told him it was entirely possible. In fact his nagging belly gave him a strong hint of another definite possibility: of an invasion force from any of the other Kings here as well. Either Aragon or Navarre, Castile, or even the King of France could capture them all. Right here, with enough troops and the element of surprise.

He ordered double duty for his chosen men, detailed to either protect or spy on each King; and he declared a 24 hour constant state of alert throughout the garrison.

Edward was very close to his sons. This was unusual for the time. They both respected and feared him, in correct proportion for a Plantagenet family that was for ever fighting another war.

The fact that he was still the leader was never in doubt. Equally well, the Black Prince, his heir, had proved himself a supreme tactical and ruthless Commander in the field and Prince John of Gaunt was a consummate politician and negotiator. The perfect team.

But the tension was building around the garrison. Every man knew the lid would blow off the pot very soon. Something was about to happen!

Every day spies reported anything suspicious. Ex-King Pedro spent the time with his dying daughter, and to his credit, didn't seem to be able to think of anything else. King Peter of Aragon and King Charles of Navarre were closeted together for hours, no doubt plotting treachery somewhere. Just as long as it wasn't here.

Despite enrolling the sharp ears of two of the Queen's Ladies in Waiting (the most fluent in Spanish and French) in an adjacent part of the garden, nothing could be gleaned from their animated tones. They were reported to be either talking Flemish, or in code.

For three days, suspicions and possible plots were discussed and guessed at endlessly amongst the English hosts. In fact, they were fairly certain they had explored every eventuality, until the first solid warning came: When guards reported the suspicion that King Abu Said and his son had hidden something bulky underneath their cloaks.

As the visitors entered the Great Hall for their 2nd meeting, they found themselves surrounded by no less than 20 guards spaced around the walls. Incongruously, if they looked, there were even more soldiers hidden behind the tapestries, some making rather lumpy wall decorations, and some even showing the toes of their boots.

Everyone, except for the old Bishop, who seemed too old to notice, expected fireworks in more than one way!

King Abu Said and his son entered last.

Although my training had taught me to keep my eyes on my Black Prince, even I, Petit-roi was taken by surprise by the sight of the Arab King suddenly throwing back his cloak with a wide arm and a flourish.

As one, the guards leapt in front of our own Masters. Whatever attack was expected, it was undoubtedly our duty to take a knife or an arrow in their stead.

The Abu Said's cloak showed a grandiose red lining, with a voluminous gaping pocket full of something wooden.

He roared with laughter at our demonstration of defence.

He found us ridiculous!

'Ho! Ho!' he mocked, and raised both arms high above his head; 'A little trust is needed here!'

But when a guard bent over to pluck the wooden piece from his pocket, the Moor slapped away the soldier's hand with full force, causing him to lose his balance momentarily, and snapped: 'Oh No! You don't, young man! Nobody touches *that*!'

Then things started to happen in a rush; at the sound of a scuffle, from behind various tapestries, the hidden soldiers emerged battle-ready. This must be their cue! At the same time, the guard nearest the Moor reached for his own dagger, deftly stepped to the side, and promptly held the dagger at Abu Said's throat.

Suddenly the Great Hall was swamped with soldiers.

As cool as ice, the Moorish King's son, who had been slowly opening his cloak, smartly pulled it shut again. Nobody had seen.

King Edward was quicker than any of them to assess the situation.

'STOP! STOP! Stand Down. I order you to take one step back!'

The Moorish King was released, grumbling that he couldn't do business with a hundred soldiers in the room. He had a point! Things had clearly got out of hand.

But King Edward wanted some answers. Just what was the wooden object in his pocket? Why was it so precious? Was it a weapon? He thought he could guess.

Slowly and carefully, while looking purposefully at Edward, the Arab drew a small wooden box from inside his cloak. So they could all see, he lifted it into the air, and carefully placed it in the middle of the table and removed his hand.

It sat there, all by itself.

Everyone sat looking at it in silence, with their own thoughts.

It was an oak casket in a dark smooth wood, about three inches square, though the corners had been worn smooth with age. It was obviously much handled, and very old.

An ancient Treasure? A Relic? Was it a force for good? or evil?

It felt mysterious, sitting there amongst them.

'WHAT IS IN THAT BOX?' King Edward demanded at last, breaking the spell. 'Is this some of your killing powder, Abu Said? Your saltpetre?' he guessed.

There was silence. No reply.

There was danger here, Edward could feel it. Was this some sort of trick? Was it going to explode in front of them?

'No Sire! It is not saltpetre.' The answer came at last.

Edward did not believe him. 'If it can kill twenty men at one go, you would slaughter everyone in this hall!' he insisted, moving his chair back.

'I protest, Sire. It is no such thing,' said Abu Said. But his host was warming to his theme. 'So! You would destroy the warriors of Christendom in one call of a cuckoo.'

King Pedro's voice boomed into the middle of the discussion:

'Peace be with you, my fair cousin. The box is MINE. Abu Said is only looking after it for me because he has bigger pockets! For God's sake, you're very jumpy this morning. You really must not insult our Muslim friend. Don't forget, he came here at my request.'

'Did he just? Are you sure he's not using you?'

The Black Prince rolled his eyes at the other guests. His father's temper was well known, but he was right this time. Abu Said, though, took well the warning not to be found out. And King Pedro went quiet.

At last they settled to their business. Nobody mentioned the box. Clearly, it was an awful ominous presence. We felt an unexplained chill in the air. King Edward shrugged off his suspicions, and swung his mood in totally the opposite direction.

For the moment, he was doggedly resolved to ignore the casket. He had an agenda, and he was determined to keep to it.

'Firstly,' he said, 'King Pedro will put his proposals. Secondly, we will rule as to their possible acceptance. Thirdly, we will hear King Peter of Aragon's accusations against King Pedro. Fourthly, I will make my judgement. The question is whether or not I will call my army, and win back King Pedro's rightful crown. Lastly, we will deal with you, Abu Said.'

As cold as ice, the Moor's reply came at once:

'Here!' he vaguely waved at the castle walls around him, 'I HAVE the formula you want.'

The King of England stood up, and gave the Moor his best enemy-stare: 'Do you? I wonder.' And he sat down again.

'Yes, I have it.' The Arab paused, 'It is well hidden.'

Abu Said's son leaned over to whisper in his father's ear. 'We can never reveal it, father. They'll kill us both if we give them the formula.'

Abu Said nodded his head. He would not tell his son, but he had never intended to hand-over the secret.

Hassim, the young Moor, was an imposing figure, in his late twenties. He was taller than his father. Surprising them all, he found his voice. 'We came here in good faith. We are under your roof at the invitation of your kinsman. We should be under your protection.'

'Of course, you have it,' said the Black Prince, taking over quickly. Something was puzzling him; and he wasn't sure what.

He hoped it wasn't the influence of that odd looking box.

'It is common courtesy,' he continued, looking at his father, who pursed his fingers, brushed his moustache away from his mouth, and ran them down his pointed beard. When he did that, we knew the storm had blown over, again.

'King Pedro, I am calling on you to open your negotiations if you please.' The Prince spread out his hand: 'We wait.'

Pedro began with a bang. 'Would you be interested in Templar Treasure?'

Back in the garden at Santiago de Compostela, the English Envoy came alive,

'At last!' he cried, jumping to his feet, accidentally knocking into the old hermit, and sending him flying.

'At last you've got round to the one subject we're interested in.' He reached down and picked the old soldier up. 'Can't you give me a shorter version from now on?' He sighed, 'Besides, John of Gaunt has waited long enough!'

'Prince John in England? How can he possibly know of our conversations here?'

'Ah!' replied the Envoy, 'because I have already sent back three messengers with your story so far! You have no idea, there is more than my career on the line here!'

124

The memory of the hermit peters out with thoughts of Prince John. He shakes his old head in confusion.

'Go on, go on!'

The old man did not like being knocked down, 'It's my story and I'm going to tell it my way' said the old man stubbornly. The envoy subsided, clutching his head in his hands in despair.

'Now,' said the hermit, 'where was I?'

'King Pedro was about to offer King Edward the Templar Treasure.'

'Oh, you think he was? Just wait and see. Patience, my friend.' He resumed his story.

'Prove it!' snapped back King Edward, 'We've all heard it before.' He started to inspect his fingernails, a common sign of impatience. 'Besides, I have already told you, I will take no evidence and no promises that are not verified.'

'That is exactly why I have asked our good Bishop Falco to speak for me.' Pedro waved towards the cleric across the table. 'He is the Templar expert! If you won't take my word, then I'll let him talk.' King Pedro promptly sat down.

All eyes alighted on the old Bishop of Lucon, hunched into his seat, four chairs away from Pedro. He had shrunk with age. He had a kindly round face, with old rheumy eyes. In the olden days, he used to bustle and hurry. Now he needed a chaplain to help him up and down, and to make up for his own failing sight. It was sad for a man who had read so much.

His voice was surprising strong, though he spoke slowly and very formally as if he was still lecturing his congregation. 'Kings, Princes, enemies, Christians, and Muslims. We are an odd mix, are we not? I especially welcome the chance to talk with our infidel friends here. There are many questions only they can answer, both about the Templars, and about our Christianity as well.'

'So, there IS treasure then?' asked the Black Prince impatiently.

'Certainly,' he nodded, 'most certainly there is Templar Treasure intact in every country in Europe. May I point out additionally, that France and Spain also have a second source of treasure, a non-Templar source, which is from an earlier date.'

'Do you know where these places are?'

'Oh yes, of course.'

'Are you going to tell us?'

You could have heard a mouse creep by. It was one of the most important silences of the 14th Century. Nobody was going to break into the old man's thoughts. He had to decide the answer for himself.

'Where to find the Templar treasure,' the Bishop said, 'is not the problem. It is what you can take with you that matters. And it is what you must leave behind, because you are a CHRISTIAN. That is of the greatest importance to our religion.'

The old man sat up as best he could and re-arranged himself in his chair. 'Let me explain this historically. It was the Pope who created the initial problem. Two hundred years ago, Pope Innocent II issued a secret Papal Bull that certain items found in Jerusalem were to be made to disappear forever.'

'What items?' asked the Black Prince.

'Heretical Holy Relics, statues of other gods, things like that.'

Geoffrey Chaucer looked up from his note-taking. 'Aha! Anything that proved parts of the Holy Bible wrong?' He had heard this rumour before.

The Bishop nodded. 'And there was a considerable amount of it.' He raised his old head to get a good look at the others at the table. He spoke clearly, deliberately, so there would be no misunderstanding:

'As a Christian today, you are expressly forbidden to touch or remove those relics.' He paused. 'Naturally, the Muslims would love to have them!'

'Why?'

The old boy hesitated and blew out his cheeks:

'They would prove the teaching of the Resurrection of Jesus Christ to be false.'

There was total uproar at the table. King Edward furiously called for silence.

'This is talk of Christian heresy,' he roared, and rose from his chair once more. 'I'll not listen to this!'

'No!' replied the Bishop, in a surprisingly deep voice. 'I fear it is high time this story was told. Then, Sire, you may judge for yourself.'

Slowly, reluctantly, Edward sank back into the arms of his chair. 'Get on with it!' he mumbled.

In the meantime, King Abu Said could see his throne getting closer.

'First of all,' the Bishop continued, 'I wish to ask: Who has Templar connections here?' Most of the arms moved on the table.

'I thought as much, so we may be frank. We will start with you, King Edward. It was your grandfather who ordered the elimination of the Templars for heresy. He imprisoned, tortured, and burnt them to death.'

The English King was surprised to be criticised. 'It was my French grandfather, Philippe IV. He was my mother's father. He told us the Templars were common thieves and heretics. It happened the year my own father succeeded to the English throne. I remember he told us that in his childhood all the boys wanted to be Templar Knights.' He blew through his cheeks, and added, 'My own father never understood why it happened.'

'What I don't fully understand is why the first Crusaders were called up by Pope Urban II?' asked Chaucer again. 'They said it was because Christians were being denied access to their holy sites in Jerusalem? Was that true?'

The Bishop nodded. 'It was, but it was much more complicated than that. It took ninety years of provocation, and two years of planning. You must understand that Muslims, Jews and Christians had lived together in peace for centuries. It came to an end when one of the Muslim leaders in Jerusalem, a certain Caliph al-Hakim, ordered the systematic demolition of all Christian churches. This eventually included the Churches of the Holy Sepulchre, our most sacred sites. At that time they had been divided into three separate buildings.

There was a round church called Anastasis above the grave of Jesus; a wonderful basilica called the Martyrium; and in the square between the two churches, a shrine over the position of the Crucifixion, named Calvarium, or Golgotha. Christian pilgrims were often robbed or slain for their offerings, for the Caliph had taken away their protection. The result was that the pilgrims stopped going to Jerusalem. Then I declare it was God himself who took a hand!'

'What do you mean by that?' asked Chaucer.

'He brought not one, but two earthquakes to the Temple Mount, to show His anger. The first one took off the golden dome covering of the Dome of the Rock. The second one destroyed the Al-Aqsa mosque. These earthquakes made the Temple Mount unstable. They also jolted the rock underneath the Dome. The rest of the raised platform that makes up the Mount was in danger of collapsing into the gigantic holes and cracks.

Up to this time, the authorities in Jerusalem had only used Muslim builders on the Temple Mount. Now the emergency meant they had to employ many of the Christians as well. What these Christian men found underneath the platform was eventually reported back to the Pope.'

The Bishop reached over to fill his tankard, and took a long draft of ale. 'It was pure chance when a hidden crypt was discovered by a handful of Christian workers under the Holy Stone.' He looked over at the Moors, and sighed: 'They realised then that the rock underneath the Dome was hollow.'

'It's a lie!' shouted the Moorish King. 'It's simply not true!' He was outraged. The Holy Rock was part of the legend of Muhammad. His footprint was on the top.

The Bishop himself now had the answer to an old question. 'So, the Muslims did not know,' he said. 'It was a jolt from the earthquake had loosened a secret entrance underneath. The cave was full of other gods, golden graven images. They were in niches all around the walls. Some with their own arches and little pillars. It is thought the Christian builders had found one of the earliest forms of prayer alcoves. In the centre of the crypt, hurriedly piled high, was some of King Solomon's treasure.'

'How do you know it belonged to King Solomon?' asked Chaucer.

'The items were identified in the Bible. The Christians managed to re-seal the secret entrance, and continued with work on the top. The visible surface of the Rock of the Dome had been damaged in the earthquakes, with fault lines showing on the central mound of the stone. The workmen were ordered to chip off the stone, until they could make a flat, even surface. They were frightened lest they broke into the crypt from above, so they did not do the work very well - on purpose. If you see it now, it is still very uneven.' The Bishop turned towards the Moorish King, who stared at him with hatred. 'So, you didn't know your sacred Rock was hollow!'

He continued: 'The entire platform of the Mount had been supported by arches and pillars every few yards underneath the surface. It had been in-filled with earth and rocks to the height of about sixty feet. Solomon's ruins of the first Temple Mount was far underneath later constructions. The earthquake opened up some places like a slice of cake. Large open vaulted stables were discovered, still mostly intact. Golden chariots were dug out; hidden tunnels were revealed; and old water cisterns were found.

These items could not be hidden from the Muslims for ever; but there was obviously a lot more to discover. The Al-Aqsa mosque was rebuilt, much smaller, because of instability over the top of King Solomon's stables. They made big plans to start major tunnelling work under the base of the Mount, but they never had the chance.'

'Why not?' asked Chaucer.

'The Crusaders arrived.'

The Bishop's chaplain signalled to his host, and King Edward called a break for refreshments. The old man looked in danger of disappearing into the arms of his chair. He seemed nearly asleep, and they all hoped he was not going to die on them. To a man, they wanted to hear the conclusion of this story. On the way out, my master the Black Prince spoke a few words of warning to his guards. 'You will not forget your vow of secrecy.' He pointed to each one of us in turn. 'These are secrets of our Christian faith. They do not go beyond these four walls!' We nodded.

'Petit-roi,' he said to me personally, 'you keep an eye on that box! Do not let it out of your sight and for God's sake DON'T touch it!'

Chapter 12 - Gunpowder Treachery

B y the time everyone was about to re-enter the Hall two hours later, the box had moved. It now sat directly in front of King Edward's chair. How did that happen?

My God! The King would take my head for this! Quickly I, *Petit-roi*, leant over to move it back to the centre of the Great Hall table.

Just in time, I remembered my orders: 'DON'T TOUCH IT!' At that stage, my fingers had got as far as being outstretched and a few inches away. Instantly I felt a jolt of a shock run across my hand, up my arm, paralysing my right shoulder. I saw a flash slithering down my torso, across my knees which buckled, sending sparks all around me on the floor.

God knows what would have happened if I had actually made contact with the box.

No more *Petiti-roi!*

Clutching my shoulder, I painfully picked myself up, ashamed and afraid.

Luckily my Black Prince entered the Hall first.

Seeing the box moved, and me in agony, he whipped his sword out of its scabbard in a clean, mean, fluid motion, the action of a much-practised medieval warrior. He yelled for the other guards, and they immediately started poking about behind the tapestries for a thief.

At last he turned to me with a thunderous look.

'Oh deary me!' exclaimed the Moorish King from the doorway as he strode into the Hall. He reached out and calming pushed the wooden box back into the centre of the table, as if it was the most natural thing in the world.

'It does that sometimes! You see, it has a mind of its own. You must understand. It reacts to Strangers!'

He shrugged, and shoved his hooky nose right in front of the Black Prince, 'I told you not to touch it!

The Prince gave ground and stepped backwards. It was an action he was not used to. 'For God's sake, WHAT'S IN THE BOX?' he shouted in disbelief.

No reply.

He turned his blond curly head towards me, with more sympathy in his eyes: 'What happened, Petit-roi ? Report!'

'There has been nobody in this room since you all left, Sire. I have been sitting here with my sword on my lap, guarding the box.' I felt my shoulder with a wince. 'I only took my eyes off the table for a second, to see who was coming in first and when I looked back, the box had already transposed itself across the table and down to the far end, right in front of King Edward's chair. It was like a Magic Show, a slight of hand, only there was no hand! There was nobody. And, come to think of it, I didn't even hear the box scraping across the table as it moved. I tell you, it was MAGIC, my Prince,' I hung my head in my confusion, it sounded like an excuse; 'Terrible Magic!' I repeated in a hoarse croak. I had let him down.

My Black Prince had healing hands from the day he was born. I had seen him mending his father's aches and pains at a touch, tapping into his own internal body-heat.

Now, he reached into an inside pocket of his jerkin, and withdrew a few folded river-reeds, which he twisted into a circle, securing the ends together. Using both hands, he gently held the ring of reeds just above the top of my right shoulder and passed them around and around in his hands; then he stopped and quickly pressed them down hard on the joint and withdrew his circle of reeds.

I was pushed to one knee wincing and would have screamed, but all I felt was intense heat. I crossed my left hand tentatively to it as I knelt there. There was no pain. I was whole again!

Waving away my supplications, my Prince ordered me to quickly rise and

131

smarten my uniform, for we could hear King Edward and the rest of his guests were about to enter the Hall. Each one was straining at the leash to hear more about the holy city of Jerusalem and Templar Treasure.

While they were taking time to scrape the chairs into position, I moved into my position behind my Master. Determined to keep one eye on the Moorish King and the other on the box in the centre of the table.

After his rest, the Bishop began anew. 'Two hundred and fifty years ago, Christian Crusaders conquered Jerusalem. They breached the walls from a hill on the north-east corner. Muslims were driven out, and denied residence during the Christian occupation. Pope Urban II ordered a new population of European Christians, mostly from France. They were builders, professional administrators, quarry men, and their families, all chosen for their skills.

Thousands of Christian pilgrims started to come to worship once more. A special Holy Order of Knights called The Templars was formed with the Pope's approval, tasked with sealing off the Temple Mount, making it their headquarters and looking after the safety of the pilgrims.

The dangerous task of repairing, shoring up, and investigating what lay below the Mount, took years. Meanwhile, the Templars lived inside the Al-Aqsa mosque. When they had made it safe, they later housed their horses in King Solomon's stables beneath it.' He looked up to make his point. 'Now you can understand how they had the time and the freedom to dig out all the deepest secrets of the Temple Mount.

It took about nine years for the terrible heresies they were uncovering to shake their own faith. The finds that affected them most were from the remains of Herod's Temple, which was being completed at the time of Christ. This temple had a short life. It was destroyed by the Romans in 70 AD.'

'What did the Templars find?' It was the Black Prince who asked the question, everyone wanted to hear the answer.

'There were items hidden in a hurry by the early Christians, presumably when the Romans came to burn it down. There were relics precious to the early Christian Church, items made within the living memory of Jesus

Christ, and items not mentioned in the New Testament.'

'Hold, Bishop!' interrupted John of Gaunt. 'Don't you think our Moorish visitors should go out at this point. This is secret!'

'It's quite alright,' interrupted King Pedro quickly. 'They know the story already!'

In point of fact he was mischief-making, because the two Arabs had never heard the story before, which Pedro must have known. They were more than eager to stay and hear the coming revelations. Why did he say that?

'They found literally thousands and thousands of pieces of evidence,' the Bishop continued, raising his old head in order to watch the faces of his audience very carefully. He was not a little fearful of their reactions: 'There were accounts of John the Baptist as the Messiah; images of a black Madonna with a black child; statues of evil pagan gods, obviously worshipped by Christians; and heretical inscriptions in Aramaic, telling of two wives of Jesus. In some ways, the most disturbing of them all was a record of the Acts of Solomon. This is mentioned in the Bible as a Succession Document, an official account of Solomon's story and his accession to the throne. I have studied it. It was written in very old linear writing.'

'Why would that be heretical?' asked Chaucer, quite afraid of the answer.

'Because it has always been quoted as the basis of the Old Testament, or a considerable part of it. Suffice it to say the writings differ alarmingly from the stories in the Bible. I tell you now, it is ONE thing to question the teachings of the New Testament, but it is QUITE another to bring the Old Testament into disrepute.'

'Why is the Old Testament different?'

'Because so many other religions also believe in the Old Testament, including the Muslims. Now, my friends, you understand exactly why I am here. I needed to be able to explain to you how vital it is that certain parts of the Templar Treasure are NEVER allowed to see the light of day again. And I mean for eternity! It's for the sake of ALL our religions.'

I could not believe what I was hearing. No wonder us guards were bound by a vow of secrecy. Certainly, we had never heard anything like this; and to look at the reactions of the others, neither had they! At last I remembered to glance quickly at the wooden box. It had not moved.

There was total silence. The Bishop mopped his brow, and continued. 'At first they made inventories, and piled the discoveries into Solomon's stables, which was the first area to be cleared. After this, according to depositions I have in my possession, the Templars went to the extraordinary length of wearing Arab dress.'

'Why would they wear Muslim robes?' asked the Black Prince.

'They were much criticised for it later. But at the time they needed to be as inconspicuous as possible when transporting thousands of items back to their homelands via the Arab port of Ptolemais, which we call Acre.'

'They were stealing!' Chaucer was incensed.

'No, not really. You see, two following Pontiffs gave them free rein. The first one, Pope Innocent II, in the 1130's, freed the Templars from any political or religious intervention, including his own. They had carte blanche to do whatever they wanted, with no questions asked. In other words, the Pope did not want to know what they were doing.' He sighed. 'I tell you something, gentlemen, no other body in the world has ever been granted total Christian immunity like that.' He paused for effect: 'I have especially brought this to show you, here,' and signalled to his helper. The chaplain leant down and unrolled a parchment. He held it out at each end so that everyone could read the contents:

'You can see the heading for yourselves. It is a Papal Bull, a decree, dated 1263. It is called Omne Datum Optimum. This is from the second Pope. It is quite long and it attempts to define the role of the Templars more clearly. But still, they are given certain concessions.

I will read two parts to you. It ordered them to: *'concentrate solely on the defence of the section of the Catholic Church which is under threat from pagan beliefs.'* Later it says: *'We grant you the right to convert, at your own profit, all that you can take away, without anyone else having a share, if that is your wish.'*

'What on earth made the Pope say that?' Chaucer was intrigued.

'What indeed!'

'Were the Templars merely thieves?'

'Oh, far from it. They financed most of the Crusades! Though they did undoubtedly remove all the heretical items to various European countries, where they could hide them in their own strongholds, for eternity, as requested by the Popes on behalf of Christianity.

Some of the gold was melted down, and used to finance ships to carry the cargo back in secret. Then these same ships were reused to transport new Crusaders to the Holy Land, to replace those returning home. Some of the treasures were sent to the Popes, but the rest were sent home on the ships.'

'What sort of treasure?' That was what interested Edward.

'They are said to have cut in half the two giant bronze columns, Boaz and Jachin, which had stood outside King Solomon's Temple. It is believed they were taken to Tomar, their centre in Portugal, where the Templars built an octagonal church inspired by the Muslims' Dome of the Rock in Jerusalem. That design became the model for all Templar masonic churches in the future. There is a legend attached to that place.'

The Bishop raised his hand to get help to rise from the table, but he kept talking slowly as he struggled to his feet:

'It tells of the Grand Master of the Templars in Portugal, hiding the Holy Grail in Tomar.'

'The Holy Grail!' King Edward scoffed, he's heard that one before! 'What I want to know is : How about that box in the middle of the table? Where did that come from?'

'That will have to wait!' replied the chaplain sharply, as he manoeuvred the old man away from his chair and leant him his arm as they disappeared out of the door.

For ten minutes, as they waited, the others sat talking quietly amongst themselves. I, Petit-roi, soon noticed each one of them glancing towards the centre of the table. But then, I was looking for those signs. There was no doubt, the box was consuming their thoughts.

Eventually they got going again, and the King of England immediately repeated his question. 'Where did that box come from?'

'That has a completely different history,' interrupted King Pedro unexpectedly.

'Isn't it part of the Templar Treasure?'

'No, It's CATHAR Treasure!' None of them understood.

'All these stories about the Holy Grail, I thought they were mere invention. What is the Grail anyway?' asked de Padilla. He was ignored

'Why did they not destroy the statues and graven images? They could have buried them. I don't understand.' The Black Prince was a practical man.

The Bishop nodded slowly, taking time to think. 'There is proof that some written items were buried. Certainly, legend tells of the men hiding papyrus writings and other effects, somewhere in the desert. Who knows, maybe they will be found in years to come.'

At last, De Padilla, felt he had something important to contribute: 'My grandfather was a Templar,' he said. 'A rockslide fell on him in the desert and he was badly hurt. Maria and I were told the story when we were children. He was helping to bury parchments in oil jars. It killed three others. It happened somewhere near a salty sea, my father told us. They preserved the bodies and brought them back home to Spain. I know one of the gravestones reads: '*Holy Knight. Buried in the sands of the Holy Land. Beloved of Jesus.*'

'Interesting!' the Bishop nodded, paused, and then continued. 'It is written that after this period, the Templars lost their faith because of the items they were ordered to hide from the rest of the world. They no longer took their oath on the Bible, but on other books. During this time, there was an explosion of building in and around the rest of the damaged city of Jerusalem, and much if it was carried out by the French masons, under Templar direction. It became almost as if the Templars were ordered to fit all the Christian holy sites to the Bible story, rather than the other way around, especially on the Temple Mount. Every structure they found was labelled Solomon's this and Solomon's that, to keep prying eyes away.'

'Yes!' exclaimed Abu Said, 'That was disgraceful. Even the foot marks imprinted on the Rock of the Dome by Muhammad when he made his ascent into Heaven. They suddenly became the footprint of your Jesus! That was the worst sort of heresy for us Muslims.'

'Are there any other questions?' asked the Bishop. 'Is there anything you do not understand up to this point?'

'Can you tell us the most important sites of Templar Treasure now?' asked Edward, his mind focused on the main chance.

'Well, it was taken to every country where the Templars had established a base, including Spain, where it was thought to be best protected at Compostela. This was where they shared the duties of looking after pilgrims with the Order of Santiago.'

'What about the other treasure you mentioned. The Cathars you said? Who were they? What had the Cathars to do with the Templars?' asked Chaucer.

'The Cathars became a separate Christian sect, not soldier/monks like the Templars. They did have similarities as fellow Christians; but in the end, they certainly differed in their heresies. You see, they were both influenced by the finds under the Temple Mount in Jerusalem. The Cathars' beliefs are thought to have been brought back home to south-west France with the French masons, who had been working on the excavations in Jerusalem. They, like the Templars, lost their faith in the Catholic Church. In other words, they turned up so much heretical evidence, they no longer believed in large sections of the Bible.'

'How come they ended up with different ceremonies and beliefs from the Templars?'

'Yes, that is true. You must understand that they both came under the influence of other religions. The Cathars particularly came under the influence of the Mancheist Movement, which had originated in Persia. It had then been taken up by the Romans. This was a dualist belief in the light and darkness in every man. To them, all Matter, or physical things, were evil. But they believed each person carried a divine light internally, which could be ignited to save their souls just before death. So long as they embraced religion. Rex Mundi was the awful devil who ruled their daily life, which explained everyday temptations and evil thoughts. Perfects (or Priests), were called out to deathbeds. They administered to the dying in order to enlighten their souls at the very end of life, and to deny Rex Mundi, ready for their journey to heaven.'

'Sounds reasonable to me,' remarked John of Gaunt.

'Well, in many ways the Cathars led an admirable life. We could learn a lot. They were God-fearing people. The landowners among them rejected their excessive riches, and they lived a life of sharing and caring for each other.' The Bishop looked around the table, 'Some people still think it was an ideal society.'

'Why did the Catholic Church hate them so?' Chaucer was mystified.

'One of the main problems was that the Perfects, the Priests, lived completely stainless lives, unlike many in the Catholic priesthood of the time. And of course there was the biggest stumbling block of all. Many of the Perfects were women! The Catholic Church would never recognise women as priests.' The old man rattled his chest with a stray cough in his throat, and leant forward to take a short draught of ale.

'There were two other problems,' he continued, 'firstly, they did not believe in the New Testament, and would not read from it. In other words the Cathars did not accept the reincarnation of Christ.'

'Why not? That was definite Heresy.'

'Yes it was, but in many ways the Cathars were more charitable to others, and more Christian in spirit than any Pope and his followers at that time.'

'What did they preach about Jesus Christ then?' asked the Black Prince, now with some trepidation.

'They believed he had two wives and three children, and did NOT die on the Cross. The second problem for the Pope, was their daily supplication to the ugly figure of Rex Mundi, the devil.'

'As long as they died pure. That doesn't seem like a very bad way to live. Why did the Pope pick on them particularly? Christian against Christian?' asked Chaucer.

'My friend, it was thought to be a purely political decision. King Edward, it was your grandfather, King Philippe of France, who saw a chance to gain the vast south-western lands of the errant Cathars. He persuaded the Pope to send in his Crusaders. This was one Christian group destroying another. Then he sent in The Inquisition to question, imprison, and torture the Cathars.' He sighed, sadly.

'How do you know all this? Is it true?' demanded Edward.

'I was born in Foix, deep in the south-west, in Cathar country. The Count of Foix played an extremely difficult role in protecting some of his Cathar friends from the Inquisition. All the while he appeared to be the vassal of King Philippe. His chaplain was Nicholas Falco, my uncle. I believe the martyrdom of the Cathars will be told throughout France for centuries to come.'

'My dear Bishop, I can see you're a Cathar sympathiser!' teased King Edward lightly.

The old man put his forefinger to his lips:

'Ssssh! There are a few of us left, Sire. My predecessor came to the same conclusion.' He looked relieved to have confessed.

'Come now, tell us what the Templars believed when they returned home.' John of Gaunt was eager to get on.

'Don't forget, Sires, the Templars were already a secret Order. They knew how to keep their own doubts well hidden. They confessed to some very strange practices. It seems they were most influenced by the graven images they found.' The old man slumped back in his chair again, quite spent.

'Do you mean the statues?' urged the Black Prince.

The Bishop nodded his assent, and mumbled something to himself.

'What was that you said?' insisted the Prince.

'Baphomet! The Sabbatic Goat!' shouted the old man. He was clearly in need of a good night's sleep.

Chapter 13 - King Solomon's Treasure

Itwas the next morning before they were all around the table once again. No one was going to miss this.

'Where was I?' The Bishop looked at his audience, scratching his head.

'Baphomet,' some replied in unison.

'Ah, yes! You see the Templars confessed to worshipping many graven images. The most infamous of these was 'Baphomet', which was a life-sized bearded goat's head, with the body of an ass. Some of them confessed to praying to a real man's bearded head on the body of a pig, but I don't think that was ever believed. These confessions were extracted under torture. We just do not know which is real. They certainly staked the fresh head of a cat on a pole each day, and placed it at eye level for their ceremonies. Several of those were recovered.

To get back to what the Templars took from Jerusalem by order of the Pope, I know you are all going to ask me what proof I have that their treasure exists.'

There was a murmur of agreement around the table.

'Perhaps I can explain this most clearly this way. All you French and Spanish Kings here around this table are personally involved. You are deep in the mire of plots to steal Templar Treasure, right now!'

A clamour of indignation flew from every corner.

'Alright then, I will give you three instances.'

With effort, he stood up and pointed at the three Kings or leaders in turn.

'**Number 1**, why do you think King Peter's father tried, unsuccessfully in the end, to get his own man into the Grand Mastership of the very Holy Order that houses the treasure in HIS region of Aragon?

'**Number 2**, why did King Pedro of Castile's father insist on a 10 year-old illegitimate son becoming Grand Master of the Order of Santiago? Much good it did him!

Number 3, why do you think Grand Master de Padilla is here?

That's because King Pedro did succeed in putting him into illegal office. They are ALL guilty!'

'How on earth do you know all this,' demanded King Edward.

'AHA! I have my contacts!'

The old man paused. 'Quite apart from all this, I must tell you, there are four people in this ROOM who have been categorically told of the existence of the treasure in one country, and where it is to be found. And,' he paused, 'there is one OTHER vitally important person among us, who has physically seen the treasure for himself.' We all looked at each other in bafflement.

It was John of Gaunt who picked up the clue first, 'King Pedro's grandfather and my grandmother were the young Prince and Princess of Spain when they were taken for a visit with their parents to see the treasure at Santiago de Compostela. We have all been told that story. There was my father, myself, the Black Prince, and King Pedro. The four of us have heard it.'

'Yes, you are right about me also, Bishop,' answered de Padilla, rather reluctantly. 'You know more than I do about the overall picture. But yes, there is a closed crypt full of items condemned never to see the light of day. We are all sworn to it. Even I will never open it.' There was silence.

'Then you defied King Pedro's ambition to lay his hands on the treasure for himself?'

'Yes, I did. Once I became Grand master, I changed my opinions, and vowed to protect the secrets of the Templar Treasure in Spain, instead of steal them.'

'That couldn't have been popular!'

Silence.

141

'Just what are we here for then? To hear nice stories? Tell us about the crypt.'

'No Sire!' de Padilla replied quickly to the first part of King Edward's questions.

He sighed, 'There are two strong-rooms with grill doors. They are full of jewels, crowns, golden chariot parts and harnesses, badges, and even golden oxen. And I hold the key to one of them.' This reminded him. He reached inside his tunic, and withdrew a rolled up document.

'I thought you might ask; I made a copy of the Templars' inventory, if you care to look over it.'

The Black Prince was the quickest, he leapt up, clattering his chair, and handed the roll across to his father. 'I must explain' said de Padilla. 'This is a list of ONLY ONE shipment of Solomon's Treasure from the Holy Land. In their busiest periods, it is estimated they sent out a shipment a month, to all different countries. There must have been more than two hundred loads taken from the Temple Mount, all being shipped through the port of Acre.'

'King Edward took a little time to comprehend the list, his lips moving. He was not a fast reader of Spanish. But eventually, he called out the contents to the others around that table:

INVENTORY of SHIPMENT from Jerusalem – via Ptolemais
Dated: Spring 1131
2 ...... bronze pillars
2 ...... capitals of copper
2 ...... ornamental festoons of chain-work
243 .. ornamental pomegranates
1 .... Great Sea of cast metal mounted on 10 oxen (2 missing)
10 ..... bronze trolleys with decorative relief
10 .... bronze basins
Variety of ornamental pots and urns (71 large/ 189 medium/ 684 small)
16 ..... gold shovels
27 ..... gold tossing bowls

56 ..... *tablets of Solomon*

6 .... *decorated gold Mahtah-Censers for Incense*

9 .... *decorated brass Miktereth-Censers for Incense*

3 .... *Teraphims – with divine properties (handle with care)*

1 .... *Holy Breastplate with jewels*

Urim

Thummim

10 ...... *cases of jewels, crowns*

25 ...... *gold chariots (for repair)*

31 .... *cast metal racing chariots – parts of*

37 .... *gold harnesses*

2,501 .. *copper badges – head of Solomon*

24 ...... *small decorative gold oxen*

53 ...... *gold ornate candlesticks*

43 ...... *gold spitting bowls*

Edward showed them the distinctive stamp of the Knights Templar that decorated the bottom of the document.

He rolled up the parchment, and tucked it into his sleeve. There were more important matters right now.

'It's not like Pedro to leave all that behind at Santiago de Compostela!' Edward said lightly. 'What a list!'

'Oh, I did manage to take some of that to finance my wars,' chuckled the ex-King of Castile. 'But I confess, that infernal half-brother of mine, Trastamara, got in my way.'

They were all quite unprepared for a sudden change of mood in the Hall; there was an explosion of words that followed:

'FOR ONCE IN YOUR LIFE, GIVE ME AN HONEST ANSWER, Pedro!' shouted Edward. 'Have you brought enough from your Treasury to pay my army, and Calveley's here?'

'NO, I have not.'

There was a communal intake of breath around the table, as the King of England pushed back his chair and held his head in disbelief.

'You clearly said you had a proposal to make. I understood that is why we're all here,' said the Black Prince.

'Yes I will pay for your army, but it won't be until we have won!' There was general commotion. 'We simply march further on to Galicia, where de Padilla and I will give you the pick of the contents of the strong-room in Santiago de Compostela, up to the value we must decide now!'

Everyone waited for a further burst of words, but, to their surprise, King Edward was running his fingers through his beard. 'Why didn't you tell us that in the beginning?' he said.

'Because you wouldn't have believed there was any treasure until you saw that list.'

John of Gaunt's administrative mind clicked into play. 'So, King Pedro, you will not even give us the monies to pay for the transport of thirty thousand men, and two thousand horse from England. Father, we cannot be expected to pay all these costs on the chance that we might win.'

'Nonsense,' replied King Edward with a wave of his hand, 'of course we will win. But it is true, there needs to be something you can use as a deposit with us. Your crown perhaps?'

'He lost it!' The Black Prince and his brother spoke at the same time.

King Pedro stood up and slowly pointed at the wooden box in the centre of the table. 'I only have THAT,' he said. 'Its value is beyond price.'

'It is the Blood of Christ!'

The Bishop looked suddenly shaken. 'Is that what you stole? I honestly didn't realise what it was.'

Slowly it dawned on the Black Prince what it might contain. Cautiously, feeling very uncomfortable indeed, he asked, 'Surely this isn't the bottle of Christ's blood you stole?'

To their dismay, the Bishop of Lucon started to shake violently. One long trembling cadaverous old finger was raised into the air as he gasped out,

'We have the REAL blood of Jesus in a vial at Poitiers Cathedral. It is our most precious relic,' said the Bishop. 'If you have stolen that...'

'For God's sake, this is a Christian abomination!' roared Edward in absolute dread. 'That box must NEVER be opened!'

'That's a pity,' said Pedro calmly, 'because this is no vial of blood; it is the world's most perfect jewel instead.' He leaned over, and to their horror, flipped the lid, exposing a deeply swirled red ruby stone. It was indeed the exact colour of dark congealed blood.

The Bishop flopped back in his chair and mopped his forehead. He looked exhausted. The assembly broke up once more, and Pedro carefully scooped up the box, and deftly tucked it underneath his arm. It did not give him a shock!

It seemed both the Moorish King and King Pedro weren't counted as strangers.

During that night, the truth dawned on King Pedro. His heir might die there. Beatrice had shared his intrigues and plots. She was his favourite and most able daughter. All he could do was to pray for her recovery. He asked the Bishop of Lucon to stay with him by her bedside. The old priest was exhausted, but she did not die that night.

The next day the meeting started once more with a statement from King Edward. He addressed King Pedro. 'IF we can negotiate the Gunpowder formula, then we will consider your offer of this fine ruby stone as an initial payment of our army expenses.

That is only acceptable to us, if you can satisfactorily explain how you obtained the jewel and why it is called The Blood of Christ. After that, we will have to come to some agreement on the value of treasure we take from Compostela.' He wagged his finger at his cousin. 'I warn you, Pedro, I shall bring my own valuers along with me.'

King Peter of Aragon suddenly felt his chance to destroy his old enemy was slipping away. He stood up and got their attention. 'I came here to accuse Pedro of Castile of heinous crimes.'

'They're no worse than yours!' came back a retort.

'Alright! Alright! Enough. Let's get this over with,' said Edward in exasperation.

'We did promise to hear them out, Father,' indicted the Black Prince.

'I know, I know. You can proceed.' He waved towards Pedro and Peter. 'We will have the accusations, then the answers, and I will give my judgment. But be quick about it.'

King Peter began his objections to King Pedro regaining his throne. **Firstly**, he said, Pedro had murdered the Archbishop of Santiago and his verger when they tried to prevent him stealing the Blood of Christ from the Santiago de Compostela crypt. **Second**, he had used his Christian army to install a Muslim King, Abu Said. **Third**, when his own nobles turned against him he had executed fifty of them. **Fourth**, he had thrown his only legal wife into prison, where she remained for many years, on the very day of their marriage. **Fifth**, he had not married any of the mothers of his three girls, whom he called his heirs. **Sixth**, he was a coward, never staying for a battle. **Seventh**, he was forever plotting to get his hands on Templar Treasure. **Eighth**, he had killed another half-brother, the rightful Grand Master of the Holy Order of Santiago and his mother, replacing him with his private prostitute's brother, de Padilla.

'For all these reasons,' King Peter concluded, 'Pedro is unfit to rule. More, he is unfit to pass on his blood to the next generation of Kings.'

The two royal Princes had the same reaction, they instantly blocked King Pedro's path as he made a lunge at his old adversary.

'That's some accusation!' admitted King Edward, although nothing surprised him. The ex-King of Castile began his reply to the charges:

'You, King Peter, accepted a bribe of one sixth of my country to depose me. You paid Calveley to join your side by offering him your eldest daughter Constanza, plus the title and lands of the Count of Carrion. You conspired with my half-brother, Trastamara, to de-throne me. You accuse me of murder, yet you have executed my only son! He was only a baby, and his mother was no noble woman, but you said she must die, 'just in case.'

'Another of your bastards,' flung back King Peter.

'Silence!' roared Edward. 'Continue, Pedro.'

'The Archbishop of Santiago and his verger were caught in a Muslim uprising. They died bravely on the steps of the shrine of St James. They managed to raise the alarm, and the Order of Santiago saved the bones of the Holy Saint.'

'That is plainly untrue!' Peter protested.

'De Padilla? Can you clear this up?' asked Edward.

'It is the truth, Sire.'

'Swear it!' demanded Peter of Aragon.

De Padilla looked at Pedro for an instant. 'I do so swear.'

Pedro continued. 'Yes, I helped Abu Said to revenge his sister's murder. We are friends. The balance of power in Castile was turning away from the nobles. They did not like it. They plotted against me. Yes, I executed them; after a fair trial...Besides, if we all stayed around this table to vindicate the mysteries of our marriage-beds and the long tales of our amours and mistresses, I think we would be here for decades.' Everyone laughed. 'Besides, my new wife was only being detained within her own apartments. It was for her own protection.'

'Why?' asked Edward.

'I happened to have a very jealous mistress. And, by the way, Maria de Padilla is now my legal wife. You will just have to accept my word for it. As for my half-brother, the late Grand Master of Santiago, he offered to fall on his own sword. Naturally, I accepted. After all, he had committed treason, and had turned against my father. He wasn't going to get the chance to do the same to me. His mother was a different matter. She had been my father's mistress, and had manipulated him to the verge of disinheriting me. I swore vengeance on that wicked woman.'

The Mistress of the Royal Household bustled into the Hall and interrupted him as she scurried by, her large skirts sweeping the flagstones as she dropped a deep curtsey to King Edward.

'Oh hurry, hurry Sire!' she cried. King Pedro and de Padilla leapt to their feet.

'What the devil is the matter woman? What's the meaning of this?'

'It's the Princess Beatrice, Sire. She's very ill.'

'We must end this session anyway,' announced King Edward, 'We will meet again tomorrow morning, if God wills.'

King Peter called across the table in aggravation. 'Stay a minute! What about my accusations against King Pedro? When will you give your judgment?'

'Oh, very well then. Case dismissed!'

Chapter 14 - The Chronicle of the Ruby

It seemed King Peter of Aragon had got out of bed on the wrong side the following morning. Having lost his personal battle to get Pedro banished or beheaded; and having been out-staged over the Gunpowder formula by the rambling priest who had hogged the table with his tales of Crusaders, Templars, and any other sort of heresy. He was petulantly refusing to come back to the table.

King Edward had to draw in his patience, and address him as he sulked under his bed covers.

'Remember, we still cannot do without your alchemy skills, Peter. We have yet to find a way to get the proper formula out of this pesky Moor; and you are the only one who will know if it is a forgery or other trick, or if it will work.'

'It will take time to test even when we do get the formula!'

'I know that, come on, I want you to help us lay a trap for this man. For I don't believe he will give up his secrets freely!'

'What is this jewel then, this Blood of Christ?' demanded King Edward as soon as they were all settled down around the Great Hall table once more.

'That's what I would like to know,' grumbled the English emissary as they settled down for another session. The old hermit grunted. 'Please yourself,' he said. 'Do you want to hear about your treasure or not?'

'Of course I do. Just get on with it, will you.'

'Right,' said the hermit. 'Listen on.'

The Bishop was ready to continue. 'Sires, this story will take some time to tell. I ask you to please bear with me.

I will go back to the Holy Land in the time of Jesus. Our tale concerns Mary Magdalene. She was also called Mary of Magdala, which was a town on the western shore of the lake of Tiberias. She was the daughter of Jairus, and sister of Martha and Lazarus.

She was older than Jesus when they met, and was very likely to have been already married and widowed once. Martha appears to have been the older daughter, and the owner of their house. According to my own research, and because it is heavily hinted at in the Bible, Jesus and Mary Magdalene married and had three children. There was a daughter Tomar-Phoebe, who later married Paul; a son, Jesus Justus, who himself became a preacher; and a second son who presumably died young.'

'Why have we never heard this?' asked Edward. There were loud mutterings from all sides of the table. The Bishop shrugged.

'The Church wanted Jesus to be pure, in every way. Why do you think the Templars and their French builders, the Cathars, took Mary Magdalene as their central figure? They found out about her in Jerusalem. The evidence was too strong. They made her just as important as Jesus himself.

Now, you will certainly accept that Mary Magdalene was present at the Crucifixion of Christ, along with two other Marys, who were both aunts of Jesus. There was Mary, wife of Cleopas, called 'Mary Jacobe'; and the third was Mary Salome, wife of Zebedee, mother of James and John. It is well recorded in the Bible. The Good Book says, in John 19: verse 29, about the last moments of Jesus on the Cross:

'Now there was set a vessel full of vinegar, and they filled a sponge with vinegar, and put it upon hyssop, and put it to his mouth.'

Hyssop was a plant whose twigs were used in Jewish rites. It had medical properties. A bunch of this was used as purification. To this she added pounded aloe-wood, to hasten the end of his suffering. This was what embalmers used to solidify the blood. A mixture of vinegar and full-strength pounded aloe-wood will thicken anything dropped into it.

However, Jesus never got to drink the aloe-wood mixture, for according

150

to St John he expired immediately after tasting the vinegar. Then, the gospel says, a number of Jews appeared, demanding that the body of Jesus and those of the two thieves beside him, be taken down and buried, because it was the custom that they could not remain upon the Cross on the Sabbath. The Roman soldiers agreed, but before the two thieves were taken down they had their legs broken. Again, it was the custom. Jesus, however, did not suffer broken legs. According to St John this was because the soldiers thought that he was already dead. The gospel continues:

'*But one of the soldiers with a spear pierced his side, and forthwith came there out blood and water.*'

The bishop took a deep breath, and when he resumed his voice was shaking with emotion. 'You see what this means,' he said. 'DEAD men do not bleed. Maybe Jesus was alive when he was taken down. The whole ethos of the Church rests upon the idea of his Resurrection, but THIS stone leaves the proof of the Resurrection at least open to question. If this becomes known, the Church would rock.'

'I said this was heresy' shouted Edward. 'But it doesn't explain about the stone.'

'I'm coming to that,' said the bishop, beginning to wish that he had kept his mouth shut. 'You see, Mary Magdalene was sitting at the foot of the Cross, and the bowl containing the aloe-wood mixture was beside her. Some of the blood from the spear wound fell into the bowl, where it instantly coagulated into the jewel you see before you. That is why it is known as the Blood of Christ Stone.

And there is one thing more that you should know: *Legend has it that if he who possesses the stone is pure in heart, the stone will protect him from all dangers. But if the possessor is evil, then the stone will kill him.*

They all looked at the stone in their midst, and then looked at each other nervously.

John of Gaunt was thinking, it reminded him of another stone.

'I'm afraid this is as very practical question. What exactly is the connection between this red Blood of Christ jewel and a mottled-green Blood Stone I've seen in all the markets?'

The Bishop nodded his acceptance of the comparison: 'As you say, the green is not a jewel. The origin of that, is when the blood of Christ fell upon the grass beneath the Cross, and turned into stone. Those stones are probably too numerous to be true. They are found everywhere now. But THIS is the one and only Red Ruby Blood of Christ Jewel in the world. THIS is unique! Beyond Price! This was the Blood of Christ, just as much as her two children were,' said the Bishop.

'How did it get here, sitting on our table?' Asked the Black Prince.

'Pedro stole it!' King Peter replied for the bishop.

'Gentlemen,' said the prelate, 'Let us get back to Mary of Magdala. There is an old fishing village on the coast of Provence. It is called Saintes-Maries-de-la-Mer. Sometime after the Crucifixion, a group of Christian leaders cast themselves out into the sea from Palestine in a boat. They trusted God to guide their craft, which had nothing but a small sail. He showed them where in the world he wanted them to preach about the new Christian church. They landed at a fishing village, which was later named in their honour.'

The old man took a sip of wine. 'In the small boat were the Three Marys from the Cross, with Martha and Lazarus. These five were all related, as I've said. Mary Magdalene brought three items with her. The Blood of Christ Ruby in its box, a carving of a fish, which was the Christian symbol at the time, and a spindly statue of a black Madonna and Child. 'It's you!' A holy man had said as he pressed it into her hand. He had obviously made it himself.

Also in the boat was St Maximim, who was later to become the first Bishop of Aix; St Sidonius, the man cured of blindness; and there was a black servant named Sara. Some people believe that St Trophomine, and a preacher called Zaccheus also came in the same boat. But they are thought to have travelled later. Certainly St Trophomine ended up in the same area; but Zaccheus became the hermit Amadour, who lived high on a rock above the Dordogne valley, a long way north.

The fishing village where they landed, was near Marseille. There turned out to be Greek and Roman settlements all along the coast of Provence. In those days, Provence was independent of France, the River Rhone being the frontier.

When the villagers eventually realised that their religious refugees were great preachers and leaders, they were converted to Christianity, and named the village Saintes-Maries-de-la-Mer. I believe that they still, to this day, have a celebration on the anniversary of the arrival of the little boat each year.'

'What happened to these people?' asked the Black Prince, stretching out his arms. He was getting stiff.

'The occupants of the vessel split up to spread the word of God. Lazarus and Mary of Magdala went to Marseille to preach. Some years passed, and her brother seems to have returned to the Holy Land. We are not sure, but there are accounts of him being killed there sometime later.

Mary of Magdala eventually retired to the Grotto of St Pilon, near Baume, and lived out her life in isolation and prayer. The locals protected her from strangers, and left her food. She always placed her ruby and its little box in a niche beside her. The Black Madonna, the gift she had been given, had a pride of place by the entrance. She became a mythical figure in her own lifetime. She was specially venerated, and they called her St Madeline. When she died, St Maximim came from Aix. Mary de Magdala was buried with her beloved box containing the stone, the carved fish, and the black statue of her son and herself. Maximim arranged for, and had constructed, four fine Gallo-Roman sarcophagi, for the bodies of Mary Magdalene, and later St Trophomine, St Sidonius, and eventually himself.

They were placed in the burial vault of a Roman Villa at St Maximim de Baume. Nearer our time, in 1280, the Pope ordered this vault to be incorporated into a fine basilica, which was built over the top and eventually became an important place of pilgrimage. Yes, that Pope officially recognised that this was the burial place of Mary Magdalene. Down the centuries history cannot be denied. Much has been written about Kings and Popes who have visited her burial place, as well as her grotto. It is undeniable. I believe a Mass is celebrated in her cave at midnight on the 22nd of July of each year.

Now we get to the story of the OTHERS, and find out how the Blood of Christ Stone was discovered. The two other Marys, the aunts of Jesus, stayed in St-Maries-de-la-Mer, with Sara the black servant. Every year the locals still remember their holy visitors, and re-enact the little boat's landing. They also remember a small CHILD who may have been Jesus Justus.

Martha, the sister of Mary Magdalene, went to preach in Trascon. She is said to have tamed a wild dragon, and sent it back to the Rhone. There is a yearly festival there to celebrate it. She was much loved, and was buried there in a church of her own name.

Maximim and Sidonius went to Aix, where Maximim became its first Bishop. St Trophomine went to Arles. He is thought to have been sent there separately by St Paul. If anyone is interested, they keep his foot as a relic.'

'Time for refreshments!' called the King. All this concentration was making him hungry.

'So, Mary Magdalene's vault must have been plundered?' said the Black Prince. 'How else could they get at the Ruby?'

'I am certain it was the Saracens,' said Prince John. Such remarks were flying across the food while they ate.

The Bishop of Lucon kept his own council, until he had their full attention again.

'WHO stole the Ruby?' demanded Edward, two hours later.

'Wait, and you will see. The Sarcophagi were safe way back through the invasion of the Germanic Visigoths in the fifth Century. Then, in 711, the Saracens started progressively conquering Spain. They swept northwards into France as far as Poitiers, and along the south coast towards Provence. With news of the advancing troops, the locals covered the burial vault, so that the enemy could not desecrate the graves, and plunder the artefacts. They did their job so well that the vault was not discovered again until the year 1240. Around that time, many French builders returned from Jerusalem carrying their own Black Madonnas. They always returned home with minor plunder. This time, they had come across a hoard of Black Madonnas when they were excavating by the north-west corner of the Temple Mount. Those who wished, had been allowed to take them home to donate to their local churches.

These builders were Cathar by belief. They came home to great religious troubles. The Inquisition had ordered the torture of many, to confess their heresies. Thousands had been slaughtered or imprisoned for their faith. Their friends the Crusaders had been turned against them by the Pope.

These Cathar builders heard the old stories of Mary Magdalene being buried at St Maximim la Baume. They also heard of her Black Madonna, and of the Blood of Christ stone. Generations of local villagers had never forgotten. Don't forget, these men were experts at excavating. They started to dig, and soon revealed the sarcophagi. What they did not know, was that they were being watched. The Saracens got wind of the jewel, and planned to steal it. The excavators found the box with its ruby, as well as a very spindly Black Madonna, along with the carving of a fish made of olive wood. The tomb inscription was faint: *'Mary, daughter of J...rus, beloved of Joseph Ben ... Daughter of God.'*

The Cathars knew the Catholic Church would destroy the Ruby. After all, it was possible proof for other religions that Christ was still alive when he was taken down from the Cross. If he was still bleeding, he was still alive. As for the Black Madonna, with its black baby, could that really be the child of Jesus? Was Jesus black too?

At last the builders realised that they were being followed by the Saracens. It became vital to take the jewel, its box, and the Black Madonna to a safe house, where nobody could use them as a religious football. Travelling westwards in the heat of late August, the Cathars were also carrying two of their own Black Madonnas from Jerusalem. They decided to make for the safest fortification they knew. This was the original Roman town of Carsac (Carcassonne), the capital of the neighbouring region of the Languedoc. It still had Cathar sympathisers within its massive walls. This was where Simon de Montfort and his Crusaders had crushed the local Cathar heresy thirty years before. De Montfort had died, and left the fortified town to the administration of King Louis IX of France. Perhaps the safest place for any heretical Holy Relic was in the lion's den! Nobody would look for it there.

Carsac was in a unique position on a crossroads between the Pyrenees and the Massif Central mountain ranges. It stood between the Mediterranean and the Atlantic, and was a natural market place and stopping-off point for passing traders. They came to and from Italy, Greece, Spain, and the Orient.

The Cathar builders arrived among old friends, on the 1st September in the year 1240. They had long discussions on how to hide the artefacts from the authorities, when, on the 16th September, there was a general panic in the town. A mighty army was a day's march away, intent on winning back their town from the King's administrator, Guillaume des Ormes and his troops. With no time for preparation, the two Cathar builders fled out of the gates before they could be closed. The siege lasted one month. Although the friendly inhabitants refused to defend their ramparts, the King's troop managed to defeat the besiegers.

Heading south, the Cathar builders were offered shelter ten miles away, on a hill above the town of Limoux. Notre Dame was a round Roman church in bad repair. They were grateful for a hiding place, and food and ale from the priest, for they realised the Saracens were following them again. They gave the old priest the first of their own Black Madonnas, from Jerusalem. She was exquisite; under one foot high; with a crown and flowing robes with braids and motifs, all arranged in the shape of a triangle, depicting the Trinity. The priest asked its origin, and was deeply impressed with talk of Jerusalem: 'We are to rebuild this church soon. Tell me, who is our Madonna?'

'Saint Marie de Marseille' they replied.

'So we will dedicate our new church to our very own Madonna, Notre Dame de Marseille'. And so it was.

The Cathar builders decided to head for the safety of the Pyrenees; but they were still forty or fifty miles away. They followed the pilgrim route from Limoux, through the hot springs of the river at Alet, and on up to the town of Rennes le Chateau, situated on a high plateau. Here they knew they would find more old friends. Unfortunately, in their absence, the town had become plague-ridden and deserted. *'Beware Plague'* was posted on the main gates. Hurriedly, they headed up the steep slope of the nearby hill to the Chateau. They were offered rest and the usual hiding place for travellers' valuables in the crypt of the church. They were advised to stay in the countryside. The towns and châteaux were falling to sieges. Even on the open roads, they were in grave danger of being picked up by the Inquisition Police.

Home for one of the Cathar builders was a small village, called Montaillou on the climb up towards the Pyrenees. Half the inhabitants were Cathars. It was a day and a half's walk from Rennes le Chateau to Montaillou. There they were treated as returning heroes. They decided to stay until the religious fervour died down.

Two years later they received a secret visit from a Templar Knight, who travelled on a donkey dressed as a monk. This precaution looked ludicrous when he stripped off his outer garment. It impressed on them the important nature of what they carried. The Templar seemed to know what they were transporting, although he never told them its name. He advised them that the only safe hiding place was at Santiago de Compostela, over a thousand kilometres away in northern Spain. He gave them letters of introduction for Santiago, IF they could get there. 'Keep to the busy pilgrim routes,' he said.

'We prefer to stay here, in our own village. We are quite safe,' they argued.

'Oh NO you are not! THIS is one of the best known Cathar villages. It is only a matter of time before the Inquisition reaches you.'

They did not really believe that warning, but they had cause to remember it one week later. News came of an ambush of eleven Church Enquirers, who had been killed by local Cathars. 'Flee now!' ordered the Templar. 'You are putting your families in mortal danger.'

Not trusting the open roads, the two Cathar builders with their artefacts, decided to split-up. One was given Mary Magdalene's own Black Madonna and Child. He made for the most holy site in France, Rocamadour, which sits above the valley of the Dordogne. This was the site of the still uncorrupted body of the hermit Armadour (or Zaccheus of the New Testament). It was true, Kings and Princes had joined the thousands of penitent pilgrims who climbed the two hundred steps on their hands and knees, with chains around their limbs. King Henry II of England went twice. Pilgrims prayed in the tiny sanctuaries built into the rock face. One of the greatest pilgrim tokens was the Rocamadour oval disk, worn around the neck, and only given to those who reached the top.

The remaining Cathar builder took the Blood of Christ Stone to the safest and most impregnable stronghold of the Cathars. It was not far away: the Chateau of Montsegur. This place had been strengthened in the early 1200's. It was impossible to take by siege, or so it was thought. 1207 metres high, the Pog, or high rock, reared vertically from the plain below. During the latter part of 1242, and the spring of 1243, more and more Cathars arrived there from outlying villages, seeking safe shelter. They had to climb up the mile-long treacherous path to the safety of the walls of Montsegur Chateau. Every able-bodied man was detailed to descend, and bring back up provisions each day. They eventually had a huge stockpile with animals, a well, and rooms full of dried food. They felt they were safe at last.

In May 1243, under the orders of Hugh des Arcy, the Siege of Montsegur started. The King of France demanded a blockade, to appease the Pope's anger. The siege lasted ten months, through a very hard winter. The besiegers were building ramps to get them closer and closer. In March 1244, a mass escape bid failed, and the Cathars at last accepted defeat. A fifteen-day truce was negotiated, at the end of which they had to choose, to renounce their faith or to perish at the stake.

During the night of March 15th, the day before the expiry of the fifteen days of truce, three men were roped down the north rock-face of the mountain unseen, and escaped. Two of the men carried Cathar secret parchments, and some small items of treasure. The third man was the Cathar builder from Jerusalem, who carried the Blood of Christ Ruby in its smooth wooden box. They parted company at the base of the rock. One went to the church at Rennes le Chateau, to bury his load in the crypt. One other headed for the Caves of Lombrive, where other Cathars had been forced to live the pre-historic life of cave-dwellers.

The builder who carried the Blood Stone headed for the most populated pilgrim route through the Pyrenees, towards Santiago de Compostela. There the Templars would protect the jewel. They would see it was kept safe at Santiago, along with their other secrets.

Too late, in 1279, the Church heard of important relics, finds and tombs in Provence. The Pope accepted that this was the tomb of Mary Magdalene. But reports of jewels and statues were proved quite wrong.

The townsfolk of Vezelay, two hundred miles away in Central France, were furious. They too had claimed the bones of Mary Magdalene for the past two hundred years. A great pilgrimage route had been built-up around the Vezelay Magdalene.

Now you have the full story how the Cathars rescued that Ruby,' said the Bishop, relaxing in exhaustion. 'And to think King Pedro has stolen it from Santiago!'

The Bishop sat down, just as the bustling Mistress of the Bedchamber came running in towards the King once more.

'What now, woman?' demanded Edward.

'It's Princess Beatrice! She's gone sire, a few minutes ago!' She wept into the folds of her skirts. 'Oh No!' groaned King Pedro, starting to his feet.

'Oh, heavens above! I must go!' cried the Bishop giving the impression of running, while still sitting in his chair. The spirit was willing. The flesh was too weak. He needed a good sleep. Eventually, he was helped by his chaplain, and exited with King Edward, with everyone else in hot pursuit, including the guards who were under very special orders from the King to vacate the Hall immediately.

Except for two men, who were slow to leave the Hall on purpose. In the hub-bub, King Abu Said leaned across the table and took the box with the jewel. He put it under his son's robe, and joined the melee around King Pedro. Nobody saw him steal the Blood of Christ Ruby.

Chapter 15 - Moorish Deception

There was no hue and cry to discover the thief who had stolen the Ruby, because nobody was allowed into the Great Hall to discover it missing. A deliberate ploy.

Nothing better than a good bit of Intrigue to heal the sulks of two Kings!

King Edward held a secret meeting with the protagonists, King Peter and King Pedro that evening. You could not have guessed it from his friendly demeanour, but he did NOT trust either of them, for he specially requested his guards' presence, OUR presence. The ex-King of Castile was heavy-hearted and subdued, but no doubt he was more than willing to talk if he felt the pull of a dastardly plot in the air.

'The question is,' said Edward, 'is there any chance that Abu Said will give up the Gunpowder formula if we don't help him back onto his own throne? …Which we cannot do, I may tell you.'

'Never! Not a chance,' replied Pedro. 'it's the very reason he has come here.'

'Well then, the next question is can YOU, King Peter, work out the rest of the formula from the part he has shown us on the parchment roll?'

'I doubt it, but could try within a few weeks; certainly not immediately. In truth, I know all that already. The 74.6% of nitrates does confirm my own tests.' He held up his right hand with its missing finger. 'That is the result of trying 90%!'

'So, we are no further on,' said Edward, 'I want that formula, Peter,' he insisted.

'Well, if I were to try,' came the reply, 'you would have to give me time to

160

do it, say about six weeks, and immunity for myself if I am to help you. I also need a promise that England will not attack Aragon.'

'Yes, I agree,' Edward replied immediately. 'And if we will not attack you. Then I must have an undertaking from you. You will not deliver that formula to Trastamara, do you understand?' He caught the eye of King Pedro, and instantly recognised the face of someone who was brewing a cunning idea. 'NOR will you deliver the formula to Pedro here. If you do, I will kill you!'

'My word is given. Aragon is neutral from now on, I swear it.'

'Pedro, will you give one sixth of Castile to Peter if he does not fight against you now? After all, it is exactly the same deal he got from Trastamara. It's only fair.'

'Fair? FAIR? Fair to lose a good slice of my kingdom? I think not. How would you like it if someone took Scotland from you for nothing in return?'

'I would never get myself into that position, dear cousin.'

King Peter sought to soothe the ruffled feathers. 'Do not fret, either of you. The formula is worthless to anyone without the resources and skills to make a weapon in which the Gunpowder can be used. For sake of argument, let's call them cannons. They will require a big smelting project that will need years of refinement, and huge investment to make enough to use in war. And there are practical problems. How do you handle hot iron to fire more than once an hour? Will it blow a hole in itself after every two shots? What is the most effective projectile to use? Could you invent a reliable gunpowder-casing that would explode on landing; or that would not blow up the cannon-men as they manoeuvred it into the weapon? The formula is only PART of the problem. There is not one of us, not King Pedro, his usurper Trastamara, or myself, who has the time, money, and skills to develop this weapon to its proper potential. THAT is the main problem'

'Thank you, Peter. I understand it better now,' Edward replied. 'am I correct in saying the formula is the most vital piece of evidence in this jigsaw? Without it, we cannot even start our experiments?'

Peter nodded. 'If you ARE going to develop this weapon, you will enhance the defence of your country, that is true. But remember the experiments will cost some lives among your own men. In this work, all mistakes cost lives.'

'Now,' said Edward, 'back to the business at hand. I have to tell you that Pedro already has a plan in action right now!' He turned to his cousin, 'You're good at that. Anything devious is your speciality, isn't it?' But before waiting for a reply, Edward continued, 'It requires my Guards, at this very moment, to practise a major case of Dereliction of Duty. But you must understand, I DON'T want to know anything about it. Suffice to say, nothing must happen under my son's roof. He is a stickler for his word. Unfortunately, he gave Abu Said his protection.' He leaned between the two men and whispered, 'Use the hunting lodge.'

In another part of the castle, Abu Said and his son were hatching their own plot. 'Save yourself, father,' said Hassim. 'If you are going to escape with the formula, at least change clothes with me. And take the Ruby with you. You will have much more chance if I stay behind and pretend to be you, in your red robe. May Allah be with you!'

That night a monk passed out of the gates of the castle. This was not an unusual sight; but this monk had a blue Arab robe hidden underneath his brown cowl, as well as many knives hidden on hooks. The wooden box with the Blood of Christ Ruby was safely concealed in one of the numerous pockets. This made him the usual rotund shape of a monk. They did love their food. The parchment roll with the Gunpowder formula was easier to hide about his person.

In the meantime, it was King Pedro who took charge of his new plan; he visited the Great Hall and found the Ruby missing. Setting up a hue and cry around the castle, he gathered the guards as he ran straight to the Arabs' chambers, and saw the occupant of the red Arab robe looking out of the window.

He directed the guards to search the rooms. 'Look for the box, for your own sake, DON'T TOUCH IT!'

162

'Where is your son?' asked the Captain of the Guard, thinking he addressed King Abu Said.

The Arab shrugged, his face well hidden in the cowl of his Arab robes.

'Your son has stolen the jewel from the Great Hall and he's GONE!' King Pedro was certain. After all he had deliberately let it happen!

'The scoundrel,' said the son of Abu Said, pretending to be his father and lowering the pitch of his voice. 'I will get him back. I need that ruby as much as you do, to bargain with King Edward. Let me go and find him.'

At that point, the English King entered the chambers pointing directly at the Arab:

'Have you stolen that ruby? What's going on here, Abu Said?'

'His son has escaped with the jewel,' replied the Captain

'Hot-headed fool! Let me go and find the stupid boy,' begged the Arab, 'I'll get him back for you.'

Puffing himself up to a very great anger, Edward thundered: 'You have my son's protection here, and I must honour his word. But I warn you, if you play me false, I will have you executed without mercy. That ruby is King Pedro's deposit to get his throne back. You will have your reward only when that is completed.'

'GO!' he ordered. 'If you try to escape, you will find two Arabs will not get far in Aquataine.'

He turned to the Captain, 'Release him!'

Whatever King Edward, King Pedro, and the Captain of the Guard did or did not know about the escape of the 2nd Arab. None of them realised they only knew half of the story. They had a nasty surprise ahead.

The young Moor, pretending to be his father, was let out of the castle to bring back his 'son', and the jewel. It felt good! He passed under the teeth of the gates of Poitiers Castle, relishing the freedom in having the drawbridge especially lowered for him. Across the open plain beneath the castle walls, he entered the Wood of the Saints (a dense forest with wide paths, all set in a canyon with sheer granite walls either side).

The very trees comforted his nerves; they were thick with undergrowth, and somehow there was safety in their numbers as they hid him with his fleeing feet, as he picked up his skirts and his speed, and ran like the wind for his freedom.

Maybe he had gone a mile or so, enough to be blown, enough to begin thinking of where to look for his father. A troop of soldiers sprang up from behind the undergrowth, a trap in front of him; and, as he turned around, they closed in behind him to create a circle. Right there, in their clutches was his Father, who was still acting the part of an overweight monk. Disguised as his son, with blue Arab robes underneath and a well-hidden face.

'Have you met your son, our fat friar here?' the Commander asked sarcastically, 'we scooped him up earlier!'

Still the soldiers did not know the two Arabs had changed robes.

The two Moors were brought along a meandering track to the hunting lodge in the middle of the dense wood, where they found King Pedro waiting. The fat friar's cowl was removed, clearly revealing underneath the blue robe and voluminous hood of the younger Arab. However, in the dim light they could not see his face. It was the older man. The wrong man!

'Aha, here we have the son!' cried Pedro erroneously.

Soldiers held both Arabs still, while Pedro felt for the wooden box, and found it amongst the fold of the blue robe. 'You're a young viper in our nest. Common thief!' he growled, drew his sword on the spot and lunged at the prisoner.

Feeling with his left hand for the third rib down, Pedro thrust the very tip of his sword in, and then pushed it with all his weight right through the body of the Moor. He gave it a half twist, and removed it, feeling the familiar sag of the body weight. In a swish of movement, he wiped the blade on his knee, bent down and searched the body urgently for the Gunpowder formula. Black anger leapt into his face as he realised that the parchment roll was not there.

'That's MY FATHER, my father! You've killed the King,' gasped Hassim, throwing aside his head covering, showing he was the younger man. 'We changed clothes so you would think you still had the King.'

King Pedro put his head back and laughed with relief: 'I've killed the King, have I? What a fortunate mistake! Now we are free to torture the son for the formula. Strip him bare, and strap him to the ladder! On his back, if you please, so I can reach the important parts. I'm good at carving out testicles.'

Pedro started fingering through Hassim's own wicked knife collection.

'You know, I find the rungs of a ladder are placed exactly the right distance apart for me to perform a very neat removal. If you understand my meaning.' The young man felt himself going dizzy with shock, and felt his limbs were not responding to his desperate wish to flee. Perhaps it was just as well he could not feel them, because he would lose a part of his body soon enough.

'I think I shall start by using one of your own knives,' Pedro taunted 'this nice curved barbed one will do the trick!'

The young man screamed in pain and terror even before his favourite blade got nearer, and nearer, and started slicing into his flesh.

'Oh well,' said Pedro, the reason for his nickname of The Cruel becoming increasingly apparent, 'since you've just lost one testicle anyway, I might as well finish the job. Then we'll start on your right hand. Isn't that the one a common thief loses? Are you ready yet to tell us where the formula is?'

'Stop! Stop! I'll tell you! It's in the monk's cowl, in the hood. I sewed it in.'

Pedro found the formula and took time to check it was complete. 'Kill him!' he ordered, as he turned away and walked out. He hadn't meant to kill the King, but that was their fault for the deception. Killing the son was of no consequence at all.

A dozen soldiers were under strict orders from King Edward to make sure they accompanied King Pedro, the jewel box and the formula, on their return to the castle.

'Here's to King Pedro, the clever old fox!' was the toast from his cousin. An echoing cheer went up from King Peter and the royal Princes. They were discussing a successful day between themselves, in an ante-chamber.

'Have you seen the formula, King Peter?'

It was on the table in front of them.

It read:

10 .... dirhams of saltpetre = 74.6 % nitrates
1½ ..... dirhams of sulphur = 11.9 % sulphur
2 .... dirhams of charcoal = 13.5 % charcoal

'We have it!' shouted Peter. Years of work and study had suddenly fallen into place.

'Thank God.' whistled King Edward.

'How did you do it?' the Black Prince asked King Pedro, now the hero of the hour.

'Oh, I set them a trap. We couldn't let the Arabs escape once they knew too much about the Christian heresies and treasure. I know you all thought I was being stupid to talk so openly in front of them. I simply made sure they knew all about Jerusalem, and how the Christians fooled the Muslims. I liked that bit best. You see, I meant him to steal it. The tricky part was to make up a convincing cover story so that he had the opportunity to take the jewel.'

'Cover story?'

'Yes, a trick. You see, my poor daughter is very ill, but she's not dead yet. Thank God! The other difficult part was to get them away from here, because YOU, dear Prince, gave them your protection while under your roof.'

'I had to.'

'Yes, yes, I know. But we just had to make sure we didn't take their monk's robes from them when we all originally arrived. In other words, we gave them their disguise to re-use. The guards on the castle gates were told to report any monks going out, but not to stop them.'

'Edward, you solved the only remaining problem by offering the hunting lodge in the woods. We could have done it in the open, I suppose, though it might have been a bit noisy. And now we come to the important part. HERE is the Blood of Christ Ruby, safely in its box.' As agreed, he handed it over towards King Edward.

Immediately, I leapt to the defence of our King, for had I not felt the shock and harm the box could give to a stranger? I flung my body full-length between the two Kings, suspecting the ex-King of Spain's intentions towards his cousin.

'Ho Ho!' roared Pedro at my antics, 'Don't you worry young man, your King is safe now. You see, the box knows when it has a new rightful owner. How do you think it has been handed down safely from the days of Mary Magdalene?' I retired uncertainly, and found my Black Prince's hand on my arm to calm me.

Pedro held it out and offered it to Edward once more: 'This is the first payment for the support of your army, as well as Calveley's Free Company, so that I can get my throne back.'

The King of England turned and walked to the window, he appeared reluctant to touch it. 'Very good,' he said, 'And you will pay the rest when we get to Santiago?'

'Quite so, dear cousin.'

'Very well then, my eldest son shall retain the jewel in safe keeping.' He signalled that the Black Prince should accept the jewelled deposit, and its box.

'Beware lest it is recognised in France! They believe it has magical powers over here.'

Before I could breathe, in one smooth motion, the Black Prince stepped forward and flipped open the domed box. No fireworks, no shocks, just silence, as he lifted the swirled red ruby gemstone to a nearby candle. 'It is just like a blob of congealed blood. Whatever its history, I shall wear it in the CENTRE of my Crown when I become King. Nobody shall steal it from there!'

'Bravo,' called his father. 'Not too soon I hope!' and they all laughed.

John of Gaunt clapped his brother on the shoulder. 'And I shall take the box,' he said.

Chapter 16 - Death and Destruction

'Despite several false alarms,' the hermit continued, as he told his story in the orchard of the inn 'the heir of Castile, Princess Beatrice, did not die until the third week of February. At her bedside for the last two days of her young life, were her father, King Pedro, her two sisters Constance and Isabela, and her uncle, Grandmaster de Padilla.

The elderly bishop had already left. Their talks had finished. King Edward deliberately encouraged the imminent death to affect the mood of the garrison. The exceptions were for himself and his two sons. He used the diversion of King Pedro's attention to make plans for the coming campaign.

Numbers, transport, strategy and dates were discussed. Edward had already allocated thirty thousand troops from England, plus the 700-strong garrison at Poitiers. The talk was all of logistics, armaments, supplies, and the marching of garrisons down from York to Plymouth, from Lancaster, Bristol, Leeds, and the Welsh Castles, as well as from London.

The seizing of sea-faring transport was the easiest. They simply announced a crackdown on 'unsafe shipping'. Any decent-sized commercial boat, whether it was English, Venetian, Greek, or from any other Mediterranean country, was seized as they discharged their normal cargo at the English docks. The crews were detained while an armed force with 'Official Assessors' checked the condition of the ship; the hull, the sails, the ropes. The safety check was NEVER passed, and the crews were promptly arrested and removed. The ship was then purloined for King Edward's army of horses, supplies and men, and taken by trusted army sailors around the coastal waters to Plymouth. Here there were warehouses of supplies for just such an occasion.

King Edward was in his element; always one step ahead; and John of Gaunt was proving himself a brilliant administrator. At any time, the army was able to respond to an emergency within a single month. Considering that most other countries took a minimum of three months to react, it was accepted that England provided the foremost fighting force in Europe, able to defend her French interests at short notice. Being an island nation, perhaps she had to.

The exact strategy for the campaign was more complex. The battleground to regain Pedro's crown, on Spanish soil, would inevitably have to be fought on the Castile border, but where? Maps were fetched, and King Edward was eager to lead the planning stage. However, to his disappointment, the two Princes flatly refused to discuss this subject. They were adamant, doggedly determined that cousin Pedro would know the lie of the land best, and have knowledge of any possible strategic advantage. It was true that they needed to be able to choose the battle-site in advance, but they could not do so; not just yet, for strategic reasons that they kept to themselves. The King found it incomprehensible that they refused to discuss it with him. He had always laid great store by 'outwitting the enemy on paper', as he called it. After all, the poring over maps and the planning was half the fun of the battle.

Edward got his own back when they came to discussing possible dates. 'We want the element of surprise,' he said. 'How soon can you cross the Pyrenees?'

However, they were still in the grips of bitter weather. February was known as the worst month of winter.

'There's no point in thinking about that until you can muster the army back home,' said the Black Prince. 'How long will that take? Another month after you get home? Then there's the shipping of men and supplies from Plymouth into Bilbao. I can't see it happening until the end of April, beginning of May,' added his brother. 'Say June for sure,' agreed the Black Prince.

'That's the worst idea I've ever heard!' roared the King. 'By May, the

Spaniards will be re-supplied by 20,000 more French mercenaries queuing up to get through the Pyrenees. Believe me, that usurper Trastamara is going to hire anyone he can get his hands on. Our only chance is to catch him by surprise, quickly,' he paused, 'and before he can double his troops.'

'How can we possibly surprise him quickly?' asked John of Gaunt.

'You can't. Even if we could get through the snow in the mountains, this garrison alone cannot take on ALL of Trastamara's army,' said his brother. 'If our troops from England cannot get there before May, the whole campaign will be lost.'

The brothers turned to the King, and watched in amazement as he cocked an eyebrow at them cheekily, picked up his scabbard, and slammed it on top of the map, pointing to the north-east coast of Spain.

'There. At Bilbao! How would you like 30,000 men, horses and equipment by the 25th of March?'

His sons looked at each other. What was he up to? 'There's no time, father!' said one. The other agreed. 'It will take us until May to get home, muster the troops, march them down to Plymouth and arrange sails and supplies, let alone make the voyage to Bilbao.'

The King let them argue themselves to a standstill. When they had quite finished, he spoke very deliberately.

'Considering I have ALREADY sent the orders to assemble the army, THREE WEEKS AGO. I see no reason to think that they will not be on Spanish soil by the 25th of March. How's that?' he exclaimed in triumph.

The two royal Princes laughed out loud. Their father was still at it, outfoxing them by a mile, as well as everyone else. He must have sent the orders to muster the army on the very day after King Pedro and his family had arrived at Poitiers.

This meant that all the while, he had intended to provide his cousin with the necessary English troops. Good Heavens! Even Pedro's TRIAL had been a pretence, because Edward had already sent for the English army to help him get his throne back.

'Now it's up to you, my sons. The two main questions are: Can you get this garrison here from Poitiers, of 700 cavalry and Longbowmen, through

170

the snows of the Pyrenees in March? And can you meet up with our army near the borders of Castile?'

'Whoa! It's not possible!' declared the Black Prince. 'That is only next month, and the mountain passes are blocked until mid-April at least. It's never been done.'

The King nodded his head slowly. 'Yes it has. And with a full army!'

'By whom?'

'Charlemagne and Roland did it.'

'That's seven hundred years ago!' protested the Black Prince.

'So?'

The Black Prince felt the quickening of a challenge. John of Gaunt felt despair. That was the difference between the two brothers.

As I listened to this extraordinary turn of events, standing within earshot in my role as bodyguard, I felt a cold finger of dread creep up my spine. I was not afraid for myself, you understand. There was nothing much wrong with my health now. My fear was for my master, my Prince, my double. You see, I knew that his illness was getting worse. Had I not seen its daily progress? Of course, given a challenge, he would take it on with all his heart; but surely the question was whether that heart would burst asunder under the strain?

Around the table for their last meal together, King Edward had Constance and Isabela of Castile placed on either side of him. The two remaining daughters of King Pedro were 12 and 10 years old. They were not the best companions for an old King, being quiet and watchful girls. But he had a personal message for them, well out of hearing of their father.

'With the help of God,' said Edward, 'we will put your father, King Pedro, back on the throne of Castile. This means that you, Constance, will be his heir.' He looked with purpose into the deep brown eyes of his dark young second cousin. She was no beauty. She had a broad brow and a sharp chin like her father's, but there was a quiet composure in the way she looked straight back him; unflinching, unafraid. He found surprising strength in the way she held his gaze. No doubt she would need that courage in the life ahead of her, if she had any.

He continued, 'However, as we know, things can go wrong. There are two promises you can both give me right now. **Firstly**, that you stay here in Poitiers, properly protected, until the battle is won. You do not need to go through the dangers of the Pyrenees in snow again. **Secondly**, if either of you is ever in need, come here to Poitiers, or to England. Girls, we are your family. Grandma England and I will always keep a place and a position for you at Court.' Poor girls, would they ever stop trotting after their father? he thought.

One of their promises would change the course of history, and the other would haunt them forever.

King Edward left France the next day, eager to oversee the preparations for war back home. The Queen and sixty lancers went with him. He leaned over the Black Prince and his brother as they knelt side-by-side for his blessing before departure.

'Don't forget, I'm sending a Valuer over with the army.'

'A Valuer?'

'Yes, to assess the amount of treasure from Santiago de Compostela. God go with you my sons.' He had no foreboding about this adventure. But he certainly should have.

By March 1st, the English army of 30,000 men, 600 horses, and waggon-loads of equipment was threading its way towards Plymouth. Like spider-legs, it came along the radius paths in the countryside through England to meet the armada of purloined ships that gathered at the great port. In truth, England was so used to sending their soldiers over the sea to France, they thought very little of the further distance to Spain. But they still had to wait for favourable winds and tides.

They had managed to conceal it well, but there was indeed a very good reason why the two Princes would NOT discuss with their father the route of the march, and the strategy of the battle ahead. Earlier, the Black Prince had been forced to admit the truth to his brother about the state of his health. The proposed long march from Poitiers, over the impossible Roncesvalles

Pass of the Pyrenees in winter, and on to Castile, was a journey of at least 500 miles.

The extra distance to Santiago de Compostela, on the north-western corner of Spain, to collect the promised treasure, was another 300 miles or more. How could he lead his troops when his own body was so bloated that he could not even get into his famous black armour? His joints were so swollen that they locked, and he had to be lifted from his horse. If he rode at the back, or in a waggon, instead of at the head of his men, they would know something was wrong. The soldiers called themselves the Invincible Army; they would follow him anywhere. He had never led them to either a compromise, or to a defeat. They would think it an ill omen if he showed them the slightest weakness.

The brothers knew they would alarm their father if he had been aware that they had already planned to travel separately from the 700-strong garrison force. They took the decision to start later than the others, and take a different route for two-thirds of the journey. We would arrive near St Jean Pied de Port sometime after the main column. There they all had to wait and pray for favourable weather before attempting the Roncesvalles Pass. I knew that my Prince must ride for hundreds of miles. How would he do it? Would he get there?

The royal brothers made their own itinerary: a mixture of masculine toughness, a sense of adventure, pride, and, what surprised me the most, a certain amount of humility. It seemed they had certain religious questions they hoped to answer along the way. Since they were on their way to Santiago de Compostela anyway, they reasoned they would embark on their own pilgrimage to the tomb of St James, or St Jago as they called it. It never occurred to them, that the small matter of a particularly irreligious bloody battle along the way would not exactly improve their State of Grace with St Jago.

They would join the suffering of the pilgrims along the holy route, for was it not true that the Black Prince was in need of a cure? Was it not true also, that there was one particular pilgrim path from Poitiers which was well known for its line of natural hot spa towns on the way to Bordeaux?

Since childhood, the brothers had been indoctrinated into the world of three memorable books. The first was a fine illustrated Bible. The second, was a set of four books in a collection called Codex Calixtinus. The Historia Karoli Magni et Rotholandi was their favourite. It was also called The Great Chronicle of St-Denis, or The Chronicle of Pseudo-Turpin.[3]

The third book the royal Princes grew up with was the Guide for the Pilgrim to Santiago, from the same collection. The author, Aimery Picard, had travelled the four main routes himself, and had spent fifteen years writing his collection.

The Black Prince ordered me to carry a pocket version of this guide, as did many pilgrims who had learned to read for themselves. In fact, far from fitting into my pocket, I had to wear its heavy pages in a form of a sling across my back. I was indeed cursed with its weight. Unslinging it was an ungainly manoeuvre, for the Prince often wanted to consult its pages. There were details of the easiest paths, the cleanest rivers with the best access (hundreds had to be forded along the way), the greatest relics to be visited, and the safest towns.

The imaginations of the two Princes were stirred. What adventures they would have, following in footsteps of King Charlemagne! They decided then and there exactly where the coming battle would be fought. Only one place fitted their purpose: the site that Charlesmagne's nephew Roland had chosen for his legendary confrontation with the giant Ferragut. It was named after the victor, Poys de Roldan. The celebrated battleground was on the Castile border, near the town of Najera, beside the pilgrim route to Santiago de Compostela.

Officially, the main garrison was told that the Black Prince and his brother would catch up with the column at the Pyrenees. They had matters of State to attend to for their father the king. The main army had to leave Poitiers by the 1st of March, to give themselves any chance to get through the mountains within the month.

At the traditional farewell feast on the night of the 28th of February, King Pedro dropped his bombshell. His two remaining daughters HAD to come with him as well! He would not leave them. There followed desperate cries about their safety, and about the perils of another ride through the snow-clad mountains. All fell on deaf ears. There was no reasoning with him. Only King Edward could have forced the issue, but he had returned to England.

Feeling a fury and an impotence that perhaps reminded him of his own diminished strength, the Black Prince leapt to his feet. All he could do was to lash out with his tongue. 'You've killed one daughter with your stupidity! Is that not enough for you?'

He was met with a stony silence. He pushed his chair away noisily: 'Now you're bent on destroying the other two.'

The Black Prince marched out of the hall. He did not want to be in the company of such a bastard, for whom he was expected to lay down the lives of many of his own soldiers in order that Pedro could regain power. For indeed, there would undoubtedly be great loss of life. A percentage of them would certainly die even before they got as far as the battlefield. The Pyrenees would claim dozens of men, horses, and vital equipment. Indeed they might all perish there. The Prince was disgusted with his cousin.

John of Gaunt had a different reaction. 'Why must Pedro take his daughters with him?' he asked himself. 'What was behind this decision?' He could not guess the answer. If he had guessed, he certainly would have slain the ex-King of Castile then and there, as he sat at the table.

Pedro was following his own agenda. He was about to break every one of the promises he had made to King Edward.

My own personal problems, which had been boiling up for some time, came to a head the very next day. My woman, Marie-Elaine, had at first been boastful and proud of my promotion to the Black Prince's personal staff, though she was not allowed to mention the real reason lest there should be a soldier in a foreign inn with a loose tongue. The fact that the Prince had a stand-in, was a state secret.

I asked if she could be given a position in the household, to be nearer to me; for indeed I kept long hours attending my Prince. She was given some work in the royal kitchens. But it was not long before her fiery temper got her into trouble. She was thrown out on her ear one night, when one of the

Queen's cooks nearly got throttled to death. I do not know who started the fight. But the Queen's favourite sauce-maker was not likely to be dismissed.

Whatever the truth of it, Marie-Elaine had to go back to camp, and so she saw me less often. At first she seemed content enough to ask me questions about my training, and all was well. But she began to resent my absence. I could not always get a message to her if my Prince wanted me late at night. She started getting jealous and suspicious 'You talk of your Prince; why does he want you so late at night?' She would ask. Then she fell back on the old standby: 'Are you visiting another woman? I'll twist her neck off!' Truth be told, I wouldn't have dared.

Our relationship was falling to pieces. I still loved her, but could no longer cope with her tempers. On two or three mornings I reported for duty carrying a bruise on my face. My Prince would cock an eyebrow at me, and make no remark. I was ashamed to be beaten by a woman; but you see, I myself would not lift a hand to her in anger. Until one night, when I lost control, and laid her out with one blow.

The very next day the order came for the army to prepare to leave camp with full kit on the 1st of March. Our route lay southwards, to the base of the Pyrenees.

I knew it was vital that the secrets of the talks were kept; for at no time were the soldiers ever told their true ultimate destination. They had no inkling that they were going over the high mountain passes, and on into Spain in winter conditions. The very idea was mad, unthinkable.

The Black Prince knew his men well enough. They would follow him anywhere...within reason. And over the Pyrenees in snow was not only unreasonable, but asking for disaster. For now, the orders read:

The Garrison of the Army of England at Poitiers,
under the command of Prince Edward the Black Prince,
will move out with all supplies at daylight on 1ˢᵗ March,
in this year of our Lord 1367.
Destination: South to St Jean Pied de Port

Signed and Sealed: Edward of England
Dated: 20 February 1367
For our God, our King, and for England!

It was as if no violence had ever happened between us. Marie-Elaine instantly became once more friendly and loving. I do believe she became empowered by the mantle of her old role as the head of the Women's Army. She swung into action, and rounded up and drilled the other women in the finer arts of carrying pots and pans, and stealing the food the soldiers were to eat along the way. They all knew how to wring a chicken's neck without a give-away squawk; but a goose was more difficult, for they hissed so. She showed them how to lasso the geese, and tighten the knot quickly before they alerted their owners with their evil hisses. Cattle had to be prodded with spikes; and sheep were so stupid, they would follow the lead female all the way back to the night's camp. It was easy for the women to divert the luckless shepherd. The trick was to identify the dominant ewe by watching the flock for several minutes. Then some of the women had to chase her towards the trap. When she was caught, she could be led by a rope, and the rest would follow. Pity the poor shepherd, caught with his trousers down. In his dreams he may have seen one woman who wanted a sheep; but he could not have conceived of a host of women taking them all.

Marie-Elaine drilled her women, she shouted at them, and she oversaw the gathering of spare weapons, utensils, spades, bedding; an endless list of things they must take with them to sustain their men folk, plus the carts and horses to pull the heavier equipment, including fake siege weapons.

So, the day came when I had to face the one conversation with her that I had been dreading for the whole week before. It started with her innocent remark.

'We'll be some sight, you and I,' she declared proudly, with her red hair spread out on my stomach. It was two evenings before we were due to go.

'Why is that, my love?' I replied sleepily.

'Well, you'll be riding at the front of your army, alongside your Prince; and I will be running at the head of my army at the back. Yes! We'll sing the songs to our marching men. We've been practising, you know.' She ran her hand through that hair of hers; that wonderful hair. 'Oh, my Petit-Roi, it will be good to be on campaign again, eh?'

I had to tell her the truth, or at least part of it. I took a deep breath.

'Except I won't be there,' I mumbled. The dreaded hour had come.

'What did you just say?' she spoke sharply.

'Orders is Orders! The two Princes and two guards are travelling later, on a different route. I have to be one of the guards.'

'YOU WON'T BE THERE! My God! What trickery is this?' She was shouting it out now.

'Quiet, my love, keep it QUIET! It's a secret!'

Then she was off and running. 'Oh my good God, not another secret! You cheating bastard. I thought you would give up with your lies when the army was on the move.'

To shut her up, before she managed to extricate all the Prince's secrets from me, and shout them out to the world, I slugged her again. Then I moved my kit-bag, my uniforms, weapons, and my cat to the royal apartments.

I could not handle her questions anymore; and I certainly was not going to tell her about the Black Prince's illness; for the soldiers would never follow him into the mouth of death in the snowy passes of the Pyrenees, if they knew. He was a God to them, indestructible. Besides, if she had realised, or if any of them had known half of the plans the Prince plotted for his men, we would have had a mass desertion on our hands.

Sunrise on the 1st of March brought low-lying clouds that were spreading their eerie fingers of mist up the river valley below the English fortress. The creeping carpet was only just below the castle. It made the assembled army feel as if they were about to march out among the heavens, into the sky. A ripple of awe passed along the ranks as they marched out of the garrison and saw the clouds. The drawbridge, protesting loudly at the damp conditions, cranked shut behind them.

They travelled under the banner of the Black Prince, although he was not with them because of matters of State for the King. It was his army of men, and they required full provisioning along the route. It was the duty of each town within the English-owned region of Aquitaine to feed them if required. This needed forward planning, and at least 48 hours warning before the army arrived. Every inn had to be emptied of other travellers, and provisions collected around the nearby countryside. Nobody was compensated if all their chickens were taken, or if their vegetables were dug up. Once out of their own territory, it was up to the woman's army marching behind to steal the daily needs for their men. I remember looking down from the tower of the Prince's apartments, as the army passed over the drawbridge beneath me.

'That sight always makes me feel proud,' said the Prince. He was standing beside me as the ranks of men and horses tramped out of the garrison. I had never before watched the army marching out. The organisation was deeply impressive. Every man knew his place and his pace, and was comfortable with whatever weapons he carried, be they pikes, swords and hammers, or longbows taller than themselves. But the biggest impression that will always stay with me was the sight of the multitude of loyal females in the Women's Army marching along behind them.

They carried spare weapons around their necks, and cooking pots dangled from their waists. Every part of their bodies was covered with provisions or bedding rolls or weaponry. They clanked at every step. They did not drag their heavy loads along, oh no! They marched out with a lightness of foot, even with a certain peculiar grace, as they drummed in time to their steps upon their pots and pans.

With a shout, 'and a left, right, left,' the women started up with the Soldier's Song, a Round that the soldiers sang in turn. On every campaign, it helped to march the miles away. The women sang through all the verses first. After that, the foot soldiers took their part, then the longbow men replied and the foot soldiers came in again. Finally the cavalry finished the song; they all sang the chorus, and then the women started again. Round it went; always with a long pause on the first word of a verse:

> Footsoldiers: *My...Shag-hair Cyclops come let's ply*
> *Our hefty hammers lustily*
> *Our hefty hammers lust'ly.*

> Longbowmen: *By...My wife's sparrows I swear these arrows*
> *Shall singing, winging, fly*
> *Thro' many a fine foe's eye*
> *Thro' many a fine foe's eye.*
> *These...headed ones with golden blisses*
> *These...silver ones with feathered kisses*
> *Thro' many a fine foe's eye...*
> *Thro' many a fine foe's eye.*

> Footsoldiers: *My...hammer's of lead it strikes a man dead*
> *As if in a dance he falls in a trance*
> *With my hefty hammers lust'ly,*
> *My hefty hammers lust'ly.*

> Cavalry: *When...back and sides go bare go bare*
> *Both hand and foot go cold...*
> *If ere ye've strappey're armour on*
> *Y're belly will live till y're old till y're old,*
> *Y're belly will live till y're old.*

> Chorus: *Y're belly will live till y're old, till y're old*
> *Y're belly will live till y're old.*

Sir Hugh Calveley was assigned the command. He rode Pheciphelies at the

head of the column, with his Free Company behind. In the middle came
Pedro of Castile, and the Grandmaster of the Holy Order of Santiago, de
Padilla. They rode in front of the 700 soldiers of the garrison. The King of
Castile was well protected.

It was an impressive mobile force. They travelled light. The riders were
in full armour, and carried their weapons, and immediate necessities, slung
over the horses' backs, and fixed behind the saddles. The foot soldiers had
their longbows hanging sideways on their right shoulders. Their weapons
were longer than the men who carried them, and their spares and personal
needs were strapped to their backs. They also wore a sword about their
waists for close-order fighting. These men did not run like Spanish foot
soldiers, for they were larger, heavier men. They marched at double-order
instead. Hour in and hour out, they travelled at the pace of a horse's light
trot, averaging six miles in an hour. The army marched all the daylight
hours of early March, with five-minute stops at convenient rivers, as much
for the horses as for the men.

The usual supply waggons and extra personnel to serve those in command,
were almost entirely absent, except of course, for what the women's army
behind them carried. One of the few concessions this Poitiers force carried
were thousands of snowshoes for the horses, to be fitted for the treacherous
paths of the Pyrenees. These had to be kept a secret for the first part of
the journey, and were well camouflaged. Accompanying these, were heavy
sacks of extra nails. They would provide grip on the snow, and could save
the lives of both men and horses. The sacks were slung either side of twenty
spare horses. Each one was led from another horse.

Every cavalry man knew how to shoe his own horse, and carried his own
tools. Five of their number bore more sinister-looking implements. These
were long heavy brass axes, to be used to dispatch dying horses, either in
battle, or in the Pyrenees. The only other addition to the force was just one
waggon, which travelled in the middle of the column. This was for the two
Castile Princesses. It also carried a mysterious load of heavy possessions
belonging to the Black Prince and his brother, John of Gaunt.

So, we watched the women singing below us as they marched out of the garrison. They saw it as their duty to sing, to keep up the spirits of their men folk, and to lock themselves into the punishing double-time pace.

'She's a magnificent leader, that woman of yours!' remarked the Prince as he watched her tied-back red hair, swinging from side to side as she marched tall at the head of her women. He turned to me to acknowledge his compliment,

'Yes sir,' I managed to reply.

'I didn't want the ladies to go, you know, but what could I do? I could not explain to them about our Pyrenees crossing. I know very well they would not have allowed their men to go at all.' He sighed. 'I would have had a mass desertion on my hands - and we have not even got to the mountains yet.' He smiled wistfully at me. 'Was I right, Petit-roi? Was I right?'

I nodded, and then thought better of it, 'Sire, you'll certainly have to tell them when we get to the base of the mountains; we know they CANNOT follow the men over the Pyrenees. Surely Sire, you could tell them to wait for the men's return after the battle?'

'It's more difficult than you think Petit-Roi,' mused the Prince. 'You see, these soldiers will never come back.'

At once I felt the chill of a truth revealed. 'You mean Sire, we will not survive? We will all die in the Pyrenees?' I faced him full on. 'I thought you believed in this mission; that it was possible?'

'Steady, steady, Petit-Roi.' He shook his head at me. 'I was not talking about our survival; that is in the hands of God. The truth is that the King has planned to evacuate most of the force from Spain by sea after the battle. They will all be going back to England.' He saw my face and continued, 'There are two reasons for this. In the first place it will be less dangerous than marching them all the way back here again; and secondly, we need fresh troops at Poitiers. We have arranged for a new consignment of soldiers for the garrison. They arrive within the next month. After the battle, only a small company of cavalry will travel on with us to Santiago to escort the treasure back home.'

The Prince put his hand on my shoulder. 'You see now, don't you Petit-Roi? These women will never see their men again. Think it out for yourself.

How can I tell them that? I dare not, or my men won't go!'

'What will you tell them, Sire?'

He turned to walk away from my question. 'Nothing. Nothing at all,' he murmured as he started to leave me there.

I hurried to catch up with him, my disappointment making me bold. 'And the women?'

He shrugged. It suddenly struck me that he had not even considered the women. It was almost as if he thought they were not <u>his</u> problem. But of course they were. He let the women help his army on the march, now he must help them.

'Sire, may I have permission to send them a message a couple of days after we have gone from the base of the Pyrenees?' I saw his expression, and quickly carried on talking before he could stop me. 'At least you could tell them to make their own way back to Poitiers. We do not have to explain why.' His eyes did not flicker a response.

'Sire?' I insisted.

'Very well!'

Sometime after that, I could hear no more singing among the surrounding hills, but occasionally I caught a swell of noise, until the army and their women had been gone for an hour or more. Much later, I heard the stories of their journey southwards from the other soldiers. Most of the first part of their journey was spent within Aquitaine, the area of southwest France under the rule of the Black Prince. The road they took was the alternative pilgrim route, due southwards from Poitiers.

This path was slightly longer than the traditional Via Turonensis. It ran between Poitiers and Belin, some 15 miles inland from the other route. After Belin the roads converged. By then they would be three quarters of the way towards their intended base at the foot of the Pyrenees.

The army's second river-stop, that first day, was on the banks of the Charante, at Charroux. Long ago, King Edward had decreed that his garrison would pray here at the abbey whenever they were marching southwards to battle.[4]

As they travelled on, the long column followed the winding Charante valley. It took them first westwards past Civray; and then south again past the Benedictine Abbey of St Amant-de-Boixe, and onto the town of Angouleme, where they spent their first night. They had marched for the best part of sixty miles, the last hour of it in growing darkness. Uniquely, the town gates were kept open for them, for they were always closed strictly at nightfall. This was the first sizeable town that could accommodate them. It had done so many times before.

That evening, most of the men were fed and watered in the various ale houses. One or two, including the tireless Calveley, visited St Peter's Cathedral. They took the opportunity to see the famous Frieze of Roland, depicting him mortally wounding Marsile, the treacherous Moorish King. King Pedro never bothered. It certainly was not his favourite pastime to go poking about in dark old churches.

The next day they pressed on southwest, past the old Templar Commandery in Cressac. There was no stopping this time, even though there were legendary frescoes all over the walls showing scenes of Jerusalem and the Crusades. They were on the long march towards the Dordogne River. They passed the 300 Benedictine monks at Sauve-Majeure, who also owned other abbeys in England and Spain. In all it took them four days to reach Belin, where the parallel routes converged. They were twenty miles south-west of Bordeaux. They were on schedule. Their destination was at the base of the Pyrenees, St Jean Pied de Port.

Chapter 17 - Pilgrim Princes

In the meantime, the Black Prince and his brother left the garrison at Poitiers later the same morning, with myself and another bodyguard in attendance. We all travelled incognito, under no flag, without fine clothing, and no black armour. The two Princes journeyed as pilgrims, simple squires, and we bodyguards as their servants. I, of course, carried the Pilgrim Guide Book in a sling on my back. But in truth, they had mighty fine horses for country squires. Two prancing chargers were not exactly normal pilgrim carriers. Perhaps four mules would have been more fitting, but there were limits to their self-denial.

As the brothers rode the long pilgrim route, they would have to think of ways in which to pass the time. The younger brother had it well planned. Conversation would be the best method of diverting the Black Prince's mind away from his aching limbs. But he did not mean the usual brotherly banter; he planned an altogether stronger medicine than that.

'I want to talk to you about your wife,' said John of Gaunt. He had worked it out before they left. He had always wanted the truth. There were family scandals from their childhood. No one talked of them. Now was his chance to hear the real story, and to keep his ailing brother mentally occupied to complete the ride towards the battle ahead. Now, deliberately, he set out to stir up a hornet's nest of trouble. It was time for answers.

But there came no reply. Instead, the Black Prince leaned over the other side from his brother, and quietly asked me to open the pilgrim book I carried for him on my back.

'I want to talk to you about your wife,' his brother repeated.

'I hear you. I thought you might, one day,' the Black Prince said, his mind elsewhere. He had just started looking into the pages of Aimery Picard's pilgrim guide. 'Oh God!' he exclaimed, 'It says here: *1 million and one steps to Santiago.*' He was reading as they rode towards the next town.

'Do you mean from Poitiers, from here? It can't be; it must be from Paris?' asked John of Gaunt, for he had read it too. It would be hard enough for his brother to get as far as the rendezvous point at the base of the Pyrenees. But how on earth would he have the strength and the stamina to lead his army through the deep snows as was expected of him? He already knew that the worst 15 mile stretch would have to be completed in ONE day, or the entire army garrison would freeze to death as they toiled through the blizzards in the high mountain passes. As if that was not enough, if they still had the men and horses left after that ordeal, the final day and a half of their journey would be in enemy territory. The pace would have to be fast and unforgiving.

As pilgrims, the Princes' first duty was to join the daily service at St Hilaire's Basilica, their favourite church. The sepulchre of St Hilaire, who died in 367, was visited by most of the pilgrims passing through Poitiers. The church around it had been rebuilt twice, after first being burnt by the Moors in 732, and then being badly damaged by a Norse attack in 833. Miraculously, the sepulchre of the first Bishop of Poitiers, St Hilaire, had remained intact. The saint's tomb struck a particular chord with the pilgrims because of his rejection and exile by the Church. He suffered for the rest of his life for his belief that Christ the Son was just as important as God the Father in the Trinity. He became a writer, and eventually was influential in helping to turn the Church back to the earlier Nicaean Code, acknowledging the Father, the Son, and the Holy Ghost. A strict adherence to the pilgrim's code of humility and charity epitomised the message passed down by St Hilaire.

A local story was told of two passing pilgrims in Poitiers. They asked for hospitality in Rue St Porchaire, but only a poor man living at the end of the street near the church offered it to them. During the night, through divine vengeance, a violent fire destroyed all the houses in the neighbourhood,

186

sparing only the one where the pilgrims had been taken in.

St Hilaire's Church, which we now approached, had finally been rebuilt in the 11th century, and re-consecrated as a Basilica under the special protection of the Pope. A hundred years later it was vaulted, as befitted a jewel of the Holy See. To the side of the great church, sparks flew from a busy forge, which was no more than a lean-to against the Basilica. But there were no horseshoes being made. We saw a prisoner was being fitted with three heavy rings forged around his neck and arms, all linked with a chain. This was a common punishment for a murderer, sentenced to carry his chains for a thousand miles to obtain his certificate of Confession and Communion at the tomb of St James, if he ever got there. This certificate was called a 'Compostela,' hence the name 'Santiago de Compostela'. At their destination, beside the shrine of St James, they were released from their chains. Daily, there was a new pile of shackles displayed beside the holy site.

The Black Prince and his brother ordered me to join them as they dismounted in the square in front of the Basilica for the service of blessing. We handed the reins to my fellow guard, and bade him stay outside. Sweeping off our wide-brimmed hats, and tucking them under our arms, we passed under familiar noble carvings around the main entrance. Here we joined seventeen fellow travellers, each setting out that day on their own individual pilgrimage. These men were of all types, and all ages. They were leaving behind their social conditions, and the comfort and warmth of home. To them a pilgrimage meant renouncing worldly goods to follow the evangelical ideal of humility and poverty. They nakedly followed the naked Christ. In the physical difficulties imposed by walking up to twenty miles a day, in the heat or the cold, in hunger and thirst, and the many uncertainties and dangers of finding lodgings, the pilgrims re-enacted some of the sacrifices of the Cross.[5]

Any woman who set out on a pilgrimage, however, was made fun of, and presumed to be on the way to an assignation with a lover. One female did arrive at the church that cold March morning. She rode pillion behind her husband, upon the horse's rump, her face fully hidden behind a black veil. She would have a bumpy journey ahead. Her man dismounted, and appeared to ignore her. She was left alone, to slip to the ground by herself. All the other travellers guessed why she was there: she had been unfaithful, and her husband was making sure she repented. In fact, they were far from the truth. She was going for 'the cure'. The left side of her face, already raw to her cheekbone, was being eaten away by a disease.

The new pilgrims setting out from Poitiers that day were joined in the chancel of St Hilaire's by the two Princes and myself. Instead of our usual long pointed pikes, we deliberately carried less visible short swords. On their arrival, each pilgrim was required to deposit some clothing and chattels for collection upon their return; if they survived the journey there and back.

All we pilgrims knelt around the sepulchre of St Hilaire for the Rites of Pilgrimage service, which started with Mass, and was followed by Confession.[6] We each placed our two indispensable companions of travel upon his tomb: the pouch, or scrip (called 'escharpe' in Old French), and our sturdy staffs. Then the priest evoked the solemn witness of St Hilaire, and blessed the two objects, which took on a sacred and symbolic meaning.

We all wore scallop shells sewn into our hats, as tradition demanded.[7] There were legends to support this custom. **One** related how they saved a Prince from the stormy waves into which his runaway horse had thrown him. About to drown, the knight called on St James to save him. Immediately he found himself miraculously on shore, and covered with scallop shells. **Another**, in the 'Liber Sancti Jacobi' said that a scallop shell was brought back from Compostela by an Italian pilgrim, which had made an enormous goitre disappear from the neck of a knight from Apulia, simply by being rubbed
on it.[8]

The Rites of Pilgrimage service came to an end with the blessing of St Hilaire, and the benediction. From that moment, all we travellers found ourselves officially placed within the safekeeping of the Church; in a state of Grace, with the peace of God.

Lining up after the service, the clergy and the rest of the congregation led us as far as the beginning of the pilgrim route, singing litanies as they went. Their chants were punctuated by the clanking of the prisoner's chains as he walked. At last they bade farewell to our assorted crowd of travellers, and left us to our individual destinies. Thus we became officially 'Les Peregrinorum' - members of a lawful company, which protected us from certain taxes and tolls, from arbitrary arrest, attacks and economic exploitation; and the safekeeping of our belongings left behind

As we started out, the royal brothers talked of the ceremony, and of their fellow travellers. They had never attended a pilgrim service before. Though their main purpose was not at all peaceful, for indeed we faced a bloody battle ahead, in truth the service in the Basilica had been most impressive. But it was the variety among the other pilgrims that caused them much merriment, and a lot of speculation for the first few miles.

Of the nineteen pilgrims and two escorts that day, there were seven riders: the two Princes, we two bodyguards, the husband and wife, and an armoured knight. The rest were walkers. This was indeed five or six mounted pilgrims more than was usual leaving the town of Poitiers each day.

The supposed tale of the cuckolded husband with his wife exercised their merry imaginations. This was not surprising. Women on pilgrimage were treated with such suspicion that the general word used for an adulterous woman was 'coquillarde' (or 'coquette'), after the scallop shell emblem of the pilgrim. But we learned later that the Princes had guessed it wrong. Then they turned their attention to the knight. Was he one of the 'Fighting Knights' of old? These were usually crusty old jousters, willing their limbs to relive their fighting days. Wanting one last tilt at their past glory years perhaps, they indeed posted a challenge with blunt lances to all-comers within a ten mile radius of their proposed pilgrim route. Perhaps they secretly prayed to St James for a glorious death from a sharper lance? This fighting knight looked ridiculous in full armour, with his visor down. They doubted he could even see the road, let alone guide his horse around the scattered boulders.[9]

We new pilgrims from Poitiers stepped onto the Via Turonensis. This was the legends-old route that ran from Paris, over the Pyrenees, to north-east Spain. There we would join the famous Camino Frances route, 'El Camino', which followed an earth-energy line under the Milky Way to Finistere ('Fin-terre' - the end of the earth). Though few of us knew it, we Catholics were using an ancient Shamanistac pilgrimage road, dating back to the days of the Druids.[10]

The walking group set off rather hesitantly behind the riders. One small wiry traveller, with good boots, turned around and doffed his pilgrim's wide-brimmed hat to the farewell committee. He flashed his bald head at them, and revealed he was in his middle years. He turned back to his purpose, and started up a tune on his merry pipe. His tune would help the walkers step along with a fuller heart. He was well known to the congregation of the Basilica at Poitiers, for he was a Professional Pilgrim, paid by local nobility to intercede with St James on their behalf. His father had been in the same profession as a young man, walking the same route for the Countess Mahaut of Artois and others, in the 1320's. His old military marching flute was used to cheer up his walking group, for he looked upon them as HIS. He knew the ropes, he was the professional. He would set the pace. He would teach them the songs. He would bolster their spirits. As he started to play the notes of the ancient pilgrim song: *Ultreia, ultreia, e su seya, Deus, adjuva nos!* He was delighted to be joined by a gangly, long-nosed youth, blowing his own tin whistle.

'Onward, onward and forward.' One by one the other pilgrims began to sing, as they joined in the marching chorus: 'Onward, onward and forward, O God, help us!'

Up the first steep hill and out of sight we walked. The pipes went quiet for a while, the minstrels too out of breath to play as they crested the mountain. The tall thin young man, who played the chirpy tin whistle, was in love. He was out to impress the object of his desire. She wished him to come back more of a man, she said, though she was careful to tie an amulet of senna, mint and rue, plaited around his wrist. It was to prevent evil and temptation, she said.

From the outset, it was clear that the pace set by the professional pilgrim, intending to cover 20 miles a day, would suit neither the prisoner in chains, nor a very elderly pilgrim at the back. He carried one staff in each hand, to help him painfully along. Together they hobbled at much the same speed. They were not much company for one another, for both muttered loudly in complaint as they went. The scratchy old man was infuriated by the clanking noise of the other's chains, and the murderer was tossing oaths into the air and catching them with his mouth. He hopped and sprang first forwards, then sideways, picking up his chains, then drooping them about his arms or his neck, or on his back. He distorted himself at odd angles and at all paces, to try to find the most comfortable method of supporting his terrible metal burden. They made an odd couple, but they did make some progress. So, after much suffering, and much swearing, they were destined to show the best of their temper to each other, eventually. The old man even ended up helping the prisoner with his load, and in doing so, in helping another human being, he found a reason to live a little longer. For in truth, he had only come on this pilgrimage to die en-route, in God's grace. It was the only place he could find it. Indeed he had led a selfish and mean existence, and had always taken much delight in making a misery of both his and anyone else's life.

One young monk, in his early twenties, showed an eager and sprightly spring to his step. He was ready for adventures outside the cloister. The portly sombre friar who accompanied him was under instruction to lessen his own belt-size, and to see his younger companion did not become over-adventurous. The elder monk thought it most appropriate that they should travel beside two middle-aged devouts. These good people spent the day muttering the longer litanies, and read from a pocket bible as they walked.

They soon stopped that after the first day; for they were forever tripping over boulders, and hurting themselves. They were a menace on the road. The monks tried to offer advice about the impending hazards coming up, but the mutterings were ceaseless, and made the Devouts somewhat deaf to any warnings. Eventually, this group settled down to tell each other stories from the bible, and managed to keep their limbs generally free from the awful gashes and bumps of the first few hours. Delayed concussion was among their injuries that day.

It turned out that the young monk should have been wearing the amulet of senna, mint and rue, like the young lover. For, indeed, he was the one who was most tempted. He found his God worked in strange metaphors. While his elder companion was telling him about the evils of women, all he found out for himself was the lightness it brought to his life if he chanced to see any female of the species. Just to get a look at one; especially a young one, filled him with irreligious longing.

Walking at the same pace, keeping themselves separated from the rest, was a white-faced group of three. There was purpose in their steps, but no anticipation of adventure, no lightness in their souls. They were a delegation from the village of Dissay, 10 miles north of Poitiers, which had been touched by the Plague. They were on a mission to ask St James to intercede to stop the dreaded deaths. Before their departure, uniquely, they were attested as not having been in contact with the Plague, and thus safe to travel. But they did not look healthy. They had been garlanded with mustard and garlic around their necks, to ward off the disease. The strings of garlic made a swishing noise as they rubbed together, and gave off a satisfying reek of protection. Their travelling companions kept their distance.

But it was the last three pilgrims, all young men, who gave us the most merriment. They said they were heirs to a great fortune; dark-haired, tousled, and as alike as pins. If they added up their brains between them, they would not make one. Apparently, their dying father had bequeathed his vow of pilgrimage to his heirs, and provided in his will for sending them to Santiago to secure the salvation of his soul.

These three had argued since they were first able to hit each other, for they had never learned to share. Their father had been driven wild with their arguing, and thought to teach them a lesson. The one who would inherit his wealth, would be the young man who was the most helpful to his brothers en-route, he said. Who would judge them? Why, St James of course. It was stipulated they should share and wear but one hat, and one mule between them. Of course, they never could agree who should mount the beast.

'You get on!'

'No, you get on!'

So, nobody rode the mule. They carried a lot of luggage, spare shoes, their favourite hop pillows, a change of clothes, and medicines for every occasion (provided by their mother). There was willow bark for fevers, opium for pain, and a deal of wine to cleanse wounds, and to drink. They all wore the hat at some time each day, but none wanted to be accused of having it upon his head for a longer period than his brothers. One problem was being able to tell the time when it was raining, or if they were in a forest. They could not find the position of the sun. So they spent every day wearing the hat for only three minutes or so each, and passing it on. One hundred paces became the exchange time. Each young man was kept busy concentrating on being ready to take and wear the famous hat. Over the course of a full day's walking, between them they wore the hat five hundred times.

All the time they dragged the stubborn mule along. It did not even carry their gourds of wine, lest one was favoured above another. In truth, the mule was King of the bunch, for they dare not even lean on him, lest they accused each other of not being worthy. Much later, they got stuck in the mountains when good weather and common sense entirely deserted them. They decided to eat their poor mule to stay alive; but they argued for so long over who was to kill it, that a passing troop did the job for them and saved themselves instead.

Deciding to start off slowly for a few minutes, in order to observe their fellow travellers, the Black Prince and John of Gaunt were particularly tickled by the antics of the tousled-headed brothers. They could only guess at the story of the hat.

Chapter 18 - The Princess of Wales

Whereas the English cavalry and longbow-men from the garrison had earlier headed due south, on the alternate inland route; the Black Prince, John of Gaunt, myself and one other guard were heading south-west from Poitiers, on the official pilgrim route, the Via Turonensis. This ran nearer to the coast.

Exhausting their conjecture about their fellow travellers, the two Princes spurred their horses and talked as they went. You must understand that as a personal bodyguard to my Prince, I was well trained to be invisible and deaf when it came to overhearing personal conversations. But this exchange between the two brothers, made me wish God had forgotten to provide me with ears.

'Your wife!' the younger Prince insisted once more.

'Yes, yes. What about her?' came the mumbled reply.

'I want you to tell me her story, about when she was young.'

There was a pause. The Black Prince's accusing voice was icy clear: 'You're raking up something that happened a very long time ago.' He turned on his brother in anger. 'Give me ONE good reason why I should discuss my wife with YOU?'

Prince John shot back his reply without thinking: 'I caught her alone with King Pedro the other day!' He clapped his mouth shut. He had not meant to tell his brother that.

'She told me about it,' the Black Prince responded calmly. 'She'd just slapped his face. I assure you, she hates the man.'

'It didn't LOOK like that.'

The elder brother shrugged. 'She's a flirt. It's harmless.'

'What are you going to do about it?'

'Nothing.' He laughed, defusing the situation. 'I just have to keep her pregnant.'

'No wonder you're bandy-legged!' laughed his brother. 'Well, you watch out!' he continued, only half joking. 'You know what they say about children of over-sexed parents?'

'What do they say?'

'They prefer their own sex!'

The brothers had to concentrate on helping their horses down a steep bank and through a rough fast-running stream. Once we were all up on the far side, Prince John found his brother, still willing to answer his questions:

'Why is she such a flirt? And why don't you mind?'

'So, you really want to hear the whole story, from the beginning?' offered his brother cautiously. He was not at all sure this was wise.

Eagerly, Prince John urged him to start. He wanted the truth. There had always been rumours about Joan, *The Fair Maid of Kent*. There had been scandals about her when she was a child.

'Tell me about that fellow, Thomas Holland.'

'Yes, well, our Mister Thomas Holland comes a little later on,' the elder Prince took a deep breath and launched into his wife's story. 'It all really started before you or I were born.'

'Don't forget, you're ten years older than I am,' said the younger brother.

The other nodded and began the long saga that would last until they got past the worst of their journey ahead. Which was exactly what John of Gaunt had intended, but good intentions often go awry. At least it diverted the Black Prince's mind away from his failing body, at critically difficult times.

His voice sounded far away, in the land of his thoughts: 'Do you know her very first memory as a child? She must have been only 2 years old at the time. She was being sprayed with fountains of blood, as she watched the executioner cut her father's head off.'

'Oh God! No!'

'Her mother had her baby brother John in her arms at the time. Joan remembers holding onto her mother's skirt, with a red river running down the material towards her fingers. It engulfed them in a torrent of blood.' He hesitated with the words, 'Her father's severed head had landed on its ear beside her, looking as though it wanted her to put it back on. She tried to, but...' his voice trailed away.

'Were they standing underneath the scaffold?'

'On it, I think.'

'That's barbaric!'

'Apparently she dreamt of it every night, until she was older. She still does sometimes. She grew up too quickly, that was the problem.'

The story was hard to tell. John of Gaunt, at times, wished he had not requested it. It was important for the Black Prince to be able to recount it in his own way. The beginning was about Joan's background, for she was their cousin. It was their family history as well.

The story of the downfall, abdication and murder of their grandfather, King Edward II, *The Weak*, had been taught to them early on, as a lesson in the destruction caused by civil war and the deceit of his family. His eldest son, young Edward III, the Princes' father, was caught in the middle, manipulated by his mother and her lover Roger Mortimer.

After the overwhelming defeat by Robert the Bruce at the battle of Bannockburn, in 1314, fought around Stirling Castle in central Scotland; the barons of England started withdrawing support for Edward II. It had happened as a direct result of his own father's policies. Edward I had been successful as the *Hammer of the Scots,* fighting constant military campaigns to subdue the Welsh as well. However, he had died, leaving Wales in a determined separatist mood and the Scots in an uproar. They were far from being defeated, having been led by William Wallace and then by Robert the Bruce.

The King's son, Edward II, the Black Prince's grandfather, was left with the problems of defeating the rebellious Scots and paying for his father's wars. He managed neither. At home, his barons and nobles refused to pay the taxes he imposed, which eventually led to intrigues, plots and civil war. His wife left him, taking their teenage son, the Princes' father, back to her homeland in France and started plotting with her lover, Mortimer, for her husband's downfall.

'The entire family deserted him,' said the Black Prince bitterly. 'With one sole exception. The only relation to stay loyal to his King was his half-brother, Prince Edmund of Kent, who was Joan of Kent's father.'

'That is why he was beheaded?'

'Yes. The King was forced to abdicate and was murdered, very horribly, in prison in Berkeley Castle. Any supporters who were left were publicly beheaded. The Queen returned from France with her lover Mortimer and put her son, our father Edward III, on the throne, along with his new French wife, our mother. They were so appalled at the beheadings and confiscation of land, that they defied the Queen Mother. They took the executed Prince Edmund of Kent's destitute wife and four young children, all under five, into their own nursery. Nobody else dared give them a home, in case they were punished for it. Eventually, of course, the young King, our father, took power himself, exiled his mother and executed her lover, Roger Mortimer.

We all grew-up together. I remember it all so well. As a very young child in the nursery, Joan's natural protectors were her elder brother Edmund and her sister Anne. I can remember them, often running into her room and holding on to her tightly, to calm her in the middle of her nightmares. I believe she would not have developed such an obsession with physical contact, if her sister had not died during the following year and her big brother two years after. It was a disaster for her.

We consoled her, but she was so vulnerable. She was now the eldest in the nursery, but somehow we felt she was in need of our care. Gradually, as awareness crept-up on us, our childish cuddles turned into secrets that, at some stage, all children desire to know. She showed us her body. I used to think it was a *thank you* for the cuddles. It was an innocent thing, no more than a game. Yet we knew not to tell the adults. It grew into probings. She liked that. It also grew into feeling games among the boys and with her.

About this time, another boy joined our nursery occasionally. He was

William Montague, the heir to the first Earl of Salisbury. His parents were friends and they stayed quite frequently. They brought their son, because there was talk of a future marriage between Joan and William Montague. They were much the same age. He also joined in our games and helped to console Joan. When they were aged ten, the *Marriage Treaty* was signed. It was agreed they were to be married when they reached the age of 17. She was to go and live with the Salisburys immediately, until the marriage.

I was only eight, but I remember such sadness in our nursery. I remember I would do anything for her. I knew then that I loved her. I was the eldest in our family and I told her I would always be her Knight on a black charger. I promised that I would always come to her aid.

So, she went to live with the Salisburys. She had always liked the son, William Montague, but they were no longer sharing a nursery together. Now they only met when well chaperoned.

The Earl of Salisbury, like his father before him, had been keen on jousting. He regarded it as high art, equal only to hunting in its suitability as a sport for the sons of noblemen. He employed a Jousting Master to teach his son to keep himself safe.'

The Black Prince interrupted his own story and nodded at his brother. 'You remember, our Mister Thomas Holland was the arms master. He taught us fencing and jousting as well'

'Ah! So that's where Holland comes in. He was a tutor.'

'He had come recommended as a champion jouster. Holland was the son of Robert, 1st Lord Holland, who was born a poor Knight who owed his advancement to his position as secretary to Thomas, the great Earl of Lancaster.'

'MY wife's grandfather?' exclaimed his brother in surprise.

'Indeed. He joined with his own retinue in the Scottish wars for King Edward II and was granted land and a title. Eventually serving as a loyal King's man in Parliament. Eventually he went the way of all loyal King's men. He was beheaded soon after Edward II was deposed. His son, Thomas Holland, was sixteen when his father was executed.'

He continued after a pause, 'Jousting was skilfully taught. It was common practice for the sons of many minor noblemen to get noticed in the lists of the jousting tournaments. They wished to better themselves. Young Thomas Holland soon became a champion and landed the job as arms master, with the Earl of Salisbury. His role was to teach young William Montague the high arts of fencing and jousting. When Joan of Kent joined the household as prospective bride, she asked to be taught fencing. This was most irregular, but the Salisburys were kindly and I can imagine her foot stamping must have been terrible, for they agreed in the end.

At first, the two youngsters took fencing practice together, supervised by Holland. But Joan so far outstripped her future husband in agility and co-ordination, that they were no longer a match for each other. Disastrously, she was allotted separate lessons, alone with Holland.'

After 45 minutes of talking and riding, the brothers ordered us to push our horses on faster. Our first night's stop was still a long way on. Joan of Kent's story would have to wait for another day. The interesting part was yet to come. Besides, they wanted to be able to follow the history and stories of places they saw along the route. Was this not one of the main reasons they came this way?

We arrived quite quickly at the banks of the River Feuillarte. There was no bridge. There would not be many along the whole of the journey, but the crossing place was simple. The river was small when it was not in flood. Many rivers would be more difficult. On its banks we passed Pontaine-le-Comte Abbey, built a hundred years before by Guillaume VIII, the Count of Poitiers. It was the home for a community of canons, who helped serve St Hilaire's Basilica.

We continued at a good pace along level terrain and passed through the sleepy village of Coulombiers. There our horses made heavy work of fording the busier and stonier river, where we found a way marker with a scallop shell, showing the tricky exit out of the water. *2 hours to Lusignan,* was carved upon it. This was meant for pilgrims on foot. It would be the walkers first night's stop. But horsemen would take less than an hour to cover the eight miles and would be anxious to push on.

It was at that point we all noticed the Black Prince had kicked his feet out of his stirrups, before we reached the town. This was a sure sign of tiredness. But we knew better than to say anything about it.

Two miles further on we came to the wide, gently flowing River Vonne, on the outskirts of the town, we stopped to water the horses. Prince John started to read from the book that I carried, of the Legend of Lusignan: *'A powerful enchantress called Melusine brought down fear and destruction on any man who mistreated the animals which served him. The beasts would be given powers to take their most frightful revenge: the man would change places with his beast.'*

John of Gaunt read more of the history*: 'Melusine founded the town of Lusignan, they say by magic, and lived there in the castle named after herself. It was believed that her descendants now lived in that castle across the river. Certainly, the Lusignan family had fought with such renown in the early Crusades that they had become Kings of Jerusalem, and of Cyprus. They had fortified and defended the town successfully against all Moorish attacks, and had founded a Benedictine priory within its walls.'*

Soon we were up and away again on what would turn out to be the longest stretch of the first day's ride, through Chenay and Chey, for we met a detour. We started-off at a trot, which was more tiring for the riders than a canter, but less exhausting for the horses. We needed to average ten miles an hour, which allowed for some walking later.

The Black Prince's health was obviously far worse than on their previous trip, only two weeks previously, when he had led the troops for the parley with King Pedro's enemies. All Prince John could do was to watch as his brother tried sitting crookedly in his saddle, first leaning to one side, and then the other. He must have been in agony. We had only covered 40 miles and had another 360 to the Pyrenees, a further 100 to Najera, a battle to fight and another 400 miles on to St James at Santiago de Compostela. Would he still be alive?

We were heading for our first overnight stop, at the *money* town of

Melle, straight ahead. The Black Prince groaned when it became clear that the pilgrim route was taking us in an extra 20-mile loop, around a vast inaccessible forest full of wolves. The locals called it *Forestaire des Enfants*, for it was quite impassable with brambles and fables were told of a witch who stole the babies of the unwed.

On the far side of the forest the abbey at Celles-sur-Belle loomed grey and forbidding on high ground above the pathway. Founded, like many abbeys, a hundred years before, its religion centred particularly on the Virgin, in an era when it was more usual to worship Christ and the Trinity. They were not accustomed to welcoming travellers, for the pilgrims were always pushing on to Melle for their overnight stop. The brothers were too.

They had good reason. Melle had been heavily fortified for over 500 years, because it produced huge quantities of coins from its silver-bearing lead mines. These were in the valley of the Beronne River, which was enclosed within its mighty walls. The mines were well guarded and not accessible to the pilgrims. But there was a Benedictine priory, another St Hilaire, which was set into the walls of the town. The priory had also constructed a hostel on the outside of the walls especially for pilgrims arriving after sunset, when the town gates were closed.

One of the monks' tasks was the traditional washing of the pilgrim's feet each night. This was a purifying ceremony to mark Christ's action with his disciples before the *Last Supper*. It also signified charity, humility and the pardoning of sins. The monks provided beds and hospital services within the walls. The hostel outside was lined with benches and two water holes for drinking. There was a small chapel at the side. The monks brought hot water as well as gruel, which was a mixture between porridge and soup. They also provided bread and wine in great flagons, for they picked their own grapes from their own vineyards upon the southerly slope. The help and aid offered followed the *Seven Works of Mercy*, recommended by the Church: '*I feed, I visit, I water, I soothe, I clothe, I ransom, I bury.*'

These larger hospitals were founded upon charity, and designed also for the many misfits in our society: the poor, the lame, the ill, and the orphans. The city of Burgos, which was much nearer to Santiago, had need of thirty such hospitals within its walls. The nearer the pilgrims got to the Shrine of St James, the more they were in need of these services. They were founded by mixed religious orders, of both monks and nuns.[11] The hospital at Melle, within the town walls, had a chapel on the ground floor. There was also a wash room, kitchen, and a large room for the monks. While upstairs were cells for the ill and infirm, along with a dormitory for the nuns.

Melle was on every pilgrim's itinerary because the monks gave out one newly stamped coin to every traveller. Most did not spend it. It became a tradition to show the coin, still new and sparkling, as part of the proof of their momentous journey to Santiago. Some of the pilgrims had never handled a coin before, let alone a brand new one. It was a shiny omen of hope amid a sea of suffering legs.

All of the 6,000 miles of official pilgrim routes to Compostela, threading through neighbouring countries, were declared Christian territory, and that included the soil at the side of the paths where some were buried. 'Whoever receives the one sent by me, receives me' were the words of Jesus Christ. They were inscribed over the doorway to many hospitals. Besides, how could you tell who was hidden under a pilgrim's cloak? It could be Jesus himself, an angel, or St James.

'I want to show you something,' said the Black Prince. Despite his tiredness, he had been reading his Pilgrim's Guide again. The priory of St Hilaire at Melle was a considered a wonder of the route for its sculpted columns. But what took his eye here was recessed into the outside wall. It nestled above the north entrance. There was a famous statue of Christ on horseback; not on a donkey, as usually depicted. It was arched overhead with more than thirty scallop shells, to signify pilgrimage.

This was a sight not to be missed. It had been created to the glory of the Roman Emperor Constantine, who had first granted freedom of worship to Christians, via the Edict of Milan in 313. The statue symbolised the triumph of Christ and Christianity over Paganism, which was represented by a small figure sitting at the feet of the horse, looking up in awe.

The author of the Pilgrim's Guide certainly knew his history. No wonder he wrote about this equestrian statue, for he had come from that region. He was a monk from the small town of Parthenay-le-Vieux, only a few miles east of Poitiers. He obviously liked the Poitou area and its people, because he constantly praised them as: *'...fertile, excellent and full of all bliss. Its inhabitants are vigorous people, good warriors, clever at using bows, arrows and lances in war, brave on the battlefront, very fast in running, elegant in their way of dressing, handsome faces, witty, very generous, generous in hospitality.'*

Then it happened quite suddenly, just as he stopped reading from the book. Exhaustion overcame the Black Prince. He slumped against the church wall and for once, asked for his brother's assistance. There was now an acute urgency for proper rest, a soft bed, linen and a soak in salted water for his swollen limbs. Luckily it was available close by.

Chapter 19 - John the Baptist

O ur small royal party left at dawn the next day. We needed the extra hours in order to complete the demanding 80 mile journey ahead. We were heading for the therapeutic thermal baths of the town of Saintes. The plan was to stay there for two nights, so that the Prince could take the cure. But first we had to get him there. Was that going to be possible?

Leaving Melle with the new coins in their pockets, the royal Princes rode along the banks of the Boutonne River. We would cross and re-cross this major river for the next six hours. Two hours into our journey, we could see the landmark of the distinctive square steeple of St Peter's Church in Aulney, looming over the next hill. We passed the gnarled arms of five yew trees, reputed to be older than Christendom, at the entrance to the cemetery. You could see very old tombstones and sarcophagi on stilts, scattered around, some in a bad state of repair.

St Peter's may have been an elegant church, well known for its Romanesque sculptures depicting bible scenes, fantastic animals, and the signs of the zodiac, but our party had no time to look. The target was to reach St Jean-d'-Angeley as quickly as possible. It turned out, however, that we had a shocking reason for stopping in Angeley, and it had nothing at all to do with the Black Prince's health.

'Here it is, in chapter eight,' said the Prince excitedly, delving once more into his Pilgrim's Guide:

'One must go and see the venerable head of St John the Baptist which was brought by monks from Jerusalem to a place named Angeley in Poitou. The very

sacred head is worshipped there night and day by a choir of a hundred monks, and is famed for numerous miracles. While it was being transported by land and by sea, this head distinguished itself by its many marvels. At sea, it chased away many storms, and on land, if one believes the book of its translation, it gave back life to several dead. Thus it is believed that it is indeed the head of the venerated Precursor.'

The story was that in 817, an Angeley monk, Felix, returned from a pilgrimage to the Holy Land, carrying the head of John the Baptist. It was an official gift from Alexandria to the King of Aquitaine, Pepin 1st. A monastery was built for it. Then, during Viking raids, the monastery was damaged, and the head disappeared.

In 1010 it was rediscovered hidden within a silver reliquary box, when the Duke of Aquitaine started the construction of a new abbey on the site. The Holy Relic attracted many pilgrims, and brought fame and prosperity to the town built to house them.

Entering the Abbey, the sound of singing monks surrounded the royal brothers, as we prepared ourselves to pray at one of the holiest sites in Christendom. One could not help being stirred by the sweet voices that filled the air; and then shocked to the core by the proximity of the real head of John the Baptist.

Nothing could have prepared us for the sight; because the head was uncorrupted, unlined, and real. What was not covered in a black beard, was flesh. The EYES were open. They were clear and brown, and looked as if they were seeing everything.

The only parts that looked dead, were the flaps of skin surrounding the base of the head, where the top of the neck had obviously been roughly struck several times, and the SKIN torn away. The end of the skin was dark purple. Part of the top vertebrae stuck out at an angle behind the ears. This provided a prop at the back, so the head did not have to rest on its chin. It was exhibited at head height, and at exactly the correct angle to look eyeball to eyeball with any tall man.

The Black Prince started fiddling inside his tunic. Suddenly, with a flourish, he extracted something completely unexpected, the Blood of

Christ stone! He had brought it with him. His younger brother's immediate reaction was one of disbelief that he should have brought it on such a dangerous mission. It was worth a fortune. If things went badly, it could be lost forever.

Instinctively, I moved closer to my Prince and his precious Ruby. All my training warned me to protect him in unexpected situations. But he waved me back urgently, out of his way. I hoped he knew what he was doing.

Back in the garrison at Poitiers, during the talks attended by the old bishop and King Pedro, the brothers had learnt for the first time that many early Christians, Templars, Cathars, and many other sects, believed that John the Baptist was the Messiah, and not Christ.

'I want to find out the truth,' the Black Prince declared, placing the Blood of Christ stone upon the edge of a high pillar, right beside the head. 'Give me a sign!' he ordered, and turned to his brother. 'You watch the head, and I'll watch the stone for an answer.'

'Is this the head of the Son of God?' he asked.

It was only a millisecond......It blinked! ...the Prince blinked too. Had that been his imagination, or had he really seen the dead eyes blink?

'I'm not sure,' he whispered. 'But something happened.'

He looked at me, and I nodded, feeling numb.

'Is this ruby-stone the blood of the Son of God?'

A stab of intense white light shot through a tiny far window and lit up our corner, pin-pointing the ruby on its pillar.

'Is it your blood?'

'WHAT ARE YOU DOING, my sons?' an urgent voice came from behind them. A senior monk was pushing his way in between the brothers.

The Black Prince did not have time to grab the Blood of Christ stone from its pillar, before the monk's eyes rested upon it. He became motionless, staring at it for a full ten seconds. The princes looked at him; the colour was visibly draining out of the monk's face. He looked ashen.

'Where is the BOX?' he whispered in awe.

'You know this stone?' The Black Prince was aghast, not only because he had absolutely no doubt that his questions had just been answered, but because this monk obviously recognised the Ruby.

'This is too public. You had better come with me.' The monk looked furtively around. The Prince grabbed the Ruby from the pillar, trying not to touch the head, and we followed the monk to his private office. He was the monastery librarian. The Princes introduced themselves, and he reached down a heavily bound volume, which was labelled 'Items Received'.

'This is our charitable donations book,' he said. He placed it before them, and gently turned the sewn pages until he reached entries for the year 1241. 'Here it is!

'Mary Magdalene's box with Ruby. 170 carats. Not to be separated. Donated on the 13th March by a Cathar Pilgrim, unnamed.'

'It was OUR Holy Relic!' said the monk decisively, snapping the book shut. 'Now, WHERE is the box?" He looked them straight in the eye.

Always the mediator, John of Gaunt played for time. 'How do you know it is the SAME stone?'

'It was here until five years ago.'

'You are saying this is your stolen relic?'

'No! Not at all' The monk sounded confused.

'Explain!' demanded the elder Prince.

The monk was silent for a while, before he began his story. 'My predecessors discovered that the Cathars and the Templars were constantly attempting to steal it from here. It was always kept in its box. Eventually we had to arrange for it to be taken to Santiago for safekeeping, it was just too valuable for our church. Several times they ransacked the church looking for the box. It just was not safe here.'

'Who took it to Santiago?'

'The Knights of the Order of Santiago. A senior knight signed for it here in our Relic Book, five years ago.' He wheeled a large flat table towards them. It was covered in a floppy yellowing binding, holding such large parchment pages that he had to ask their help to hold half of it, as he tenderly turned the pages. He looked this way and that to reach the date he wanted:

'Here it is: 15th September 1362.'

There, unmistakably, was the Grand Master's seal of the Holy Order of the Knights of Santiago.

The Black Prince let out a cry, 'De Padilla! So THAT was how King Pedro stole it, through Grand Master de Padilla.'

'Yes,' agreed John of Gaunt, 'and the Ruby never reached Santiago at all. The fox.'

In a flash, Prince John reached over, grabbed the Ruby firmly out of his elder brother's hand, held it out towards the monk and said, 'We obviously must return this to you, Friar.'

The Black Prince conferred in furious whispers with his brother. 'You have NO RIGHT,' he said. 'The Ruby is MINE! Traitor!'

'Try trusting me, brother,' was the slow quiet response.

'Where's the box?' asked the monk cautiously, for the second time. He wanted an answer, but he made no move to take the proffered jewel.

'I sent it back to England. We don't have it.'

'Is that true?' The monk clearly had difficulty believing this.

Both Princes nodded.

The librarian friar gently backed away, looking down at the wooden boards of the floor, as if his life depended on where he put his feet. 'Without its box to protect it, any man can steal that jewel! We DON'T wand it here! For God's sake, you must take it to Santiago. KEEP IT!'

Coolly, Prince John retracted his offering and cocked an eyebrow at his brother as he turned away smiling.

Back down in the church again, we passed John the Baptist's head once more on the way out. Without the least warning, Prince John held his closed hand out sideways towards me, 'Petit-roi!' he meant me to take the jewel unnoticed. I fumbled with it and nearly dropped it.

Outside I asked him the question: 'Tell me, Sire, what would have happened to the head if I had dropped the Blood of Christ stone? And what would have happened to the stone, if the head had seen it?'

My master shrugged, 'Inconclusive, I'd say!' quite undisturbed and we passed on. I know what I thought. My knees felt like jelly.

'We wish you adieu, Friar. We must depart.'

The monk bowed slightly as we walked past him, sighing deeply as he turned back towards his den and hurried away to see the disarranged state of his most precious books.

We were soon on the way again. Daylight hours were precious. We still had three hours of hard riding to get to the next destination, the Roman town of Saintes.

We made good time, until we were forced to abandon the path. Hooded monks guided our little party on a detour to miss the village of Fenioux, because of a new outbreak of the dreaded Plague. The Black Death was feared in every man's heart throughout Europe. In England alone, twenty years before, it had been responsible for the death of between a third and a half of the entire population. It was still a terrible threat.

From a distance, riders could see the tall pyramid-shaped spire of Fenioux's Lantern of the Dead, that watched over its sad cemetery. Nobody was moving in Fenioux.

At last we arrived at the shores of the great Charante River and its ancient town of Saintes, that the Romans called *Mediolanum Santonum*.[12] The Princes had two cousins and their grandfather's very old half-sister, within its safekeeping. Here the brothers were cosseted and spoilt. Our horses were tended, re-shod and fed only the best. The Black Prince was lowered into the abbey's own thermal baths for immediate relief from the terrible swelling of his joints. The next day the baths were repeated and a visit to the sarcophagus of St Eutrope was arranged. Consecrated by Pope Urban II in 1096, St Eutrope Church was built over his resting-place. This tomb was one of the main reasons for the Black Prince taking this particular pilgrim route. It was noted for its cure for dropsy. His doctors could not confirm that his illness was dropsy, for his swellings were more dramatic than anything they had previously seen. They had also never before had a patient who refused to rest, let alone one who was set to ride many hundreds of miles.[13]

Leaving early on the fourth day, the Black Prince faced his toughest task so far. There was a ten-hour ride ahead and not ten hours of daylight in the sky. Blaye was our next destination, at the arm of the sea at Gironde, where the rivers Garonne and Dordogne began. This was where we would have to take a boat upriver to Bordeaux, to continue on our pilgrim route.

My Prince felt free in his limbs and declared himself fit to ride ten hours. But when we got to the imposing defensive fortress at Pons, we had been on the road for more than four hours, when it should have taken us three. We realised our horses had been too well-fed by the abbesses at Saintes. We would not be able to get to the river crossing at Blaye by nightfall.

By walking the horses most of the next three hours, we eventually arrived in the early evening, beside the tower in the village of Plassac. This was an unexpected stop. But the inns were used to pilgrims and hopefully more prudent with the feeding of horses. As we pulled into the yard of the first hostelry, I remember we passed a jostle of people dressed up in odd costumes. They were obviously on their way to the village festival.

After a warming meal at the inn, the brothers were entreated to join the throng. It was dark outside and we were handed candles with holders to light the way, following the innkeeper and his family.

This was the Festival of Death. What they were enacted was the *Dance of Death*. Laughing excitedly, the people entered the village graveyard through the main gates, as all their ancestors had done. They took their places in a line around the cemetery walls. The dead had noisy company that night.

John of Gaunt nudged his brother and nodded towards the far wall. A thickset man, quite bald, was standing on one leg and one wheel. He had a wheel for his left leg. It appeared to be attached below the knee with a spring, a harness and a strap.

Suddenly, the air was without sound. Nobody spoke. To our left we saw a set of thirty candles being carried shoulder-high into the graveyard, through an entrance from the east wall of the church. Gradually, a procession of twenty monks filed into the middle of the cemetery. They stopped and gathered in a small clearing in the centre, this was the only part with no graves.

One monk stepped forward. In a loud ringing voice, he delivered a short eulogy on the certainty of death. He ended by saying: 'I am here to teach the truth, that all men have to die and must prepare themselves to appear before their Judge.' The villagers seemed to know every word, for they cheerfully said it with him. Wild applause and calls of praise signalled the end.

Five agile dancers, dressed in luminescent skeleton costumes, cavorted over and around the tombstones, all over the cemetery, playing the fool to the crowds. When they had visited every gravestone, the dancers joined a troop of some thirty men and boys from the village. They were dressed up to enact six different apocryphal daily scenes, in the form of *Dances of Death*. Some acted as skeletons, representing the dead, while others dressed as the living.[14]

In the first scene, there were peasants wearing farm clothes, dancing with forks and rakes and hay. Two or three were drinking deeply from flagons of wine and one young man was hitching his trousers up. Out from the hayrick appeared two *skeletons*, which picked up their implements and worked alongside the farmers. One drinker noticed the dead men, screamed and fell down dead himself. The young man with his trousers half way up his bottom, tripped and fatally hit his head on a rock. The skeletons helped to carry the bodies away.

The second scene described men on a construction site, building a church. They had stones, ropes, tools, wooden scaffolding and a cross for the top. One man passed a large boulder to an important looking master mason, who danced around it, inspected its shape, measured its size and approved its use. The boulder was handed along a line of dancing men, up the scaffold and down again. Every second man was a skeleton. The stone was passed faster and faster from hand to hand, until the scaffolding fell down. All the skeletons survived and all the workers were dead.

The third scene was Hunters in the Forest, where the prey escaped when the hunters shot each other by mistake. The prey were a group of skeletons.

The next two scenes were single tableaux. Skeleton horses carrying skeleton corpses to the hunt and Peasant girls with wide frilled skirts, dancing with Death. Finally, all the villagers and the dancers trooped out of the graveyard, to enter the church, for the very last enactment of the evening. A skeleton started at the altar and danced down the aisle. It held out its arms and received an infant from the baptismal font.

Eventually the dancing was over and the revels began. The villagers were in full swing, when the two Princes decided to make their way back to the inn. They were tired and the rough red wine we had drunk with our meal was making my master's joints swell alarmingly. As luck would have it, the innkeeper considered himself to be a physician regarded with awe locally. He was very gifted at bleeding the sick. Taking it upon himself to help his guest, who was obviously unwell, he asked the Black Prince for some details.

'How old are you? Which planet were you born under? How long have you felt like this?'

When given his answers, he shrugged and spread his hands. 'Ah! But of course, the 15th June. All my Geminis are feeling unwell this week.' He pulled a long pathetic face, a bit like a spoilt child. 'Ask anyone in the village! It's quite out of my hands.' But quite quickly he obviously thought better of it, wanting to offer something, at least to these important-looking young squires. 'I have some woodbine, that's the proper stuff. Guaranteed cut under a waxing moon. I could pass it over you three times. That'll do the trick!'

'No.'

'Well, if you cannot sleep, squire, my wife has some carrots in the kitchen. I'll mix them with the white of a fresh egg from our Jemima in the yard. You'll sleep for two days.'

'No! Leave me alone!'

'I'll get her to boil some heather for you then. You can put it on the top of your head when it's still warm. It's great for a headache!'

'It's not my head that hurts. Go away.'

Getting desperate, the innkeeper-cum-physician trotted out his speciality of the house. 'I could bleed you a little, if you wished...' He saw their expressions. 'Or a lot.'

They sent him packing. The Prince felt worse.

As we set off at the trot the next morning, eager to get going, the man with the wheel on one leg passed us at speed, flying along on his unique cycle. He was a pilgrim. He had the knack of shifting his weight onto the wheel, and rolling along. We watched him in morbid fascination. He managed a fast and furious pace as long as the path was smooth, hard, and level. The man had his own way of dealing with the boulders. He had perfected a side-step, a quick lunge onto his right leg to sway his body around the obstacle, and then back again to the wheel-leg. It was a sort of high-speed dodge. He had obviously become extraordinarily skilful at controlling the wheel. We wondered how he would cope with a hill. I am ashamed to say, we cantered along behind him to catch up and see.

The answer came at the next downhill section. As he slowed at the top of the slope, he kicked his left leg (the wheel-leg) behind him, landing fully on his right leg and hopped down the hill. At a much slower pace, but in total control. How on earth was he going to be able to hop uphill?

We were soon enlightened. The man stopped at the bottom of the slope. He withdrew a leather strap from his clothing and passed it between two top spokes of his wheel. Fastening it tightly to the spring on the stump of his leg. Now he could walk up the hill with one leg and one immobilised wheel.

The early evening of this fifth day found us at the tomb of the Patron Saint of Travellers, St-Romain-in-Blaye, where the abbey looked out over the wide expanse of the Gironde estuary.

The Pilgrim Guide said: '*On the rocky slopes of the antique Blavia, lived the hermit Romain, the evangelist of the area in the 4th century. After his death in 385, a basilica was raised in his name. The patron saint of travellers, St-Romain, saved from shipwreck all those who called on him in danger on the waves and by the 7th century, a famous cemetery surrounded the basilica.*

This was the burial place of Caribert, son of Clotaire II (584-629), and it was here that Charlemagne, back from the disastrous ambush in the Pyrenees, in 778, decided to bury his nephew, valiant Roland.

A community of regular canons of St Augustine watched over the sepulchre of St Romain and Roland, exciting the fervors of generations of pilgrims. They came here to make the dangerous two-hour boat trip up-river and across the estuary to the old Celtic town of Burdigala, or Bordeaux.'[15]

During the crossing the next morning, we discovered that we had to hang onto the horses bridles to steady them, to soothe their fears, for the waves were choppy and the waters were rough, the tide strong. The horses were unsettled and stamped at the planks of the small boat, making it unstable. The whole experience was dangerous. The brothers knew very well that horses were not able to vomit. If gases had built up in their stomachs, they could have become seriously unwell within minutes. The animals needed exercise to relieve the pressure. Hence their stamping in the boat. If they developed this colic, they would have a better chance if they jumped overboard and swam.

According to the guide: *'after crossing an arm of the sea and the Garonne, one arrives in the Bordelais where the wine is excellent, fish abundant, but the language is rough.'*

With relief, we landed our four horses on the outskirts of Bordeaux. It was mid-morning. I will never forget the mound of raw meat, wool and bones that greeted us beside the river as we landed. We saw feral dogs and wolves vying for the tasty dark-red flesh of horses and mules, growling over strings of offal and sinew between them. There was a fresh mound of dead horses every day, where these pilgrim-carriers had succumbed to the rough crossings. It was an all too common sight in Bordeaux. The odour was atrocious. I believe the inhabitants never became accustomed to the smell that came from their side of the river. Indeed, our royal group had to find a way around this terrible sight, for our horses would go nowhere near it. And even more time was lost as we had to give our mounts an extra hour to find their land-legs. They were staggering, and looked depressed.

While we waited for the horses to recover, the brothers left their horses behind with us, and wandered off into the centre of town unescorted. They arrived at the tomb of St Seurin, a bishop of Bordeaux in the early 5th century. An abbey was built over the sepulchre.

'It was to this abbey church that Charlemagne brought Roland's ivory horn, split by the power of his breath as he vainly called for his uncle's aid in Roncesvalles Pass,' said the Guide.

214

Chapter 20 - Steamy Affairs

We had to have fit horses to tackle the next stage, southwards across The Landes, a daunting million square metres of Atlantic sand dunes and lakes. This huge triangular wilderness was dreaded by pilgrims. The sands of the well-trodden path were loose and unstable. Even the hundreds of thousands of pilgrim feet could not anchor the shifting surface.

The elderly and infirm counted each stride carefully to pass the time. It was reputed to be 150,000 steps in shifting sands, to the welcome hot spas in the town of Dax, on the southern edge of The Landes. However, it was nearer 200,000. If they were heavy-footed, they took two steps forward, to one step sideways or back. If they trod more lightly, they could take the ridges at a scamper, only to fall sideways after a cluster of small strides.

The Princes' horses could get more grip, because they had been shod in Blaye with sandbar shoes, which stretched across the base of their hooves. They found it easier than pilgrims on foot. Frequently, however, with the weight of the horse, the entire side of a dune gave way, and rider and horse rolled to the base. Mules and donkeys, on the other hand, had an uncanny ability to skip fleet-footed over the top of the sands; a miraculous gift thought to be embedded in their history from the deserts of the Holy Land.

For centuries, the Atlantic rollers had piled up a line of dunes along the coast. They became the highest in Europe. Westerly gales blew the sand ashore, creating a bare desert that increased every year. The wine pickers to the south-west of Bordeaux used open-weave panniers, so that the sand on their grapes would fall through the holes.

Each early September day, a line of donkeys were trained to stand in the Garonne River carrying low-slung baskets on each side, to sluice the grapes clean. Nobody liked sand in their wine.

As the royal party headed out into the dunes we by-passed the priory hospital of Cayac De Gradignan, run by the Hospitallers of St John of Jerusalem. They had no need of their services; not just yet. This would be by far the most difficult part of their journey to the Pyrenees. If there was anywhere along the route that required John of Gaunt to divert his brother's attention away from his aches and pains, it was here, it was now.

He had to get him talking again.

"Tell me more about Thomas Holland.'

'Where did I get to?'

'Joan was about to take fencing lessons alone with Holland. That was disastrous, you said.'

'Ah yes!' the Prince was quiet for a while. He needed to find the words to tell the story in his own way. Later John of Gaunt would remember the gist of it only too well. Afterwards, he was never able to look at his sister-in-law in the same way again.

Holland was 25 years old; a fine looking young man, with an excess of downy red hair on his arms and chest. He was strong in the trunk and neck, but his face was fair, and pleasing to the ladies. However, his position made it imperative that he was trustworthy with women; and he was. His reputation was clean.

Joan was missing her hugs, and the closeness of a boy's body. These were the consolations she had experienced in the royal nursery, particularly from myself, since I had been the closest in age. Nothing ever would have happened between them, if she had not confided to Holland why she was upset one morning, and revealed her constant nightmares about her father's severed head. How could she possibly have known that he too had seen his own father beheaded, for the same reason? He had fought alongside the deposed King Edward II. Holland's father was beheaded two years before Joan's.

216

This forged an immediate and emotional bond between them. He was the only other person she knew who could share the aftermath of her terrible nightmares. He told her much more than she already knew about her uncle, Edward II, and his unfaithful queen; his forced abdication, and his death. He also explained how King Edward III, as a boy, was manipulated by his mother. He told her that there had been over two hundred honourable knights executed by the queen and her lover, Mortimer.

As she got older, the Earl and Countess of Salisbury allowed their son, William Montague, more access to his future bride. She was happy, and William loved her. Already, on occasions, in the middle of hiding games, she allowed him to unfasten the laces of her dress, to run his fingers around her darkening nipples, and feel how the swelling mounds of her breasts were growing. For her small favours, not yet truly awakening his young body, he adored her; and followed her around like a puppy. In his innocence, he totally accepted that Holland as well had fleeting access to her favours. The whole thing felt natural. No sense of guilt entered his head, either for himself, or for her and Holland.

Young William Montague was not jealous, because he was sure of her as his future bride. The King had signed the document, and he felt proud to be marrying the King's cousin. For Holland, of course, it was a test not to become aroused…and he did not succeed.

Holland and his two young charges played elaborate game scenarios along with their jousting and fencing. Of course Joan of Kent did not joust, but the ritual she was delighted with, was to act as the favoured beauty in the royal box, and to accept the scarves or crested pennants of the combatants, before their horses thundered down the lists at full tilt at each other.

So time went on, and young Montague learnt the etiquette, and loved to claim back his pennant from his fair bride-to-be. Many were the scenarios they acted out to enliven the required two hours of practice at arms each day, and household servants were frequently called in to act as extras. Occasionally, the boy's parents were given a performance. It was often a fairy tale. One was a fable about a succession of suitors who had to kill a fierce bull which protected the beautiful Princess locked up in a tower.

Precision with the tournament lance was required from young William Montague. He played all three suitors. The first two had to miss the 'bull' (a padded-up Holland) in different ways; and the third was the handsome Prince, who had to score a hit in exactly the right place, between the bull's shoulder blades...which he succeeded in doing. Whether he had to climb a tower, and bring his Princess down, or even have time for a quick fumble at the top, history does not relate.

We don't know who had the idea to play the game of 'Weddings'. First, William was the groom, and Holland was the groom's father. One household servant played the best man, and another, the vicar. Ten acted as choristers and bridal attendants, and the rest played the congregation. They staged the mock wedding in the church, when the chaplain was absent. There could not have been much work done that morning in the Salisbury household, for there were upwards of 35 players in this particular enactment. William and his 'bride' processed into the vicar's room, and were shut in there for five minutes, as was the custom; usually, the vicar was there too, signing the register, but not this time. There were just a few minutes for a fumble, before they were released.

Then the roles were reversed. Holland became the groom, and William Montague delighted in ceremoniously giving the hand of the bride over to the new groom. All went just as before, up to a point. The words of the marriage ceremony were read out by the 'vicar', and the correct responses were made. The 'bride and groom' repaired to the vestry, and the door was symbolically locked behind them. This time, however, the mock vicar stayed OUTSIDE.

As Holland turned around, anticipating his customary fondle, he discovered her attempting to remove every stitch on her body. Very tenderly, he started to help her. He lifted-up her full-length dress and her under-shift as one garment, rolling it up her lithe athletic body, and up past her exquisite navel, which seemed to be winking at him. With a shock, he realised that she had teasingly placed a small opal stone in its confines.

He was instantly aroused, though thank God, he was gentle with her. Up and up he slowly drew the dress, revealing more and more young flesh until it slipped over her head and fell to the floor. Her breasts were filling, her nipples were dark and sharp to the touch; her shoulders and neck were long and graceful, and her eyes searched his eagerly. Her whole body throbbed with excitement and invitation. She read his face, and knew there was something different. He took her hand gently from its resting place on his thigh and moved it. Now she could feel the difference. She found that day that she had power over him, and it was a lesson she would never forget. In fact she became addicted to it.

In a minute he was unbuttoned, and he had the presence of mind to turn away from her and jam a chair-back against the door knob. Outside, in the body of the church, the statutory five minutes were adjudged to have expired. But the door was found to be jammed. More worrying still, the noises from within the vestry were loud and unmistakable. Panicking servants, who understood all too well what was going on, diverted William Montague away from the area around the vestry door.

Then, in walked the vicar; the REAL vicar. Forced into action, one bright spark indicated to the others to join him in an orderly queue outside the confessional box situated along the middle of the side aisle.

'Good turnout for confession' said the vicar, climbing into his usual seat behind the grill. There must have been a lot of sinning in the household while he was away.

Oh dear! Now he could remember the last time he had numbers queueing up like that.

It had happened years before, when the old Earl accosted three house-maids in the same night, watched by a long string of peeping-toms; household members who found themselves inspired to treat each other in exactly the same way.

'I'll soon learn the truth,' he thought.

Well, he never did. For not one of his congregation dared to admit their fears that Joan of Kent, the King's nubile cousin in their midst, had been de-flowered ahead of schedule. As indeed she had. Each invented a different sin to confess to. It was not that difficult. The household was governed, on a daily basis, by an habitually inebriated steward who never noticed pregnant maids; and the Countess seemed to suffer from failing eyesight in this regard.

Upon hearing the vicar's voice, the young couple in the vestry dressed hurriedly, quietly removed the chair that jammed the door, and crept out of the side entrance of the church. Standing around the corner, by the confessional box, all the household servants heard was the faint creaking of the old vestry door. The current servant saying her confession spoke up a bit.

'The incident was buried, but not forgotten,' the Black Prince continued. 'Young William Montague, the future groom, was unaware of the facts, but he did harbour a worry about why the vestry door was jammed, and he could not quite understand why he had been advised not to tell the vicar about the 'play marriage' they had just enacted. Something smelled fishy, but he kept it to himself for many weeks, until one night, when he found himself awaking with a wet bed underneath him. He had been dreaming about Joan, his young bride-to-be.'

Suddenly, he developed an uneasy feeling about the noises he remembered hearing from the other side of the vestry door. Probing in the most roundabout way he could contrive, he asked his senior tutor to tell him the facts of life, and eventually confessed to suspicions of something happening between Holland and Joan. The tutor, who had never liked the enactments, and who had always thought the arms master had too strong an influence with the youngsters, recommended an investigation into the matter. He felt sure it was mostly in the imagination of young William. After all, he had just entered an impressionable age. However, there was always the encouraging possibility of getting Holland dismissed.

The Earl of Salisbury refused to take the matter seriously, but the Countess was horrified. She was ever the drama queen. Her imagination leapt into over-production, as usual. For once, she was correct. The deeper they probed, the worse it looked. She was left with the option of either removing her son from his marriage contract, and telling the King and queen the reason, or simply dismissing Holland and saying nothing, pretending it had never happened. She chose the latter option.

Despite his suspicions, her son William could not bring himself to believe that Holland and Joan indulged in sex. His mother's inaction proved the matter to him. William Montague was in denial. Nobody had been truthful with him. He was the one victim in this saga. He still loved her, and said so. She was sweet to him, but now she loved Thomas Holland, though she never said that to her fiancé.

Foolishly, his mother and his tutor instructed the household to keep their secret from him.

The Countess of Salisbury was a coward. She could not face the wrath of the King and queen. Holland was banished, complete with jousting lances, to a war in far-off Prussia. He managed, somehow, to smuggle a note to his love: 'I'll be back!' it read.

While the Black Prince was recounting his wife's early adventures, we were riding through the middle of the dunes of the Landes region. As we progressed, we crossed a welcome bridge at Blin, where the River Eyre turned southwards. Thereafter, the route kept within sight of the river. At last we completed the 30 miles of tortuous shifting sands. The horses were exhausted, and our pockets and boots had filled with sand every time we fell down the side of a collapsing dune. The other bodyguard was suffering with sand in his eyes. We stopped twice at lakes along the way, before his eyes recovered. All of us, horses included of course, were grateful for the opportunity to drink.

At last, a small Romanesque church hove into view. This was the town of Mons, which held an important key to the legend of King Charlemagne. Once again, the Black Prince found an entry in his pilgrim's guide that drew his attention away from the tale he was telling. I was getting practiced at reaching behind my back, and swinging it down in one motion.

'...in the small Roman church in Mons the pilgrim will find the bodies of scores of valiant knights, brought here for burial by Charlemagne, in 778, after the massacre at Roncesvalles Pass in the Pyrenees.

Read the graves dear pilgrims: Oliver, Gondebaud, King of Frisia. Ogier, King of Dacia. Arastain, King of Brittany. Garin, Duke of Lorraine and many other Kings and nobles, but their names are not clear.'

Dismounting outside the old cemetery gates, the brothers handed their horses over to us, and knelt before a row of raised sarcophagi. I could see that both felt the presence of these brave legendary knights, as strongly as if they were brothers before a combat. They were overwhelmed with the feeling that their pilgrimage was no accident, no last-minute idea. They had no doubt; it was written in the stars that they should arrive here, and mingle with the Knights of Charlemagne. Indeed, Charlemagne had been the greatest King of Europe and beyond. He himself had crowned all these men, and made them Kings as reward for their knightly service to him. He had loved each one as a son.

Standing there, surrounded by these knights, the royal Princes acknowledged they had always had an ambition to follow in the footsteps of Charlemagne. Now they knew it was right. They renewed their vow. From now on they would stop where he had stopped, and they would pray where he had prayed. And eventually they would fight on the same battleground that he had fought upon.

It was an hour before sunset when we left the little churchyard, and rode the last four miles into the village of Saugnaiq-et-Muret. Here the oblong stone church, with its tiny hospice on the side, offered stabling, food and a rough straw barn, for we found the inn was already full.

Despite everything, we managed to leave before sunrise the next morning, because the light sands showed up in the dark sufficiently to be able to see. We had to cover forty miles, before we could get relief at the hot springs of Dax. The problem was that the base of the dunes had notorious patches of quick sands. There would be no time for talking. The Princes would have to concentrate every step of the way, to get themselves and their horses through. Had we made a mistake by leaving in bad light? Would the Black Prince have enough strength to reach Dax, at the end of the Landes?

The wind was blowing easterly, and cold. Occasionally it swirled and picked up sand in a funnel. The conditions were dangerous. Several times, the horses shied away from white bones, and skeletal faces were revealed in hollowed-out pits created by the wind. It became obvious there were hundreds of dead pilgrims on all sides; all picked clean by the sands and any lucky bird.

If pilgrims died in The Landes, they could not be buried with a cross beside the route, for they would not be found. This was the one place not to die. A special service was held in Bordeaux every day, to give benediction to the pre-dead, just in case.

For the first hour, the wind was blowing one mound of sand quite bare, and creating another. It became a lottery. If the wind had chosen to remove the dune we were walking on, it would have annihilated us. But our luck held, and the wind died down.

It was a good thing we had no way of measuring our progress, for we had only gone one mile in the first hour. Ignorance was sometimes bliss.

Prince John decided our horses would make better headway by walking along the shallow river-bed of the Eyre, which was still flowing slowly in the right direction. The bottom was not too stony. We trotted and cantered in mid-stream for the second hour; something we could never have done on the shifting sands of dry land. Eventually our watery road turned eastwards, and our royal group had to abandon the river.

Stumbling sideways, the brothers lost count of the number of times they were delivered a faceful of sand as they hit the ground. At least they were soft landings. It was a slow nightmare, even though we were riding on horses.

'I don't fancy the chances of the man with the wheel,' muttered the younger brother through gritted teeth.

As if placed for rescue, every two hours there was an oasis to be found, with a hostel or a tiny village settlement perched on rocks, beside welcome streams. We passed village churches decorated with scallops. Some were dedicated to St James the Apostle of Galicia, with unlikely names like Herbe-Fanee, Escource, Onesse-et-Laharie, Lesperon, and Taller. Sometime after this last settlement, the young bodyguard who had suffered earlier with sand in his eyes, had to stop. His horse had collapsed on the water's edge. However hard we strained, we could not pull it up onto its feet. I had to drag my fellow bodyguard away from his unfortunate horse, for there was nothing he could do for it now.

Our exertions were making the Black Prince look grey and vacant in the eyes. I knew the signs; he was looking ashen-faced. It was immediately obvious that the remaining four riders and three horses had to get to Sax fast, before he passed out. It was well past dark, but there was a clear three-quarter moon.

We started off on our feet, because the horses were exhausted and impossible to ride. The town of Dax could be clearly seen only two miles further on. The sands began to clear from the path. Grass and stones were underfoot again. Looking down at the loose rubble on the road as we trudged along, we suddenly realised what that meant: at last we had got through the Landes. Our numb endurance seemed to be almost over.

Within ten minutes of walking beside his horse, the Black Prince started to feel his senses slipping from him. He had the sensation of his legs walking on their own. They refused to respond, though he vaguely knew his brain was past giving them orders. He didn't care anymore. He staggered for four paces, and half-succeeded in turning sideways to reach out for the horse's saddle beside him. His knees buckled as his feet came to a stop up against a rock. He saw the ground rising up to meet him. His eyes saw things for the last time, in slow motion.

With horror, I saw my Prince fall, but before I could react, my horse reared away in fright. Suddenly, the critical moment was passed, and I found I could offer no help to the one man I was there to protect.

He fell, folding inwards around the small boulder. It was not a large rock. Did his foot manage to feel his last step? It was smooth and round, not more than ten inches high, no doubt eroded in the past by the sands of the Landes. His body had wrapped itself untidily around the boulder, right in the middle of his horse's legs. One arm and one leg were splayed out at oblique angles. Within a minute, a scene that had been full of movement, became a dreadful stillness. It looked so final; so definite.

The picture looked unreal, falsely posed. It was as if this boulder was taking the full responsibility for being the final barrier to the great Prince's life.

224

Chapter 21 - The Order of the Garter

As the Black Prince lost consciousness, he had a last vision of his horse scrabbling on the loose stones to miss his body as he fell. On the narrow path, there was no room for boulder, body, and the horse. Instead of panicking, the gentle giant of a horse halted stock-still. Deliberately, and very slowly, one by one, it lifted each huge hoof right up to its elbow, extracting its iron-clad foot from beside the head and the limbs of the body, and placed it out of harm's way.

Unfortunately, as the last hind hoof was lifted up, it released the Prince's head, which banged downwards, falling sideways, ear uppermost onto the exact piece of road where the horse planned to deposit his great heavy hoof next.

If John of Gaunt had got there in time, he might have been able to divert the hoof at the last moment before the inevitable impact on his brother's skull. In the meantime, I was still busy struggling with my own horse. Despite my curses, it went on rearing so violently it was spinning completely around. I had little chance of staying on; and no chance at all if I jumped off without being crushed beneath its feet as well. I could only cling on grimly. To make matters worse, the other bodyguard on his feet got knocked over in the melee. It was some time before I could dismount safely.

The quickest reaction came from the Black Prince's own horse. The stallion bent its fine black head to peer below his belly, and saw the new position of his master's face. He reversed the downward motion of his hind leg, and snatched it up again. It had came to within an inch of the human skull, just above the Prince's cheekbone. The horse abandoned his intention

225

of standing on all four legs. He stood solidly enough on three, with his left hind foot quivering in mid-air, well above his beloved master.

Trusting the charger not to move, Prince John flung himself awkwardly between the front legs of the horse, and plucked his brother from the ground. With my help at last, he half-carried and half dragged him to his own horse. For a few seconds, he lowered his brother to feel his pulse. And found nothing. Past caring now what was broken, and what needed attention, we flung the still body face-down on to the front of his saddle. Prince John mounted, and stuck his spurs deep between the fur-covered ribs below. He felt nothing now for his own horse. He did not care if he killed it. Despite its earlier exhaustion, it was forced to try to gallop. Every second counted. How long could a man live without breathing, until he was finally dead?

I followed at the fastest pace I could, not even stopping to pick up my colleague; he would have to walk. I was leading the Black Prince's horse, and sending wicked curses down upon my own. I felt that I had failed my Prince in his hour of need. Now it was all too late.

The spires of the town ahead seemed to be just in front of us. However, on rounding a corner, I realised there was a deep, wide river in the way. Dax was on the far bank of the River Adour. We had to cross a bridge a good half a mile further up. John of Gaunt's horse, with its two passengers, galloped past a small church as they clattered on to the causeway. Prince John was hanging on to his brother's body, struggling to keep it from falling, holding it by the belt around its waist. He pulled to a stop at the far end of the bridge, and was met by many willing hands outside the Bout-du-Pont hospital.

Here, they were used to every human drama, placed as they were at the end of the Landes region of the Pilgrim Route. One of their tasks each day was to count the pilgrims as they entered the town. Only then could someone tally up the number of daily fatal casualties, swallowed up by the sands, for Bordeaux also counted those who set out.

In my panicked state, I imagined there was always a chance that the pounding endured by a body as it lay face down across the saddle of a galloping horse might re-start the heart. Or it might make matters worse.

As I brought my two horses across the bridge, I saw the inert body of the Prince being handed down carefully from his brother's quivering horse, and placed on to a canvas pole-bed, to be checked over. If they could find a pulse, that would mean the patient could be hurried away uphill to the hospital for full medical help. If there was no pulse, the Death Chamber downhill by the riverbank would be the Black Prince's destination. There, the lying-in chamber for the dead, with wooden boxes in a row, and a priest, awaited the nurse's judgment. With his head in his hands, John of Gaunt could not bear to look, wanting to delay the inevitable. 'What do you want to do with your horse?' I asked him gently, trying to get him to move off it. He seemed totally unaware that it was lying down beneath him, and he was still sitting on it. It looked dead to me. He did not even glance down.

'Kill it!' he replied in a low voice, and raised his head. On looking up, he saw the stretcher bearing his brother disappearing around the corner at the run, going uphill. 'He's alive!' he called, jumping to his feet, and running up the hill after it.

He did not leave his brother's side all night, and gave no thought to his horse until the Black Prince asked after both their gallant chargers the next morning. He was sitting up in bed; he looked well, and was eager to know what had happened. He was also in full voice, demanding an immediate hot spa bath.

I disobeyed my orders that day, managing to revive the fallen horse with a mug of ale, and had nursed all three into willingness to graze on the spring grass around the hospital stables. We all stayed at Dax for a week, both for the 'cure', and to await the arrival of the Royal Troop of Guards; for Dax was indeed the end of our personal pilgrimage. There were thirty hand-picked knights scheduled to escort the Princes in full pomp and splendour to be reunited with their army awaiting them at St Jean Pied de Port.

The two sons of the King of England had arrived...Just. From now on, they would follow the same route as Charlemagne; but there would be no more stopping at churches, and no more stories from the Pilgrim's Guide. Now they had to concentrate on passing through the Pyrenees, and fighting their battle to regain the throne of Castile for their cousin King Pedro.

227

While he rested, the Black Prince had plenty of time to finish the story of Joan of Kent, his wife. Again, his brother would have no difficulty in remembering the gist of it, for the rest of his life:

'Thomas Holland was banished, but he did make a personal promise to come back to Joan,' reiterated the Black Prince.

'What did the Countess do next?' asked his brother.

'Well, she quite rightly blamed herself for what had happened. For the first time, she saw clearly the lax supervision within her servants' quarters. She dismissed her drunken steward, and brought in harsher controls for her household. Life was not nearly so much fun working for the Salisburys after that.

The Countess discussed the problem with her husband, and sent Joan back to the royal nurseries, back to the King and Queen. To explain this, she dishonestly blamed her own son's 'dangerous and besotted state' with his intended bride,claiming that she feared he would be unwilling to wait until they were married in six years time, when the girl would be seventeen.

The King and Queen were delighted to have Joan back in their nursery. She was their favourite pretty cousin. This time, there were more babies to look after, and Joan was old enough to help. Luckily, this recipe for a catastrophe never did materialise into the dish of disaster it might have done.

Between the ages of twelve and sixteen, Joan of Kent grew up to be a breath-taking beauty, extremely desirable, with long auburn hair to her waist and dark eyes. The queen indeed caught the King gazing at Joan one day, and wisely removed him from temptation.

At that point, the queen started to turn against the girl. Joan clearly posed a danger for any married woman in the royal household. Every man was besotted with her beauty; though none dared touch her.

Originally, her return to the nursery had been welcomed by all, especially myself. She was a wonderful carer for the babies (there was a new one every year or two), and she had the undying devotion of every boy in her care. I thought of myself as her protector. I was the next eldest in the nursery, and I defended her honour constantly against the rude jokes of the younger ones. However, the whole affair was cloaked in innocence, for she secretly swore never to let anyone else but Thomas Holland play with her in that way again.

Wisely, she kept the whole story to herself, merely discussing occasional points of biology, mostly with me. I swore eternal fidelity to her, and said I would always protect her. Thus far I have kept my word.

In January 1344, when I was fourteen, I was invited to my first Royal Jousting Tournament at Windsor, given by my father. The stands were full, and the skills were applauded. In their turn, both William Montague and I handed our pennants to the beautiful Joan of Kent. From that day on, the public called her the 'Fair Maid of Kent', and news of her beauty spread throughout England.

The tournament lasted for two days, but came to an abrupt end when William Montague's father, the Earl of Salisbury, was accidentally pierced by a lance when his horse tripped. He fell sickeningly, skewered to the ground by the weapon and breaking his right leg, hip, shoulder and arm. The Earl had been a famous warrior in his day, and a jousting champion, but luck was not with him that day.

Amazingly, he lived one more day. But, on the 30th January, the Earl of Salisbury died from his wounds. They never dared to remove the lance from the old knight while he was still alive. It stuck up towards the ceiling as he lay dying in agony. At the age of 16, William Montague became the second Earl of Salisbury.

The following year, young William was called up to fight in France. So, on the 20th June 1345, William Montague, second Earl of Salisbury married Joan, the Fair Maid of Kent. It marked the end of nearly seven years of betrothal. At least they would have a few months together before he had to go to war. Joan accepted her fate because she liked him a lot; but she kept him frustrated and dissatisfied with the access she gave him to her bed. She secretly longed for her first love, Thomas Holland.

Whatever else was not quite right, she did love the grand balls she attended with her husband, as the new Earl and Countess of Salisbury. They were a glittering young couple, and Joan's beauty and flirtatious bearing

THE UNBELIEVABLE MYSTERY OF THE BLACK PRINCE'S RUBY

ensnared every man on the dance floor. The King famously danced with her on one occasion, when she suddenly stopped in the middle of a gavotte. Deliberately, she reached deep up inside her full-length dress, and loosened a pretty blue velvet garter from around the top of her right leg, from her thigh. The other dancers stopped, gasped, drew back, and watched as she kicked the garter off with an energetic flick of her graceful ankle. It flew into the air, and landed in the middle of the dance floor. Instinctively, all the dancers made a circle around it. The King and Joan were left standing in the centre, looking down at the offending piece of clothing.

My father threw his head back with a great belly laugh. There were roars of mirth, while everyone else joined in. At last he caught his breath, and then announced in a clear solemn voice, 'I formally declare, whosoever shall pick up this heavenly garter, shall be invested with the robes of the First Order of Chivalry in our great land. It shall be called The Most Noble Order of the Garter.' And then he picked it up himself, ordering her husband, William Montague, to be the second recipient.

In 1346, her husband and I travelled to France with the bulk of the cavalry. We saw our first battle at Caen; and were in camp just before the battle of Crécy. As fate would have it, our commander was the 32-years-old Thomas Holland, Joan of Kent's lover.

Holland came to my tent to instruct me on the next day's tactics, and there he met William Montague face to face. Expecting congratulations, William told him he had married Joan of Kent, his long-time betrothed. Holland, who was not lacking in courage, told him straight out that his marriage was not legal, because he had bedded Joan himself, years before. He knew the law was on his side...I had to jump in between them to avert bloodshed.

After our astounding victory against overwhelming French numbers at Crécy, the two claimants for Joan of Kent were ordered home to sort it out. Holland sent a petition to the Pope to annul her marriage to William Montague. The wheels were in motion.

Furious and humiliated by both Holland and Joan, William made the mistake of asking her whom she preferred. 'Thomas Holland,' she replied without hesitation. William had thought she loved him. Angry and hurt, he

230

lost his reason and shut her up in his house as a prisoner.

Thomas Holland had been looking at the law books. They said that if a sexual liaison had taken place, and there was a witnessed ceremony of marriage, then it must be legal. So it became public knowledge that intercourse had happened.

The King and Queen washed their hands of her, and refused her pleas to be rescued. The Pope had her examined and questioned, and called the Salisbury household servants as witnesses. Eventually, the pontiff declared that her marriage to William Montague had to be annulled; and that Thomas Holland was her legal husband.

William Montague was ordered to release her. He refused. But I had made a childhood promise to Joan, and I led the rescue party. I might have thought it would happen, she promptly married Thomas Holland in a proper religious ceremony, in case their future children were tainted by their unholy wedlock. I was the only other person she would confide in. Stifled by royal protocol and stuffy ritual, I swallowed my pride, and quietly thought her daring and determination were beacons I could relate to.

My parents decided that I too, must marry. But they had not reckoned with my flat refusal to be the least bit polite or charming to the gravel-faced foreign Princesses they constantly produced for my perusal. Some I even refused to talk to. I made sure that none of them would want me as a husband, and I made it quite plain that I would never accept any of them. However, I remember there was one Princess who had some spirit, and who showed commendable fortitude in her determination to become the future Queen of England.

The Princess of Greece was not to be put off. She was made of an altogether stronger metal than the others and her face showed it. To call her ugly did not do her justice. There were the remnants of pretty skin beside her cheeks, but the rest had been twisted by a disease. She was left with a hare lip and sunken jowls. Maybe she had survived the Black Death. They got her out of there. I did promise to marry someone, eventually, but I would choose my OWN bride, in my OWN time.

The unfortunate William Montague went back to war, licking his hurt pride. He married another, two years later, fought in the Languedoc raids, and was a commander at the battle of Poitiers in 1356. Ironically, and terribly, he was destined, years later, to joust against his only son, 33-years-old Sir William Montague, on 6th August 1382. He killed his own son in a similar freak accident to the one that killed his own father, with a lance through the body. Thereafter they were known as the 'Jousting Salisburys'.

Joan and Thomas Holland were married for 12 years, before he died in 1360, in Normandy, of a swollen gut. They had two hot-headed sons, Thomas and John. Joan was left penniless after his death, for the Holland properties were fully mortgaged. She and her two sons, aged three and six, were given royal lodgings close to my own residence. She and I started living together almost at once, much to the horror of my mother. She rounded up the Archbishop of Canterbury, who gave me a formal warning that if we wanted to marry it would not be legal, nor would any children be legitimate, because William Montague was still alive. Luckily he was overruled by the Pope, and within months we were married quietly.

Poor Mother. She was now forced to look on Joan as the future Queen of England. It was unthinkable. But the most she could do was to persuade the King to send us to France to look after Aquitaine. So here we are; out from under her feet. And we've been happy, thank God. Joan still flirts outrageously, but that's all there is to it, and we've had two great sons. He sighed, 'Tragically now, only one.'

I had listened to every word. My Black Prince had told the whole of the incredible tale of his wife, The Fair Maid of Kent, in stages throughout our nightmare journey along the Pilgrim Path to the base of the Pyrenees. I knew John of Gaunt had drawn the adventure out of his brother deliberately to divert his attention away from his ailing body.

Now, I, 'Petit-roi', his personal guard and his double, believed I knew him best, for I dressed his swollen and aching body each morning.

Looking out upon the mighty Pyrenees, I believed with all my heart, that my Master had no strength left to do anything but die between those wicked snow-covered peaks.

It was not only my Prince who was in danger from this folly. Our whole garrison from Poitiers would perish. How could we survive the elements? For I was firmly told by another Pilgrim, this was indeed high season for the deepest snowfalls. How could we possibly miss a complete disaster?

Chapter 22 - Decimation

W ell, that was a nice bit of tittle-tattle,' said the emissary, tossing a chicken bone over his shoulder. 'I enjoyed that. But I don't know that it gets us much closer to the quest for the treasure, and that's what I'm really interested in.'

The hermit rose to his feet. 'I have to tell my story as I remember it,' he said, 'or I'll not be able to tell it at all. Anyway, it gets exciting from this point on.'

He subsided and carried on:

The dreaded avalanche from a thousand feet above, swept down from the top of Orisson Peak. A slice of snow, no more than ten feet wide, detached itself from the top of the mountain, sliding, onwards and onwards, faster and faster, towards the struggling column of men. As it gained momentum and speed, the weight of more snow increased the width of the avalanche to 150, and then 300 feet. Noiselessly, it slipped down the mountain towards the toiling, jingling army below. Three abreast, the horses came on, every step an effort through the snow. Prized longbow men followed them, in columns of four.

We were travelling along a high ledge, halfway up the mountainside. The climb was hard. This road had been hacked out by the Romans over a thousand years before. But it was now so deep in snow that it required each step to be inserted up to the knee, and then extracted with effort. The going was strength-sapping for both men and horses.

As we toiled and struggled for every foothold, I could not push my black humours away. My mind played and replayed the terrible scene with Marie-

Elaine the evening before. I was tormented by my thoughts, they would not leave me alone.

You see, in my wisdom, I had decided that the time had come for me to seek out my woman, and bid her one last farewell; though there was just a very slim chance I would be back to her one day.

I was all set to catch up with her, to vow that if she was nice to me, if I did not die in the mountains, or in a Spanish field, and if I was sent back to England, I would return. For she was the only woman I knew, and all those years ago, she had taught me to be a man.

I approached the Women's Army equipment base. 'Marie-Elaine, have you seen her?' I asked a pretty chit of a girl with pouting lips. She sat with her legs far apart, tying a breastplate of armour to a shoulder epaulette with a strip of narrow leather. She raised her head, and weighed me up for a few seconds. Then she stood up, and brushed herself down with her hands, and made a suggestive swish of her hips at me. 'You're her old man, aren't ye?'

I nodded, surprised at the tone.

'Well,' she continued impishly, 'ye ain't any more, love.' And she gave me another wiggle. 'Perhaps ye fancy a different dish?'

I shook my head and turned away puzzled. Normally the women would not dare encroach on Marie-Elaine's territory. She would tear them from bust to bottom.

And, what was she saying?

'Oh...my good God,' I saw my answer soon enough, just around the corner. Marie-Elaine was wrapping her wondrous red hair around and around the slight neck of an enraptured youth, as she lifted her right leg high and curled it around his torso. I had loved the feel of her doing that. It was always a prelude to the ultimate goal. Suddenly I felt weak at the knees, sick in my stomach and hot in my face. The pain I felt was as sharp as the wound of a pike.

The favoured young man was turned away from me, so I could not see his identity. But it mattered little whoever he was, for Marie-Elaine definitely saw me standing there. I was the onlooker, the outsider, as she deliberately laughed at me. I saw her well enough, as in the throes of her heat she laughed in my face, with her mouth opened wide in her passion: 'Aaaagh!'

I lowered my head and stumbled away. She had got her revenge.

Bewildered, that night I played and replayed that scene in my mind. The only question that still remained was: why had I bothered to seek her out? The only possible answer I could give myself was that I had missed her. I wondered at my own stupidity. I still loved her. God help me.

Toiling along in the deep snow, the army received no warning of the avalanche heading their way. There was absolutely no chance to save ourselves. It was a lottery of who lived and who died in that instant. Even if we had heard it coming, nobody would have had the time to get out of the way, because a faster pace was simply not possible in those conditions.

The path was already proving not only deep, but treacherously slippery underfoot.

The Black Prince's army was strung out for nearly a mile. Toiling, cursing, occasionally stopping to help each other as one lost a foothold and fell harmlessly sideways onto the snow. Two horses sat down on their haunches, like dogs, and rolled over. They had not slipped; it was their hearts that gave out. Perhaps they were too old for this kind of terrain.

They hardly delayed the riders behind, for they simply rode around the twitching four-legged humps, while others helped to push them over the edge. Down and down they fell, tail-first through the air, their heads screwed sideways as if to look where they landed. They were still just alive as they fell.

With the snorting and grunts of horses and men, nobody heard the silent killer cascading down from above.

The avalanche measured a hundred yards across when it hit us. The enveloping snow swept twenty-six horses and riders away down the ravine, 1,000 feet below. All of them were surprised, alive and screaming. Seven other horses panicked amidst the swirling clouds of snow, bumped into their comrades and leapt into space, disorientated by the avalanche. This sent another ten scrabbling for their feet and falling over in the snow. In the mayhem, with men, weapons and horses all over the path; another five lost their hind legs over the edge and followed their companions to eventual oblivion.

Dark bodies of horses and men tumbled down the face of the mountain amidst the white deluge. They bounced against jagged icy ledges and slid across an outcrop of rock below. They disappeared out of view, to crash into the white-clad valley floor. The remaining soldiers rushed to lean over the edge of the old Roman road to see the fate of their comrades. They could hear cracking sounds below, as the bodies hurtled into the tops of pine and spruce trees. In the path of the avalanche, there was no living thing left. They had been there, in their innocence, one minute before. All that could be seen now was a mound of snow heaped across the middle of the track, taller than a house, cutting the army neatly in two. The soldiers on the other side were cut off.

There were curses and shouts aplenty. When they had marched out of camp that morning, leaving the women behind, these men had absolutely no idea they would be required to grapple with the *evil spirits* of the Pyrenees. Why, they had been heading in a westerly direction when they left St Jean Pied de Port, and that was towards the sea. It happened to be usual camp procedure when they were to be gone for only a day or two, that the women would not be needed, so the soldiers carried their rations on their backs.

Two hours down the road, they were ordered to wheel sharply left-handed, onto a wide grassy area at the start of a southerly path. They were looking straight up onto the gigantic raw stone and snow-covered mountains of the Pyrenees. Thousands of feet above them two snowy eagles dived and swooped in a graceful dance of courtship. The birds shrieked at each other, the soldiers heard it clearly, even though the King and Queen of all the birds were more than two miles up.

Here, within sight of the threatening presence of overhanging rocks that were more than half a mile high, the Black Prince halted them and signalled that they should be drawn-up, into orderly ranks. He removed his helmet and turned, ordering me to remove mine. 'Come with me,' he said quietly.

Side-by-side we cantered up and down the lines of his soldiers. We changed places at the end of each row. Sometimes he rode on my right and sometimes on my left. Strangely, as if they knew it was required, our horses stayed in step, rocking to the canter at the same time.

We rode down the ranks to gasps of amazement, to questions, to whistles, to consternation amongst the men. Why? For we had the same curly blonde hair, the same face and we were no different in our bodies, for I had just been delivered of a fine decorated suit of armour, coloured black, just like my Prince's.

At last we pulled to a halt in front of them and he spoke to me quietly:

'You ask them! Go ahead, ask them this:

AM I YOUR PRINCE OF ENGLAND?

AM I MY MOTHER'S SON?'

I cried-out the words he gave me and raised my clenched fist in the air. I was proud of my acting. The deep-bellied roar that issued forth from every soldier was almost primeval. It was a roar of naked aggression and man-to-man love. The tidal wave of noise hit my senses.

I think they must have seen me drawing back a step in total surprise. I had never heard such a basic cry of human manhood, a cry of nearly a thousand deep voices.

They saw me and they thought I was him. I withdrew. So THAT was what it felt like to be the Black Prince!

He was delighted. He threw his head back and laughed to the skies. He signalled behind him for King Pedro to ride-up closer. He leaned down and replaced his helmet, urging his great black charger forward, to stand within good view of his men. Then he made it rear-up high and kept it balanced, on its two back legs. Holding on with his left hand, he drew the mighty Sword of State, a weapon of immense length and held it aloft to catch the glint of the morning sun, as it reflected off the snow on the mountains above. As he drew it out, the swell of the cries of support grew to match the importance of the mountains. Indeed the mountains came to him, for they echoed and echoed and echoed.

The Black Prince brought his great horse back down to earth, returned the sword to its scabbard and raised his hand to quieten them. There was total silence within three seconds. What power he had over these men. He did not want to take up any more time. The job had to be done now. He raised his voice to be heard by them all:

'I AM Prince Edward of England, and I AM my father's son!'

He allowed them to bellow their approval for a few seconds only. 'You will always know it is me. See! Look! I have three black feathers on my helmet and,' he pointed to me, 'he wears only one!'

'Now, I have good news for you, my brave men of England. Know this: we have tricked our enemies, we have deceived the French!'

He allowed the whoops of exultation, but not for long. 'We have succeeded in slipping past the French army, for they are not yet out of their winter beds. Thirty thousand Englishmen are on the way. They are coming to meet-up with us. I tell you, the invincible army of England is on the high seas now, as I speak!' Again he had to stop their roars of support.

'We march to Spain, to regain good King Pedro's rightful crown. Tell me, my soldiers, must England's army win the war without us? I tell you, my brave garrison of Poitiers, they need us to lead them, to show them how it is done. Did we not win at Crècy and at Poitiers? We fight together, we have never lost, whatever the odds.'

He was whipping them up into a froth of fervour. They were trying to cheer, but he would not let them.

'The battle is over there!' He pointed over the mountains. 'Three days march away. Shall we join them? Shall we lead them?' Now he did want their reply, but first he waited for silence once again. 'Tell me my men! What are fifteen miles of snowy passes, to seven hundred of us, when the might of the army of Old England is braving the tempest seas as we speak?'

There were shouts of 'We go! We go!'

'Our most important vow this day, is to protect the Princesses of Spain and King Pedro, for they too face this mountain. THIS IS MAN'S WORK! Let us pray.' He bent his head:

'Our Lord God, keep us this day and guide our hands justly. Your Will be done. For God, for the King and for England!'

They replied: 'For God, for the King and for England!'

The Black Prince swung his horse to face the mountains and pointed once again, 'THERE is our road to battle!'

Amidst their cheering, he silenced them for the last time. 'Come, my men of England, ARE YOU WITH ME?'

He spurred his charger towards the mountains, leaving the orderly ranks to wheel sideways and close-up, into marching order. He did not look behind. He could tell they were following him as soon as they struck-off on the very first step.

They started with 700 voices in unison. There could be no mistaking his army's marching song:

> *My...Shag-hair Cyclops come let's ply*
> *Our hefty hammers lust'ly*
> *Our hefty hammers lust'ly*

Three hours later, I was riding with my Prince and his brother at the head of the column, when a roaring noise came from way above our heads.

The avalanche struck us without warning, as a thundering noise echoed around the canyon above and below us. With pounding hearts, we turned to race back, and saw it only too well. A heavy avalanche of snow had fallen across a narrow strip around the bend behind us. It took us some time to get back to the scene because of the debris. The blockage of snow covered the path completely for a hundred yards. There could be no way through. It had cut our troops in two.

Sir Hugh Calveley was already there with a muster of spades, working to dig into the obstruction from the far side of the avalanche. He was with the stranded half of the army. 'They were my Company men,' he cried. 'My Men! If God was in need of them, they would wish to die in battle. Not like this!' Every survivor of the Free Company dismounted and knelt to pray, with one hand holding on to their restless horses.

The Black Prince arrived back. 'How long...will it take...to get...through?' he called out to the other side, kicking the snow. His voice echoing around the valley.

'Two...or three...hours, Sire!' echoed back the answer from Calveley on the other side.

'Oh God!' he groaned, 'What a disaster!' One hour could mean the difference between getting through and freezing to death. Three hours, or even two, would be a death sentence for those on the other side of the avalanche.

My Prince turned to his younger brother, 'Go! You lead the front section onwards,' he ordered. 'At least you will get half of them to our destination! Somehow we've got to reach the top of the pass by sunset, or we'll all die out here.'

John of Gaunt replied wearily, it was the obvious: 'NO! I fear it is YOU and only YOU, who can lead these men into battle now. They will follow you, even if there is only half an army left.'

The Black Prince nodded absently. He was thinking. He knew he had a decision to make on his own, because his other commander, Sir Hugh Calveley, was 100 yards away on the other side of the snowfall. Maybe he could get fifty men from the front-end to help dig out the snow from this side, while he continues on with an even smaller force. Or he could leave with all men available and hope the obstruction would take less time to dig through.

The main problem was the width of the road itself. Not everyone could work at once. Also, the roadblock was made of fresh unstable snow, which shifted under a man's weight. They would lose more soldiers if they tried to clamber over it.

John of Gaunt took action. He called six of his own guards to his side and spoke to his brother urgently: 'I have a plan. GO! GO now! Take every man you can. You never know, we could be one hour behind you. GO!' he ordered. The reply came in a curt nod. The great black stallion turned around. The marching order was given, 'Forward. Faster!'

The Black Prince could see and it did not surprise him, that the soldiers were reluctant to leave their companions.

The day had started out so well. They had at last got the clear visibility they had been waiting for. The men had been in good heart and after the first song, some of the finer voices had sung *Se Canto que Canto*, the love song of the Pyrenees Mountains, as the climb got steeper and more difficult:

Aque los montagnos .... *These wonderful mountains*
Que tant haoustes sount ....*That are just so high*
M'empachian de bese .... *Prevent me from seeing*
Mas amours ou sount .... *My love far or nigh*

Then they sang the Pyrenees Pilgrim Song:

To climb and climb up Roncesvalles,
Eight thousand steps to the top of the hill.
If you glide like a bird - you may fly,
If you walk like a pilgrim - you will touch the sky.

Prince John beckoned his aide to stay behind with him. This was my fellow
bodyguard on the journey from Poitiers. Later he told me what happened.

'You once said you like to climb rocks. Is that true?' Prince John asked
him, 'I need to get a message to Calveley.'

'Yes, Sire. But it won't help here. This snow is too soft. I'd slip right-off
the rock face. I do have another idea though. I could try tunnelling through
the centre of the snow, along the path.'

'It might cave in.'

'We'll see, Sire. The heavier the weight of snow, the more chance there is
of compaction. It should hold together if the hole is not too big, as long as
it follows the line of the inside edge of the path.'

Prince John clapped him on the back and turned to project his voice out
into the echo chamber of the ravine. 'Calveley, dig a tunnel through...on
the inside.'

After two minutes, the reply came echoing back. 'Understood, Sire!'

John of Gaunt and his six personal guards each stripped-off their armour,
took out a flat scoop from their tools and fixed it onto their staff. Alongside
his men, he dug at speed, in a frenzy, crouching low. They found the
snow easy to tunnel into, but much more difficult to move out of the way.
Gradually, they slowed to an efficient sustainable pace and worked out the
fastest method to remove the snow, as they dug. Six were digging, while

one fetched a horse to pull their manteaux along the ground, tied together. The snow was heaped on top of the cloaks and carted away by the horse. Soon they had to make the hole bigger, so that the horse could enter the tunnel.

As they burrowed deeper into the remains of the avalanche, Prince John had no time to think of the consequences if the snow did cave-in. After three-quarters of an hour, it was the Prince himself who launched his spade at the snow wall ahead and uncovered a head and a helmet, a body and a wild-eyed dead horse. Shockingly, the horse moved, its back end lifting up and up...Surely it couldn't be alive? But no, it was the tunnellers from the other end who had reached the horse as well and were pushing it through.

'STOP!' he yelled with all his force. 'Stop!' The two bodies were so large, the snow would certainly cave in if they were removed.

'Dig around them,' he ordered, trying to calculate how much width they had left on the path underneath. It was a gamble they had to take. Gingerly, they cut the tunnel towards the outside of where the path should have been. One spade-full too far and they would slide down the mountainside collapsing the tunnel.

The dead horse's frozen eyes were staring at them as they scooped away the snow beside its head. Prince John leaned over and placed two snowballs over its eyes, but the icy blindfolds slipped to the tunnel floor. On the next stroke of his scoop, he clashed spades with someone on the other side. Clearing the hole, Calveley's head came through and he saw the Prince stripped to his undergarment. They clasped shoulders, wordless, weary friends.

Within an hour and a quarter from the start, they had all got through, except for the waggons at the back. They had orders to return to St Jean Pied de Port. The Women's Army could use them to get back to Poitiers. The two young Princesses, King Pedro's daughters, were transferred on to the front of the saddles belonging to their uncles de Padilla and Prince John of Gaunt. At last, the second half of the Black Prince's army got under-way again.

Prince John had difficulty with the 13-years-old Princess's hair. He had been given Constance, the older daughter and she was obviously a practised rider. She had a tall, slight body that moulded into the swing of the stride of his horse. Her hair was shiny, black and long enough to sit on. To be comfortable, Constance twisted it at the end. Placing it behind her on the saddle, on his lap. With one hand, he easily held onto the light lithe girl in front of him, feeling he had the best of the bunch. It reminded him of eight years before, when he and Blanche had married as raw youngsters and he had first felt the suppleness of a woman. He wished he didn't have his armour on. He did not think to ask why King Pedro had not taken either of his own daughters([16]).

The ground was starting to re-freeze in the early afternoon cold. This made the conditions underfoot easier. The horses and men did not sink down so far at each step. To make a better pace, Calveley ordered every foot soldier to hang onto a horse's stirrup to tow them along.

They made faster progress. But, two hours later, the light was starting to go. Their half of the army had to find a way to increase their speed even more. Soon, the temperature would freeze the breath they inhaled, their lungs would contract with the freezing air and each one of them would come to a stop, choked into an ice-block.

The breakthrough came as soon as the horses were able to trot. The ground was slippery, but fairly solid. 'Foot soldiers, mount up! I want two men on each horse!' Calveley ordered.

'We cannot, sir,' came the replies. 'We cannot ride.' 'We're too cold, sir.'

The giant of a man was angry now. He was fearful of not being able to save these men from the terrible fate they faced. They had to force themselves to make the effort.

'You'll just have to hang on!' He ordered the riders to dismount, to help the longbowmen into the saddles and then to remount themselves. The great wooden longbows they carried were a real hazard for those trying to get a leg over their horses rump.

'Hang onto your passengers!' he called out, gripping his own incumbent with one huge arm around the soldier's scrawny waist. Calveley's other hand was guiding his horse. It was fortunate that there were just enough horses to go around, otherwise the Pyrenees would have gained many more victims as the night rolled in. At last they reached Puerto de Ibaneta, 3,000 feet high, which had been the crossing point over the mountains since the 8th Century BC. Here, Our Lady of Roncesvalles Hospital, run by Augustine monks, had room for them all.

We greeted them with disbelief, having all been convinced we would never see them again.

The only other visitors were Basques, local villagers who had come for a family burial. They carried a small round gravestone, only about a foot and a half in height and carved with an ornate cross. The body of the deceased was balanced between them, without even a coffin. In the cold, the body stuck straight out like a stiff board, frozen into shape. Two men played their own notes on a txirulas; a sort of three-holed flute.[17]

There was a warning in the Pilgrim's Guide:

You are warned. The Navarrese and the irreligious Basques, not content simply to rob pilgrims, have been known to ride them like donkeys and make them perish.

As the English soldiers sat down to eat at long oak tables that evening, we were joined by the group of Basque mourners. By tradition, they had buried their dead in the small graveyard at the side of the hospital. These people spoke in a very strange tongue.

Some men in the army of the Black Prince, could speak French, Spanish, Latin, Italian or a little Greek. These were the languages they were used to, but the sound coming from the mouths of the Basques was completely incomprehensible. We found ourselves listening to one of the least understood languages in the world. It was based directly on Palaeolithic words, rather than a European vocabulary. And it was said that the Devil only mastered three words, after seven years of study. The Basques ate quickly, stepped out into the cold and returned to their homes.

Because it was their custom to entertain pilgrims, the Augustine monks offered their visitors the story of Charlemagne and the Death of Roland. They told it in a singsong voice, accompanied by a lute:

'Charlemagne was the first great Christian warrior King. At the time of this story, he had already conquered Anjou, Aquitaine, Bavaria, Brittany, Constantinople, England, Flanders, Lombardy, Maine, Normandy, Poitou, Provence, Poland, Romania, Saxony and Scotland, all in the name of Christianity. But Spain held out, in Infidel hands.

In the year 777, Soliman ben Alazabi, the Muslim Governor of Barcelona, promised Charlemagne three strongholds south of the Pyrenees, if he could liberate his country from the tyranny of their ruler, Abd Al Rahman Al-Daklil, the Emir of Cordoba.

In 778, Charlemagne's army entered Spain. As he rode through Roncesvalles Pass, he symbolically raised the Cross of the Lord, to stay there planted till the end of time. Then, bending his knee, he turned towards Galicia and prayed to God and St James.

As his army progressed through Spain, Gerona, Barcelona, Huesca and Pamplona, every smaller town they passed, opened their doors to Charlemagne; and hundreds of Christian slaves were released. But they met fierce resistance at the town of Saragossa, where a difficult siege began, which lasted for two months. Then came the news that the whole Muslim army was marching towards them, led by the tyrannical Abdal Rahman Al-Dakil.

Charlemagne's nephew and favourite, Roland, advised him to stand and fight. Roland's father-in-law, Ganelon, a senior general, thought his son-in-law a dangerous hot-head and persuaded Charlemagne to raise the siege, withdraw and return with their proper siege weapons. They could take Saragossa the next time. The disagreement between the two advisors became personal. Ganelon conspired against Roland with the Basques.

Leading his army of 100,000 men, Charlemagne successfully re-crossed the Pyrenees. They were a few hours ahead of Roland, who commanded the 20,000 men of the slower rearguard accompanying the waggons and baggage.

As Roland's men passed through the narrowest cut of the Roncesvalles Pass, they heard a cacophony of whistles. Birdsong? In the winter? 120,000 Basques ambushed the rearguard, jumping down from the crannies and ledges above. Ganelon had told them Roland was coming. They were all killed, except for a group of sixty valiant Knights, who organised themselves on the narrow path and held out against all odds. Among these was Roland, with his magic sword called 'Durandal', given to him by an angel. Anyone he touched with the sword was killed.

The only fear he had, was of an attack from behind. They might get his magic sword before he could strike them. Legend told that he tried to break it before he died, smashing 'Durandal' repeatedly against a rock. He only managed to break the rock. The clean cleft in the mountains was called 'Roland's Breach', where he split it.

The Basques could not kill him. His sword was too magical. But the legend said he died with the effort of blowing his trumpet to summon help from Charlemagne. The veins in his head burst apart.

The King buried many of his lost troops in Roland's Chapel at Roncesvalles and called it 'Holy Spirit'. From there, their spirits would always be able to see the hole in the rocks above, Roland's Breach. Grieving, Charlemagne took his nephew Roland's body back to the Abbey at Blaye, on the shores of the Gironde, near Bordeaux.

After his defeat, Charlemagne was despondent for months. In a dream, an angel of the Lord came to him, advising him to gather together an army of 53,066 young girls. He dressed them as soldiers and trained them to the lance. They re-entered Spain and the Muslim Kings were afraid. They preferred to surrender and convert to Christianity, rather than fight an army of women.

The legend grew. The girls returned to their homes, stopping to rest on the way. They planted their lances in a field, whereupon a miracle took place: the lances had grown branches and leaves the next morning.'

Ever since the time of that great Christian warrior King, pilgrims had planted crosses on the hill where Charlemagne had done so, and knelt in tribute to Roland and his dead soldiers. The Black Prince and his army also placed a cross to remember their perished comrades. Early spring was no time to be in the Pyrenees Mountains.

There were beds for all of us. The hospital was vast and empty at this time of year. The Commanders horses were stabled and the rest were corralled in the yard. Every man and every horse lay down where he was, except for Sir Hugh Calveley's giant charger, which was too large for its stable. It had to sleep standing up with its knees locked. This was the last time the army had shelter before the battle. It was the final night of comfort upon this earth for many of our valiant comrades.

The Black Prince, whose life revolved around assessing acceptable risks and casualty rates as commander of the army, called for a headcount before dawn the next morning. He learned that 51 men had been killed or seriously injured, 38 of whom had fallen down the mountain, as well as six who were missing and must have been buried in the snow. Seven had frostbite, unable to continue. They had lost 45 horses as a result of the avalanche, 38 having been swept away and six buried. The remaining two had heart attacks. Three horses were lame, but could be replaced from the hospital stables.

The Black Prince did his sums and reckoned the losses at under six per cent. That was a very acceptable figure, considering what they had been through. 'We can only hope,' he said to me before we mounted our black horses, 'and pray, that the battle ahead will be won with so few fatalities.'

Unfortunately, it was not.

Chapter 23 - The Gamble

King Edward sent over the main force from England, via Plymouth to Bilbao on the north coast of Spain. They landed on March the 26th, spending a further two days gathering supplies. On the 29th they embarked on the four-day march to the pre-arranged rendezvous point at Logrono, on the frontier between the two kingdoms of Navarre and Castile. There, they waited for the arrival of the Black Prince.

Travelling with the English troops was Geoffrey Chaucer, who carried a capitulation treaty for the enemy Trastamara to sign, when he was defeated. This awarded him certain lands in France, provided he surrendered his claim to King Pedro's crown. There were also treaties for his supporters and other Kings to sign. Peace treaties with England.

Also accompanying the English army, was King Edward's personal valuer, to assess the quality and quantity of the Templar Treasure to be taken from Santiago de Compostela. He had been instructed to load it on to waggons for the trip back to England. He was to take enough to pay the army, the garrison from Poitiers and Sir Hugh Calveley's Free Company, plus enough to make the King of England think that the whole adventure was worth his time. Say, ten times the cost of the army.

Three days later, their Commander-in-Chief, their beloved Black Prince arrived on his black stallion. He rode (just like St Francis of Assisi some 140 years before) past the three defensive towers and over the twelve arches of the stone bridge across the Ebro River, into Logrono. We rode behind him.

He had managed to join the two armies, one from England and the other from Poitiers. Now, they were a formidable force of over 30,000 men. They had never lost a battle under the Black Prince. Morale was high and their commander was well.

News of the English army landing in Bilbao had taken the enemy, Trastamara, by surprise. His spies in England had been tricked with false information that King Edward was about to fight in France. The usurper himself was in Burgos, the capital city of Castile, not far away. But his supporters and their soldiers would take longer to muster. Moreover, Bertrand du Guesclin, his indispensable general, with his hired band of French mercenaries, was unaware and unprepared. Caught on the wrong side of the Pyrenees. This was exactly how the Black Prince wanted it. He had gambled that General du Guesclin and his mercenaries had returned home to France for the winter.

Having achieved the element of surprise, the English found themselves with a few days to prepare for the battle ahead. The priority was to scout the battleground. It was all very well picking-out a suitable place for his army to fight, from a book about the legend of Charlemagne and Roland. But now he had to check it out.

In 778, when Charlemagne brought his army into Spain, most of the towns and villages opened their doors and prisons to him, releasing their Christian slaves. The town of Najera was ruled by a giant called Ferragut. Legend said he was a Moorish Lord and nine feet tall. Ferragut not only had Christian slaves, but also boasted of Christian Knights in his prisons.

Seeing that the giant was cumbersome and heavy on his feet, Charlemagne gave his nephew permission to challenge the giant to a personal duel. Roland taunted the giant from the top of the hill (ever since called Poyo de Roldan). After several attacks, Roland could not outwit his adversary. Both men were tired and arranged a binding truce, that both kept while they slept.

Before they commenced to fight once more, they started a religious debate, both agreeing that the victor in the duel would be the holder of *The Truth*. They started to attack each other again and finally by the grace of *Lady Luck*,

Roland managed to drive his dagger into Ferragut's navel. This proved to be the giant's only weak point, for he was covered in clever flexible armour. Charlemagne and his army entered Najera, freeing the captive Christian knights and slaves.

The question remained: was the Poyo de Roldan as suitable for two armies as it had been for Roland's man-to-man duel?

I, Petit-roi was still beside my Prince, the Commander-in-Chief, when he took his generals to Roland's hill, near Najera, to find the answer. It was six miles away and I remember that King Pedro was not with us. On the way, we passed the hospital of St John of Acre at Navette, with five decorated arches in its magnificent doorway. Undoubtedly this hospital would be where we would have to carry the wounded, bury our dead and mourn our comrades after the battle to come, for Najera was close by.

We had been told that the Poyo de Roldan was a grassy rounded hill, set in the pasture on the right hand side of the pilgrim road. But we found out something even more important: there were TWO similar grassy rounded hills, half a mile apart. Which one was Roland's?

They looked alike. Both were over 250 feet high, with a single tree three-quarters of the way up. The difference was that the one on the right was topped with a barely visible, overgrown, yellow/brown rock. At ground level, behind, there was a strip of narrow spruce forest, which ran between one hill and the other. Both hills were broad, about three-quarters of a mile around the base, but the most interesting detail was revealed when we inspected the back of the right-hand hill. It was lightly wooded, with scrub that camouflaged a wide pit. This was a large hole in the side of the hill, where it had been mined for yellow iron pyrites, known as *Fools Gold*.

The mine could have been Roman. It was so deep, that no trees could be seen from the front or sides of the hill. No wonder Charlemagne chose it for a battle. There would be room to hide his cavalry. The other hill had no tell-tale rock and no mine.

'I want a path made, in and out of this hole!' ordered the Black Prince. 'And

251

I want the trees removed, except for the outside ring. My scouts tell me that we have four days to play with. I want it done in two! I want the road blocked, pilgrims and all. They can be corralled inside the town walls. I want no spies to see what we are doing. Tell the men to approach from the back, out of sight, through the spruce forest behind.

'There is just one action I definitely DO want everyone to be able to see, so they can go back and report it to our enemies. I want you to build me large trebuchets and a battering ram. By the way…They don't have to work!'

When we returned to the camp, we found that King Pedro and his daughters were missing! It was Prince John who pointed them out in the distance, climbing the rocky path, along a high ridge. They were making their way up a tortuous stepped path to Clavijo Castle, which overlooked our camp at Logrono. Its massive walls dominated the view over a wide valley below, stretching to the south and the west for over fifty miles. West was towards Santiago de Compostela.

The Black Prince snapped, 'I want him HERE! Where we can keep an eye on him. Where is the guard I left with him?'

'He is watching him from here, Sire.'

'Well go and tell the King. I won't have him wandering off.'

'We understand it is his own place, Sire. Clavijo is his castle.'

'I forgot he's in his own country,' replied the Prince, hesitating… 'Clavijo is NOT his base, I know it isn't.'

'They say he has a woman there. Well two actually, mother and daughter.' The brothers laughed out loud. What a surprise! At that moment a messenger rode up with a timely message: 'King Pedro is sheltering his daughters in the castle,' he said. 'He will await your instructions there.'

They noted there was no invitation to take a comfortable bed, or eat with him. 'Poor girls!' muttered Prince John. 'Now, I order you to get King Pedro down here, for I need him in battle. Whether he likes it or not.'[18]

'At this moment, we must find out where the enemy is,' the Black Prince turned to his leaders, 'and watch out for spies.'

The report came back. Trastamara was in the city of Burgos.[19] The gamble the Black Prince was prepared to take, was that Trastamara would not wish to subject his capital, to a destructive siege. His spies would already have told him of the arrival of the two English forces at Logrono. Without a doubt, he would be content to stay safely behind the massive walls, until more of his army could join him. In particular, his Commander in Chief, Bertrand du Guesclin, with his 250 French mercenaries. But it would be at least another two weeks before they arrived.

Du Guesclin was a clever and devious practitioner of warfare and, like Sir Hugh Calveley with his English Free Company, he brought the best and most expensive professional soldiers to the battlefield. Though numerically few, they invariably swung the fortunes of war, in favour of whoever paid , them. Indeed, Du Guesclin and Calveley were firm friends. There was much respect between them. No wonder King Pedro had lost his crown, when both mercenary leaders had fought together for the usurper Trastramara.

If the methods and politics of the mercenary leaders had been inspected, they would have been revealing. They would even create acts of war for any paid-up King or mogul, but somehow they contrived never to fight each other. If they happened to be on the same battlefield, on opposing sides, they made sure they did not clash. Officially, they both needed their own monarch's approval, but often neither the English nor the French King knew where they were, or who they were fighting for at any one time.

The Black Prince had spectacularly succeeded in getting his own troops over the mountains. Also, his soldiers had cleverly filled in the avalanche behind them. Thus, he had cut Du Guesclin off, on the other side of the Pyrenees. The enemy Commander in Chief would delay any plan to muster his French mercenaries at St Jean de Pied de Port and attempt to cross the mountain passes, until the snow was manageable, probably in mid-April. Usually Trastamara relied on Du Guesclin's leadership.

The question was, how could the English army persuade Trastamara to leave Burgos and come-out to fight, before reinforcements and the French mercenaries arrived?

The Black Prince had formulated his battle plans as he rode along

THE UNBELIEVABLE MYSTERY OF THE BLACK PRINCE'S RUBY

the route from Roncesvalles. He had three objectives. **Firstly**, to draw Trastamara and his army out of Burgos, within one week. **Secondly**, to intercept any reinforcements travelling towards Burgos, from King Charles of Navarre at Pamplona. And **finally**, to trick Trastamara into fighting on the battleground of the Black Prince's own choice, Poyo de Roldan, where the English were laying their traps in advance.

He knew the usurper's spies would be lurking around the town of Logrono, reporting back on the size and strength of the English camp. Loudly and in full public view, trees were logged from a wood nearby and dragged into a pasture beside the pilgrim path. Here, a noisy group of soldiers worked on the logs. They hammered loudly and sang at the tops of their voices, while building three siege-engines and a battering ram, within two days. The engines had wheels stripped from local waggons and long throwing arms, meant to pitch stone or rocks at defensive battlements. The only difference between these imitation trebuchets and the genuine article was that they were built with fixed balancing arms, instead of free-swinging ones. They were decoys. The machines could not have thrown the mayor's cat for three feet, let alone a heavy rock 1,000 feet. What is more, they could not travel the least distance, let alone the two days march to Burgos. They would have toppled over the first stone they met, because of the size of their wheels. They would normally be equipped with small wooden wheels for stability. But they did LOOK fearsome enough.

The Prince gambled that the Trastamaran spies would be convinced enough to fly back to Burgos with the news that the three siege engines and battering ram were ready. And that the army was preparing to march on Burgos itself, equipped with provisions for a terrible siege.

My master the Black Prince, had in the meantime, sent me out on a mission with just twelve men. We were not in uniform and had orders to spy out the land at Pamplona. Others were sent to Burgos, to mingle in the town. King Charles of Navarre, Trastamara's ally, had heard the unexpected news that the English garrison from Poitiers had been seen to by-pass his town. Now he was busy gathering his soldiers to join-up with Trastamara at Burgos.

'Sire, he is planning to slip past Logrono via a forest to the south, out of our sight,' I reported back to my Prince two days later. He laughed at my appearance, for I had rubbed my fair hair in mud to disguise myself. It had occurred to me, that King Charles of Navarre might recognise me if I was captured and believe that I was the Black Prince.

Sir Hugh Calveley and his mercenaries were ordered to travel quietly by night, with muffled hooves, to the intended battleground at Poyo de Roldan. They camped in the forest of spruce trees and commenced their preparations, which included the access path into their hiding-hole at the back of Roland's Hill. They were to be the surprise element. Their skills would be wasted, if the rest of the English army got drawn into a battle elsewhere, or got out-manoeuvred themselves. What a gamble!

At last, after five days, we were able to rejoice. The news from the other group of spies came back. Trastamara and 22,000 troops and cavalry, had left Burgos and were heading eastwards towards us. We had drawn them out!

As my Prince had predicted, they wanted to protect their city of royal tombs and pilgrims, from a siege which would ruin much and kill many. By the time the message reached the English commander, our cavalry had already surrounded the King of Navarre's 3,000 foot soldiers, in the forest south of Logrono. The officers were executed on the spot and the men were given the option of stripping themselves of their arms and armour, or being killed. They chose to strip and ran back to Navarre. We loved it.

If they had been wise, Trastamara's army from Burgos should have travelled just a few miles from their capital city and then stopped and waited for either the English enemy, or for their Navarrese or French reinforcements, whichever came first. They did neither, they marched on. Why were they so foolish to let the English enemy dictate the site of the battle to come?

The answer was because my Prince was a clever tactician. The enemy repeatedly saw the English forces in the distance, drawing them on. Their advance scouts went missing. They had no idea that the cavalry ahead were deliberately teasing them. The English allowed themselves some minor skirmishes on the second day. Several of our men were lost, but it was all for a greater purpose, which was to encourage Trastamara into a trap.

If only the Usurper could have had his Commander in Chief, Bertrand de Guerclin, in charge. He would never have fallen for such a tactic. As it was, Trastamara believed that he was pursuing a retreating army. This was one way to defeat King Pedro. Now, he believed he would get to kill him at last.

Chapter 24 - The Battle of Nájera

In the early morning of the third day, Trastamara's Castillian army arrived at Najera. They found the English lined-up, waiting for them outside the nearby village of Navarrete, around the Poyo de Roldan. At last they could see the English were going to turn around and make a fight of it. This was the proper way to decide the fate of a crown. Trastamara was fully confident of victory, especially since the number of enemy troops looked not much more than his own.

He knew the formal ritual ahead, the age-old convention before a battle. Each side would be allowed time to choose their own ground and line-up their troops in their chosen order. He was quite content to occupy the second hill. That was his half of the battleground. The enemy had already got charge of the first. He did not see the difference between the two hills.

The fighting would not start without a Parley between the two sides. Peace terms would be ritually offered and were always rejected at this stage. Much pomp and blowing of trumpets followed, before the bloody butchery could begin.

The only tactical decision that Trastamara took before the fighting began, was to send scouts out to investigate the narrow spruce forest that ran behind the two hills. On hearing the report that there were no enemy troops to be seen there, he arranged to deploy 1,000 of his foot soldiers around the back. He would blow his distinctive low-pitched horn as a signal, as soon as the mayhem of war had commenced. They were to attack the enemy hill from behind.

Every detail of this battle was orchestrated from the start. First of all, full courtesy had to be shown, each to his enemy. This was, after all, a fight for a crown, a kingly contest. All colours: flags, pennants, matching shields and horse-coverings, crowns, decorated armour and fashioned helmets, were paraded in front of their opponents, each in turn around their own hill.

The English displayed themselves as if it was a tournament, adorned in all their finery, with cavalry knights and noblemen carrying their family shields and wearing tunics over their armour. All were in the colours and designs of their own coats-of -arms. The colours were predominantly red and yellow, though there were white, mid-blue and gold on display.

They followed twenty trumpeters, blowing their horns from horseback and twenty drummer boys, beating the time as they marched. Next came the royal standard bearer, with the lions upon the yellow-and-red flag of England. The Black Prince was in front of his two commanders, Prince John of Gaunt and Lord de Lucy from Egremont, who led the pike-men; followed by King Pedro.

The noblemen came next, then the knights and the cavalry. Last of all the longbow men, displaying their six-foot bows, showed off their fearsome weapons. The English only took half an hour to parade around Roland's Hill, because thousands of foot soldiers did not join in. Those without adornments, were clearly not invited to the party.

Commanders and noblemen had elaborate helmet covers. The Black Prince wore his Italian-made black armour, decorated with fleur-de-lis and lions, with his victory badges commemorating the battles of Crécy and Poitiers around his hips. Everyone else's armour was grey, silver coloured. He wore the *Black Prince's Crown*, specially designed to go around the outside of his black pointed helmet. For display purposes only, he proudly wore his personal symbol of a fur-clad lion, around the top section of his helmet, attached inside the circle of the crown.

Prince John wore a stuffed peregrine falcon on his helmet.

A dozen courtiers, known as Kings of Arms, stood at the rear. They were not dressed in armour, because they were not there to fight. They were official observers of a battle, watching from a distance and reporting on the casualties of knights, by recognising all their coats of arms. Running alongside all this finery, were twelve senior heralds of the royal household. They also carried messages between the two sides. Their rules of conduct were strict. They were not allowed to act as spies. These men wore short tabards in the royal livery, with hose for easy running. They would be the ones who gave the signal to commence the battle and they would be the ones who counted the dead at the end.

The Spanish looked on at this procession and happily did their turn around their own hill. This was led by Trastamara wearing the disputed crown, followed by his nobles. This time, the procession took a lot longer. All the Spanish soldiers joined in. All twenty-two thousand of them.

Pilgrims on the way to Santiago de Compostela stood all day beside their route, transfixed by the sight of such splendour and colours, no doubt hypnotised by the raw promise of blood. That day, they forgot the ritual of putting one foot in front of the other and simply ignored their mission. It was as if their lives were suspended for a day. The townspeople of Najera, two miles away, had seen the Spanish army pass. Gradually, in twos and threes, they added themselves to the back of the marching line, following on behind. They were not going to miss this! They arrived in droves and crowded behind the defensive walls of the village of Naverrete, jostling along the parapets to get a better view of the entertainment. This was something to tell the next generation. Some started moaning, when they realised that it might be their own sons about to fight out there.

By mid-day, battle still could not commence. First, a formal *peace* had to be offered. In the space between the two armies, with one on each hill, a tent with a carpet, a table and two chairs was painstakingly set-up. This was for the *signing*, if there was to be one.

Trastamara and his two commanders rode forward, carrying their document and met face to face with the Black Prince, King Pedro and Chaucer, carrying the English peace plan. Chaucer read out the main details:

Trastamara is offered land in France,
if he renounces the crown of Castile.
King Pedro's claim to the throne was not disputed.
He is a legitimate son of his father and Trastamara is not.

Trastamara offers the English in return,
to execute King Pedro and not return to Spanish soil.
(He went on to diatribe about the unsuitability of Pedro as King)

Both sides refused to sign, withdrew to their positions and the tent was removed. Tunics, fanciful helmet covers and their crowns were taken off. Flags were placed standing at either side, to be claimed later by whichever side was the victor.

At the top of the Spanish hill were the usurper and his messengers. Down the sides were half of his foot soldiers. Around the base were the cavalry and in the front ranks were the rest of the foot soldiers. The Spanish archers placed themselves in between their lines, ready to start their running scissors movement. It was a tactic they had learnt from the Moors. They called it *Las Bourras* (the executioner). It was a manoeuvre performed at the run, by their long-range bowmen, who were equipped with standard short bows for ease of movement. They had arrows which were twice the usual length, with red-tips with what the Arabs called *az-zarnik* (the natural mineral *realgar*, or red arsenic). A conventional arrow fired by the short bow, had a range of about 150 feet. More if it was flighted. By using the longer arrows and weighing them correctly, they could shoot over 250 feet. They killed any living thing the arrows touched, either instantly, or sometime later from poisoning. This manoeuvre was made all the more devastating because of its mobile nature.

Usually, as the range of these specialist arrows was further than that of most enemy weapons, the Spanish/Moor tactic always allowed them to fire first. Three rows of archers at a time ran, through the front ranks of foot soldiers, from both wings. They stopped and let loose their volley of deadly arrows, some kneeling, some standing. They fired sideways into the centre of the enemy's front line, striking them where their armour was less protective.

As the next three lines of archers took their places, the first wave ran sideways along the front of their own soldiers, firing towards the outer wings of the enemy line as they went. They could fire about ten arrows each, before they turned back and re-entered their own lines. They continued running in a circle and re-entered the fray, where they had started.

This Scissors tactic prevented the opposing force of foot soldiers from moving forward, as they were assailed from each side at once. The standard reply was to charge the Spanish with the cavalry, anything to bridge the gap and bring them within range. However, this tactic led to appalling loses of men and horses. For as soon as the cavalry reached the Spanish lines, the archers had run back out of sight, to reveal that the front line of Spanish foot soldiers had planted their lances, with their tips angled towards the enemy. The charging horses had their bellies ripped open.

Trastamara, previously guessing that the English might take-up the cause of King Pedro, had been training his army in their barracks at Burgos all winter, perfecting their scissors movement.

But Spanish troops had never met the longbow men of England, with their six-foot bows made of tough bending yew. The Spanish may have been proud of the 250 feet range of their poisoned arrows, but had they realised that the English longbow could shoot at least 200 Yards, they might have been less keen to run to the front, in ever-changing circles.

King Pedro was ensconced on top of the rock, on the Poyo de Roldan. He had left his girls behind at Clavijo Castle, with de Padilla to guard them. Two of us were assigned to guard Pedro. Myself, Petit-roi and Prince John's bodyguard.

'I trust you most. Keep a close eye on King Pedro!' ordered the Black Prince. 'I will not allow him to leave the battlefield,' I protested. 'I want to fight, Sire!'

'I CANNOT afford to lose you.'

'Let me protect your back, Sire.'

'Did you not know, Petit-roi…I AM INDESTRUCTIBLE!' He mocked

261

me.

We had a good view of the battle. To King Pedro's very obvious relief, he was not required to fight, but he did have to be present if they wanted to crown him later. He had longbowmen around him in a semicircle. They were so numerous that they covered most of the slopes. At the base were the foot soldiers in the middle, with cavalry on both wings. At the head of each wing were the two royal brothers, the Black Prince and John of Gaunt.

Also, there was one other unit of cavalry on the English side, but they were completely invisible. They were hiding in the old mine at the back of the hill. It was Sir Hugh Calveley's Free Company of mercenaries. Only THEY could teach their horses not to whinny and give away their hiding place.

If only the usurper Trastamara had the assistance of his usual general, Bertrand de Guerchin, the French mercenary leader. He might have remarked on the absence of his old friend Calveley and suspected a trick. He would also have told him about the incredible range of the English longbow. Undoubtedly, he would have moved the Spanish army front-line back one hundred paces, out of harms way.[20]

In front of the Poyo de Roldan, at last, the heralds officially started the battle with a blast from the trumpets. Immediately an excited clamour arose from the Spanish side. Throughout the day, as it unfolded, they would curse, shout and encourage each other, yelling constantly. The level of noise was the sound of an undisciplined army and it added to the fog of war, where every soldier could only fight the man in front of him. He could hear no orders above the din and was not able to attack elsewhere, swing the line, or even to stop fighting. He was only required to kill, or be killed. Sometimes, if they failed to recognise a uniform, they killed their own men.

The English, by contrast, fought silently and moved forward together in groups of twenty men, swathing through the enemy line. They fought in front of them, at the sides and behind them, all at once. They fought as a unit. In order to swing their line of attack, a raised pennant at the end of a sword was held high from the centre of each group and pointed in the direction of the new attack. This message was passed down the line. Each unit would close-up with the next, to replenish their numbers, keep their shape and to make their change in direction.

As soon as the Spanish order was given to commence battle, Trastamara blew his low-pitched horn to signal the 1,000 foot soldiers, despatched to the spruce forest. Ordered to attack and kill King Pedro from behind. He noted that Pedro had archers around him and that they were facing the front.

The Spanish archers began their scissors movement and started running to the front of their lines to gain ground, bringing the enemy into shooting range. The English longbow men could not only shoot two and a half times further, but they could fire their arrows over the heads of their own soldiers, because they were still standing on a hill. From this position they had a huge advantage.

Volley after volley of English arrows struck the running Spanish archers, before they themselves could get into range. Within a few minutes, 500 enemy archers were dead and the rest were unable to come out and face the barrage. Their front-line soldiers was starting to turn around, to escape the torrent of arrows.

Trastamara had heard nothing yet from his troops in the wood. He ordered his foot soldiers to retreat and his cavalry to charge. Anything to get to grips with the enemy.

Suddenly, we could see the danger for our troops. From the top of our hill, it was obvious that the balance of the Spanish army was different from the English. Trastamara had three times as many cavalry as we had.

But the Black Prince read his intentions and swung both wings of his cavalry towards the centre, to the front of his own troops on foot, in order to protect them. He did not want them subjected to a full attack by the enemy cavalry. Not just yet.

Now the two sides were truly locked in battle.

There was something fascinating about watching our English army at its best, when it was attacking on all sides. The English cavalry formed around their Prince, whose black armour had the distinct disadvantage of making him the very first target of an enemy attack. The enemy cavalry were numerically three to one. The clash of combat resounded off the walls of the fortified village of Navarrete. The watchers gasped in awe. They could barely hear themselves above the noise of battle. The clash of lance against armour, the sharp bite of sword against sword resounded. Then it was sword against armour and finally, armour against armour, as even the fallen cavalrymen clashed body to body, each in their own deadly, mortal combat. Even when they had killed their opponent, the soldiers must turn to do it again and again.

They dragged their exhausted bodies to face a new foe at every turn, dripping with sweat from every crevice in the armour, driven on by pure adrenaline and the will to live. There were loose horses, dying horses, men and horses screaming. All the normal, grotesque, deafening noises of war.

We saw Trastamara's mistake now. He did not follow-up his cavalry with his foot soldiers. The English archers were pinning them back out of range. They were unwilling to move. He should have come down from the top of his hill and led his men forward at the run. At least half of them would have got through. Enough to overwhelm the hard-pressed English cavalry, many of whom were fighting dismounted.

Trastmara must have known that this would be his best option. But he probably reasoned that there was no point in exposing himself, when he was the one who wished to go on wearing the crown.

It was John of Gaunt who had a respite around him first. He looked up and thrust his lance in the air with his helmet on the top. It seemed a foolhardy action in the middle of a battle, but it was the agreed signal for the English foot-soldiers to advance. The beleaguered cavalry badly needed their assistance.

Trastamara decided to deploy another 2,000 troops through the spruce forest, even though he had heard no trumpet signal from the first wave. Certainly, he could still see King Pedro on the top of the other hill, so they had not got to him yet. Their reception committee awaited them, hiding in the mine. But there were fewer than 150 of them, the Free Company having lost so many in the Pyrenees.

Sir Hugh Calveley was responsible for the situation and he knew that

King Pedro was vulnerable from behind. In fact, he and the Black Prince had planned it that way, to make Pedro himself the target. The plan was to withdraw him when the time was right.

The narrow forest covered some two miles in length, but it was only 100 yards wide. By his calculations, the enemy would only get 50 men walking in a row, for no doubt they wished to stay hidden from English view. Over rough ground, pushing branches and undergrowth apart as quietly as they could, each man would need at least five feet of space in front of him. What the Spaniards had not been able to see, was that Calveley's men had cut down the trees along the far side of the strip of forest, funnelling all the soldiers into a narrower section only ten yards wide, which stopped abruptly beside the back of Roland's Hill. There were no trees at all for 200 yards, though this could not be seen either from the side, or the front of the enemy's hill.

The enemy soldiers were caught unawares. They started to pile-up, one behind another, ten deep, in the ten-yard wide section, delay and indecision plaguing their movements. Either they had to expose themselves, run for 200 yards with no cover, climb up the hill to kill King Pedro and escape; or they must retreat. From where they stood, peering out of the undergrowth of the forest, the hill looked abandoned at the back, though they could still just see King Pedro near the top. He was inviting bait. But we were there too. It was our job to see that he was always within sight of the enemy, but out of range. As they watched, we moved him about on the hill, dangling the carrot.

Suddenly, ten at a time, they broke cover, crouched over, running quietly, for they wore no armour. They were spaced closely behind each other and they spread-out, crossing the open ground, heading for the whole span of the back of our hill. They planned to attack en-masse.

Within two minutes, we found that 600 Spanish troops had exposed themselves without cover and had already reached the bottom of the hill. By the time the first line had clambered half way up, all 1,000 of their unit had left the forest and were in the open.

We had to keep our nerve. I could see that King Pedro was starting to panic. I knew what he was capable of, he might try to kill us, his guards and flee if he could. I swung my sword and touched its tip against his gullet and growled: 'Stay, or I'll kill you. We are under orders, Sire!' He froze, and did not try to move again. Now I knew he would watch me. I was his other enemy and I dare not drop my guard.

It was then, when the enemy soldiers were out in the open, that Calveley's men picked them off with their own arrows. The trumpeter was among the first to die. The longbow men at the top received their expected orders from the mercenary leader. They turned around, and let fly a barrage of killer shafts, aiming at the enemy troops furthest away, to prevent any escape. They loaded, and re-loaded from their quivers. The bodies piled up, until there was nobody left alive. Calveley ordered his cavalry to mount up, and led them downhill to the clearing.

The second wave of 2,000 Spanish troops entered the forest, and had to wait until they got to the end, before they realised the fate of their comrades, whose bodies littered the clearing ahead. If Trastamara had sent his mounted troops through the woods, they might have fared better; but foot soldiers were usually preferred when the thickness of the undergrowth was not known.

Calveley heard the crashing among the trees as the next wave of enemy soldiers entered the forest, and he led his men at the gallop unseen along the outside of the wood. They turned sharply inwards before they got near the Spaniards' own hill, and blocked the way back for the 2,000 troops.

He knew that if the enemy advanced into the clearing, the English longbow men's arrows could reach them. If they retreated, they were funnelled into equal oblivion. Realising they had little chance, the Spaniards panicked. Many of them broke out of the line of trees at the back, and tried to escape with no cover. Here they found a precipice, with a river far below. There was no way around. Many jumped and died on the rocks. Some were luckier, and landed on their softer comrades. They ran home.

Calveley made sure there was not one single messenger left to report back to the Spanish leader. Then, as bold as brass, he quietly led his men to the far end of the forest at the rear of the Spanish lines, and halted at the side of the enemy's hill. Nobody realised he was there. He ordered his horses to lie down.

Trastamara thought his troops had succeeded, because King Pedro was gone! He was no longer on top of the other hill. This view was strengthened when a whole company of dead horses was pointed out to him. They were by the entrance to the forest.

They were not his cavalry. His forest troops must have killed them. Good for them. Again, if only du Gesclin, the French mercenary leader had been with him, he would have known that 'dead horses' were a particular Calveley trick. Though the English Free Company had fought for him the last time, Trastamara had never seen these tactics before. He was completely taken in.

In the meantime, the Black Prince and his men were gradually pressing the enemy on to the back foot. He felt the first glimmer that the tide of war was turning. 'They're signalling to you, Sire,' one of his troop yelled across to him. An insistent trumpet blast stood out from the background noise of the battle. It came from behind him on the wing, where he had first lined up with his cavalry. It was the agreed message he was waiting for. Again and again the trumpet sounded. It was the signal from Calveley to his Commander in Chief, to come and join up with his Free Company.

'Take command here!' he shouted to his Commander, Anthony de Lucy, who was fighting beside him.

As arranged, he extracted a hundred men from his mounted unit out of the line, in order to turn them to gallop up their hill behind them.

We were still guarding King Pedro, and my Prince obviously intended to head straight towards us. We watched, as he swung around; and, by chance, he met the cutting side of a Spanish lance.

Chapter 25 - Saved by the Blood of Christ

We were watching from the top of the hill, when the Spanish lance sliced across the Black Prince's chest. If it had been a full-on thrust, in spite of his armour, it would have killed him. The lance had been well sharpened and it caught his breastplate, dented it, right in his stomach.

I saw my Prince collapse on to his horse's wither, with his weight in front of the saddle. His brother, who was next to him, was quick-witted enough to grab the edge of his armour and prevent him from falling. Another Knight snatched hold of the horse's reins and pulled it out of the fray. He started to lead the horse uphill, towards us. Frantic to help, I slid down the hill.

At this stage there were two important considerations: **firstly**, the Black Prince had to be attended to and **secondly**, the royal cavalry must ride on to support Calveley. For the sake of the battle, the second action was the most pressing.

Not caring a scrap for either royal crowns or family feuds, Prince John stayed with his brother and handed the temporary command over to another. Quickly, he called ten of the Knights to surround them. He did not want English troops to see their *Commander in Chief* gravely injured. Then, he ordered the remaining 90 cavalry to gallop around to the back of the enemy hill and report to Calveley, for further instructions.

John of Gaunt and I between us, let the slumped weight of the Black Prince down on to the grass. We laid him on his back. Immediately he started convulsing, trembling and jumping inside his armour. I struggled to remove his helmet and unstrapped his dented breastplate.

When Prince John lifted the visor, he suddenly realised his brother's twitching and jumping were not because he was dead, with his nerve-ends severed. No, he was alive, but fighting for every breath. He had been struck just below the chest and was severely winded. I was astonished, for a blow like that would normally kill a man.

I reached in and inserted my hand in order to remove pressure from the stomach area, to help his breathing. I felt a square of leather next to his skin and removed it out of the way. Withdrawing it, I discovered a damaged leather pouch in my hand. I gave it to Prince John to hold and he saw immediately what was inside. He gave a quick intake of breath. It was the Blood of Christ stone.

The Black Prince had carried it into battle as his talisman. It had indeed completed its task. The Ruby had saved his life, by deflecting the edge of the enemy lance away from his heart.

The only obvious sign of damage that we could see, was an abrasive knock to the jaw. I started massaging his stomach, for he was still in distress. My Prince yelled out in agony. I could feel that his ribs were broken and withdrew my hand hurriedly. No wonder it hurt. I did not want to make it worse. I knew if he bled from the mouth at this stage, then we would know that his lungs were pierced.

He was amazing. It took barely five minutes for King Edward's eldest son to catch his breath again, gingerly put his armour back on, remount and join his cavalry at the back of the enemy hill. It must have been agony for him to ride, with all the jolting up and down in the saddle. But he did not flinch. Occasionally he put his hand to his jaw. 'I swear I will ennoble anyone who will rid me of my toothache,' he announced loudly, riding back to battle.

Just after the Prince was wounded, while some of the cavalry were being removed from the front battle line, a gap was momentarily opened up. Into the hole in the English defence, poured ten enemy soldiers. They isolated Anthony de Lucy, the new commander and hacked him off his horse. The royal brothers had turned away and were not aware he had been slain. His second in command was shocked into action and took charge. He gathered help and rescued the body from being hacked into ever more tiny pieces.

Trastamara, on the top of his hill, ordered all the troops around him to advance. Five hundred followed him down the hill. He mounted his horse and led the men himself, having spied the break in the ranks of the enemy, where the horses lay dead. This would be his finest hour. He was convinced that King Pedro was taken and now he would conclude his business here. What a victory this would be.

Trastamara ran his men across to the side of the field and cried 'Charge!'

He ran them right into Calveley's trap. The *dead* horses suddenly rose up, with their riders attached. The Spanish felt they were fighting ghosts. They were terrified. Then Trastamara heard a noise from above and looked up the hill. He saw King Pedro laughing at him. He digested the terrible truth in one glance. He saw that the full weight of the English cavalry was galloping down the slope, to cut them off from behind. They, indeed, were no ghosts.

The odds were still stacked against the English, but most of the Spanish troops made no fight of it. This was not war, this was magic! This was the devil's work. They fled. Many did not escape.

Trastamara surrendered and was captured alive. He was disarmed, brought to watch proceedings from the rock on Roland's Hill and his armour removed.

As royal guards, we were no longer needed for King Pedro, so we were assigned to watch Trastamara. John of Gaunt's young man, who liked rock climbing, was my fellow guard once more. Just then, my master rode up. He was looking weary. He replaced me with his favourite aide, a boy of only sixteen years old.

'I want you to take my place, I need to rest.' He must have been hurting badly. He walked off the field, passing me his helmet, with the three feathers as he limped away. His soldiers closed about him in protection. I climbed onto his charger, the fiery beast.

The heralds ordered the trumpeters to blow for the end of the battle. The noise was distinctive. Slowly, everyone ceased fighting. Some wanted time to finish-off the enemy soldiers they had at their mercy. They all looked up

CHAPTER 25 - SAVED BY THE BLOOD OF CHRIST

to get the verdict. King Trastamara had conceded defeat by his capture.

'King Pedro will be crowned King of Castile!' the King of Arms announced.

The victors lined up, with the two Princes (one of whom was me) and Pedro at the front. Slowly, we rode over to where the enemy flags were waving in the breeze. One by one, we picked them up, broke the poles in half and threw them to the ground. Then we rode to the centre.

The King of Arms collected the crown of Castile from its resting-place and proceeded to place it on King Pedro's head.

Time passed quickly, as the congratulations continued on the field. The heralds started their gruesome task of identifying the bodies of knights and noblemen, from the coats of arms on their shields and tunics. Numbers were counted. Fathers, sons and family members were mourned, for many of the knights were related to each other.

It was three quarters of an hour, before John of Gaunt gathered twenty of his troop and marched them smartly up to the top of the hill, in order to escort ex-King Trastamara into custody and eventually into exile. But all he found at the top, were the bodies of the two royal guards. His brother's young favourite aide and his own rock-climbing bodyguard. Trastamara, a prisoner of trust, had used a hidden knife to murder the guards.

'It could have been me! It should have been me.'

Apparently he had run down into the mine and found a way out by the river, far below the forest. Trastamara had escaped.

I broke the news to my resting Prince and handed him back his armour and his horse once more. He looked grey. The fury of the two Princes was black, instant and cruel in its intentions. They swore to plunder and kill any living thing that harboured the man who killed their two favourites. These young men were from the noblest families in England. Each had shared every triumph, every sorrow of their Princes. They had shared love with their masters, perhaps more even, than a son.

As they gathered their weary cavalry to chase the fugitive, they called for hunting dogs from the village. My master looked tired, but he kept his wits and remembered to order a fifty-strong troop, to provide a guard for

King Pedro. 'Better keep him safe, while Trastamara is on the loose,' he said. They were ordered to escort the King, his daughters and de Padilla back to camp, where they would be best protected.

Trastamara's flight had been witnessed by many from the village. The royal brothers rode with 200 cavalry and I went too. I witnessed their fury and resentment growing with every mile. Besides his ribs, his toothache was fast adding to the Black Prince's temper.

They would lynch him. They would torture anyone who helped him. They would burn them out. There was no punishment hellish enough for the underhand slayer of their personal favourites.

With the dogs on the trail, we saw a group of ten or twelve men running downhill in the distance. Trastamara's distinctive yellow tunic was among them. They ran through a copse and, in our full view, the fugitives entered the monastery of Yuso, a quarter of a mile ahead.

The Black Prince had no thought and no care for the most precious relics of Spain's first saint, St Millan. Our troops galloped through the two archways at either end of the monastery wall. Riders, armour, horses and dogs overwhelmed Yuso monastery by every door available.

Trastamara had run this way because he knew the Cogolla Valley well. Its sides were full of graves. It had two monasteries built within sight of each other. This one, Yuso, was in the valley and Suso was the other monastery, on the far side of the same valley. It had been built a quarter of the way up the forested hill. From childhood, he knew Suso best, because Saint Mallin had lived in the caves beneath it and people liked their final resting-place to be as near him as possible. Three Queens of Navarre were buried there, along with his own mother, the late King of Castile's most beloved mistress. He knew the caves below it like the back of his hand. When he was escaping, he met others fleeing for their lives. He changed tunics with one of them in the copse and ordered them into Yuso monastery. He himself headed for the cover of the woods and Suso monastery, on the far hill.

Our cavalry entered Yuso at the gallop. We caused chaos as horses slithered around corners and galloped up aisles, while dogs gave tongue around the cloisters. The horses went through the refectory where the tables were laid. They knocked over the beehives in the garden and galloped over the vegetables.

'Trastamara?' I yelled at the cowering monks, 'Where is Trastamara?'

We found the Abbott and his books in the scriptorium. He was hauled before the Commander in Chief.

As they went, some knights had knocked over chairs, tables, hospital beds and candles in the chapel. We were ordered to round up every living being there. There were local poor asking for food, fishermen paying their dues, the sick, the holy and the odd escaped Spanish soldier. Not one of them was Trastamara.

Everything was sacked, destroyed, smashed and trodden on. Decorations and carvings were ripped down, such was the fury of our attack. It was madness. The Abbott knew nothing and it took time for our leaders to realise that he was speaking the truth. In the meantime, the chapel was starting to burn. The fire spread to the Chapter House, the Abbott's house, the kitchens, the lavatorium and the dormitories.

Eventually, we left the monks to bewail their beloved monastery. We had failed to find the usurper. We believed he must have died hiding in the chapel. Indeed, we might have expressed some regret at Yuso's destruction, if we had realised that we had just destroyed the wrong monastery. Disastrously, Trastamara had escaped through the caves of Suso.

We rode back to camp, where cartloads of injured were being transported to Our Lady of Acre hospital at Navarrete. There was no hurry for the dead. The noblemen would be pickled in spices to preserve their bodies. Important knights would be buried in individual graves at the hospital. Poor knights would share a grave and the ordinary soldiers would be buried in great pits around the outside of the battlefield. Dead and injured horses were dispatched and burnt on giant foul bonfires. The village people of Navarrete mourned their sons and husbands. They went around wearing a protective cloth over their faces. The stench lasted for weeks.

The Black Prince was at the end of a long day. He needed to rest his ribs and seek some help for his sore jaw. Prince John took charge of the camp and asked to see King Pedro. But he was missing, along with his escort party.

Scenting a problem, Prince John ordered me to take ten soldiers and ride back to Clavijo Castle. That was when I saw the escort party, waiting below his castle. They had been sent a note earlier, telling them to wait, '*King Pedro would be down soon.*' I was sure they had been duped. I took all the men along the high ridge, up the rough steps and into the precincts of the castle.

Immediately, it was obvious he was missing.

A servant handed me a letter. It read:

To Prince Edward, Commander in Chief, or to Prince John, second in command.
We will see you in Santiago de Compostela.
We have some business to attend to before that.
Signed: Pedro of Castile.

It occurred to me that there was not one word of thanks for putting him back on his throne and no explanation for his behaviour. The letter confirmed it. They had given us the slip. Pedro and his family had disappeared along a narrow path, down the opposite side of the hill. This path was impossible to see from the Logrono side. It clearly led into an area of small hills and valleys, providing ideal cover for anyone sneaking off unseen.

'Now we have lost King Pedro!' I reported back to Prince John.

He looked puzzled, 'Why on earth did he want to go without us knowing?' We both had suspicious minds. He was the one who put it into words. 'Could it possibly be true? Suppose he does not intend to go to Santiago at all? Suppose we never get the treasure?' He was becoming agitated.

'Back in Poitiers, why did he insist on taking his girls with him? They would have been safer left behind. Was that something to do with the Templar Treasure as well? Or?' he sighed, 'is there any treasure at Santiago after all?' The questions went round and round in his head. There was obviously something very wrong.

He determined to report to his brother at once, where they both agreed on one thing. Pedro had better turn up at Santiago, or they would not be able to get their share of the Templar Treasure. They would not be able to pay the army, Sir Hugh Calveley and his Free Company and, even worse, they would have to face the unforgiving fury of King Edward of England.

The army stayed around the battlefield for another week. They buried their dead and the heralds made up their death lists. The embalmers moved in and worked on lines of bodies, brought into the hospital nearby. There were ten skilled practitioners. They were never required to carry arms. Their tools were incense, myrrh, aloes and musk spices.

If there was a fault in this delivery line of bodies to be embalmed, it was with the ordinary soldiers who were ordered to pick them up from the battlefield. They did not always have the time, or the stomach, to check they had the right head with the right body. Maybe it had been kicked some distance away, in the melee of battle.

The embalmers themselves were generally little men, who liked nothing better than to have a shattered body to re-arrange, an arm to stitch back on, or somebody's head, if they could find the right bits to fit. If not, another would do just as well. They were not too fussy whose it was.

It was wise that the King of Arms was there to make sure the torso corresponded to the coat of arms. At least part of the body was the right person. The embalmers were part of the English army and present at all major battles. They worked on the noblemen and the knights. The King of Arms personally carried everyone's instructions as to the disposal of their body, should they die in battle.

Two of these men were the Royal Embalmers, personally paid by the King. Their task was to preserve whatever was left of the Black Prince or his brother John of Gaunt, should they get killed on the battlefields of foreign shores. The tools of their trade were very different. They offered, uniquely, the very latest in preserving techniques. They carried honeycombs with them, linen cloths, strips of heavy lead, a length of cord, clay, a coffin of oak and a tassel.

The normal tradition was that if *neither* of the royal Princes was killed, the services of the royal embalmers could be offered to the most senior nobleman to die in the battle. In this case, that was the 3rd Commander in Chief. When the Black Prince heard that his close friend, Anthony de Lucy from Egremont had been killed beside him, he gave permission for him to be *preserved like a Prince until Judgement Day*.[21]

The royal embalmers got to work. Anthony de Lucy's body was clothed in a simple linen loincloth. His organs were not removed. (The Black Prince had requested to have a tight cord of penitence placed around his own neck in death. But this was not the wish of Anthony de Lucy, so it was not present.)

The next layer was an inner linen shroud. After that, the embalmers worked with a large heated pot beside them. They melted the blocks of beeswax, until it was thick and viscous. On the first day, they dipped another linen shroud in the melted beeswax and wrapped it tightly around the body. The problem with this method of preserving a body, was that the embalmers had to be very careful not to burn their own hands. Then they left the beeswax to dry overnight.

By the second day, the wax coating had dried smooth, hard and tightly wrapped around the body. They then added a third layer beeswax and left that to dry also. This time they added a funeral tassel at one end, as a decoration. It was in the royal colours of yellow, black and red. After another two days, the body was neatly wrapped around many times with linen and twine. The next layer involved a similar process, except that it used lead.

They melted the lead until it could be carefully poured all over the waxed body. Anthony de Lucy's had to be turned, in order to be completely enclosed in its new wrapping of lead. Like the wax, the lead hardened, taking the body's shape.

The ingenious thinking behind this method of royal embalming was to counteract the effects of moisture and air, which normally caused bodies to decompose. The lead sheath kept out any moisture, while the three beeswax coatings excluded any air.

When the two embalmers were satisfied with their work, they placed the heavy leaded body in an oak coffin with iron clasps. Packed the inside spaces tightly with clay, so that the body would not move and get damaged in transport.

The coffin needed ten men to carry it to a double-axle waggon and two horses to pull it. Thus it arrived on home shores, with the returning English army and was formally escorted by carriage, with an escort of twenty soldiers, northwards to St Bees Priory, for burial.

Chapter 26 - Savage Revenge

'So they didn't get the treasure, then,' said the Emissary. 'All that fighting and dying was for nothing. I must say, if you'd said THAT at the start I could have been on my way a lot sooner. I suppose you know you've wasted a great deal of my valuable time?'

'My oath, you're an impatient fellow,' said the old man. 'All this stuff has been mouldering inside me for years, and now it's finally coming out I'm damned if I'll stop before I've finished. Don't you want to know what happened to Trastamara and the evil King Pedro, let alone the treasure?'

'Oh, very well,' said the envoy, resigning himself to his fate.

'King Pedro,' said the hermit 'was laughing like a madman as he spurred his horse until it grunted with the pain.

'Faster, damn you, faster!'

'It would have been an easy task to follow King Pedro's tracks. The horse's blood drained freely onto the dark earth, as he wounded it every time he spurred the poor brute for more effort. He wore long sharp wheels at the ends of his spurs.

Malicious joy flowed through his veins. His royal blue blood stirring in his cold heart. First of all, he thought, I have some scores to settle! He was free. He was the King. And he felt cruel today.

Pedro had plotted it well. A dozen loyal troops from Clavijo Castle accompanied him. The Grandmaster de Padilla and his daughters had been ordered to take a parallel path, two miles east through a village, for he did not wish them to see what was about to happen.

Pedro's grand design was to encroach upon a certain Diego de Vivar and his family during their midday feast. This husband and wife were traitors. He wanted to show them what he could do, one by one and child by child. What sweet revenge it would be.

This Diego de Vivar had originally proved to be a strong commander of his army. Pedro had promoted him as a young man. He had risen from being one of his favourite aides, through the ranks and eventually took charge of Castile's army. The King had treated him almost like his own son. He had been his protégé and distant cousin, for Diego was a descendant of the legendary warrior *El Cid*, Rodrigo Diaz de Vivar and his wife Chimene. She had been of royal Spanish descent, being the daughter of King Alfonso VI.

Pedro had liked the idea of the blood of El Cid leading his army. Like him, the great El Cid had the Moors as his allies and was called *szidi* by them, meaning *Lord*. But Diego de Vivar, his protégé, had betrayed him and Pedro would never forgive him. This was the man who had planned to lead him into a trap, with a plot to kill him, no less. This was the thanks Pedro got from his favourite.

The conspiracy was discovered. De Vivar had been wounded, but managed to escape. What was worse, he had taken half of Pedro's army to fight on the side of his enemy, the usurper Trastamara.

Pedro had planned this scene every step of the way through the Pyrenees and every step back again. He was in luck. Fortune smiled on the vengeful that fine April noonday. The King of Castile knew they loved their feast-days in the forest. He knew, because he had eaten with de Vivar family many times. After all, today was *San Jose Day*, Mother's Day in Spain.

He could see the smoke rising from their favourite outdoor feasting place in the middle of the wood ahead. He knew that they liked to celebrate their feast days in the open air. The children felt there was excitement about. It was as if the year was waking up again after the long winter. It was a rare treat to eat outside and the woody glade was perfect at that time of year.

Now that fidelity was past, this particular example of disloyalty deserved punishment. More than punishment, a mad terrible retribution.

The little family were easy prey. There were only two servants. What a pretty sight they made. The sun filtered through the trees on to the small clearing and shone on the children's hair, as they chased each other around a wooden table, hewn from the forest about them. There sat Diego, darkly good-looking, laughing at their antics, helping himself from the table. He was a man in his early 30's, with wavy short hair and features that appeared too fine to belong to a warrior. He had been such a pretty boy as a child.

I'll soon change that, thought Pedro to himself. He won't have much face left by the time I'm finished with him. Look at him now! While he eats, his whole family is at play. King Pedro stroked his long chin. He has no weapon about him. He was in no hurry, now that he knew the man was his.

His wife must be sick, for she looks so pale and painfully thin. Then Pedro remembered her smile. She had the warmest smile. Why had she smiled at him, her King? She had encouraged him. Pedro had simply taken what he thought was on offer at the time.

She was a savagely beautiful woman, with red hair. It was not the flaming orange colour of the Western Isles, but a darker richer hue. It was as if she washed her head in the deep red soil and dipped it in the old black holes of the peat bog. She always wore it wild and free, down past her navel and temptingly wavy. Her husband loved her like that.

Once, over a year ago, before her husband's defection, Pedro had spied on her; watching while she bathed. Lust overcame him. From that point on, she only had to make one small move towards him and she would be his. And it happened! All she did one day, was to smile. It was an innocent, open smile which lit up her face. Pedro totally lost control. Leopard-like he sprang on her, pinning her to the ground, raping her savagely, ignoring her screams.

Much later, he was surprised to discover the sting of deep scratches down his own loins. He had no memory of her terrible fight for her virtue. But she was not dead, was she? She was not hurt, was she?

He had no comprehension that perhaps a woman would prefer to die. He had no conception of doing wrong, of being evil. He had these uncontrollable urges and was used to taking what he wanted. Was it not true that Kings, through annals of time, had taken what or who they wanted? What was wrong with that? Besides, they seldom wanted it again from the same beauty twice.

Later, he completely failed to connect the husband's betrayal with his own actions. Why should a man protect his wife? All men should be more like him. They should have several wives, although, his weren't really married to him. He had devised a sort of service for these occasions, if the women insisted. It was simple. They just said a few words and the silly females thought they were the Queen. That was their stupidity. He idly thought he had about ten of them around the country. For the life of him, he could not remember half of them now.

Now, this husband had betrayed him. He and his family were first on his list for retribution, every one of them. Pedro could not think why he had ever fancied the wife. Look at her now! Wan and thin, with a short, ragged hair rather like a nun's crop. He had snatched off a proper nun's habit a time or two, and liked it. Now, she had a baby strapped to her side.

If he caught some man stealing one of his own women though, no man had ever dared, he supposed he would really breathe a sigh of relief to see the back of her.

Hidden among thick undergrowth, Pedro savoured the domestic scene before him. Sweet-smelling vapour curled into the air from a giant *olio* (a solid four-legged cauldron), which stood gigantically astride a comely fire. This was out-door eating of the most tempting kind. The huge pot was a good five feet wide and deep enough to take wild hog meat a-plenty, a whole skinned deer, or maybe half an ox. It was so large the children were not able to see into it.

This day the cauldron contained a fine hog's head with tusks, tail and trotters, which had been separately cut from the carcass. First it had been de-whiskered by singeing, but the eyes had to be protected, for they had to stay clear to prove it was a new kill.

Into the pot went briny water from the forest pools, with square slabs of oatmeal bannocks, bacca berries, wartleberries and roots of wild garlic. A swan and a heron had been plucked. Their heads had gone to the dogs, but their webbed feet were still attached for identification, for the swan was considered too rich and fatty for the children. Each was stuffed with herbs ground with vinegar and sewn up inside the chest cavity with long strips of cat intestines. Apparently the abundance of kittens around the stables had their uses.

The last ingredients of the *bisque stock* were leeks and onions, to make it tasty, along with a ewer-full of *bishop*, the same warm spiced wine that was used to slake the thirst of the adults at the table. The children preferred to drink mead, made with fermented honey and water. Each trencher plate was laden with hunks of black bread, made with molasses and used to soak up the spicy gravy.

It smelt so good. It was time to have some of that. Calling out to *Alecto*, *Tisiphone* and *Megaera*, the three goddesses of vengeance, the King and his men galloped into the clearing. They planned to stay their killing weapons, until they were face-to-face with the father first.

But the very first thing they were confronted with, was the bold gaze of a solid two-year-old, a very young warrior, who walked sturdily in their direction, challenging them all to mortal combat. Wielding his toy sword, he stomped towards them. Some infant instinct kicked in, perhaps it was the blood of El Cid. He wanted to get at this big bad enemy.

King Pedro bent low in his saddle and scooped up the boy. For his trouble, he received a blow on the nose from the little wooden weapon. Stung into action, he signalled one of his men to take hold of a wriggling leg. He then simply veered his own horse to the side sharply, pulling the little boy apart. The tearing of bones and sinew followed. They cracked and split and gave way surprisingly easily, like twigs. Others grabbed the father as he ran towards them, bellowing with disbelief and grief, while the wife, baby and two older children dived underneath the table.

'Don't kill him!' barked out the King, releasing the bits of the child he had held.

The soldiers speared the father firmly to a Spanish oak tree, through both shoulder blades. Pedro wanted Diego de Vivar's head and genitals untouched. With his eyes, he had to be able to see and understand every form of torture about to be enacted upon his family. Pedro had invented a long list of those. As for his genitals. Well, that would come later.

The little boy had been a mistake. A missed chance to gouge, or mangle, or to impale like his father. Pedro would not be so hasty with the other children. Besides, the woman's new baby was an extra bonus he had not counted on.

He used every method of torture he could think of. The wife, damn her, was given the *bastonada*, beating on the soles of the feet, followed by the *garrotear*, a good throttling. Nobody fancied her bag of clattering bones any longer. She looked dreadful.

The eldest girl was set on the grill above the cauldron to yell. Eventually, quite deaf with the shouts and moans of the father and quite exhausted with the drama of it all, they flayed him and boiled him in the pot. But first they removed his genitals and flung them in like a sausage and pieces of black pudding.

Drunk with revenge, Pedro took a draft of the warm mulled soup in the cauldron. Nothing had ever tasted so wonderful. Something caught his eye as he dipped the ladle into the pot. A small body surfaced, navel first. It was the baby, of course. The King looked away and suddenly realised he had seen a tiny penis. Then the awful possibility struck him. Was this HIS boy, the product of his rape, twelve months before. He had always wanted a son to inherit the throne of Castile. Now he had one and had just boiled him alive. Pedro lost his mind. The part that was not lost already.

A day later, in the mid-afternoon, the Black Prince and John of Gaunt gathered up a dozen of us and diverted us from our route. Our scouts had heard horrors reported by locals. There were fearful tales of *black magic* in the forest. Nothing, in any of our lives, prepared us for the scene in the clearing.

The fire beneath the huge cauldron had gone out. Otherwise everything was exactly as it had been left, except for the smell and the carrion crows. Every human body-part had been flung into the pot and cooked. There were arms with tiny hands, faces with no noses, a knee with no foot and a breast with a hole for a nipple. A boar's head appeared to be eating something, not an apple, but a tiny child's head. Quite obviously, somebody had put their own hands in the pot and arranged the pieces to look insanely dramatic. A couple of rib bones and the remains of two adult legs were lying on the churned-up grass below the pot. They had been eaten. By the perpetrators? By wolves? Or pecked clean by crows?

My stomach would not take it and I was not the only one. Not daring to guess, or even to communicate to each other, the brothers retreated and sent in their official body-experts to disentangle the remains in the cauldron. They were ordered to liaise with the local village chief, to collect names and to help bury the victims.

The Princes were silent. They did not even take command of their own vanguard, as they resumed their ride towards Santiago de Compostela. They left the ordering to others.

In war you see everything, they say. But this particular form of torture, with its killing and then eating, must have been done by a deranged lunatic. In truth, as soon as they heard the names of the victims, the true identity of the perpetrator was obvious. But neither brother would let the name pass his lips. Each kept it to himself.

Coincidentally, they both felt a rare need for urgent advice from their father.

As of that moment, they refused to deal with this animal. But if they had to collect the Templar Treasure from Santiago, how were they to proceed?

The beauty of Santiago meant nothing to them now. The sanctity of the great church meant little. The history of the pilgrim path passed them by. They let nothing invade their thoughts, except for the coming collection of the promised treasure. Somehow it had to be achieved without dealings with, or sight of, King Pedro. Surely Grandmaster de Padilla and the two girls were not implicated in this? The Princes were disturbed and sick with loathing.

As it happened, they need not have worried unduly. King Pedro had never had any intention of meeting them there, or of giving up the treasure. Indeed, we waited a week in Santiago for sight of him. He had simply hoodwinked us all.

After that, I noticed that something caused the Black Prince's illness to start once more. I supposed it was his low spirits that triggered it. The dreaded aching, swelling illness had returned. This time it would last many years. It never left him again.

Just after that time, I, Petit-Roi started feeling unwell with stomach cramps. Then half of the troop went down with it. I kept well away from my master. He was ill enough already. Later on, I heard the story about Prince John and Mr Chaucer.

Praying at the altar of St James, John of Gaunt knew in his heart there was treasure in the crypt beneath his feet. He was certain. Was he really to lose it now?

They had fought a war, ousted a King, marched their army through the Pyrenees in winter and risked the very life of his brother to be there. Kneeling, he swore revenge.

Frustration and anger made him vocal in his condemnations. He called out against King Pedro and blamed his God for letting it happen, until other worshippers were alarmed and upset by the dark mutterings from the fair-skinned warrior in the corner. He was on his knees for two days, before he surrendered himself to more penitent reflections and asked his God, 'Why? What do you want of me?'

It was young Master Chaucer who came to his rescue and calmed his troubled soul. Earlier, Geoffrey Chaucer had taken the pilgrim route from the battlefield alongside his silently brooding prince. But it was his first time upon a pilgrim road and he experienced a sensation, more akin to his master's earlier wonder, at the history and folk tales of the old path. As they travelled from village to town, seeing their fellow pilgrims, Chaucer was captivated and driven to write notes on the stories they told at night. It would be some years before he could put those notes to good use. Though his *Canterbury Tales* were written about the pilgrims to the shrine of St Thomas a'Becket, the first germ of the idea and some of the tales, came from the route to Santiago.

Chaucer was a man who knew how to turn a diplomatic phrase into an attractive proposition. After all, that was his job. He wisely let his master fling his anger at the altar for as long as it took to become more rational, before he interrupted. 'Sire, have you considered, my Prince, that perhaps God does not want you to take this Holy Treasure?'

'Why ever not?' was the hurt reply.

'Perhaps he thinks you would use it unwisely, for your own gain, to increase your lands in France perhaps.'

'What's wrong with that? There will be plenty left-over when we've paid the army.'

Chaucer shook his head. 'To fund the fighting of one Christian country against another?'

The Prince's response was bitter, 'If the Almighty thought we planned to misuse *His* treasure from King Solomon's Temple, if this is the sign of *His* mighty displeasure, I tell you it will count for nothing. For the retribution from our father will be worse. Indeed, a more earthly hell!'

'Sire!' Chaucer was appalled at the blasphemy.

'Stay with me a while, Master Chaucer!'

So they sat in the presence of St James and talked of the futility of war. 'We have just put the wrong man back on the throne of Castile,' admitted the Prince.

'I know,' replied Chaucer.

That night, Prince John had a particular dream, which was repeated night after night. He confided in Chaucer, who was widely read and knew something about the interpretation of dreams. It was not a fearsome dream. It was curiously detailed, with colours and lights. He felt sure it must have a meaning. 'I stood at a long table in the middle of an orchard with young apples and medlars on the trees,' the Prince recounted. 'There was a large cornfield behind it. A swarm of bees flew past my head and landed in the cornfield. I don't like buttermilk, but three or four tankards of the stuff were laid out on the table for me to drink. As I was drinking it, I remember a bright ray of sunshine that came from behind a cloud and shone on to the table. It was lighting up an onion for me to eat, but I gave it to a child. I found it difficult to drink the buttermilk, because I had to use my gloved left hand. I was worried because I had lost my right-hand glove. I could not drink without a glove.'

Chaucer went away to work it out. Soon, he returned to ask many questions.

'How near was the cornfield?'

'In the distance, on rising ground. But I remember it was easy to see where the bees landed, among the heads of corn.'

'The fruit in the orchard, was it ready to pick?'

'It was green, not yet ripe.'

'Did you eat any of the onion yourself?'

'No.'

'Was the buttermilk palatable?'

'No! I hated it, but I had to drink it. Why did I have to use a glove? Tell me!'

'I will,' Chaucer paused. 'You must understand, we have no way of telling the order in which these predictions happen to you. Let us take it slowly, line by line. **First**, an orchard with ripe fruit indicates an inheritance now. An orchard with unripe fruit indicates an inheritance later on.

Second, a cornfield indicates sea adventures. A faraway cornfield on a hill means distant deep ocean travel and rough seas.

Third, bees mean your children. A swarm of bees does not indicate you will have hundreds of children. What it does mean, is that your descendants will cover the land. As for the bees landing in the cornfield, this is extremely significant! It means that your descendants will find fame on the open oceans.

Fourth, I must separate the items on the table. The buttermilk is an ominous sign and there is so much of it. I am sorry to say that this indicates death and more than one death. But it is not your own.

Fifth, the onion is a vegetable we would all like to dream of. It denotes the finding of treasure.'

'But I gave it to a child!' exclaimed John.

'Then I fear it is your children who find the treasure,' he sighed and continued. '**Sixth**, the ray of sun is a very serious matter. It represents the will of God shining from afar. This is a definite warning to you.'

'A warning? Of what, for God's sake?'

'Exactly! The treasure has to be used for the benefit of God, to spread his teaching to far-off places. The warning is clear. It must not be used for the benefit of man alone. And **lastly**, the losing of the right-hand glove, I fear, is more emphasis on grief.'

What he did NOT tell his master, was that a lost right-hand glove really meant the death of a beloved wife and the desperate unhappiness afterwards.

John of Gaunt was perplexed by his dream. So, he would not get his treasure after all. His children might, but what was the good of that? It would not pay the army right now. On reflection, the rest of his dream was more interesting. Certainly his father would die at some point, as well as others in his family, he supposed. That was normal. He could deal with grief.

At least his own health would hold out and his children would prosper to carry on his blood-line. What more could a man ask for? Travel across the wide ocean? That was something to ponder upon.

The inheritance part troubled him. It seemed unlikely, though he supposed his wife's inheritance might count. Certainly she would inherit her father's enormous land holdings and wealth upon his death, at some later time. That would fit.

Overall, the signs were good and he decided that the best course of action was to keep an eye on that treasure. You never knew, he might come up with a dream of eating the onion himself the next time.

Eventually the Prince had to return to the present and deal with the main problem. There was no money to pay the troops, or to repay Calveley and his merry men, who liked gold. There was no money even to pay for ships to take them home. John of Gaunt sold his Prince's coronet to get passage back to England for himself, his brother and his men.

The Black Prince had offered his Blood of Christ stone, but his brother would not let him sell it. That Ruby was the one good outcome from this whole madcap expedition. What was more, the royal brothers connived to keep it from their father.

After all, they thought they had glimpsed a hint of its power. They were determined their father would not be allowed to take it, to be sold to a dealer to help to pay for the troops. They felt a heavy responsibility for the Ruby, not because it was valuable, but because if it fell into the wrong hands. They swore to keep it safe. As promised, the Black Prince would put it in the centre of his crown, where it would always be guarded. They believed in its promise. It would protect them and their descendants forever.

So they told their father they had been forced to give up the jewel to the monastery containing John the Baptist's head, which was nearly true, though the King remained suspicious.

At once, new and terrible taxes were raised in England to pay for the Spanish War. The people blamed the King and his temper was awful to behold. He swore revenge on King Pedro. He issued directions to Calveley to find him, however long it took and issued an execution order. As a member of his own family, King Edward saw it as his duty to rid the world of this man. He did not speak to either of his sons, until the deed was done.

Chapter 27 - Spy for England

'So I was right, there was no treasure after all!' *The young Envoy was in the garden listening to the hermit's story. What a waste of time!' He leapt to his feet, turning his chair over violently, and commenced pacing up and down the long narrow strip of grass. So this was the end of it. He had come on a useless journey.*

'Oh, I didn't say that!' the hermit replied quietly, almost to himself. He disliked noise, he was not used to it.

'What did you say?' Suddenly the hermit found the younger man's face right up against his own.

He started back and caught his breath in surprise. Then he blew out his cheeks and said wearily, 'I do wish you would sit down, young sir, and let me continue my story.'

Edward of Alpath picked up his chair and slid himself onto it reluctantly. He nodded curtly and asked what happened next.

'That was when they put us in the monastery.'

'I do not understand,' snapped the Envoy, 'who is US?'

'Well, there were sixteen of us in a terrible state. They said we had dysentery. That's a killer! We were told we would not be fit for at least a month. The problem was, the ship was due to sail for England within the next two days. I understand Prince John left some little money with the Abbott, to look after us and for our return to England later. We were already in the isolation part of the monastery hospital, so the Princes had to leave us there. They went home.'

'Without the treasure?'

He nodded, 'Without the treasure.'

Three weeks later, Sir Hugh Calveley arrived at the monastery, and asked to see us soldiers about our travel arrangements. By then, six had died and the rest of us were not yet fit enough to go home. I had started thinking of Marie Elaine again and wondered if there was any chance she would still welcome me. After all, Poitiers was the only home I knew.

Calveley was a giant of a man. I especially remember the size of his hands. We must have looked a pretty miserable bunch. I wondered why he had come himself. Surely our homeward journey could have been handled by others? I kept the question to myself. We were honoured to see him, and it certainly raised our spirits.

I was the most senior English patient there. He should have seen me first; but instead, he chose to talk to me last. I wondered why, but soon found out. The answer was both unexpected and unwelcome. It turned out that the true reason for his visit was more to do with espionage, than with travel arrangements.

He shook my hand, 'First of all, Petit-Roi, I must confirm how much you already know about this story. May I ask you questions?' Intrigued, I consented.

'I understand, you saw the cauldron in the woods full of human body parts. Is that true?'

'I am very much afraid, I threw up, sir!'

'Ah, so you did see it! I was not there, as you know. Well, that confirms that point.' He lowered his voice so we would not be overheard. 'The Black Prince tells me, you were with us for the Templar Treasure revelations by the Bishop at Poitiers?'

'Yes, sir. I was one of the guards around the table.'

'You know the full story?'

'I carried the inventory list of the Templar Treasure for my Prince. He wanted it in order to identify the pieces when we got here to Santiago, Sir Hugh. The valuer needed to know they were authentic.'

'Have you memorised any of that list?'

'Yes, sir. It is in here,' I tapped my head. 'My master made me learn it, in case anything happened to the parchment.'

Calveley surprised me by pulling the very parchment roll from beneath his cloak. He looked hard at me for several seconds. 'Name me some of the pieces' he challenged.

I relished this, for there was precious little wrong with my memory, then. My body may have been weak with dysentery, but my head still worked. 'There were twenty-five gold chariots,' I told him. 'But they were in need of repair. Then there were thirty-one cast metal racing chariots, or at least parts of them and thirty-seven gold harnesses. Also I remember ten bronze trolleys with decorative relief, fifty-six tablets of Solomon and...'

'Thank you, that is enough!' He laughed. 'You'll do!' His message to me and to me alone, was this: King Edward wanted my services for two very particular missions. I had to *stay* in the monastery at all costs.

My *first* mission was to keep my ears open for any news of the whereabouts of King Pedro and to report it back to Calveley. He put a giant hand on my shoulder. 'Maybe it will not surprise you to know that my orders are to kill him!' He saw my face light up. 'We all feel like that, my friend,' he said. 'It seems he will get justice after all. So, I will have my spies out and we will get news of him as soon as possible. But *you* may have the best chance. We know he likes to come here to Santiago. You must report to me immediately if you see him here, or know where he will be. Keep your ears open.'

Finally he told me he had endowed the Abbey with enough money from the King to keep us longer if necessary and to pay for any unforeseen circumstances. I was feeling unsure about all this. I supposed it was *me* who was going to be the *unforeseen circumstance*.

'How do I get a message to you Sir Hugh?'

'We have thought this one through quite carefully. You may not like it, but this is how the King wishes it to be handled. You must stay here and become a monk!'

I gasped.

'Sir Hugh, I beg you, I cannot! I am not in the least religious. Maybe I am a bit superstitious before a battle, but that is all. Sir, I beg you.'

'Stop! Stop!' The great man was sharp-eyed and severe. 'You do not understand. This is an ORDER, soldier. You cannot disobey your King.' Then he softened a little. 'Do not worry Petit-Roi, I will try to think of some other guise for you. But this is your duty. You have been specially chosen for this mission.'

'But why must I stay here, Sir Hugh?'

He sat down heavily beside me, 'Because of the *second* mission we have for you. The *first*, as you know, is to report news of King Pedro. The *second* task concerns the Templar Treasure here in this crypt.'

I stared at him, feeling every muscle tense. A shiver cascaded down my spine.

'You must locate the key to the correct crypt, open it and identify the pieces from the inventory list in your head.'

I looked at him incredulously. I could not believe my ears. What was he asking me to do? Was it to steal the Holy Treasures from Jerusalem. All on my own? He saw my face.

'You only have to identify them. We would not want to rush in and remove the *wrong* treasure, would we?'

'What if I'm caught?'

'Oh, please don't get caught Petit-Roi. I hope you understand clearly, you must identify the treasure, put the key back and get a message to me.'

'Will someone steal it later?'

'Oh Petit-Roi,' he sighed, 'you know full well that King Pedro promised us some of that Jerusalem Treasure, to pay for the army and for my mercenaries. We will have to take what is owed to us later.'

'How long must I stay here?'

'Oh, not long if you can complete your tasks successfully. You will obviously have to be here to show us where to get in.'

My head was in a wild state as I tried to make sense of it all. 'How do I get a message to you Sir Hugh?'

'We need to discuss that, you and I, right now. The problem is, I have not been able to set it up yet.'

I thought quickly, 'Another monk here, perhaps?' I suggested.

'No, we have no contacts at all within these walls. I have asked, but it appears we have no time to infiltrate someone. I am afraid you can trust NOBODY inside this monastery,' he paused, 'your contact will have to be someone outside.' He sighed and added, 'I have been asking around and of course, apart from working in the fields and burying the dead, the monks do not go out themselves. This presents a dilemma.'

'So, who can be my contact?' I was getting confused.

'Well then, the two options are *either* someone working among the vines, where a stranger might be obvious, *or* among the beggar hermits outside the walls, who are visited every day for a medical check-up.'

This was extraordinary. I had been distantly aware of our army marching past so many hermits along the pilgrim path. They became almost invisible to us. They were just old beggars with a roof. If I had thought about it at all, I presumed they slept elsewhere, had a hot meal and returned during daylight hours to their chosen patch to beg. You can be sure of one thing, I had no inkling of the true life of an old hermit and how it would become inextricably entwined in my own.

Sir Hugh Calveley and I agreed that the most practical contact for me was among the wayside hermits. That would be the least suspicious way.

'Anyway, it will not be for long,' he reassured me as he turned to go.

'And then?' I addressed his back, before he reached the door. I was still troubled.

He swung around and raised one hand, 'Ah, I knew there was something else. I believe your Black Prince wishes to make you a Knight. How about that!' He reached me and shook my hand energetically. 'So you see Petit-Roi, you have to get back.'

Back where? I wondered. The giant mercenary leader left us.

Three weeks later, one more of us had died, two had taken ship for England and six waited for a passage along the coast to get themselves lost in the French city of Bordeaux. They had had enough of the army.

Before they left me alone among the strange Spanish-speaking monks of Santiago, Calveley himself returned for a meeting with the Abbott. He managed to pass me a small package with a note inside. It read:

4th hermit east of monastery. He is your contact.
Leave a message addressed to 'Wilhelm' and
leave this red cloth visible beside his shelter.'

The piece of deep-red cloth inside the parcel, was the size of a large book. So, they had set up my message service. Instead of feeling relieved, my brain began to race. This was also my escape route out of this monastery. I suddenly realised how vital to my life was this scrap of cloth. I carried it hidden as my second skin from then on.

The day after the others left, I was still without a plan of action. I found myself with mounting unease, when I was summoned to see the Abbott.

'Your commander gave me to understand that you wish to stay here for a while.'

'Yes, sir.'

'Well, now that you are quite well, I fear you have to leave! You see, we need the bed.'

I knew the hospital had sixty beds, and only two of them were occupied. Of course, he knew that too. Now what was I to do?

The problem was that I had not yet prepared my speech to him. I had no idea how to handle this. I found myself falling into the snake-pit. All I could think of doing was to try to persuade the intractable Abbott that I was devout enough to stay. I knew nothing of religion. I couldn't even quote good phrases to impress him. However, my King had ordered me to stay. But how?

'I understand that money was left for me to remain here?' I had to say something.

'No! No! Only the sick, or the monks live here.'

I felt my legs fill up with lead as I said, 'I MUST stay, sir.'

'Call me Brother, if you please.' He was only just keeping his temper in check.

'Unless,' he changed his tone and continued more slowly, looking me up and down, 'unless you are trying to tell me something.' His voice became quieter. 'My son, could it be that you have found a calling to join our brotherhood? Could it be that you wish to become a monk? Is that why you do not want to leave us?'

'Yes,' I replied miserably.

'Yes, Brother,' he corrected. 'So you have found your vocation at last. You would not be the first. Well my son, we will have to school you in our ways. I warn you, it is not a simple life for a soldier to take on.'

My thoughts lurched to the nightly scourging I had heard through cell doors, to the silence that was kept for twenty-three hours each day, to the constant working, praying cycle of life, all performed in a strange language. I bent my head to my fate and the Abbott took that for supplication. He blessed me and called for help to begin my lessons amongst the novice monks.

What had I done?

I did not grieve for my past life, for I hoped this chapter would be short and I would soon return to it. But I did grieve for my cat. She was old and defenceless. She had always lived in my kit bag and hidden herself from view during daylight hours. Now, I was not allowed any possessions. I was given no warning. They threw away my uniform, my kit bag and the personal seal of my Prince, which had always given me free passage anywhere.

They said my first test of obedience was to stand and watch them burn it all in the courtyard. At the last possible moment, my cat jumped out of the smoking bag and fled between the legs of the senior monks. Consternation broke out. A cat! How did *that* get into the monastery? Thanking God for at least one thing, I bowed my head to look obedient and unprotesting.

I hoped and even prayed she would find her way back to me somehow, but in my heart I knew she would never return after such a scare. Besides, how could she possibly get back in? Two days later, I overheard two monks talking. 'They caught that cat around the kitchens, you know.'

'Thought they would. Did they dispatch it?'

'Of course.'

'They don't like animals here.'

'I know.' And the brothers walked on.

My heart bled for my cat.

You ask, what was it like for me? I was a prisoner here in a monastery and there was no God. I truly believed, at that moment, that I was at the low point of my life. God help me! It was just as well I did not know that I was not even half way there.

As novice monks, we spent tedious hours at lessons. I did not listen. I was no good at decorating bible scripts and I was a bad worker at the vines. The bees stung me, seeming to know my heart was not in it. I was lazy threshing the corn; and dropped the food in the kitchens. The only skill I had to acquire was the endless chanting in the chapel, for the older monks were deliberately placed in between the novices. They pinched us if we did not make the replies and they reported us if we were incorrect or not loud enough. I suffered beatings on my feet enough to train me well at chanting.

After several weeks, I was allowed to join in the evening scamper to collect, or bury, the pilgrims along the route into Santiago and to check on the wayside hermits.

Now I was able to study them properly. They appeared to be stuck in their cross-legged position and were in the most dreadfully unkempt state. Their hair was matted and tangled and some of their beards were over two feet long. These curled up in their laps as they sat motionless all day. They were a disgrace. Why did the monastery not take them in and tend to the poor old men? Was it not meant to be a house of God?

I railed at the inhumanity of it, at the sight of them. And I railed even more when I saw the treatment my fellow novices were permitted to dole out to them. Officially, they were supposed to check that none of them died each day. Unofficially, they took glee in taunting the poor old devils, pretending they were dead, when they were obviously asleep and throwing them (as they woke up) to the wolves that waited in the nearby forest. I was sickened with it all.

The only interest I had was to identify my contact. The fourth hermit eastwards from the monastery. He did perhaps look slightly younger than the others, but not much. Where on earth had Calveley managed to find a suitable replacement? I never knew the hermit's name. None of them shared their name. But I caught his eye each time I passed with the hand-cart.

An astonishing thing happened to me one evening. My hermit signalled that he had something for me and managed to hand-over a small box as I pretended to check out his breathing. I hid it under my habit. It was Calveley's writing again, it just said:

'The Black Prince heard you lost your cat.'

There was a grey kitten inside!

So, life went on in the monastery at its usual pace and it began to dawn on me that I would never get the opportunity to spy for England. Nor indeed, ever to get out of the place again. My movements were too regulated and monitored. Somehow I did not feel too desperate. I had my kitten. I hid him in an empty cupboard and made sure he had a night time escape hole at the back. He seemed to understand that he had to be quiet.

By chance one day, fifteen months later, I was passing the Abbott's room on the way to collect a book from the library for my senior tutor monk. I overheard a conversation through the door, which stood ajar. I would not normally have bothered to stop, except that I heard the magic words *King Pedro*, as I walked by. I looked sharply up and down the narrow corridor and ducked into the long shadow beside the door.

'...grand tournament,' I heard. 'The full court will be there and King Pedro is to initiate several new Knights.'

'The whole country is over-run with Knights. We don't want any more,' said the Abbott sourly. 'It takes more and more money to support them.'

'Well, I'll tell you this my dear Abbott. If the rumour is true that King Pedro himself will be jousting, no man would dare try to defeat him!' 'Ho! Ho!' replied the Abbott, with one of his false laughs. 'He would probably eat him alive!' They both laughed at that one.

My blood ran cold. So they both knew of the King's reputation. Pedro must have boasted about it. The voice continued, 'Yes indeed and now the good burgers of Burgos have a month to prepare our lists. To feed the noble and the good coming from every corner of Spain. You are invited Abbott. We need a bit of God's presence. Here is your summons. It will be the social event of the year.' There was a rustling of parchment from within.

'By the way, the King asks you to dine with him privately the evening before. The security around him is immense. He will be in a well-guarded tent outside the city walls.'

'No doubt he wishes to talk about taking more treasure,' replied the Abbott ungratefully. I slipped away with my ears ringing. Burgos it was, in a month.

The next day I made sure that I was the novice who checked on the mortal status of the fourth hermit eastwards along the pilgrim path. I smuggled the red cloth into his hands, along with a written note addressed to *Wilhelm*.

Chapter 28 - Lost and Found

Late the next evening, my luck held even further when I spied an old foe.

He was disappearing through a dark gap in a wall beneath our dormitory, and descending a spiral staircase that I did not even know existed. It was the Grandmaster of the Holy Order of Santiago, and uncle to King Pedro's daughters, de Padilla. He was not dressed in all his finery and gold seals, but I knew him instantly, even though I only saw him sideways as he swung around to slide through the narrow opening.

I had noticed many such old stone steps down to lower levels in the monastery. I had never been able to investigate them. But this one had a secret door.

I had my arms around two old cloaks full of soiled straw, for I had been changing the bedding. They were awkward companions, and I could hardly see where I was putting my feet as I slowly crept down the stairway. I was making my way towards a trap-door in the floor, down which we normally threw the dirty straw. I suddenly heard a noise below me, and looked around the side of my ungainly bundles. I saw a long rusty key in his hand. He knocked it against the narrow doorway as he squeezed through the gap. As I watched, I realised he was trailing large loose sacks in his wake. Was he intending to fill them? The wall closed behind him, and a foot pedal beside it clicked up into a recess in the wood panelling. No wonder I had never noticed it there. 'Is he collecting some of the Templar Treasure?' I asked myself. It was possible. I must follow him.

One thing puzzled me. There were always guards at the entrance to the monastery. Why would he not have protection, if he was collecting treasure? Was this a secret mission of theft?

Thank goodness nobody saw me, as I hurried to empty my load. I could hardly leave a pile of soiled straw at the bottom of my staircase. It only took me twenty seconds to return to the hidden pedal in the wall. I levered it down, so I could tread on it, and the narrow secret door opened noiselessly. I was thankful that the hinges must have been kept well-greased to make no noise. With the thought that this meant they were well used, the hairs on the back of my neck told me I was on a dangerous trail; but I <u>might</u> be in the right place.

I discarded my sandals, and crept down the steep stone steps in my bare feet. I was determined not to be heard. I was feeling my way noiselessly around and around the wall of the tight spiral stairs. It was pitch black, for I had no light with me.

It seemed to go on for ever. Suddenly, my heart leapt into my mouth. I was just about to tread on one of de Padilla's trailing sacks. That would have given the game away! I had caught up with him. Now I could see his faint candle moving as he descended ahead of me. I stopped and composed myself. It could not be much further down.

Inside my head, I was remembering my orders: to locate the key; open the crypt; and identify the correct treasure. Well, in order to find where the key was kept, I would have to follow de Padilla back up again to its hiding place. That would be extremely difficult, for I did not have the right to roam the monastery wherever I wished. A novice would be questioned and punished if he was seen in the wrong place. I put that out of my head for the moment. That problem was for later. At least de Padilla was going to open one of the crypts. Was it the right one? *That* was the question.

I realised that I would have to slip into the crypt with him, in order to identify the pieces of the Jerusalem Treasure, the Templar Treasure, Solomon's Treasure, whatever they wanted to call it.

De Padilla carried only one small candle, which gave little light, and much shadow. This suited me well. When we reached the bottom, I slid myself successfully into the deep shadow, against the curved wall of the crypt. The holy knight ground the ancient key around inside the lock with both hands. The iron bars, which served as a doorway, opened inwards. He stepped inside, and I saw the light of his candle moving forwards towards the middle of the underground cave. I could not guess how large it was.

I felt my way gingerly to the open entrance and raised my right foot in order to follow de Padilla, when I bumped straight into him as he came back to lock himself in! Looking back on it later, it was a miracle we did not both have a heart attack at the same time.

But an attack of a different sort, we did have, there and then. It was a full-blown fight to the death. I suppose I presumed my strength would prevail. It always had. But I found that I had grown soft with *monking* and praying. My muscles would not provide me with the power I needed, even though my head told them what to do.

The Grand Master went for my arms and legs. He knew what he was doing and I had no weapon. He was stronger but less agile. I could only dodge him for so long before my strength ran out. He caught me twice with the edge of his sword, once on the arm and once on the leg, but I held on to my senses while he chased me for the killer blow. I was hurting and nearly at the end of my tether, when he slipped in the middle of an awkward turn. His left leg went sideways away from his body and he fell without being able to save himself. He hit his head on the stone floor. It bounced sickeningly.

I too collapsed right beside him. My right leg and right arm had become too numb to stand any longer. Or at least that is what I thought, until I heard a guard entering the spiral steps, with the sound of a sword in its scabbard clattering along behind him. He must have heard a noise, or maybe he was due to join de Padilla down here anyway.

Looking back on the incident, I do not know how I did it. But, exhausted and badly hurt, I just had time to scramble into a dark alcove I had previously felt in the wall near the fourth step from the bottom. At least my head was still working. The guard took one look at the Grand Master and ran for help.

Praying that I would not be seen, I limped back up the stairway somehow and found my bed for the night. In the meantime, de Padilla had been brought into the Abbott's rooms. After half an hour he regained his senses and was asked who attacked him, for he had drawn his sword in the crypt. In front of the apologetic Abbott and a room full of agitated monastery inhabitants, he replied 'It was a monk!'

Triple locks and triple guards were installed around the crypt. And I still did not know if it was the right one.

Somehow I had to hide a limp and a useless arm. It was a few days before I worked it out in my head. De Padilla must have lost his memory, for any competent swordsman would have been able to recognise the feeling of slashing one arm and one leg of his adversary.

They watched us all. I had to find a way to walk with a very bent left knee, to appear not to limp. Nobody seemed to notice that my height had shrunk by several inches inside my vestment. As for my right arm, I cannot tell you the silent screaming agony I put myself through at night in my bed. I determined that I must drag the broken limb across my body to the centre, low down. This would be the required place for my right hand to meet my left, in the prayer position. Inch by inch, I moved it. Each inch caused me intense pain from the broken bone. Every tiny movement called for more naked bravery than I had ever had to summon before. The knowledge of the agony of the next inch and the next inch.

By early morning the deed was done and my bed was dripping from the straw mattress with sweat. The pain was unbearable, but I had to get up. I had to shuffle among the monks and be anonymous. They were obviously on the lookout for weeks, for anything suspicious amongst the monks.

In order to get out of handcart and pilgrim duty every evening, I feigned another attack of dysentery. I urgently needed time to rest and set my bones. It occurred to me then that even if I had been able to identify the Templar Treasure, there would have been no way for me to send a message to confirm it.

Several weeks later, there was talk among the monks of a new King. The rumour spread. King Pedro was dead! Apparently, the French mercenary leader De Guesclin had murdered him. Clever Calveley, I thought. I bet they did it together.

'King Trastamara is back,' they said. So, now the world knew he had escaped the fire after all. To think, we had destroyed the monastery at Yuso for nothing. Time passed slowly for me as I pondered on the fact that I still had the second half of my mission to complete, or I just might have to stay there forever.

I healed slowly. My leg mended itself at an angle, so I was left with a small permanent limp, which I found simple enough to disguise. But my arm was another matter. It was set solid in front of my body and had become a positively useless hindrance. Not able to put up with it any longer, I eventually showed my arm to the physician, telling him I had suffered a fall some time before. He insisted he re-break it.

The Abbott asked why that was necessary. 'He cannot dress himself, brother,' replied the physician.

'Good God man, he does not need to tie a cravat, he only needs to pray.'

'Well then, he will not be able to work on the vines or write a script'

'That is more serious.' The Abbott paused to think. Bells started to ring in his mind and he began to grow suspicious of me. 'You got it in a fall, you said?'

'Yes, brother,' I murmured.

There was nothing he could prove, but I could tell he harboured a quiet suspicion of me from that time on. They said I screamed the monastery down. I did not remember anything. The re-setting of my shoulder blade, my forearm and elbow, was done the next day. The physician knew his job. He ordered rest and a sling for two months.

I was summoned to see the Abbott as soon as I was well enough. He said nothing, except that my injuries had been entered into the *Big Book* of the Monastery. He showed me:

Name: .... Brother Petit
  Assigned work: .... No outside duties

I was a prisoner. It was official. I could never again get a message to my hermit contact outside. I had no way to report the treasure.

The physician may have mended my broken bones, but he could do nothing to mend my spirits. I spoke to nobody. I sat and mumbled my responses. All feeling was lost. I think that was when my mind started to slip.

It was just after that time, the Plague hit the monastery. It wiped out over half of the monks, including the Abbott. Those who survived were given cells of their own. I remember very little about it, except that it became easier to have my cat.

In my despair, one day meshed into another; and one week into the next. Eventually, one year became another; and before I was aware, eight or nine years had passed since I had arrived. In the middle somewhere, I took the oath, and sleep-walked into becoming a full monk. Everything would have continued like that, probably until the end of my life, if news had not reached the monastery of the death of the Black Prince in England. My beloved Prince was gone!

It awoke me from my daytime sleep-walking, and I sat clutching the cat in my bed, under my one rough coarse blanket. No doubt he wondered what was the matter with me. But he never struggled in my arms. He was clever. He had found a way out from his cupboard, down a hole into thick undergrowth below. I fondly thought the cat was too shy to be seen by others; but of course, I was wrong. Some of them had spied him, but I was lucky, and they kept quiet. Perhaps they thought I was mad enough. I certainly did not talk at all. Perhaps they were worried about me.

My Prince, my Master. I grieved and moaned to myself. Now what was to become of me? Had everyone forgotten me here? Then I remembered the treasure and my mission.

I fetched the key. It was as simple as that. I spied it lying on the new Abbott's table and I recognised it instantly. I waited until midnight and limped silently past the sleeping guards. I was not afraid. This was something I had to do, whatever the consequences. And I was aware that I must complete my mission before my mind slipped back into nothingness once more. I would not get another chance. If the treasure from Jerusalem was not in this crypt, then I had failed. I would die for nothing in this prison

THE UNBELIEVABLE MYSTERY OF THE BLACK PRINCE'S RUBY

of a monastery.

I remember passing the sleeping guards, turning the key quietly with the greatest difficulty. But at last, I stepped into the cave. I had taken a holder with six candles to light my way. The first objects I saw were spread out across the middle of the crypt, from one side to the other. This created a barrier to the other items that were stacked on the far side. I bent to wipe the greyness off what looked like a slender pole of wood, for everything was thick with dust. As I began to run my hand along its length, a golden shaft of light burst between my fingers. The brilliance of it lit my face and the crypt around it came into its glow. I gasped with amazement. There were two poles parallel to each other. They were identical. Running my hand further along their length, the wood revealed a tapered shape that ended with what looked like a high-sided cart. It was part of a golden chariot. It was not wood. It was pure gold. It was one of many, strewn across the centre of the crypt.

Dream-like, I stepped over the golden shafts and drew my breath at the sight of chests of jewels. Full-sized golden oxen and written tablets of stone covered with incomprehensible inscriptions. So here was the Templar Treasure. Some items were missing, but the rest of the contents of the list in my head were stacked right there, in front of my eyes.

I don't know how long I spent down there. But I do know I have never been so happy in my life. Can you believe, I found religion in that crypt? Despite being surrounded by it in the monastery, I identified a higher order of believing, down there among the treasures. It came to me. Maybe Jesus had touched some of this. Perhaps he had wiped away the dust with *his* hand, just as I had and seen the Holy Treasures of Solomon for himself.

Was some of it from *his* time? I did not know enough of the Bible to say. I did remember that Solomon was earlier, but were some of these pieces from the time of the Crucifixion?

I wondered at it all. Somehow, I felt an inner peace, as if my life was now complete.

After a while, I started to puzzle out a logistical problem. How had they carried these large objects, chariots and all the other golden wonders into the crypt? I began to look for a recently built wall. I reasoned there must have been another entrance to the underground cave.

It was my cat that gave me away.

I had been gone too long. He followed my scent down to the entrance of the spiral staircase and began scratching at the secret door. As the cat passed the sleeping guards, he must have brushed his fur against a leg, for they woke up.

They laughed, seeing a cat, presuming he was after a mouse. What fun to see what he was up to. They released the pedal and tip-toed behind him down the stone steps. My cat greeted me and I picked him up, telling him of my treasures. I was glad he had come.

The guards landed on me without warning and stuck my poor shoulder through with a sword. Instantly they plucked the cat from my loosening grip and threw it high into the air. I saw all four paws stretched out sideways as it flew towards the treasures.

There was the faintest *meow* as he landed, deeply impaled on a golden spike, at the top of a golden pineapple.

Because of the Plague, a new Abbott would deal with me. My old adversary would have tortured me for the truth, for he would have remembered the King of England's soldier whom he had suspected of attacking de Padilla. This Abbott treated me as a common thief, an opportunist, who had worn the monk's habit in order to steal anything I could find. Sadly, it had happened before and it would happen again.

The monastery record books were incomplete and in disarray, for most of the senior monks had died. So there was no record made of this breach of security, because the new Abbott did not wish to blot his own copybook.

I was thrown out of the monastery of Santiago. The great complaining west gate was shut behind me, as I nursed my shattered shoulder, sitting on the pilgrim road. They had thrown me out to die. I had no money and no bed. I was a broken ex-monk.

The sole thought I had in my head, was that I could now complete my mission. I still had my piece of red cloth. Perhaps I could go home at last.

I dragged myself eastwards along the path and stopped at the fourth shelter from the monastery. It was empty. My messenger was gone. I realised with a jolt, they must have given up on the treasure and given up on me, probably years before. Why had I been abandoned by my King, my country, Prince John and by Calveley? You see I had *no idea* how long I had spent in that place.

There was nothing else I could do.

I have lived there ever since.

At last, the old hermit looked up at the strange-eyed younger man, the Envoy from Prince John. His old eyes flashed. 'Answer me! Why did Prince John leave me there? Did you not want the treasure after all? After all I have been through.' His voice broke. His rheumy eyes could not manage tears any more. He sighed and added quietly, 'The rest of the story you already know. My mind slipped away again and my 'brown fur' arrived.'

He did get his answer. It was full of the political troubles that had hounded England during the intervening years and the struggles of Prince John of Gaunt to rule the country, for the new and rebellious young King, the Black Prince's younger son.

The Envoy started the explanation, 'We had the Plague most terribly in England too. It must have been about two years after Prince John left you here in the monastery.

I remember it hit London particularly badly and the ladies and gentlemen of the King's court were told to go to their country houses. Prince John was busy again with the King, but he sent his wife Blanche home to her father, the Duke of Lancaster. Tragically, both Blanche and her father caught the Plague and died.'

'A few days later, the King received a message that King Pedro had been executed in his tent in Spain. They say King Edward did not know whether to rejoice, or to cry, because the events had all happened the wrong way around. If the treasure had been found first, before King Pedro's execution, its removal might have been possible. But after King Pedro died, all chance of collecting the promised treasure to pay the army appeared to be gone.

After all, his reinstated rival, King Henry of Trastamara, would certainly *not* keep Pedro's broken promises.'

The old hermit reacted instantly and jumped to his feet. He was angry. *'Why didn't someone come and get me out of here then? Tell me why?'*

The younger man put his hand out to calm him and replied carefully. 'Because King Edward came up with a masterful plan of his own to get the treasure,' he said. The old man sank back down into his chair. This had better be good, he thought.

'The King ordered the grieving Prince John to marry King Pedro's daughter Constance, who was the rightful heir to the crown of Castile.'

The envoy turned to the old man beside him in the garden. 'You will remember Princess Constance. She was the girl he carried on the front of his horse, when you rode through the snowy Pyrenees?' The hermit nodded quietly. He thought he was starting to get the picture. *'Why did he have to marry her?'* he asked. 'Because they would be legally entitled to call themselves the *King and Queen of Spain*. King Edward reasoned that the other King of Spain, the usurper Trastamara, had been defeated once by the English army. All they had to do to defeat them again, was to re-run the Battle of Najera. Then his son Prince John would be handed the key of the treasure crypt at Santiago.

So, they got married and they did become the King and Queen of Spain. At least, that is what they were called in London. Trastamara was still the King over here. But outside events overtook King Edward's grand plan. There was a new King in France at this time and news came from Poitiers that he was challenging and winning back hard-earned English lands. Troops were needed urgently for the continuance of the war in France. For the first time, a French King was using a professional army and paying De Guesclin's mercenaries himself.

The biggest problem for the English at that time was their army commander, the Black Prince. He was still suffering from his illness, which the doctors seemed unable to cure. Prince John, who had obeyed his father and married young Constance, was ordered to lead the English defence of their territories along the West of France. It was a disappointment for the King, but their claim to the Spanish throne had to be delayed until the English army had finished in France. There would simply be a delay in claiming the Templar Treasure.

The English army in France never lost a battle under the Black Prince. But, under the command of Prince John, they never won one. He was no strategist and no tactician. His father kept telling him to go on fighting, as more Englishmen were killed and he was blamed by the people, when they found that so many of their men-folk did not return from France.

Eventually the army lost most of the English lands, except for their strongholds in Bordeaux and Poitiers. They had to sue for peace, which meant even more taxes. Prince John returned home a deeply unpopular figure and went back to helping his father run the country.

When his brother the Black Prince died, the King was inconsolable and fell into a melancholic old age. He appointed Prince John to rule in his name. The old King's heir was now the Black Prince's young son, seven-year-old Prince Richard. He was the younger brother of little Prince Edmund, who had died at his birthday *Jousting Tournament*. But Prince John of Gaunt was still very unpopular with the people of England. They became suspicious of him. Rumours spread that he was going to claim the throne for himself and by-pass the young Prince. They said he was just waiting for his father to die. Stories circulated that he would seize the boy when the time came.

When King Edward did finally die, two years later, there was a rebellion brewing against Prince John. The people learned that the old King had decreed that his son would rule as Regent for the new King, nine-year-old Richard II. An angry crowd marched on London to confront Prince John. They would have lynched him if they could.

It was the new King's mother Joan of Kent, the Black Prince's beloved wife, who stepped forward bravely to address the rebels. Amid the tumult of noise, she called for quiet. 'My husband, the Black Prince, trusted his brother,' she said. 'And made him promise on his deathbed, not to usurp his son and heir. Look!' she said to the murmuring crowd. 'Look over there!'

At the side of the gateway where she stood, some of the greatest nobles in the land were assembled to support Prince John. The lines of nobles

310

parted in the middle and allowed a curly-headed boy to walk through them to stand beside her. It was the new King, Richard II.

'God save the King! God save the King!' rang out around the crowd. The boy looked at his mother and beckoned for his uncle, Prince John, to come forward. A gasp was heard from a thousand lips, as Prince John unbuckled the belt of his own scabbard and sword. He removed it from around his waist and laid it carefully in the young boy's open arms. Then he bent one knee, lowered his eyes and paid homage to his King.

The cheering started at the back of the crowd and rose like a wave to encompass them all. The noise grew and grew as, one by one, the nobles presented their swords publicly to their new King, until there was a tall pile of arms on the ground in front of the boy. The rebellion was over before it had started.

'*Why didn't Prince John send for me?*' pleaded the hermit once again. All these things were happening over in England, meanwhile he had been forgotten in a Spanish monastery.

'Oh, he did! One of his first acts as Protector of England was to send a messenger to the Abbott.'

'*Here?*' the old man was astonished.

'Yes, but he was told by the new Abbott that you were not there and that nobody could find your monastery records. There was a three-year gap in most of the books. He presumed you had died of the Plague, along with half of the other monks'

'*That was not true!*'

'I know, I know. And Prince John took it very badly too. He blamed himself. You see, that meant the end of his plans for the Templar Treasure. It was useless unless somebody could prove it was here.

Then he got embroiled in domestic politics for many years, while his nephew, the young King, grew up into a rebellious, easily-led teenager. The lad surrounded himself with young men who turned him against all his uncle's policies at home and abroad.

Eventually the young King insisted on taking power for himself, before he officially came of age. Suddenly Prince John found himself free to pursue his own claim to the throne of Spain. But first, he sent me on *this* mission. I was his senior aide.

'Mind you dig out the records of that monastery,' He ordered me. 'I want you to check and double-check that Petit-Roi is not still there, poor man.' In other words, I was to see if I could either find you somewhere, or prove that you had died. 'If I know monasteries,' he told me, 'there has to be a list somewhere.'

As I bowed to take my leave, he added, 'if you DO find him, for God's sake tell them he's your father or something. Make some excuse for wanting him.' He waited until I looked up again and then stared hard into my eyes and said, 'For the sake of England, do not tell the monks you are looking for their treasure.'

The Envoy paused and looked at the old hermit. 'So here I am. As you see, I was just doing as I was told.'

The old man sighed. 'And now, what happens to the treasure? Does he still want it?'

'Oh, he has plans for it alright. But they involve his children and future generations, using the funds to sail across the open oceans to discover new lands and claim them for Christianity', he said.

'Ah!' said the hermit, thinking about it, 'Treasure to spread the word of God.'

'Yes, that was the dream that I understand Chaucer interpreted for him.'

The old man kept his thoughts to himself just then. How could you sail into the open ocean, when everyone knew it was *not* possible? It was madness. You would fall off the edge of the world. But he could not help but mention it later that night.

'Maybe not, old timer. Some people think the world is round, though I have to admit the Church is opposed to the idea.'

'That is not true!'

The envoy put up his hand to stop the older man saying any more. 'Perhaps our voyages will prove the point, one way or the other.'

The next day, the old man found the Envoy packing up his belongings.

'Are you going?' he asked with some concern, for he did not want to be left

behind, not ever again.

'You're coming too,' replied the young man.

'Where are we off to?'

'Well, I'm going home. Don't worry, Petit-roi! I'll see you get a place.' He tutted and shook his head, *'Petit-roi* cannot be your *real* name. You must have been born with an English name. What was it?'

The old man scratched his head. 'I've tried to remember, but nothing comes.'

That afternoon they had an hour together in the garden before the carriage transport that was due to take them to the ship to England, sailing the next night.

'You know most things about my life,' started the hermit, 'tell me about yours, young man. Tell me about your home.'

'Well, I lived in Arden. They called it *the centre of England.* I was brought up by my grandparents, beside the great Forest of Arden. My grandfather was still working as a deers-man for Prince John. Everybody from the surrounding villages had the right to cull the deer and wild boar to feed their own families. The Prince ordered it. Mind you, we were not allowed to sell the meat. I remember two families were turned out of their houses for selling it in the market. There were strict rules.'

'Why did your grandparents bring you up?'

'Both my parents were dead. My father had been killed in the war. I never saw him and my mother died when I was born.'

'Which war was your father in? Perhaps I knew him?'

'Crécy...' he hesitated, 'yes, I believe it was Crécy.'

'What was his name?'

'Robert of Alpath.'

The hermit looked up quickly, 'Why are you called *Alpath,* when you were brought up in Arden?'

'My father was an Alpath man. He went to war before I was born. My mother came to Arden to have me at her parents house. She intended to go back, but she died having me and I lived with the old couple in Arden.'

'What happened to your father's house at Alpath?' The hermit's questions were getting more urgent.

'Oh, it had no roof the last time I saw it. I used to play there as a child. I remember, it had the tallest doorway of all the houses in the village. It was only half an hour away from my grandparents house.'

'Tell me about your childhood.'

'Like all small boys, I used to dream my father was a grand knight. I thought of nothing but jousting tournaments and how he would sweep me up on to his charger.'

Something stirred in the old man's head. 'Robert of Alpath,' he murmured.

'Did you know him then?' the Envoy asked keenly.

'YES, young man, I believe I did!'

'Tell me, tell me! What was he like?'

'Well, first I must ask you two questions,' he paused. 'Did he have eyes like you?'

'Yes! Or so I've been told. The colour came from his mother, I believe. Tell me you DO remember him! You remember his eyes, don't you old man?'

He ignored the pleading tone and continued with his questions. 'And what was your mother's name?'

'Anne of Arden.'

The hermit let out a deep puff through his cheeks and touched them with his hands. 'She used to tell me about my eyes.' He bent his head. 'I fear they are old and dim now.'

He raised himself up and straightened his old back as best he could.

'I remember now. I remember it ALL. *I am ROBERT OF ALPATH!*' Anne was my bride, for just one month.'

'YOU ARE my father!' exclaimed his son.

The young man was watching the forests and fields slip past the window of their carriage that evening. There was a certain rhythm to the swing of the coach and the hooves of the horses, as they clattered towards the coast. A movement attracted his attention within the carriage. He noticed the old man, his father, was keeping the rhythm with his hand and nodding his head. He was saying something, singing quietly. He caught the tune:

My....Shag-hair Cyclops come let's ply
Our hefty hammers lust'ly
Our hefty hammers lust'ly

****

III

Part Three

EPILOGUE

T he Black Prince hid the existence of the Blood of Christ stone from his father, King Edward. At court in Poitiers, his jeweller and armourer were father and son. They were secretly given the commission to mount it as the centrepiece of a bejewelled helmet/crown that could be worn into battle. It was made to fit around the top of his helmet. The stone was called 'The Black Prince's Ruby'. And that is its name today. Its history is an adventure in itself, but it does not take long to tell.

First the Black Prince died, followed by his father, old King Edward. The Prince's nine-year-old son became King Richard II and he inherited the Black Prince's Ruby in its crown.

Thirty years later, in 1415, King Henry V (John of Gaunt's grandson) wore the battle crown at the victorious Battle of Agincourt, where the ruby stone itself withstood a direct blow from the French Duke of Alencon and saved the King's head. (Just as it had earlier saved the Black Prince's heart.)

In 1485, Richard III (the great grandson of John of Gaunt) wore the crown at the Battle of Bosworth Field. It was knocked off his head. The King was killed and the crowned helmet fell under a bush.

It was retrieved and used to crown King Henry VII, on the battlefield. He was the first Tudor King. The battle crown was then placed into protection, as part of the Crown Jewels.

In 1654, the Republican Oliver Cromwell melted down the crown and sold the Black Prince's Ruby, reputedly for the sum of £4.

At the start of the restoration in 1660, Charles II recovered the Ruby and set it in the front of the Crown of England. All the pieces of royal jewellery that could be traced were then taken to the Tower of London for safekeeping. Despite this, the Crown Jewels were successfully stolen from the Tower, but recovered immediately. It was thought to have been a test devised by the King, for the robber went mysteriously unpunished.

The Black Prince's Ruby is still part of the Crown Jewels and is one of the most prized gemstones in the world. It is the central deep red stone on the front of the Imperial Crown of England. It is shown on the coffin at the funeral of a Monarch, worn at the Coronation, the State Opening of Parliament and on all other state occasions.

Can you crack - 'The Black Prince's Code' ?
E1p a45 et1em - 'Vj2 Dn1em Rt3pe2'u E4f2' ?

15vj4t'u P4v2 - 3u 3v vt52?
Vj3u d44m 3nn5uvt1v2u vj2 f1pi2t 4h ur2pf3pi a21tu 4h t2u21tej 3pv4 vj2 O3ffn2 1i2u. 1 v3o2 4h f22r u5r2tuv3v34p 1pf e2tv13p d2n32h 3p T2n3i345u T2n3eu.
5pf45dv2fna vj2a d2n32x2f vj2 Dn1em Rt3pe2'u T5da y1u ht4o vj2 Dn44f 4h Ejt3uv.
D5v h21t p4v - y2 p4 n4pi2t f4 !
3p vj2u2 f1au 4h i2o4n4ia 1pf t1f34o2vt3e f1v3pi, vj2 t5da y3nn d2 t2x21n2f v4 d2 1 Ur3pcn ht4o vj2 D1f1mjuj1p o3p2u 4h 1hij1p3uv1p.

N4pi n3x2 45t in4t345u M3pi !
J1x2 1 d3v 4h h5p, da ej1nn2pi3pi 4vj2tu v4 et1em 45t e4f2!

Notes

CHAPTER 6 - THE THRONE OF CASTILE

1   These were a race of Arabians and North Africans who had occupied most of Spain since the 700's. The Moors had brought their Muslim religion with them, along with their learning, universities, architecture and agricultural improvements.

CHAPTER 7 - A QUESTION OF LOYALTY

2   Spain was divided by Caliphs, ruled by the Arab Moors and separated by Christian enclaves to the north, each with its own King. Singly, their strength was limited, but with a cause to unite them they could be a problem. If that cause was his cousin King Pedro and his underhanded dealings with his neighbours, then the problem could be lethal to English interests in next-door Aquitane. The danger would arise if they sided with France against England. The unresolved war over territory and trade would undoubtedly be lost.

CHAPTER 16 - DEATH AND DESTRUCTION

3   This was written by Olivier d'Iscans in the 1100's. He was a monk from the Poitou region, near Poitiers, who took the nom-de-plume Aimery Picard. He declared the story came from the writings of Turpin, a friar from St-Denis, near Paris, 350 years before. Turpin was known to be one of Charlemagne's twelve peers in the Song of Roland, the pilgrim's marching song.

    This Chronicle contained the legendary history of King Charlemagne and his nephew Roland, telling of their expeditions through Spain in the late 700's. Many knightly households brought their sons up on these adventures. It was reputed to be the most popular reading of the Middle Ages.

4   The Abbey of St Saveux at Charroux was founded in 783 by King Charlemagne and Count Roger de Limoges. Such was the prestige of this church that four Holy Councils were held here to discuss church teachings. The first one was in 989, when the wording for the new 'Institution of the Peace of God' were agreed by the Pope and his Cardinals. This place was a natural magnet for soldiers and pilgrims alike. Without exception, St Saveux was the best-endowed church for Holy Relics. It had over seventy within its walls. Every time a man saw the vial of the Holy Blood, along with the fragment of the True Cross, he knew God was by his side. It was just the reaction any commander would want for his troops, as they marched towards an uncertain fate.

CHAPTER 17 - PILGRIM PRINCES

5   This voluntary exile was most often taken in the hope of the curing of an illness or an infirmity when they arrived at Santiago de Compostela. There they prayed for the miraculous gifts of St James the Apostle. Very often, a promise of a thanksgiving pilgrimage was made when a man was upon his sick bed when he thought he would not recover. Once attested, that vow had to be kept. Only a bishop could release him from his promise to God.

6   This service was enacted on every day of the week, throughout Europe. One church in every town held the same service for new pilgrims setting out to Santiago.

7   The clothing for the pilgrimage was entirely functional. The men wore knee-length tunics underneath a coarser sleeveless overcoat, which was a looser fit and slit at the sides. On top of this came a large collar, which covered the shoulders as far down as the elbows. This also incorporated a hood for extra protection against the elements, along with either a cone-shaped or wide-brimmed hat. Almost above all in importance, the pilgrim on his way to Santiago carried the emblematic scallop shell. In the sea off the Galician coast, near Santiago, lived molluscs with a bivalve shell, of the genus *Pecten jacobaeus*. Their legendary dedication to Venus gave them their name: 'Concha Venera'. The shell was interpreted as a symbol of good works coming out of an open hand and became the sign of St James' miraculous power.

8   Such was the demand for scallop shells, that the Galician shores became denuded. The bishops of Compostela eventually allowed the shopkeepers on St James Cathedral Square the exclusive rights to make and sell approved reproductions of the shells. These were usually in lead or tin, and were nailed to posts as way-markers along the routes, as well as to pilgrim church walls and doors. Scallop shells became the common insignia of all pilgrims to Santiago. In later times, the culinary dish 'Coquille St Jacque' would be named after the scallop shells of Santiago de Compostela.

9   The only people officially allowed to go on pilgrimage were free men who were of age, unmarried and not subject to paternal authority. They should not have received Holy Orders and should be able to freely make a vow of pilgrimage.

     This group did not include those who had to ask permission from another, before being allowed to depart. These included serfs, who had to ask their Lords, minors who needed parental permission, monks who had to get the consent of their superiors and clerics, who needed permission from their Bishop.

10   In the 11th Century, Compostela rose to the ranks the most famous pilgrimage shrines in Christianity, along with Jerusalem and Rome. By the end of the 12th Century, it was even more popular. The very word 'pilgrim' came to mean only those going to Santiago. The writer Dante Alighieri (1265–1321), in his work 'Vita Nuova', gave the meaning of the Latin 'peregrinus', as 'stranger, traveller and exile'. He wrote: "One can understand the word 'pilgrim' in two ways, one wide and the other narrow. In the wide sense, one calls a pilgrim whoever is outside his homeland. In the narrow sense, one calls a pilgrim

only he who is travelling to the house of St James, or is returning.

On this subject, it must be said that there are three ways of naming people who go on the service of the Most High. They are called 'Palmiers' when they go beyond the sea, from where they so often bring palms. They are called 'Pilgrims' when they go to the house in Galicia, because the Sepulchre of St James is further from his homeland than that of any other Apostle. They are called 'Romieux' in so far as they go to Rome."

CHAPTER 18 - THE PRINCESS OF WALES

11 These were mostly Augustinian and Benedictine. Then there were the Hospitalers and Military Orders: Templars, Antonins, Knights of St John of Jerusalem and the Knights of the Order of St James of the Sword (otherwise known as the Most Noble Holy Order of the Knights of Santiago, whose Joint-Grandmaster was King Pedro's brother-in-law, de Padilla). Most of the hospitals were built by donations from the wealthy, from Princes, Lords, and former pilgrims.

CHAPTER 19 - JOHN THE BAPTIST

12 Saintes was founded by Agrippa in the year 20 BC. It stood at an important Roman crossroads, with the ruins of a great amphitheatre outside the town. The brothers had planned to visit the river's right-bank. There, by tradition, the Abbeye-aux-Dames was run by Benedictine abbesses from all of France's greatest aristocratic families.

13 According to the Pilgrim's Guide:
'Eutrope was the son of the Emir of Babylon, Xerxes, and Queen Guiva. As a child, he went to Galilee to see Christ, whose miracles he had heard about. He was there for the miracle of the loaves and fishes. Later he left home for Jerusalem, because he believed in the new religion. After the Crucifixion and Pentecost, he helped Simon and Thaddeus to found a church in Babylon. The Apostle Peter later sent him on a mission to Saintes, which he converted from Paganism. Pope Clement predicted that he would become a martyr. In later years, he converted the daughter of a local Prince, Eustelle. The Prince was furious, and had him killed. He was buried by Eustelle and the Christians in Saintes, and has been ever since worshipped as a holy martyr.'

14 This kind of dance was played out through the whole of Europe. In Spain it was called 'La Danza General de la Muerte'; and in Italy 'Trionfo della Morte'. It was macabre black humour; country people's reaction to the terrors of the Plague.

15 Bordeaux was founded by the Celts in 300 BC. It first traded in tin and then Italian wine in the Christian period. Its own vineyards were first planted up, in the 1st Century AD, with a vine from Albania, on the wide-open shores of the Garonne River.
Known for its university from 300AD, Bordeaux later became the capital of Aquitaine, and under English rule.

CHAPTER 22 - DECIMATION

16 John of Gaunt married his passenger, Constance of Castile four years later, in 1371.

Thereafter they claimed the titles of King and Queen of Spain.

17 These fiercely independent people claimed an autonomous region north and south of the mountains. For hundreds of years they had pillaged the routes. They built 3-storey wooden towers with enclosures for their sheep and goats, to watch out for the unwise marching the pilgrim routes on their own.

CHAPTER 23 - THE GAMBLE

18 The history of Clavijo was steeped in Spanish legend. It was the most important site in the story of St James fighting for the Christians. By the year 844, the Muslim Moors had taken over the whole of Spain from the Visigoths, except for one Christian enclave called Asturia, which was part of the modern regions of Castile and Navarre.

King Ramiro 1st of Asturia had been attacked by the army of the Muslim ruler, Abd Al-Rahman II, and severely defeated at the battle of Albelda. He retreated to the nearby hillside of Clavijo to spend the night, where St James appeared to him in a dream, telling him to take up the fight again the following day, and assuring him of protection. Trusting in his dream, the Christian King mustered what men he could, and attacked the overwhelming Muslim forces once more.

During the battle St James, the Apostle himself, came to the rescue. He appeared as a Christian holy knight, mounted on a brilliant white charger; and led them to victory. He thus freed them from the obligation to provide one hundred virgins to the Emir. This had happened annually for the previous 64 years.

This was the first recorded appearance of St James in support of the Christians' fight against the Moors. Thereafter he appeared frequently, and always on the winning side. He ensured the progress of the 'Reconquista', the Christian re-conquest of Spain. His flag and his presence were carried from battle to battle over the years, as the Christians began to win back their land. Clavijo was the second most precious site in Spain after Santiago de Compostela, where St James the Apostle was buried.

19 This had been the capital of the Kingdom of Castile since 1035. It spanned across two rivers, with wonderful churches, royal tombs, and 32 pilgrim hospitals. At that time the cathedral was being extended, and a new cloister built. On the other side of the river Arlanzon was the abbey of Santa Maria la Real, which was also known as Las Huelgas Reales (from 'holganza' meaning leisure), because it was built on a well- known site for royal entertainment. It was founded in 1187 by Eleanor Plantaganet, who was sister of the Crusader King, Richard the Lionheart, and of King John of England. She was the wife of the King of Castile, and she endowed the abbey for young women of royal or noble Castillian blood. The royal households of both England and Castile had either ancestors or relations buried there.

CHAPTER 24 - THE BATTLE OF NÁJERA

20 In the Middle Ages, battles were normally fought with 3,000 - 5,000 men on each side. Sometimes there was an imbalance, as at the battle of Poitier in 1356. There, 7,000

English soldiers faced 18,000 French. The English had won with better communications, greater discipline, and the brilliant diversionary tactics of the young Black Prince. He famously had the battle won before midday, and captured three times as many men as he had soldiers still standing up. He had cooked up many a surprise for his enemies over the years; it was his trademark. But the Spanish had never faced him in battle before. Both sides had huge armies in the field. It was a fight for a crown. The Castilians were content with their 22,000 men, compared to 30,000 on the English side, after all, they were the ones being invaded. They had God and St James on their side. And they had the advantage of being on home ground.

CHAPTER 25 - SAVED BY THE BLOOD OF CHRIST

21 Anthony 4th Lord de Lucy, last lord of Cockermouth, was born in 1330, the same year as the Black Prince. They had served as young men together at the battle of Crécy. His family lived in the north-west of England, at Egrement. Historically, these northern areas were harried and disputed by the Scots. They called them the 'debatable lands'. King David I of Scotland, in 1315, followed by Robert Bruce in 1322, destroyed and pillaged St Bees priory, Egremont Castle and much of Cumberland and Northumberland.

Lord de Lucy's family had commanded three generations of English resistance.

After that, there was an uneasy peace with the Scots, and Anthony de Lucy had overseen negotiations for the ransom of King David II of Scotland, on behalf of King Edward.

Relinquishing his command there, Lord de Lucy wished to take his chances to fight abroad, where there was excitement, spoils and ransoms to be won. As long as you stayed alive.

Young nobles of his generation were welcomed in Prussia, to help the Teutonic Knights, who were dealing with serious uprisings in the forested area east of the Vistula. Each Knight had to equip himself with armour, a horse and 15 soldiers; very like Crusaders in the past. It was King Edward's not-so-secret mistress, Alice Perres, who loaned £500 to Lucy for his expenses. She was astute enough to charge a hefty interest rate, but not quite as much as the Jewish loan sharks.

The King granted him his licence in January 1367, but only on the condition that he (and others like him en-route to Prussia) should first travel in the opposite direction to fight for his friend the Black Prince, in Spain. He was given command of the 30,000 troops travelling from England; and fought in the position of 3rd Commander, after the Black Prince and John of Gaunt.

When he was killed at the battle of Najera (or Navarrete) he was embalmed like a Prince and returned to St Bees Priory to be buried, as per instructions given to the King at Arms.

His recently excavated body is now known as "The St Bees Man".

About the Author

Hon. Sarah Macpherson (also writes under Conolly-Carew) is a researcher and historical author of 3 books, many articles, lectures, radio and TV interviews.

Now in her late 70's, Sarah regards The Black Prince's Ruby as the most controversial book of the last few years.

It is well known that her late Majesty The Queen was intrigued by the mystery surrounding this precious jewel, which sits in the centre of The Imperial Crown of England.

The research for The Black Prince's Ruby began in France and Spain over 15 years ago.

This story leaps into uncomfortable territory.

As always, for an historical novel, it is up to the reader to decide.

Also by Sarah Macpherson

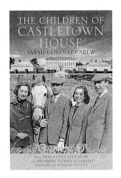

The Children of Castletown House - 2012 Ireland's largest and earliest Palladian-style house, was built for William Conolly, Speaker of the Irish House of Commons in the 1720's. Written by the children who grew up there, the Hon. Sarah Macpherson (Conolly-Carew), her sister Baroness Diana Wrangle & their brothers, the Hon. Gerald Maitland-Carew & Lord Patrick Carew. In this fascinating history, the character of the house is brought to life through its former residents, together with stories of the chance survival of the house through the Civil War, and tales of visiting royalty.

M' Lady's Book of Household Secrets - 2013 During the eighteenth century ladies of high society kept handwritten notes on remedies, gardening and household tips in their personal House Book and it became fashionable to exchange the most successful with friends and neighbours. Very few of these fragile House Books have survived and this compilation celebrates the recent discovery of two: one from Lady Talbot of Lacock Abbey and the other from Lady Louisa Conolly of Castletown House. This charming compilation is full of fascinating information and useful tips and gives an insight into the lives of those living in the grand houses of the eighteenth century.

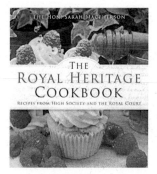

The Royal Heritage Cookbook - 2015
During the 18th century, ladies of high society kept handwritten notes on recipes and it became fashionable to exchange the most successful with friends and neighbours. This charming book is a compilation of fifty of the best recipes taken from the archives of the country houses of Britain and Ireland. Each recipe is shown in its original form accompanied by an up-to-date version created by our team of professional chefs, so that the recipes can be recreated today.